A SCAPE GOAT FOR MURDER

A FRANKIE CHANDLER MYSTERY

JACQUELINE VICK

Copyright © 2022 by Jacqueline Vick

All rights reserved.

No part of this book may be reproduced in any form or by any electronic or mechanical means, including information storage and retrieval systems, without written permission from the author, except for the use of brief quotations in a book review.

Cover Art by GoOnWrite

ISBN 978-1-945403-50-7 Print

ISBN 978-1-945403-49-1 eBook

In memory of Martin Lerma, one of the good guys.

ONE

Sometimes Life with a capital L steps in and kicks you in the teeth, making your priorities excruciatingly clear. A speed lesson. I got mine the third week of September, about six weeks shy of my wedding.

"AND IF HE doesn't stop piddling on the floor, I'll have to get rid of him."

Bart Waller's droning diatribe over his new morning ritual of mopping tinkle from the kitchen floor was getting on my nerves. I couldn't see why it bothered him so much. It wasn't a great floor. The beige tile was the cheap stuff that comes on a roll. It went with the white Formica countertop and wood cabinets in need of a coat of varnish to cover years of wear.

The room smelled of scrambled eggs and stale coffee. The former still clung to the dishes in the sink. Not my idea of the Ritz.

As the man continued to complain, I slipped a quick

glance out the kitchen window over the sink. Not a single cloud dotted the September Arizona sky. Our flight from Phoenix's Sky Harbor airport tomorrow morning should take off without a hitch. However, as I feel it's my responsibility to clutch the armrests and hold up any aircraft I'm in, I kept the weather under close watch.

"And then I stepped in it," he continued.

Biting my lip to hold back my opinion that any man who ran into piddle two weeks running should learn to watch his step, I put an end to his comments. I still had to get my cat, Emily, to her sitter and pack last minute odds and ends. After that, I would sit on my couch and sweat nervous perspiration until my fiancé, Detective Martin Bowers, and I arrived in Loon Lake, Wisconsin, for his first in-person meeting with his future in-laws.

"Be quiet," I snapped. "Please." Holding up one hand, I switched to the airy-yet-somber tone most people expected from a pet psychic. "I need silence to connect with Sparkles."

He was a beautiful roan—the dog, not the guy—with his liver-colored base coat lightened by strands of white and speckles of liver throughout. His snout was mostly gray, but that wasn't a surprise in a ten-year-old dog. Neither was his inability to hold it all night. Heck. I sometimes woke up with a need to tinkle, and I was only in my mid-thirties.

After slipping a glance at my watch and confirming I had wasted too much time on this appointment, I opened the imaginary yet intimidating wooden door I used as a mental gateway to stop random messages sent by animals from sneaking into my head.

Every creature has its own signature vibration. Sparkles gave off a sweet flutter. Once I created a path of light between the dog's mind and mine, I sent him an image of this same kitchen at night. Then I focused on the doggie door and raised my eyebrows.

Sparkles lowered his head. His long ears covered his eyes in shame.

My head drooped in sync with Sparkles', and my limbs trembled along with the dog's. With extreme clarity, the animal showed me the fastened lock on the doggie door. I exclaimed with disgust.

"What's the matter?" Bart whispered the question.

"If you block off his access to his toilet, where do you expect him to go potty?"

A vibration from my back pocket warned me the persistent caller who'd already tried to reach me three times during this appointment hadn't given up. I ignored it.

Bart barked out a laugh. "You think I lock him in?" He strode to the door. "I unlock this door every night before—"

He paused, fingering the fastened lock. "I don't understand. I—oh." In an act of feigned confidence, he puffed out his chest and cracked a grin. It wasn't difficult to read his genuine emotions in the micro-expression that escaped before the grin. Guilt. Embarrassment.

"We had a raccoon get in a few weeks ago. He was after Sparkle's food. Or she. I'm not sure. How do you tell the difference between a male and female raccoon?"

His babbling confirmed it. This man was up to his neck in a puddle of his own making. I ignored his attempts to divert my attention.

"And how long ago did Sparkles start relieving himself on your floor?"

He coughed. "About the same time."

To his credit, especially after the comment about getting rid of the dog, he cried out, fell to his knees, and pulled the cocker spaniel into a hug.

"Sparkles, Daddy is an idiot. I'm so sorry. And I was just venting. I'd never let anyone take you from me."

The spaniel's short tail thumped a beat on the floor. He gazed at me over his "daddy's" shoulder, eyes bright. Dogs were so willing to forgive. I, however, cared little for my fellow human beings and resisted the urge to express my disappointment with a slap to the back of Bart's head. People. Ugh. Other than my best friend, Penny, and my fiancé, and my parents, of course, I could do without most of them.

As I tapped my foot, waiting impatiently for the love fest to finish, I ran down a list of what I had left to do before my plane took off tomorrow morning. Before I drove my cat to the sitter's house, I had to clean the litter box. Last minute toiletries were on my bathroom sink, left out so I wouldn't forget to put them in my carry-on. I needed to shower tonight, since it was an early flight.

When my client stood, I cleared my thoughts and gave him a professional smile. "Do you have questions?"

"None." He took his wallet off the counter and pulled out a fifty-dollar bill. "Thank you so much."

"My pleasure," I said, accepting my payment.

I'd made it to my car but hadn't opened the door when my cell phone rang again. "Mother," I said through gritted teeth. I'd already suffered a flurry of phone calls with reminders to pack a dress for dinner with the Douds, Penny's family. And earrings. And makeup. My mother planned to traipse me, her engaged daughter, past her friends like a calf in a 4-H competition. More like a mature cow. Most of their daughters had wed in their twenties. It had taken me a decade longer to find my mate.

I snatched my phone from my back pocket and cleared most of my irritation from my tone. "I can either finish packing or spend my entire vacation on the phone with you."

It wasn't Mom. The clear alto belonged to Detective Juanita Gutierrez.

"Get to Holy Cross Hospital. Now."

And then she hung up.

TWO

A woman in blue scrubs seated behind a gigantic plexiglass wall looked up, startled, as I burst through the automatic doors to Holy Cross Hospital's emergency room waiting area.

"Martin Bowers," I panted.

"You need to wear a mask."

While I fumbled through my purse with one hand, I pulled my t-shirt over my face and repeated my question.

"I'm afraid I can't release information about our patients."

"He's here." I hooked my mask over my ears. "Detective Gutierrez called me."

"Your party is over there." She nodded toward the back corner of the room, just past a security desk also surrounded by Plexiglas, where a burly young man in uniform typed on a computer. A group of Bowers' coworkers huddled together. Rather than waste time arguing with the receptionist about the appropriateness of the term *party*, I crossed the room.

On my approach, the recently promoted Sergeant

Smitty O'Reilly looked up. His features softened, and the others turned around. Smitty's former partner Detective Taylor stood next to him, wearing his trademark black leather jacket even though the temperature outside had reached the nineties. On his other side, Detective Juanita Gutierrez looked like a bored model. She had on a black suit, of course, since she wore nothing but black suits.

The leader of the group, though the shortest man present, Captain Joe Southerland, settled his sharp eyes on me and stepped forward. He grasped my hand in his and squeezed.

"Where is he?" I asked.

"The doctors are with him now."

I took them all in with my frantic glance. "You look like you're at a funeral. What happened? Did someone shoot him?"

"No, no," Captain Joe soothed. "Nothing like that."

My shoulders relaxed. "Thank God." I glared at Gutierrez. "You left me hanging, so I assumed the worst. What happened?"

No one answered. Smitty shuffled his feet.

"Well? He's too healthy for a heart attack, and if he was prone to strokes, I would have given him one long ago."

Black Humor Frankie had stepped to the forefront to battle my fears. I told her to shut up.

After a slight nod from Captain Joe, Gutierrez stepped into the role of spokesperson. "He fell."

I gaped. "Fell? You mean tripped and sprained his ankle? I am so going to razz him about that."

She hesitated and looked to Captain Joe for approval again before speaking. "It's more serious than that. He's still unconscious."

"Unconscious? He fell over something and knocked himself out? Where did this happen?"

Captain Joe cleared his throat. "Someplace off Interstate 17."

"Someplace? Where?" I blinked a few times, imagining Bowers alone in the desert, surrounded by hungry buzzards. "Who found him?"

"We got an anonymous call," Smitty said, so happy to answer one of my questions that he made it sound like a treat.

"Anonymous?"

They exchanged secretive glances. I'd get no more details from them.

"What did the doctor say? He'll be okay, right?"

Instead of a confident yes, Smitty said they were still waiting to hear. The bubble of hope that surrounded me popped as if Gutierrez had jabbed it with a pin. None of them would say with certainty that Martin Bowers would be fine. Which meant he might not be.

As reality slammed into me, I gasped for air, fighting my desire to be sick. Bowers might be hanging on to life by his fingernails. I choked back a sob and turned away.

Then I realized I had skin in the game. Squaring my shoulders, I marched back to the front desk and confronted the receptionist.

"I'd like to see Martin Bowers. I'm his fiancée." My tone brooked no arguments.

She gazed at me, wary.

"No one goes back there but the patient."

"But I'm his fiancée." I pointed at my engagement ring. "We're engaged to be married. To spend the rest of our lives together." My voice rose. "We have faced down a priest in pre-Cana, survived countless phone calls from my mother demanding decisions on bridesmaid dresses, flowers, and cake. We're on our way to visit my parents tomorrow so he can meet them face-to-face. *For the first time.*"

Her wariness turned into resignation as she prepared to battle the hysterical loved one.

"I had to come up with a menu for a hundred people," I wailed. "That has to count for something!"

Suddenly, Gutierrez had her hand on my shoulder. She steered me away from the desk. "You must hold it together, Frankie. For Martin."

Her words felt like a slap.

"But you won't *tell* me anything," I whimpered. My voice dropped to a low, threatening growl. "Why won't you tell me anything?" I turned back to the receptionist, who, in her blue scrubs, might have been a nurse. Or a med tech. "Don't you ever watch television dramas? The man in the coma wakes up when he hears his loved one's voice. Bowers *needs* me to talk to him so he can wake up!"

Gutierrez took a firm hold of my arm and led me several steps farther from the desk. She looked over her shoulder at her coworkers. "Meet me in the cafeteria in twenty minutes. We'll talk. Okay? Until then, all we can do is wait."

She followed my gaze toward the double doors that separated the waiting room from the critical care area. "It will take a while for them to tend to him. We'll have a quick cup of coffee and come right back." Assessing me correctly, she sealed the deal with, "It's been a long morning. I need some caffeine."

Frankie the Pleaser gave in, but I didn't follow the detective back to her silent cohorts. Instead, I took in my surroundings for the first time.

To the right of the cop crowd, a television hung from the wall and broadcast a talk show on low. None of the occupants in the blue chairs that lined the room were interested in how to stretch their school lunch budget.

An elderly man and woman held hands. The way their gazes remained glued to the double doors, they waited for news.

A few chairs down, a woman in her thirties typed on her phone while two young children hung from her arms and legs. A third child sat in a chair and watched a cartoon on a small screen. The squeaky characters set my teeth on edge.

The final occupant sat close to the entrance, across from the double doors. A sturdy man, he wore his red flannel shirt untucked over his jeans. His elbows rested on his knees, and he looked down at his folded hands.

I squeezed my eyes shut and opened them again, but the room hadn't changed into the airport gate, and I wasn't standing in line with my honey, ready to board a plane.

Bowers didn't belong here. My fiancé was only in his late thirties. He was strong. Healthy. The emergency room was for doddering old people and drunks in bar fights. Gang members, maybe. The woman with the children was the exception. Maybe her husband worked in construction and fell off a building. I gasped. Maybe Bowers fell off a building. Was that what happened?

If he fell off the Wolf Creek Police Department roof, that would give him a concussion, but why would he be up there? With the latest COVID protocols, were they forced to have office meetings on the roof?

No. That wasn't right. Captain Joe said Bowers fall happened somewhere off Interstate 17.

When the double doors separating us from our loved ones hissed open, everyone, including me, looked, but it was only a skinny homeless man. I assumed he was homeless by his matted hair and the large amount of dirt on his clothes. And he was mumbling about his shopping cart and how *everything better be there.*

As he exited the building, a short, thin man in blue polyester slacks and a beige shirt gave him a wide berth and strode to the reception desk.

"Did they bring Detective Bowers here?"

He spoke with a soft accent. Greek, maybe, judging from his dark hair, aquiline nose, and olive skin. His face wasn't familiar. Curious, I inched closer.

"We can't give out that kind of information, sir. I'm sorry."

He jumped when I put my hand on his arm. "Are you a friend of Bowers? I'm Frankie, his fiancée."

After debating whether to take my proffered hand, he clasped it in both hands. "I'm sorry."

My eyebrows shot up. "Sorry? About what?"

"About what happened to him."

"What *did* happen? Were you there? Did you see? Tell me."

He shook loose of my grip. "I just heard something on the news."

"How do you know my fiancé?"

"We're old friends. More like acquaintances now, but I liked him." He motioned toward the main thoroughfare. "I dropped off a fare nearby and had to pass the hospital on my way home, anyway. I wanted to see if he was—how he was."

I looked over my shoulder at the back corner where the cops were in conference, their heads leaned together and their voices low. "Do you want to wait with us?"

He passed a hand over his mouth. "That's nice of you, but I must get going. I just stopped by." He pulled a wallet from his pants pocket and dug out a receipt. After borrowing a pen from the receptionist, he scribbled something and held out the paper. "Please call me if he makes it."

"Makes it?" I repeated in a whisper.

Realizing he'd been too blunt, he blushed. "I meant when he gets better."

"Sure."

On the card, he'd written *Mr. G* and a phone number. When I looked up to thank him for his concern, he was gone.

The interior doors opened again and a man in blue scrubs walked out. Everyone froze as he scanned the room before approaching the woman with the kids.

"Mrs. Donato?"

She gave him a trembling smile. He leaned closer and spoke in a murmur. She gasped and covered her face. The oldest child set down his tablet and stood, placing a hand on her knee.

"Mom?" His voice carried the fright of a youngster whose world was about to change.

She reached out and clutched his hand, laughing through her tears. "Daddy has gas."

That brought a round of fart noises from the younger two and laughter from the surrounding adults, grateful to get a break from their worries.

"It stinks, doesn't it?"

My head jerked to my left to find the stocky guy standing next to me. Up close, I noticed he had one thick eyebrow, like a gigantic caterpillar. He grinned.

"I didn't mean to startle you, but I heard what you said. That your fiancée is in there." He nodded at the double doors. "I'm Gary." He offered me a fist bump, which is no less annoying than a handshake. "My wife is back there. Like I said, it stinks not being able to be with her."

"Is it serious?"

"Everything's serious when you're three months pregnant, right?"

"I wouldn't know," I murmured.

"How about you? Is your guy going to be okay? I mean, I'm sure he will be." He said it with false enthusiasm, as if he had appointed himself my personal cheerleader. I didn't have the energy to fake an answer.

He put his hands on his hips and blew out a stream of air. "It's in God's hands now, right?"

I stared, numb. This stranger had just summed it up in nightmarish finality. I couldn't help Bowers, and it was killing me.

THREE

I made my way around the building and entered the front doors. Two women sat at the Welcome Desk. The long-haired one motioned me over and instructed me to sign in.

"Where are you going?"

When I told her I wanted the cafeteria, she gave me directions down the hallway to my right.

Detective Juanita Gutierrez must have cut through the ER, because she beat me there. Spotting her wasn't a problem. Other than hospital employees and one middle-aged couple, we were the only customers here.

I purchased a cup of coffee from a cheery old lady in a hairnet to give me time to consider my approach. First, I needed to hear what happened to Bowers, both a general recap and the specifics about his injuries. How serious they were. And where it happened, though that was more from curiosity.

As I approached her, Gutierrez disconnected a call and set her cell phone on the table.

"Sorry I'm late."

"I just got here."

I glanced at her phone. "Was that about Bowers?"

She tucked the phone into the pocket of her suit jacket without answering.

Pleasantries over, I got to the point. "Tell me what happened to Bowers."

"He had an accident."

"What kind of accident?"

"He fell."

I leaned forward and folded my hands on the table. "Tripped over the curb? Fell from the top of a building? Be more specific. I have a vivid imagination. The truth will hurt less."

She considered me for a moment. "He fell down a rocky slope. A hillside."

My eyebrows crept up. Rocky slopes didn't just pop up in suspect's backyards. "Not in Wolf Creek."

"Somewhere off C—" She paused. "Off Interstate 17."

"Isn't that outside your jurisdiction?"

"He was taking another look at an old case that had a new lead."

"And that's what he was doing there?"

Her full lips pressed into a thin line. "We're not sure why he was there."

My fingers went to the necklace Bowers had given me for my birthday. As I toyed with the Cross pendant, I reviewed the minuscule amount of information she'd given me.

"I don't buy it."

She shook her head. "There's nothing to buy."

"Bowers didn't just slip and fall. He is as sure-footed as a goat."

A powerful ZING vibrated in my chest. I sat back. I've never understood why I sometimes picked up signals from Juanita Gutierrez, just as I did from animals. However, that electrifying current in my chest meant I had hit on something.

"Goats," I said, stating a fact.

Her eyes popped open, and I saw panic there. "What's this about goats?"

I wasn't about to tell Gutierrez I could sometimes read her when her emotions ran high. She wouldn't laugh it off. But what did goats have to do with Bowers' fall? I'd find them, and once I had those goats in my sights, I'd question the little critters until I had the entire story.

She was giving me an odd look, and I realized I was smiling. Reverting to a frown, which under the circumstances wasn't difficult, I leaned forward and looked her in the eyes. "Tell me about his injuries."

"I'm not a doctor," she snapped.

I wrapped my hands around the Styrofoam cup to give them something to do and placated them by pretending the cup was Gutierrez' throat. "I'm not asking for a diagnosis. Just a report. You give reports all day, don't you? I'll get you started. Did he hurt his arms?"

"His arm? I don't know. I don't think so."

He had a concussion, which meant he must have hurt his head. "His neck?"

"It's possible."

My fingers clutched the cup so hard, coffee overflowed onto the table. With images of a paralyzed Bowers dancing in my head, I ignored the mess and gritted my teeth. "His legs? Did he break a leg?"

"I can say that he hurt his leg."

Legs weren't necessary. He could live without legs.

Could I live with a legless Bowers? It didn't take much thought. Definitely. My difficulties dragging details from the detective was starting to tick me off. "His hands? Toes? Are they okay? What about his nose? His pinky finger?"

She ground her molars together. "I can't say, but here's someone who can."

FOUR

A tall man in dark blue scrubs approached our table. I couldn't see his mouth and nose behind his mask, but his warm, brown eyes showed intelligence. "Detective Gutierrez?"

She was already standing. "Doctor Lerma."

Doctor. My breath came faster, and I stared, unable to speak. Shaking off paralysis, I jumped to my feet. "How is he?" I held out my hand. "I'm Frankie Chandler, Detective Bowers' fiancée."

He nodded in my direction but didn't shake.

"I'm happy to say we got the bleeding from the open fracture under control. We'll have to operate, but with his head injury, I scheduled surgery for tomorrow afternoon so we can keep an eye on him until then. There isn't enough bleeding on his brain to worry me. He should absorb it, but we like to be cautious."

Finally, someone willing to talk. "He'll be okay?"

"He had a terrible fall, but he's young and healthy. I wouldn't recommend he try it again," he added with a chuckle.

My shoulders sagged. "Thank God."

When I turned to Gutierrez, I expected to see relief. Maybe a smile. Instead, she held the doctor's gaze. He flinched first.

"He's not out of danger, but I like to stay positive."

"What kind of danger?" I demanded.

"Um, the dangerous kind."

"Is he conscious? Can I see him?"

Shifting his gaze from me to Gutierrez, he seemed to regret his original sunny prognosis. "No. Not possible. Hospital rules. Can't have people running around the corridors unsupervised. Dragging in germs and disturbing the patients. Chaos. Anarchy." He put the brakes on his rushed explanation and dropped his chin, summing it up in one succinct word. "COVID."

Since scientists, politicians, and the medical world were constantly changing the rules about virus safety, it was a tough point to argue. "May I have his cell phone? I need to call his sisters, and I don't have all their numbers."

The doctor and Gutierrez exchanged another glance. I snapped my fingers to get his attention. "Why do you keep looking at her? *I'm* the fiancée. If you've got anything to tell, tell it to me."

He cleared his throat. "I'm afraid there wasn't a phone among his possessions."

Another ZING from Gutierrez.

"Where did it go?" I asked, struggling to remain polite.

She spread her hands. "He might have dropped it when he fell."

"Tell me where it happened, and I'll go look for it."

"We're taking care of that."

Goats had a reputation for shoving things. Maybe Bowers' fall was an accident, though I couldn't figure out why he'd be hanging out with goats. Unless goats were only part of the equation.

I stepped up to the doctor and pointed to the spot on my body where a rampaging goat would hit me if it took me by surprise. "Did Bowers have bruising on his lower back?" I didn't know how big the goat was, so I covered my bases. "Maybe at the top of his thighs? Matching bruises." I had horns in mind.

"Why?" Gutierrez asked through tight lips.

His brow wrinkled. "His injuries are consistent with a tumble. There are lots of bruises everywhere." His eyes opened wide. "I get it. You're asking if I saw two handprints on his back. No."

Gutierrez made an angry noise. "Ridiculous."

"How about on his stomach?" I persisted. "Or hip?"

He ignored the detective's glare and considered my question. "No. I can say there weren't any specific marks suggesting a fight. Unless you mean his broken rib, but that might have happened in the fall."

I hissed in a breath.

The doctor glanced at the clock on the wall behind the serving counter. "Time to get ready for my next surgery. If you have further questions, leave them with the nurse."

No goat butted Bowers off that hillside. No way. If a set of horns connected with my fiancé hard enough to send him flying, it would have left evidence.

As Dr. Lerma hurried away, Gutierrez grabbed my arm. "Listen, Frankie. I'm sorry you're going through this. Deeply sorry. Your focus needs to stay on Bowers' recovery. Okay?" She clenched her teeth. "You're not talking to any goats, so drop it."

"Goats?" I fluttered my eyelashes. "What goats? Is goat police slang for something?"

She let go of my arm and said she had to get back to work.

That made two of us. Even though I was her coworker's fiancée, she'd keep me in the dark. Fine. I didn't need her help. When Bowers woke up, he'd share the details with me.

Until then, she'd given me something to focus on. Find the goats. Nothing could have prepared me for where that simple task would lead me.

FIVE

Bowers' sisters needed to hear about their brother's condition. I had June's phone number and debated calling her from the hospital, but if the call got emotional, I didn't want to fall apart in front of strangers. According to Dr. Lerma's report, I couldn't do anything for Bowers right now, anyway. And I had to find some goats.

As I unlocked my front door, I got a hitch in my breathing. Bowers had purchased this beautiful door, including a fancy lock, after my ex-boyfriend, Jeff, had kicked the old one down—to rescue, not molest.

Emily greeted me, rubbing her furry body against my legs. I swept her into my arms and buried my face in her fur. My cat loved Bowers. I was pretty sure she preferred him to me, though I'd never asked.

Carrying her to the blue-and-white checkered couch my parents had gifted me when I moved to Arizona, I sat on the center cushion under a painting of a Gambel's quail and dialed June's number. As soon as I heard her voice on the line, the floodgates opened, and a wail rose in the back of my throat.

"Frankie? What's wrong?" She drew in a breath. "Is it Marty?"

As the eldest Bowers sibling, June had raised her baby brother and her six younger sisters after their mother passed away. Bowers was the baby of the family and the only boy, which made him the precious pearl. His sisters guarded their little treasure like Cerberus, the guard dog at the gates of Hell.

"What happened?"

"He fell."

Silence. "Our Marty fell? Was he drunk? He used to get pie-eyed as a teenager, but that's a long time ago."

"Not drunk." I blew my nose. "Sorry about that. He was working."

"You mean he tripped?"

"No. Fell."

After I explained what little Dr. Lerma had told me, June flew into fix-it mode.

"Don't worry about a thing. I'll call the girls. You just take care of yourself and Marty."

"June, what if he—" I sniffed.

"Bite your tongue. I remember when Thunderbolt, the ornery nag the kids learned to ride on, tossed that boy out of the saddle. He landed in a heap and didn't move. Thought he broke his back. Well, as soon as he caught his wind, he got right back on her. Marty is tough. He's going to be fine. You remember that."

"Yes, ma'am."

My parents were next.

My mother answered the phone singing a ditty about how she planned to smoosh my face and cover me with kisses when she saw me tomorrow. "Did you pack something warm? The temperature dropped to fifty degrees last night."

"We—we aren't coming."

Silence. "I'm sure I heard wrong."

And that's when I decided to lie. If I told my mother the truth, at least as far as I knew it, she and my dad would be on the next plane to Phoenix. They'd arrive with warm hugs from my mother and words of encouragement from my father, and I'd cling to them like a child. Parents have that effect when life gets rough. It's safe to fall to pieces because they pick them all up and paste you back together again.

But Bowers needed me. I'd convinced myself the key to his recovery lie in finding out what happened to him. Once I knew that, as well as the extent of his injuries, I would help him make a complete comeback. To do so, I needed to talk to some goats, a quest I'd never share with my parents. Unless I wanted my mother to arrange a full exorcism, I had to stay strong and keep my plans to myself.

Forcing out a chuckle, I said, "Bowers, silly man, fell and hurt himself. He can't travel right now."

To my parents, both in their seventies, falls were serious business. "Did he break anything?"

What would keep him off a plane? When they were Bowers' age, my parent's generation laughed off things like broken arms and legs. Though uncomfortable, they would have taken advantage of early boarding for invalids and told everyone how nice the stewardess had been. I took a chance that a broken rib and the accompanying difficulties with breathing and moving might garner their sympathy.

"He took a tumble down a hillside. Broke a rib or two and took a knock on his noggin. He's in the hospital, but only so they can check him out. Make him wriggle his fingers and toes. It will be difficult for him to get around, so we need to delay our visit."

As I relayed each piece of my version of what happened, sticking as close to the truth as possible, she shouted it out to my father, not exactly as I'd said it.

"Martin is in the hospital. He fell off a mountain!"

"A hillside." Quick to correct her, I blanched at the next line.

"He might be paralyzed," she added.

Could he be? No. The doctor would have mentioned that possibility. "He's going to recover," I said, clinging to June's prediction. "But not by tomorrow morning, which is why we have to cancel our flight."

She summoned my father to the phone.

"Is Martin all right?" he asked. It was a simple question, but I had no answer. I almost broke down and told him the truth. Why shouldn't I have the comfort of my parents during this nightmare?

"He'll be fine," I said, refusing to focus on any other option. "We just won't make it this weekend."

"That's good," he said. "Very good."

As I held back a flood of emotion and tears, my throat ached. Fortunately, Dad didn't expect a response. A clatter and shuffling noises told me my mother had picked up the second phone to join the conversation.

"What do we do now?" she asked.

"We have a lot of cancellations to make, Beverly. People to notify. That's going to take some time."

My mother gasped into the receiver. "What are we going to do with Aunt Betty? We'll have to entertain her ourselves. Albert, don't cancel any events. We'll just explain when we get there."

"People might resent an engagement party without a bride."

"You planned an engagement party for me?" Bowers and I intended to make the rounds and meet my relatives and my parent's friends, but an engagement party...that I didn't expect.

My father, sensing he had fumbled, said, "Who, us?"

"It was supposed to be a surprise," Mom grumbled.

"Thank you." My throat tightened again.

"You tell us when Martin is ready to travel." My mother called to someone in the room. "Get off that right now! I'll get it for you." Returning to me, she said, "Betty is standing on the ottoman, trying to reach a book off the top shelf of the bookcase. If she breaks a leg and has to rehab here, I'm moving in with you." They hung up, leaving me, once again, alone.

SIX

At midnight, I shut off my computer and went to bed. Not that I expected to get much sleep. I was too worried about Bowers and too determined over my next move.

Earlier this evening, I'd tried to force down a microwave dinner. As I jabbed at the minute button, it's possible, with my mind wandering and stress level rising, I slammed the button too many times. Maybe twenty. I'd had to scrape the crunchy noodles from the cardboard container with my bottom teeth, and my kitchen reeked of burnt spaghetti sauce.

Staring across the kitchen table at Bowers' chair, the one he sat in whenever we ate dinner together, I found it odd that my fiancé's colleagues wouldn't tell me what happened to him. The doctor wasn't much help, either. His story kept changing. First, he made Bowers sound like a naughty boy who had escaped a horrible fate. Then he opted for caution and stopped short of telling me not to get my hopes up.

All I saw was his broken body at the base of the cliff. The image played over and over. June might be watching the same movie. To keep my sanity, to save Bowers' sisters from suffering from uncertainty, I needed to *see* what happened to him. The truth was most likely not as dramatic or horrible. And since Bowers couldn't tell me himself...or could he?

Closing my eyes, I imagined a floating road made of lights; an information highway. I sent the stream out the door, swooping around cars and corners as it hurtled toward its destination. Bowers' hospital room. Once at Holy Cross, I had to get creative about his whereabouts, but I figured a man just out of surgery would be asleep on a recovery floor. A normal sleep. Not a coma.

Bowers. It's me. Frankie. Dr. Lerma mentioned a concussion. Did that mean memory loss? I better clarify. *Frankie, your fiancée.* I flashed my favorite picture of us, one where I wasn't eating. *That's me, you lucky dog. Anyway, you're in the hospital right now because you took a fall. A big fall. Duh. Otherwise, you wouldn't be in the hospital. So, do you remember how you got there?*

Nothing. Opening my eyes, I sighed and slumped my shoulders. There were two times I'd connected psychically with Bowers. Both involved animals, and both were accidents. I tried to repeat the process, but Bowers' response had put an end to that. He said he knew what I was up to because *it tickled*. Obviously, I would not gather the details from my fiancé via mental waves. I'd have to rely on old-fashioned legwork.

The only information I had about the incident came from snippets of conversation. Chief Joe said the accident happened somewhere around Interstate 17. And Gutierrez let slip the importance of goats.

But what would I do when I found the goats? Even if they showed me what happened to Bowers in detail, how would that aid in his recovery? To my surprise, Optimistic

Frankie came out of hiding with a suggestion. One that might work.

I reconnected to what I hoped was Bowers and sent images of me sneaking around and exhibiting general nosiness. Just in case goats had something to do with his case, I placed one at my side. Remembering how Gutierrez had warned me off talking to *goats*, as in plural, I added a few more.

Look at me, Bowers. I'm sleuthing. Interfering. Making a nuisance of myself. The only way to stop me is to wake up, get out of that bed, and come stop me yourself. I did not go so far as to stick my thumbs in my ears, wiggle my fingers, and give him a taunting raspberry, but I made it clear the only way to put an end to my antics was to do it himself. In person.

My mood spiraled directly into pity party territory. Unlike Bowers, I didn't have a gazillion sisters to talk things over with. My best friend, Penny, was still a newlywed, so her time belonged to her new husband. My mother was available, but I feared the phone call would end with her on a flight to Phoenix, and all my resolve would dissolve. Without Bowers to talk to, I was alone.

Grandma Chandler used to say, *"Frances. You can't feel sorry for yourself if your busy."* Putting her advice into practice, I set my dinner aside and powered up my computer. Who would have a goat? A petting zoo? But why would anyone put a petting zoo on a slope where kids might injure themselves? Other than me. It made little sense.

Old McDonald had a goat on his farm, at least in the version my mother sang to get me to sleep. Which I never wanted to do. I imagine she added a lot of animals to the original list. I was a tiresome child. However, if the goats were one of many animals on a ranch, I'd never track them down. But what choice did I have?

When I typed in *farms in Maricopa County*, the results showed me U-Pick type farms for a variety of fruits, horse farms, and farmland owned by different colleges.

One listing caught my eye. An actual goat farm. I made my search more specific and gaped at the results. People raised goats. Who knew? Some were dairy goats, some were for meat, and others were raised for their coveted mohair.

I came up with nine potentials. Then I brought up a map and looked over Interstate 17. That narrowed the results to five. After switching the view to satellite, I squinted at the screen and studied the topography, searching for any rise in the land.

Three farms met my criteria. They were all skipping distance from the 17, and they all had hills of varying heights on the property. I wrote down the names, impatient for the morning. One of them held the answer to what happened to Bowers.

SEVEN

The mockingbird that lived in the neighbor's tree greeted me as I dragged myself from the muddled state that follows bad dreams. At two in the morning, I'd jerked awake with a pounding heart, giving a cry that sent Emily scampering off the bed. Somehow, I'd returned to a restless and unsatisfying sleep.

In the morning light, shapes and forms from my nightmare drifted away like dissipating fog, but I could still hear Bowers' desperate calls for help. Naturally, it being a nightmare, I couldn't find him.

As my feathered friend ran through a litany of cheerful calls, I cracked my eyelids open and smacked my lips, trying to rid my mouth of the taste of cardboard. The call of a cactus wren followed the rattle of a house finch, ending on an up sweep that sounded as if the bird were asking a question. My morning Caruso finished with the clear whistle of a goldfinch. Pretty impressive, especially if you were a female mockingbird. The larger the repertoire, the more attractive the mate.

I didn't often wake early enough to attend the performance, but today was special. My limited knowledge of farmers came from Penny's family farm in Wisconsin and June's Arizona farm, which was more of a homestead. Every person who raised animals or worked the land or grew a garden had one thing in common. They rose early. Therefore, I was dressed and out the door by seven am, late by farm time.

Namaste Goats was located off Baseline Road in Gilbert, which wasn't that close to Interstate 17, but it had a hill. A second farm, Falling for Goats, was also in Gilbert, but located farther south on Val Vista Drive. The third goat farm, Bennett's Grazers, was up in Cave Creek. After studying the map on my phone, I began with the closest two. That way, if I struck gold, I wouldn't waste time with the third.

As I drove, the enormity—and possible futility—of my task tickled at my brain. Bowers was in the hospital in only Heaven knew what condition, and I was off to talk to goats. If there had been any chance of seeing him, I would have had my fanny planted in the hospital lobby, waiting for the summons.

The idea of being a few floors away from my fiancé almost enticed me into making a U-turn. After all, what could the goats do but show me the awful accident? Except it might not be an accident, and if it wasn't... "Somebody has to pay."

Wincing at the anger in my voice, I wondered if I was out for vengeance. Normal Frankie wouldn't consider getting back at someone. Retaliation took too much effort. However, the injured party was Bowers, and I vowed to find the culprit if one existed. Then I'd see if I was capable of violence.

After forty minutes on the road, I drove my car through

a light-blue arch and wondered if I had the wrong place. The white wooden sign said Namaste Goats in big letters, and there was a barn of sorts, but it was smaller than expected and the landscaping looked too perfect for barnyard animals.

I left my car in the small lot and scanned the area for four-legged creatures. Mostly, I saw the two-legged variety, both male and female, and the majority wore stretchy exercise clothes. Following the human herd around a square white building, I caught snatches of conversation from the two women ahead of me. They were both in their fifties. The plain-looking brunette wore a long t-shirt advertising a family-owned pizza parlor over her black bike shorts. Her friend, the one with highlighted blond curls, wore makeup and earrings with her robin's egg blue leggings and a pink and blue exercise bra.

"I haven't laughed this hard in a long time."

"Laughter is so good for your immune system. Women's Universe says so."

I'd heard of dinner comedy shows. I even knew a cruise ship comedian. Maybe someone had come up with a way to make exercise fun.

Around the corner, the desert landscaping morphed into a lush lawn of trimmed grass fenced off with crisscrossed bamboo. Beyond the fence, a mound of dirt and gravel rose into an unimpressive slope. If this was the place of Bowers' fall, that incline was more dangerous than it appeared.

With my attention on the scenery, I careened over Miss Highlights, who had plopped into a sitting position on the ground. The lawn didn't have the soft cushioning of my childhood front yard. It was fake turf on a layer of gravel. Or concrete.

"Watch it!" Miss Highlights unwrapped my leg from around her shoulders and threw it off.

By the time I struggled to my feet, both women were lying face down on the ground. Afraid my flailing limbs had taken them both out, I bent and peered at them.

"Are you all right?"

They didn't answer, but a quick search for help showed me people dropping to their faces in slow motion. Though the idea of exercising from a prone position appealed to me, the sight of sprawled bodies gave me the willies. Were they suffering from a mass hallucination? Were they *drugged*?

Sniffing the air, I detected jasmine and frankincense. But hadn't I heard a news story about a beautiful yellow flower called Angel's Trumpet that contained a potent narcotic? Were there other flowers, indigenous to Arizona, able to deliver the same results? Something my sniffer couldn't detect.

I covered my mouth and nose, jumped over Pizza Shirt Woman, and backed away.

"Can I help you?"

A tall, slim woman with sandy-colored hair smiled at me. If I'd been wearing a leopard print leotard, I would have smiled too, but from embarrassment. The name tag stuck to her flat chest said Tamara. Her breathy voice sounded as if she needed a hit of oxygen. Other than that, she didn't appear to be suffering any ill effects from breathing the air—no sudden desire to fall flat on her face—so I lowered my hand.

I'd decided not to ask direct questions about Bowers until I confirmed whether the human residents of the farm were friend or foe.

"Um, I'm here to see the goats."

"Ah." She folded her hands into a prayer position.

"Many people like to observe their first time. If you would move over there, please. Only paying customers get the foot massage." She giggled. "Or should I say get massaged by feet?"

Had I stumbled across some sick orgy? A cult that rendered their victims unconscious and then abused them with their feet?

My head whipped to the left at a chorus of baas. Goats.

She let out a breathy giggle. "They may be small, but they're *very* active. Now, if you would move?"

After directing me to the area outside the fence, Tamara stepped to the front of the lawn, took in a deep breath while sweeping her arms to her sides and above her head, and then lowered her arms with her palms pressed together as she exhaled. She clapped her hands twice. The gate opposite where I stood opened, and a dozen dwarf goats leaped into the arena. After warming up with a few kicks, the little critters swarmed the delighted participants.

Miss Highlights and Pizza Shirt moved to their hands and knees and were instantly rewarded. Two goats mounted their backs—one goat per back. The animals stood and bleated, looking like explorers who had just conquered Everest.

Everyone wore bright smiles except the few who hadn't been stomped on by goats. One man stretched out his arm and wiggled his fingers, attempting to entice a brown doe who was playing coy.

I'd opened the gateway into my mind this morning and I sent a rush of highways to the hairy masseuses. Just as I connected, a loud rumbling echoed from behind the hill. Three dirt bikes mounted the crest. The riders paused to observe the goat action. One of them yelled *Namaste* at the top of his lungs, and his friend's laughter egged him on to add *Nirvana!*

Tamara had a set of lungs on her. "You're interfering with our life energy, you half-wits!"

Pizza Woman shook her fist. "Noise pollution!"

By the pitch and snark of the responding howls of laughter, I figured they were teens. The one on the green bike let out a whoop and descended the hill in a wheelie. He must have hit a rock, because his back tire wobbled, and he flew over the handlebars. Even Tamara cried out in shock as he bounced and rolled down the hill, landing in a heap of limbs.

In the silence that followed, I sprinted toward the motionless form, my feet spurred on by visions of Bowers in the same condition with no one around to help him.

As I reached the biker's prone body, he let out a groan. The face under the shield belonged to a teenager. Dazed, he blinked his brown eyes and coughed.

"Stay still." I patted the air to demonstrate in case he'd knocked all his common sense away. "You might have broken something."

Despite my pleas, he sat up, let out a breath, and refusing my extended hand, clambered to his feet. His friends whooped and laughed with relief.

"That was amazing!" one called. "Do it again!"

He set off to retrieve his bike without acknowledging my concern. Most of the formerly collapsed bodies had come to the fence to watch the drama. As they turned away, some mumbled comments about how the kid deserved it. The nicer people expressed gratitude that he hadn't been seriously injured.

One by one, they dropped and resumed their prone positions on the artificial turf. Still connected to the animals, my chest flooded with joy. The little hairballs were excited. Though they didn't say so in words, the goats considered the human beings their personal playthings, sent for their enjoyment.

Disgusted, I turned on my heels and walked back to my car. I'd heard of foot fetishes, but hoof fetishes? Besides. No way did one of those little pygmies knock Bowers off a hillside. Not that the slope next to Namaste Farms was much of a hill. If that biker survived his fall, so could Bowers. Granted, my fiancé hadn't been wearing a helmet, but the kid hadn't even sprained a wrist.

On to the next farm.

EIGHT

Back in the car, I dialed the hospital and asked for Martin Bowers' room. To my surprise, the receptionist transferred the call. At least I'd now know which floor he was on.

Apparently, it was the anonymous floor. The nurse who answered the phone only said, "Nurse's Station."

"Which floor is this?"

She answered with a question. "Who's speaking?"

"My name is Frances Chandler. My fiancé is a patient. I'd like to speak with him."

"I'll transfer you, but next time you should ask the operator to transfer you directly. What is his name?"

My voice was breathless with excitement. "Martin Bowers."

"You can't speak with him," she said without further explanation.

Panic took hold. "He's still not awake?"

"They're prepping him for surgery."

"Surgery? Already? What time is the operation? Dr. Lerma didn't say."

She reluctantly confirmed surgery was scheduled for

two o'clock. That left me plenty of time to visit my second destination, Falling for Goats.

The name promised more twisted people fawning over cloven-hooved imps, but the entrance was off a dirt road, and the property looked like the desert version of a respectable ranch.

The parking lot was a large area of dirt without designated spots. As I got out of my car, a man in overalls exited a single-story building. With potted plants on either side of the doorway and white lace curtains in the window, I pegged it as his home, which seemed somewhat informal for a business.

He approached me without speaking, so I waited by my car with my hand on the door handle in case he wasn't friendly.

As soon as he reached me, he said, "How can I help you?" He kept his volume low, like a parent whose colicky infant has just fallen asleep.

What was he selling? An experience like Namaste Goats? Or would he expect me to load an animal into the back seat of my two-door car? I kept it simple.

"I'd like to see your goats."

He nodded. "Are you looking for meat?"

I gasped and took a step back. "If you mean do I want to eat your goats, I don't."

His smile showed relief, and he gestured toward a pen. "Then step this way." He proceeded to tell me about their feeding and exercise routine, stressing how well cared for they were. In my desire to catch the attention of my subjects, I wasn't listening, though I did hear the word *Tennessee*.

My footsteps slowed to match his pace, and as we inched our way to the pen, I noted the hillside behind the house. Like the one at Namaste Goats, it was more of a rolling hill than a steep, jagged drop, and the many cacti and shrubs dotting the landscape would have broken Bowers' fall long before he hit the bottom.

"Do you get many visitors here?"

"We do a steady business," he said. "Most review the pictures on our website and set up a meeting."

I wondered what the meeting ritual entailed. "What are they looking for in a goat?"

As we arrived at the pen, the residents moved forward to check us out. They were cute, but nothing special.

"Looks. Personality. Mostly the latter. Some people like 'em as pets. I've had petting zoos inquire, but I don't want people laughing at them."

The billies and nannies came in a variety of colors, from a mix of tan and white to white with black spots. Two had snow-white fur. Some came with horns. Some did not.

I felt a tug as one super cutie with dark brown fur nibbled on my shirt sleeve. Leaning over the pen, I scratched behind his ear, and he rewarded me with soft bleats.

Suddenly, my cell phone rang. I'd turned the volume on high while I was in the shower this morning and had forgotten to turn it down. Mistake.

The goat leaped twice, seized up, and toppled onto his side. His legs stuck out, stiff, making him look like he was in rigor mortis.

"Oh, shoot. I'm so sorry." I jabbed at the buttons until I disconnected the 800 number. "Did he hurt himself? Is he okay?"

The animal struggled to his feet and strolled away, flicking his tail. The farmer raised his brows. "I assumed this is what you were looking for."

"A goat having a seizure?"

He laughed. "Not a seizure. These are Tennessee Fainting Goats. They have a myotonic gene. It's hereditary. They get stiff when startled."

"The poor things!"

"It doesn't hurt them."

"You're sure?"

"Yes."

"Positive?" A lot depended on his answer.

"Positive."

"Good to know." I took a deep breath and opened the doorway into my mind. The noise that greeted me was frantic and jumpy. Since I had limited time, I needed to send out a general request for information about Bowers. I broadcasted a a movie that showed what might have happened to him. Nothing prepared me for the response.

My arms and legs shot out, stiff. As I tipped back on my heels, my limbs wouldn't respond. One firm step back and I'd regain my balance. Instead, I toppled.

"What's going on?" The farmer swung into the pen in one jump.

My limbs relaxed, but the fall had knocked the wind out of me. Coughing, I got to my hands and knees and peered through a separation in the fence. Every single goat had collapsed with shock. As they struggled to their feet, I searched their minds for recognition. Any response.

I got one, but it was from the farmer. A request to leave.

NINE

Entering Prickly Pear Bistro usually lifted my spirits. Who wouldn't smile at booths, tables, and chairs reflecting the pinks, greens and purples of the namesake cactus? Or the savory smells of salty bacon and cheese, fried chicken, and fried eggs for those who like breakfast all day long. The clink of silverware as diners relished every bite. The cheerful chatter of the staff as they treated the regulars like family.

As a bonus, my best friend, Penny, owned the restaurant. We considered the center booth along the window our spot. Every time I walked in, I felt I'd come home.

But not today.

Penny spotted me from behind the counter. It was easy to mistake my friend for a naive pushover. Her sunny disposition made people think she was an innocent, and her fresh looks didn't help her case. Today, she wore her white-blond hair in two braids and wore a pink blouse with her jeans. She raised her hand in greeting. The crooked smile slipped off her face, and after whispering to Ann, her senior waitress, she rushed to meet me.

"I can't stay," I began, but she shushed me and made me sit down, taking the bench opposite me. After making a signal to the waitress, she gave me her attention.

"What's happened? You're supposed to be on a plane to Wisconsin."

As I started my story, she grabbed hold of my hands and squeezed. Somehow, I made it to the end without crying, but we both had tears in our eyes.

"Frances, I am so sorry. What can I do?"

My lips trembled as I attempted a smile. "Tell me everything's going to be all right."

If it sounds like I was pressuring my friend to be perky, I wasn't. We were opposites. In my world, neon signs dotted the landscape. Warning signs that flashed, revealing every conceivable danger on the horizon. Penny saw pretty lights.

"What did the doctors say?"

I harrumphed. "Doctor. As in one. He's doing surgery on Bowers' leg this afternoon. All he said was they were watching him."

She snorted. "Watching him do what?"

Even though she was kidding, she'd hit on an excellent point. "That's just it. I don't know. They won't let me talk to him or see him. They won't tell me anything about his condition." I threw up my hands. "I can't even tell you if he's conscious."

"Can't you call his room? They *must* let you call his room, right?"

"I've tried, but the nurses stonewall me every time." My eyes narrowed. "I suspect the receptionist is in on it, too. She wouldn't answer when I asked what floor he was on. I mean," my throat constricted, "if he's not in ICU, that would be a good thing, right?"

She frowned. "That sounds extreme. Did they tell you

why they weren't talking? Maybe they don't know anything yet. No. That's dumb. The hospital should know his condition. Did you tell them you were his fiancée?"

"Repeatedly."

"You didn't get fiancée privileges? Those monsters." Her voice carried and caught the attention of several diners. Penny, true to form, searched for a positive spin. "Maybe their hands are tied. It's possible you have to be married before they consider you a family member. Legally, I mean."

My head drooped until my forehead rested against the cool table. "What if he's in the morgue?"

"Frances! They'd tell you *that*." She leaned back and smiled. "Ask Detective Gutierrez. I realize you aren't best friends, but in this situation—"

"I did. She won't tell me anything either, except that he fell while working. Somewhere off the 17."

She wrinkled her nose. "That's outside Wolf Creek's jurisdiction."

"A fresh lead came up on one of his cases. That's all Gutierrez would say. She's not even sure that's why he was there."

"There? Where's there?"

"Wherever he fell."

"They won't even tell you where it happened?"

I lifted my head. "It's a conspiracy."

Ann set down my usual corned beef hash and a cup of coffee. She gave me a look of concern but didn't interrupt us, confident that Penny would fill her in later.

"I don't get it." Penny said. "Don't the police have to tell their supervisors what they're working on? And where they're going? If they don't, they should."

The savory smells of hash steaming from my plate made

me aware of how hungry I was. The first mouthful confirmed it.

"I just want to know what happened," I said, my voice tight. "I've been searching for where it happened. The only thing I'm sure of is it has something to do with goats. I've already hit two possibilities."

At the mention of my animal communication skills, Penny clasped her hands together and her eyes shone with the fanatical devotion of a groupie.

"And? What did the goats say?"

"Nothing." I shoveled in more hash and talked with my mouth full, too tired to care. "People are screwballs. The first place I went, the people were cavorting with goats."

She tightened her lips. "Define cavorting." Having grown up on a farm, Penny had strict rules regarding human-animal interactions. Animals raised for food were fine to eat, but cruelty and misuse raised her hackles.

"There were all these people, and they threw themselves on the ground and begged these miniature goats to stomp on them."

"Yikes!"

"It was too bizarre. Seeing them all enjoy it made me sick. They just lay there in the grass, waiting and hoping for the goats to jump on them."

Her brow wrinkled. "What was this place called?"

"Namaste Goats, which sounds pretty harmless."

When she could no longer hold it in, she threw back her head and let out an unnecessarily loud cackle. "Frances, you are priceless." She wiped away a tear with the back of her hand. "That was goat yoga."

I'd heard the term before. but it sounded too silly to take seriously. "That was yoga?"

"It's supposed to be beneficial. The laughter and the

massage the goats give you with their cloven hooves helps you relax."

Embarrassed by my ignorance, I moved on. "Oh, yeah? Well, what about the second place? The goats fainted." I didn't mention my role in knocking them flat.

She nodded. "Sacrificial lambs."

"Not lambs. Goats. Aren't baby goats called kids?"

"Sacrificial Lamb is what sheep ranchers call a Tennessee Fainting Goat. They use them as a decoy. If something comes after the sheep, the goat faints and the wolf, or whatever, gets the goat. Not the sheep."

I gaped. "The poor thing dies because of a genetic disorder?"

"It's inconvenient for the goat." Noting my expression, she patted my hand. "Think of the baby sheep that gets saved."

Farm women are pragmatic when it comes to life and death.

"Detective Bowers is in the hospital under the care of doctors and nurses. He's being looked after. That's the important thing. So, you don't find out how he got there. What's the worst that could happen?"

Penny had offered me a chance to vent my fears. I took it. "What if his recovery depends on knowing what happened? If his brain won't unscramble unless it has the facts?"

"His brain is scrambled?" she murmured.

"He might spend years in a stupor, obsessing over what happened. Or what if he develops a phobia and can't walk outdoors because he's afraid he'll trip over his feet and fall? I mean, I'm not that outdoorsy, but it might be nice to go on a nature walk once in a while."

"Frances—"

I was on a roll. "Or what if someone did this to him? No way will I let anyone get away with hurting Bowers. Even worse, his subconscious might not want to recover unless it's sure whoever did this is behind bars."

"You're deep diving down the rabbit hole and creating the worst possible spin on what happened." She took my hand again. "What does your gut tell you?"

Why would she trust my gut? I certainly don't. But when I inhaled a slow breath and closed my eyes, considering all that happened since yesterday, one thought jumped up-and-down, hand raised and begging for my attention. I opened my eyes.

"Something stinks."

"Then you need to assume something odd has happened."

"And then what?"

"You've got good instincts."

"I do?"

"Follow them. And don't let anyone tell you you're wrong. Including you. You don't give yourself enough credit."

Penny was right. Too much depended on my next steps to allow Insecure Frankie to take the lead.

I glanced around at the patrons. "I don't suppose you would like to come with."

I'd never made the offer to let her watch me at work before, but I was feeling lonely, and that made me generous. Her face lit up and dimmed in succession.

"We're having dinner with Kemper's boss."

"That's okay."

"I'd love to, but—"

"It's okay, Pen. Really."

Ann stepped up and asked if I wanted dessert. "You look like you could use something sweet."

Surprised, I realized I'd cleaned my plate. "Thanks for the offer, but I have to get to the hospital. Bowers goes in for surgery at two."

The waitress checked her watch. "You better get a move on. It's twenty 'till."

We stood, and after squeezing the air out of me with a hug, Penny reminded me that she and her husband, Kemper, were at my disposal. Anything I needed, I had only to call them.

Knowing how Kemper would do almost anything to avoid talk about psychic communication with animals, I hoped that scenario would never arise.

TEN

As I approached the main entrance to Holy Cross hospital, the long-haired woman from the welcome desk stood outside in an animated discussion with another woman who looked familiar. Her long-sleeved bohemian dress in a brown and rose floral pattern gathered at the wrists and cinched at the waist. A wide tan ruffle brushed her ankles. Her hair was hidden by a broad-rimmed straw hat.

My feet slowed when I saw what she held in her arms. A small white pooch. Windy.

"Dymphna?" I said, my voice cracking.

Dymphna Bowers traveled to her own tune. She wandered in and out of jobs with the nonchalance of an independently wealthy woman, which she was not; had all the characteristics of a woke vegan even as she enjoyed her steak; and never, *never* went anywhere without her precious miniature poodle, Windy. Some might say she was a nonconformist. In my opinion, she was an oddball.

Bowers' middle sister twirled to me and smiled. In a voice just above a whisper, she said, "Frankie, tell this woman that my Snuggums is a therapy dog."

Dymphna had the bad habit of using a soft voice that only dogs and neighborhood gossips could detect. Because of that, the flowing fabrics she favored, and the way she moved and held herself as if she bordered on anemia, I'd dubbed her Ghost Woman.

She *said* whispering was a habit. In my opinion, she did it for attention. And to annoy people. And to fool them into seeing her as helpless when the woman possessed shooting trophies and once threatened to put a bullet between the eyes of a very bad man.

The hospital employee, used to dealing with lung patients and shaky old people, had no trouble hearing her. She narrowed her eyes. "I don't see a vest on that dog."

Windy's pet mom tittered. "She doesn't have one. She's naturally empathetic."

"No vest. No entry."

Dymphna propped up Windy so the canine's face rested against hers. The animal had packed on a few pounds, and I heard Dymphna's grunt. "Isn't the naughty woman being silly?"

Windy leaned her head back and stared at me upside down, willing me to take her away and give her a treat. Maybe a small roast.

"Do you know this woman?" the welcome lady demanded.

Bowers' surgery was scheduled to start any minute. What if, just as the anesthesiologist told him to count backward from one hundred, he tore off the mask and called my name? Or held up a hand and refused to go on unless he heard my voice? I couldn't waste precious moments playing referee for his flighty sister.

And embarrassing as it is to admit, it occurred to me that Dymphna Bowers might be a jinx. Her own boyfriend had died last year. Murdered. Not that death was contagious, but I was feeling a tad superstitious right now.

Dymphna and I locked eyes, and I saw the change when she realized her fate. Her sleepy orbs popped open so wide her long eyelashes almost brushed her hairline.

"Never met her."

Instead of letting me pass, which would have been the gracious thing to do, Dymphna stepped forward and blocked my path. "Liar. You called me by name." Her volume moved way above a whisper.

"I was praying to Saint Dymphna. She's the patron saint of people with nervous disorders and anxiety. Mental illnesses. I took one look at you and said, 'Oh, Saint Dymphna, help her.'"

She didn't need me to explain who she was named after, and I left her gaping and breezed through the entrance. A few steps into the room, a voice called my name. On the couch in the center of the lobby sat the man from the ER. The one with the wife.

"Gary?"

He stood. "We're moving up in the world."

"Excuse me?"

He gestured around the room. "This is a step up from the Emergency Room."

I motioned toward the welcome desk. "I need to find out what floor the surgery is on so I can wait there."

While I talked, he shook his head. "Not going to happen."

"It's not?"

"If you even look at the elevators funny, those women will tackle you. No one's allowed on the floors except patients and staff."

He settled back down on the couch and patted the

cushion next to him. Though I desperately wanted to be alone with my thoughts, I couldn't find a polite way to reject his offer. With one last longing look at the bank of elevators, I sat down.

The entrance doors slid open, and I tensed, but instead of an angry Dymphna—with or without the dog—an elderly man in jeans and a gray, long-sleeved t-shirt strolled in with a brindle pit bull sporting a royal blue vest. As the man signed in at the desk, the remaining welcome woman, the one with the spiky blond hair, produced a treat for the pup.

"Gently," the man said, and the dog took the small bone-shaped cookie in his teeth without gobbling. As he chewed, his golden-brown eyes connected with mine, and my heart ached. What would make a dog that sad?

"The children's cancer ward is expecting you, so if you could go there first. The kids are very excited."

"Right-oh. Are you ready Bruce?"

The dog shook as if he'd just had a bath, held his head high, and wagged his tail, prepared for battle. He looked over his shoulder as he trotted to the elevators, and I sensed his resolve to make those children smile.

"A pit bull," Gary said. "An unusual choice."

"Not really. Bullies make excellent therapy dogs."

He watched Bruce enter the elevator. "Isn't that something?"

My phone rang. It was June.

"Excuse me. I have to take this." Grabbing my chance, I escaped Gary and wandered toward the wall of windows. "Hello, June."

"Did Dym make it there? As soon as I told her about Marty, she grabbed that dog of hers and took off in my Suburban."

"What time was this?"

"I didn't reach her until about noon."

"She couldn't make it here in two hours."

"You don't know Dym. There isn't a speed limit she hasn't broken. I'm a little worried about her, driving while distracted about Marty."

My little snub was about to bite me in the behind. "I might have seen someone who *looked* like her in the parking lot."

"I feel so much better. Could you do me a favor and recommend a few hotels to her? Nothing fancy. She doesn't always plan ahead."

About to name a few inexpensive chains, Polite Frankie rapped my forehead with her knuckles. I argued that I hadn't invited Dymphna, so I wasn't responsible for her comfort. She pointed out Bowers' sisters were about to become mine. Drat. She had a point. It would comfort Bowers to have his family around him, and it would irritate him if he discovered I'd shoved Ghost Woman off to a cheap motel.

"She can stay with me."

"You've got enough going on right now. I'm sure you have some decent places to stay in the area."

"It's settled, and if you argue, I'll plug my ears and sing. Trust me. You don't want me to sing."

"It would be a relief to know she was with you. Are you sure it's not too much trouble?"

"Dymphna can take the couch. Besides. I won't get much sleep. It will be nice to have company. Would you call your sister with the good news?"

Relieved when she said yes, I gave her my security code, the one for the fancy lock Bowers had installed. I also told her where I hid my spare key, since the door required both methods to gain entry. Just to be sure, I verified my address.

"Are your parents there?"

Ah. My parents. The ones I'd lied to.

"They had to take care of a lot of stuff. Cancellations. Explanations."

"I can imagine."

Her tone said June had a low opinion of parents who didn't abandon protocol and rush to their daughter's aid. It wasn't fair.

"Mom was ready to book a flight, but I talked her out of it. People are funny. If my parents rushed to my side and left them hanging without a warning and an explanation, they might hold it against Bowers."

She accepted my assessment of human nature. "Call me as soon as his surgery is over."

After I hung up, I settled onto a single chair to discourage Gary from joining me, which left me with a few prayers I remembered from childhood. I hoped they were good enough.

ELEVEN

"Miss Chandler."

I jerked awake, disoriented by the orange glow that filled the lobby until I connected it with the setting sun illuminating the windows. How long had I been asleep?

Dr. Lerma stood over me. With his mask on, I found it impossible to read his expression. I jumped to my feet.

"How is he?" My voice trembled.

"He's in recovery. We put a nice piece of titanium in his leg to hold the bone together. We can't do anything for the broken rib but let it heal. As for his concussion…well, concussions are funny."

I released my breath in a long stream. "So, the surgery was successful?"

Above his mask, his eyes took on a wary expression.

"Let's wait until he wakes up and has an examination."

"He's going to recover."

"I can't predict the future. People respond in different ways."

"I'm sure he'll be fine." Dr. Lerma's caution made me react with certainty. "Can I see him?"

"I'm afraid not."

It took effort to keep from throwing a fit. "You have phones in hospital rooms, don't you? I'll settle for calling him."

"I'm afraid, in this instance, they—I've recommended no phone calls. I don't want him disturbed."

"You're afraid of a lot," I snapped.

The long-haired welcome woman had returned from her argument with Dymphna while I was sleeping. On hearing my tone, she rolled her eyes, and the blond woman reached for the phone, ready to speed dial security.

Something was off. At my comment, the doctor stiffened, and I knew he longed to defend himself. When he first approached me, he'd talked about titanium and broken ribs as if they weren't a big deal. Now, he was Mister Cautious. His odd behavior added frosting to my layer cake of anxiety.

"I know you don't have a crystal ball, but surgeries are either successful or unsuccessful. Can't you even tell me that?"

Something flashed in his eyes, but the doctor kept his cool. "I understand it's difficult, but for the next few days—"

"Days?"

"I'm afraid that's final." The doctor's tone was gentle but firm. "I'll let you know if there's a change."

As Dr. Lerma walked away, Gary popped up at my side. "Is your fiancé on the mend?"

"I'm sure he is." I didn't want to bring the guy down.

His head tilted to the left. "They're giving you the runaround, too, huh?"

"Is your wife going to be okay? And the baby?"

"They're keeping her under observation. I suppose I should be happy because there are doctors looking after her, but I'd like to see her. Give her a hug and a rub on the belly. Wouldn't it be funny if they were released at the same time?"

"That would be nice." My response lacked enthusiasm.

Grabbing my hand, he said, "Why don't we pray together?"

I tried to reclaim my hand, but he had a firm grip. Mortified, I stared as he leaned his head back and closed his eyes. "Father God, I bring you my new friend, Frankie." He peered out of one eye. "What did you say your last name was?"

I didn't remember giving him my first name, but if I had, it was enough. "Frankie's good."

He nodded and squeezed both eyes shut again. "Her fiancé —" He peered again. I didn't like slogging Bowers' name around to strangers, so I said the first thing that came to mind.

"Twinkie." Twinkie? Maybe I should have taken Ann up on her offer of dessert. In for a pound, I made up a first name, too. "Um, Joe. Twinkie is my pet name for him."

From then on, he kept both eyes fixed on me while he prayed. "Heal Joe, er, Twinkie from—" So caught up in his communing with Heaven, he forgot his own strength and squeezed my hand until it hurt. "I need to name what he's battling. Prayer works better when it's specific. What brought him here? A sudden illness? Cancer? Or maybe an accident?"

This was getting too personal. "Um, all the above?"

The prayer wrapped up quickly after that. Gary didn't seem to hold a grudge. He chucked me on the shoulder.

"Stay positive. Your fiancé will be all right."

"Don't you want to pray for your wife and baby?"

Startled at the suggestion, his eyes opened wide. He

gave me a broad smile. "Nice of you to remember them. They'll be fine. I can feel it."

The only thing I felt was a need to check out the final goat farm. If those weren't the right animals...I wouldn't consider that possibility.

TWELVE

Before going anywhere, I sat in my car and dialed Seamus McGuire, owner of Canine Camp and my official pet sitter. It helped that his doggie day care was on the other side of the Prickly Pear Bistro, making drop off and pick up a breeze.

Once I updated him on Bowers and promised to call as soon as I knew anything more, I headed north for Cave Creek.

With a forty-minute drive and no desire to listen to the radio, I spent my time pondering our canceled weekend trip, something I hadn't dared to do since Bowers' fall. Right now, we should be schmoozing with my relatives and avoiding Aunt Gertrude's pretzel salad at all costs.

About Aunt Gertrude. Would my aged relative hold a grudge? For a brief time during her visit, Bowers suspected her of murdering her rival in baking and love, and rightfully so. Considering how many times she lied to him by omission, making him more suspicious, she should give him a pass.

Tonight should have found Bowers and me dining out

with my parents, followed by a girl's only night thrown by Penny's cousin, Gina Bradley. With her long legs and reddish-brown hair, she would be the most beautiful woman in the room. I supposed her presence would bring Penny's older brother Robby to Loon Lake, since he and Gina had been an item since my friend's wedding. Once news of Gina's adoption came out, people stopped worrying about three-headed children and endorsed their romance.

Mother had mentioned several potlucks with church groups, her crochet group, and neighbors. She'd even scheduled dinner with her parish priest, Father Jakius. Now that I attended church weekly, maybe he wouldn't try to sneak in an exorcism. Not that he knew I could communicate with animals for real. My many years of faking it, the years I spent away from the Church, and the brief time I lived with my ex-boyfriend, Jeff, gave my mother all the ammunition she needed to call for a cleansing.

As I entered Cave Creek, my assumption that every artisan in Arizona lived in Wolf Creek flew out the car window. The town's unique zoning appealed to free spirits of every type. Metal flowers leaning out of buckets, statuary frozen in time, and bright paintings displayed on easels outside of galleries gave the tourists lining the main thoroughfare something to admire.

I turned left off Cave Creek Road onto N. Pinto Road, a side street that meandered past a few extensive properties equipped with horses and houses. Past a bend, I came upon a small corn field on the left. The stalks ran within a yard of a gravel driveway that bore a hand-stenciled sign next to the street. Bennett's Grazers.

My insides did a little dance. I was closing in on my target. Soon, I'd see what happened to Bowers. I'd decide what to do with the information later.

Passing the entrance, I reached the end of the road about a hundred yards farther down, where it petered out in what would someday be a cul-de-sac once they built more houses. Not that the developer was having much luck.

Halfway between Bennett's and the end of the road, on the opposite side of the street from the farm, stood the charred remains of a new home. Since the builder's sign still stood out front, I assumed the structure had been in a work in progress when it burned. Only the blackened frame and a few hardier boards remained. Not a good advertisement for Bright Star Construction.

The air coming in my car reeked of wood ash and smoke. I cranked my window up, thanking God the fire hadn't spread into the surrounding desert. Oh, yes. There is enough scrub and grass in the desert to feed a fire.

Once I turned the car around, I rolled up and parked next to what I believed marked the location of Bowers' accident. As I got out of the car, I shaded my eyes against the descending sun.

Next to the property, to the right of an enormous barn in need of paint, the ground rose to a menacing crest. The face was a sharp decline dotted with boulders and the occasional saguaro cactus. I drew in a sharp breath, imagining the results of a downhill tumble. This had to be the place.

Bennett's Grazers covered more area than the first two goat farms I'd been to, at least six acres, though it was hard to tell what land belonged to the farm and what was wild desert. And that assumed the cornfield belonged to Farmer Bennett.

A careworn house stood back from the road about fifty yards. Closer to the street, overlapping the length and width of the barn, chicken wire reinforced a fenced area. The tops of heads and horns moved within the pen. The goats. My steps quickened as I covered the ground between us.

After one last scan for witnesses, I opened the gate and slipped inside. The occupants crowded around me, nibbling on my shirt and butting me gently. The unfortunate reaction at Falling for Goats convinced me to keep the movie of Bowers' fall in reserve as I prepared myself to communicate with the herd. Unfortunately, the goats had other things on their mind. Food.

Come and get it? Come and get it? Come and get it? The phrase, delivered in hopeful tones, assaulted me as the animals gathered around, bumping me so I struggled to remain standing. Several of them stared at the ground, but all I saw was a mixture of sawdust and straw...until it wasn't.

My feet skittered backwards to avoid the jumble of kitchen scraps—banana peels, lettuce leaves, fruit cuttings, orange peels, and tomatoes, all diced into small pieces and mixed in with oats. As everyone put in their greedy two cents, the pile grew by layers until it stood taller than me.

"No. *No* come and get it," I said, shaking my head for emphases. The pile disappeared.

I got an image of the tissue in my pocket right before a brown doe jerked it from me and gobbled it up.

"Here goes nothing." I took a gentle approach and sent an image of Bowers walking up the hillside. Two goats swiveled their heads toward the gate, and I learned there was a patch of clover around the back of the barn.

Though curious, the goats didn't have much else to tell me. That's what I thought before I clutched my stomach, feeling a burn.

This was it. They had news about Bowers. Had someone punched him in the stomach to disable him? Is that how his attacker managed to get him over the edge?

A long, loud belch escaped my lips. At the same time, a goat with a stomach resembling a full water balloon expelled gas. She eyed one of the little goats hopping around the periphery and turned her gaze on me as if to ask if I was expecting, too. That the animal knew she carried a kid in her belly shocked me.

When two more goats eyed the latch on the gate with hope, my frustration leaked out.

"You *must* be the right ones. You're my last option."

As I ran my fingers through my hair, a sharp ZING penetrated the skin between my shoulder blades. Turning slowly, I locked gazes with Detective Juanita Gutierrez.

THIRTEEN

Detective Gutierrez strolled up and placed her hand on the fence. "I told you to stay away from the goats."

Caught red-handed. After considering my options, I distracted the detective with some bluster. "You're just ticked because I figured out where Bowers fell."

With my attention on the goats, I hadn't noticed the sandy-haired, thickly built man wearing a denim shirt and jeans headed my way from the barn. Raising one hand, he hailed us. "Can I help you?"

I climbed over the fence and landed on my feet just as he reached the pen.

"It's usual for people to come to the house before they mingle with the goats. Actually, most people don't mingle."

He brought with him the stench of sweat, and his brown eyes weren't pleased. He wasn't alone in that sentiment. Another large man, this one with a long, dirty-blond ponytail wearing a plaid shirt and overalls, stepped out the open barn door. He didn't come closer but leaned on the door frame and watched, waiting. I might have interrupted them in preparing the goats' feed, or fixing a plow, or any of the long list of duties I remember watching Penny's grandfather do.

Gutierrez didn't step up and explain her presence, which made me wonder if she had an agenda. I didn't care. Now that I had an opportunity to find out what happened to my honey, I planned to squeeze every bit of information out of those goats, and no farmer was going to stop me.

Rubbing my chest as if it ached, I let my shoulders slump and my lower lip protrude. "I had to see for myself." I sniffed. "My fiancé fell on your property. I'm not sure exactly where." I made a show of searching the surrounding landscape, turning my head left to the farmhouse and barn, right toward the open desert across the road, and up to the peak of the hill behind his house.

"They found him over there." He jerked his chin toward the area at the base of the hill. "Do you want to see it up close?"

"No, no." Afraid he would move me away from the goats, I put the back of my hand to my forehead. "I've changed my mind. I can't bear to see where it happened. It's enough to feel his presence. To know before he fell, he was looking at the same things I'm looking at. Like these precious goats."

I reached over the fence and stroked the ears of the closest one. The farmer's eyes popped open, and he held up both hands. "You can't sue me. He was trespassing on my land."

I narrowed my eyes. "You knew he was here, um, Mister...?"

"Del. Del Bennett. Not until it was all over. I saw the ambulance and police cars and went to find out what was going on. Why was he here?"

Gutierrez sent another *ZING*, one that sent me stumbling back. Even though she wasn't aware I could feel her emotions, I resented the assault anyway and glared at her.

"Whoa, little lady. Are you feeling faint?"

I fanned myself. "It's the heat." And it was hot, about ten degrees warmer than Wolf Creek.

"We were just about to move the goats into the barn."

Ignoring his invitation to leave him to his duties, I sighed with heart-wrenching sadness. "I'm not interested in suing you. Though maybe if you had seen him and called for help earlier, he wouldn't have suffered so much." I threw back my head and cried out. "When I imagine him, all alone and in pain, it gets me right here." I thumped my chest, holding back tears over the thought of him, alone and in pain.

He scratched the spot behind his ear. The same spot Emily likes me to focus my fingernails on. "No disrespect intended, but that's a lame reason for breaking into my goat pen."

My shoulders lifted and dropped with a dramatic sigh. "I came here to find closure."

"Closure." He grunted. "Did he die?"

His bluntness made me gasp. So did the additional ZING Gutierrez belted me with. She didn't want me to talk about Bowers. At least not say that he was alive. My lips parted, but the words wouldn't come. "He—the doctor said—" Actual tears came.

"Sorry to hear that." He leaned against the rail. "Pierre didn't mean to hurt anyone."

I followed his gaze to a large, white billy goat with horns that curled. A patch of brown hair formed a pattern on his left side that resembled a handprint with splayed fingers. He stood by himself, scratching his rump against the fence-post. "Pierre?"

"That's better than his real name. *Monsieur Pierre mon Petit Crotte*, which is even stupider." He pronounced it *Monsoor Pierre Pet It Crot*, but I'd had enough high school French to realize he meant petit, like petite. I didn't know what a *crot* was. If I had some downtime later, where I had absolutely nothing to do, I'd look it up.

"I got him from a pastry chef in Scottsdale whose girlfriend doesn't like goats." He grabbed the fence and shook, testing its strength. "He must have gotten loose. Goats manage it all the time, especially the smart ones like Pierre." When he looked directly at me, his brown eyes lacked warmth. "I don't understand what your boyfriend was doing around here, but Pierre must have seen him as a threat and butted him over the edge of the hill."

"Speaking of Detective Bowers' fall," Gutierrez said, speaking for the first time, "I have a few questions for you, Mr. Bennett." She held up her badge.

He glanced back at the barn. "Like I said, we were just about to move the goats to the barn. Will it take long?"

While they talked, I wandered closer to the billy, numbed by the possibility that all this was an unfortunate accident. When I gazed into the goat's eyes, the disconcerting rectangle irises surrounded by gold unnerved me, but I held my ground. This goat wasn't getting the gentle treatment.

Hesitating, I wondered if I wanted to watch Bowers careen down that hillside, breaking things on the way. Watch without the ability to help him. I squeezed my eyes shut, realizing there was no other way to find out what happened that day.

Directing my mental highway at the goat, I sent him an image of Bowers followed by what I imagined my fiancé's fall looked like. The creature stiffened with recognition, and my heart lifted. Finally. I had a witness. And if it turned out the goat had butted Bowers over the edge...well, it was only an animal.

Before I posed my question, Bowers stood with his back to me. He had his hands on his hips, and from the position of his head, his gaze was directed toward the bottom of the hill. My hand reached out for him. At the same time, a hand reached out in my vision and shoved Bowers between the shoulder blades. And he was gone.

I inhaled air so fast it set off a choking fit. Grabbing the top rail for support, I doubled over and panted until my breathing returned to normal. My heart rate continued to beat a high tempo.

Del called to me. "Hey. You're not going to be sick, are you?"

Unable to meet his gaze, I motioned behind my back with my hand to let him know I was fine. With another deep breath, I sent Pierre a series of images, trying to get the goat's attention on the person who pushed Bowers. He sent back an image of...an eclair. My mouth filled with the sweet taste of custard, and I wiped away the crumbling flakes from my chin. They weren't real, but I felt them.

"What's she doing?" Del asked.

Gutierrez stared at me. "Allergies?"

It was my fault. I must have confused the goat with too many images. Repeating a streamlined version of my question, my mouth watered over the return image of a decadent chocolate croissant. My jaw clenched as I tried again only to have a tart cherry turnover thrust under my nose. Unfortunately, I knew what this meant.

Turning on my heels, I stalked away, tossing my thanks to the farmer as I left.

Gutierrez caught up to me before I made it to my car. "What happened back there?"

"You said it yourself. Allergies."

She grabbed my upper arm. "If you learned anything, you need to tell me."

Would she believe me if I told her Bowers was pushed? Especially when that information came via a four-legged animal? I thought not.

"I have nothing to say." I pointed my gaze at her hand. "If you're through, I need to call the hospital again."

Unless she was prepared to declare her belief in my psychic abilities, she had no choice but to let go of my arm. I made it into the car before I broke down.

FOURTEEN

The tears stopped when I realized the importance of Pierre's tidbit of information. Someone pushed Bowers! That one fact was all the motivation I needed to keep going. Someone out there had harmed my honey, and I wouldn't rest until I put a face to the hand.

I knew Bowers' job was dangerous. Law enforcement personnel regularly ran into criminals, both the merely annoying and the extremely nasty. Drug addicts and pushers. Pimps. Thieves. Drunks ready for a fight. The always dangerous domestic violence calls. Add to the mix violent activists who railed against, ambushed and attacked the police. The same people who would wet themselves if they were faced with the decisions officers had to make in seconds. All of them threats he was trained to meet, unlike a sneak attack in the open desert.

The image of a hand reaching out to injure my fiancé played out in front of me until I wanted to scream. Now that there was someone to blame, I wasn't sure if I sought justice or revenge. I just knew I wanted the person attached to that hand to suffer, and I wanted to cause that pain. Since I didn't know what case Bowers was working on when he met with his *accident*, as the police were calling it, there was only one way forward.

Gutierrez had shown up at Bennett's for a reason. If she only had follow-up questions, why not ask them over the phone? Trailing the detective was as perilous a proposition as approaching a straining, red-faced baby. Both could land me in a lot of poop. With no information to go on, I didn't see how else to track down the person responsible for Bowers' fall. And I would track them down. So, I followed her.

Intent as I was on keeping tabs on the detective's car, I hadn't paid attention to where we were headed. Gutierrez entered a neighborhood of low-rent apartments. The buildings were depressingly similar—grungy yellow paint and small balconies. Though an occasional tenant spruced up his or, more likely, her space with potted plants and strings of lights, most residents used them for storage. Bicycles, boxes, and unused furniture were crammed into the tiny spaces. On one balcony, laundry hung over the railing.

The detective pulled up to the curb, got out, and surveyed the area before crossing the street to the building opposite. She stepped off the path and onto the first-floor patio of the unit second from the end. The one with two brown wicker chairs and a small matching table.

I slipped out of my car, making as little noise as possible, and jogged to the hedge dividing two apartment buildings on my side of the street. Since the hedge stood about five feet tall, I had only to crouch to remain out of sight.

A skinny guy with dark, shoulder-length hair and a solid black t-shirt stepped outside the sliding glass door, leaving it open. He held something in his left hand. Medium-sized and dark. Was it a weapon? If so, Gutierrez didn't flinch, though with a nickname like Python, it probably took a lot to scare her.

After a few minutes of interrogation, the detective held something out. Something small, like a business card or photograph. Much head shaking followed until he accepted it. Gutierrez turned and walked away. Just in case she planned to case the neighborhood, I remained hidden until she returned to her car and drove off.

In my keyed-up state, I continued to crouch as I hurried across the street until the driver of a passing car called out.

"What are you up to?"

My eyes met the suspicious glare of a Hispanic woman of middle age driving an older model Toyota. She recognized skulking when she saw it. I figured she was somebody's mom. Placing my hands on my lower back, I straightened with a groan.

"Sciatica."

She wasn't convinced. "Do you live around here?"

I motioned toward my destination. "Visiting a friend."

She waited until I got to the patio and waved before moving on. Peering through the glass, I saw no movement in the dark living room. Maybe the guy was taking a nap. I rapped lightly on the glass. A shadow shot off the floor, and the same guy answered, holding a video game controller.

The controller threw me. In my world, video games meant teenagers. He looked to be in his late twenties, yet here he was in the middle of the day playing make believe, or shooting things, or whatever they do in video games these days. *Super Mario* was as far as that phase took me.

"What do you want?"

His voice had the impatient whine of a teenager. I

wrote him off as suffering from arrested development and adopted a stern, motherly tone.

"Excuse me, but I'd like to ask you a few questions." I fumbled it by adding a conciliatory, "If you don't mind."

"I'm not interested."

He reached for the door handle, but I stepped inside.

"It will just take a minute."

My heart pounded against my ribs. For all I knew, this guy was a mass murderer, and I had entered his lair. I adjusted my footing half in and half out of the apartment.

The living room smelled of popcorn. A half-eaten bowl of it sat on the coffee table in front of the couch, along with a glass of soda. I assumed it was soda. There were bubbles.

I decided the guy lived with his mother. The glass sat on a coaster. The room, including the dining area at the back, was neat. A crucifix hung on the wall over a small table with images of the Blessed Mother and candles bearing images of the Sacred Heart of Jesus. And another, better smell drifted from the kitchen. Spicy smells like whatever seasonings real cooks put into taco seasoning or chili.

Ignoring my growling stomach, I forged ahead. "That woman who just came here. Detective Gutierrez. What did she want?"

He gave an exasperated groan. "Are you a cop, too? Get out. You can't come in unless I invite you."

"That's vampires."

My limited knowledge of vampires impressed him. His eyes lit up. "You know about vampires? Oh, man. You play *Elder Scrolls*? 'Cause I'm stuck. My character keeps turning into a vampire and then I run out of juice and can't do anything."

"That's a bummer."

"You don't know the secret, do you? I'm not a weenie. I

refuse to look at the cheats, but if someone *tells* me the secret, that's all right."

We were speaking two different languages, but I needed his help. "Don't vampires need blood?"

"Well, duh. But the game won't let me drink from anyone. The villagers chase me out of town before I can attack. It sucks."

"Drinking someone's blood sounds personal. Is there anyone close to your character who might agree to it? Family? Friends?"

He thought this over, then plopped onto his couch to face the large screen affixed to the wall. "I do have a servant. I wonder..."

We wasted the next five minutes while he made his way back to where his servant lived. After getting her to sleep somehow—I wasn't paying attention because I didn't care—he let out a whoop as his character drained her of some blood. From the changes on the screen, his guy was good to go.

"Oh, man! I can't believe I didn't think of that. Thank you. Do you want a snack?" He gestured to the popcorn bowl. "I have microwave pizza puffs."

"No, thank you."

"Yeah. They taste like crap." He glanced up. "I owe you. What were you asking?"

"About the cop that just stopped by. What did she ask you?"

With his eyes focused on the screen and his fingers jabbing at his controls, he said, "About some other cop. One who stopped by a few weeks ago."

"Detective Bowers?" I tried to keep my voice casual, but it wouldn't cooperate. It didn't matter. His eyes remained on the screen with his lips parted in concentration. I repeated myself.

He tapped the controls a few times before he turned his head and narrowed his eyes.

"Yeah. That was him."

Success! This puny nerd held the answer to my personal quest. I could feel it. "What did *he* ask you about?"

He stood and puffed up his chest. "I don't know that I want to tell you. Who are you, anyway? Are you sure you're not a cop?"

His attempt to intimidate me fell flat. A man playing video games loses his fierce edge.

"I'm Frankie. Detective Bowers is my fiancé. Someone hurt him, and I want to return the favor."

He shook my hand. "I'm Enrique, but everyone calls me Gator. That sucks. I mean, I'm not in favor of cops, but I guess they're people, too."

"They are. I wouldn't be here except I love my fiancé and can't think of any other way to find out what happened to him. Now, what did he ask you about? He was working on an old case. I'm not sure what. Were you a witness in any of his cases?" I struggled to phrase the next part without hurting his feelings. "Were you, um, involved?"

"Involved? You mean, am I a killer?" His gaze remained steady until, uncomfortable with the silence, I shifted my feet. His hands rose to shoulder level, and his fingers curled one by one. When he pulled back his upper lip to reveal a nice set of teeth and growled, I jumped. He dropped his hands, laughing. "Only of vampires." He blew out a breath. "He came here last week. It was the day we—I assumed he was asking about something else. But he only wanted to find Chopper. I haven't seen that dirtbag in weeks, and good riddance."

"What did Bowers—Detective Bowers want with Chopper?"

"He didn't say."

"Does Chopper have a name?"

"Eric. Eric White."

I admit it was a reckless move, but I made an assumption based on the interest the police were showing in Gator and Eric. "Are you, I mean, is he one of your gang?"

He closed his eyes in a pained expression that said I had injured his feelings. "We are not a gang. We're a group of guys that hang out together. And sometimes we work together on odd jobs."

"You mean like painting houses?"

"Tech jobs."

"You work in tech? I can't even operate my cell phone. I don't suppose—no. So, Eric White is a friend of yours and now he's missing?" I made my voice sympathetic.

"Not a friend." While he pretended his answer satisfied me, I waited. Finally, with great reluctance, he motioned toward the apartment's interior where the bedrooms were. "He was my sister's boyfriend. He used to bully her, but when it came to Eric, she had no sense."

A female voice blared out, *"I'm leaving your butt behind, Gator."*

Backing out the open door, I scanned the room. "I didn't realize you weren't alone."

He grinned, pleased about something. "That's my ham radio." He waited. From his expectant expression, I thought he might want applause. I congratulated him, and that seemed to be the right response.

"It's my baby."

"Three, two—"

Gator responded to the girl's threat with an impressive

leap, spinning midair so he landed on the couch facing the television screen. "I need to get back to the game. We're playing as a team." He straightened his shoulders and lifted his chin in a challenge. "I'm glad Eric took off. The guy was bad news. I hope you never find him."

Little did I know how prophetic Gator's words would be.

FIFTEEN

Shadows of clouds dotted the navy-blue sky by the time I got to Wolf Creek. The orange glow surrounding Four Peaks marked the sun's final resting place for the day.

In anticipation of a long weekend away, I'd emptied my refrigerator of anything that might spoil, as well as leftovers. If it were only me, I'd be happy digging through my cupboards for crackers or chips, but I had a guest to feed. I swung into the Safeway parking lot to do some quick shopping. Since I hadn't dropped off Emily at her sitter's before getting the call about Bowers, I still had her food and bowls at home, but the kitty food level was dangerously low.

As soon as I wrenched a shopping cart free, I realized I had no idea what Ghost Woman liked. Chicken, for sure. June raised them and served them for every meal. Did Dymphna crave a change? Maybe a hearty steak? But what cut of meat was best? It was after six o'clock. How long would it take to cook a steak? Maybe I should have picked up fast food. It would be convenient, something her sudden visit was not.

Stop it. You're the hostess even if you don't want her in your house.

Bowers' family would soon be my family. They were suffering, too, and so far, I'd neglected the visiting member. I'd bring home healthy, delicious food. We'd gather in the kitchen...and starve, unless Dymphna cooked. While we ate, we'd chat like sisters. At least the way I *thought* sisters might chat. Exchange hair and makeup tips. Maybe she would expect some cute engagement stories. I'd have to make them up.

From the number of people here, it seemed most of Wolf Creek hit the grocery store on the way home from work. Instead of tearing through the aisles, I crawled behind an old woman holding herself upright with her cart. It would be breakfast time before I got home.

I headed for the meat counter first. A mustached butcher in a white coat leaned forward to show a middle-aged woman a set of ribs. He cradled them in his hands for approval, the way one might hold up a precious newborn. He didn't get it. The approval, I mean.

"The membrane is still on." The woman twitched her pointed nose. "I'm not paying for membrane."

He turned and went to work on the ribs with a slim, pointed knife.

Membrane? What the heck was a membrane? The palpitations started as I realized I'd need an anatomy class before anyone could trust me to order meat. When a younger man in a white jacket came to the counter and asked if I needed help, I gave a panicked giggle.

"Silly me. I wanted cheese. You don't have any cheese, do you?"

He hid his contempt as he directed me to the dairy section, which reminded me I needed milk and eggs. In my hurry to escape, I suffered a head-on collision with a young woman in skintight jeans that looked as if a grafitti artist had painted them on. If so, the artist had remembered to get the area between her cheeks where the pants disappeared.

"Watch it," she snapped without looking up from her phone.

"Sorry," I mumbled, even though I wasn't sure the blame was mine.

I made it to Dairy without further incident and added cheddar and Parmesan to my cart. Who doesn't like cheddar and Parmesan?

A memory of the Bowers family gathered in the living room for tea sent me to the coffee aisle. Once there, my vision blurred.

Did Dymphna like black tea? English Breakfast or Irish? Or would she want the calming effects of Ginger Tea? Or chamomile? Or lavender? Crimony! Who knew tea came in so many flavors? I chose the English and the chamomile and dashed over to the cookies to find a tasty treat for dipping. There weren't any crumpets. Were crumpets members of the cookie family? I grabbed the vanilla wafers.

After tea, Dymphna would want to talk about Bowers. She would share his childhood exploits with me, certain I'd want to hear about his first steps, his toilet training, his good grades, and his high school prom. I'd need something dipped in chocolate to keep from falling asleep and selected a box of chocolate covered cocoa snaps. Two boxes.

On to dinner.

Not being a cook myself, I always shopped with a list of ingredients copied from the recipe I planned to make. And I only bought what I knew I'd use. There wasn't a book on my shelf with a hundred ways to cook leftover potatoes, or family recipes passed down and memorized. I was incapable of grocery store spontaneity.

After my experience at the meat counter, I swept a pile of frozen dinners from the freezer shelf into my cart and snatched one of each type of canned vegetables. Fresh veggies and fruit would rot if I chose something Dymphna didn't care for, so I skipped the produce section.

As I cut through the stationary aisle, bright, colorful boxes caught my attention. My guest planned to eat and sleep, which would take up enough of my precious time. If I brought home various amusements, she might not expect me to hang out and chat. I selected a brain teaser, sure it would drive Dymphna mad. I added a puzzle. The cover had a ridiculously serene backyard looking over a lake. And there were flowers. Lots of flowers. Just sorting the pieces would keep her busy.

After paying an astronomical amount of money for two bags of groceries, an amount that made me rethink having children—I'd heard they eat three times a day—I loaded the bags into the back of my hatchback and got inside. A weird, unpleasant smell greeted me.

My fear of mice chewing through my engine wires kept me from leaving leftovers in the car. And the smell hadn't been here thirty minutes ago.

A prickle ran up my neck as I turned toward the back seat. I wasn't alone.

I yanked the door handle and fell to my knees on the pavement in my hurry to exit the car. The only other people in the lot were an elderly couple three rows away. Too far away for their hearing aids to pick up my screams. By the time they shuffled the distance, I'd be dead.

The security lights, so bright I could name the interior color of the car two spaces down, gave me a boost of bravery.

That and a family of four stopped their cart behind a minivan across the aisle. If things turned bad, I'd trade him the children for my car.

I rapped on the window. "Hey. Wake up." Light reflected off the glass, making him a shadow. A shadow that didn't respond, so I rapped harder. "I've got guests. No time to play around. I'm not an Uber, so get out."

Pressing my face against the window, my gaze landed on the neat dark hole in the center of his forehead. My rapping petered out, and my entire body shuddered. I stepped away from the car. As soon as I could control my trembling legs, I ran.

SIXTEEN

The first patrolmen to show up were Officers White and Stockton. White was a slim, young, dark-skinned man with short-cropped curly hair. His partner was in his early fifties with slicked back blond hair and graying sideburns. Neither of them was especially tall, but Stockton had a stockier build, which struck me as hysterical in my fragile state of mind and made me giggle all through my statement.

Once they were through with me, which was not as soon as they would have liked, they invited me to sit in their SUV while they secured the scene and waited for a detective and the usual assortment of crime scene people to take over.

I'd have little to tell the investigating officer other than the obvious. Still, I tried to make sense of this latest development. A dead man sat in my car's back seat. Why? And who? I admit I didn't get a good look before I scrambled out the door.

Replaying the last two days in chronological order didn't help. Bowers was injured. Mr. G showed up at the hospital. I discovered the witness at Bennett's Grazers, but the goat refused to talk until I plied him with pastries.

Before he fell, Bowers had visited a gamer named Gator and asked him about Eric White. The latter was a dead end, since his friend hadn't seen him in weeks. And now I had a dead body in my car.

If I knew what case my fiancé was clearing up, it would help.

Officer White rapped on the window to tell me the police required my presence. The detective on call was Gutierrez.

"Can't you find something else to do other than find dead bodies?"

A rhetorical question, I assumed.

"I don't know how I'm going to explain this to—" She took a deep breath and exhaled, lowering her shoulders. "Captain Joe is going to be upset." She shook that image out of her head and pulled out her regulation notebook and pen. "Have you ever seen the man before?"

"Seen him? Like have I met him? Why would it be anyone I know?"

"Calm down. Did you get a look at his face?"

"I noticed the hole in his head. But I doubt if I knew him." I stressed the last part because I didn't want her to make me look. Which she did.

The photographer stepped back and let me pass. It took a few minutes for me to talk my eyeballs into pointing themselves at the corpse, but when they finally cooperated, I swore. "Son of a donkey!"

The detective performed her good deed for the day by steering me away from my car. "Who is it?"

"He said his name was Mr. G."

"What does the G stand for?"

"No idea."

"Is he a friend of yours?"

Tilting my head, I gave her a look that questioned her sanity. I wasn't known for my people skills. Penny was my best and only friend. Bowers was my friend, but so much more. Did Seamus McGuire, the owner of Canine Camp and my go-to pet sitter count? His girlfriend, Bethany, the remora who clung to him, didn't like me, so we saw little of each other. Maybe Seamus only counted as an acquaintance.

Gutierrez snapped her fingers in front of my eyes to get my attention. "Friend or not, where did you meet him?"

I crossed my arms over my chest to stop my shivering. It didn't work. "The same place you met him."

She glanced at my car as if she'd missed something. "And when was that?"

"In the emergency room. He came in and asked about Bowers."

Her thick, manicured eyebrows drew together. "Yesterday? Why didn't you tell me?"

"Tell you what? That I talked to a person?"

"What did he ask you?"

"If Bowers was okay."

"How did he know Martin was injured?"

"He heard it on the radio. Or maybe the internet. He said he'd heard, and he had just dropped off a fare in the area and had to pass the hospital on his way home." When she didn't respond, I added, "It was nice of him to be concerned."

"Where had he met Martin?"

I recalled the conversation. Had he mentioned high school? College? "I don't know. He said they used to be friends. Maybe they lost touch. What does it matter?

Whether they were school chums or football team members, it doesn't explain why that man is dead in my car." As I spoke, my breathing quickened, and my volume rose. When the two patrolmen glanced my way, I clapped both hands over my mouth to hold back the shriek.

Once she finished jotting down my answers and perusing the page, she slapped the notebook shut. "You're free to go."

"Go? Not until someone tells me what's happening. Why would someone kill a man and leave him in my car?" The volume was up again.

She made a shushing motion and stepped closer. "Don't let this out. We don't want a panic. You mentioned a fare. That means he was a taxi driver. Someone has been killing taxi drivers and dumping them in people's cars."

After scanning the parking lot, I said, "I don't see a taxi. He might be an Uber driver."

Her teeth ground together. "And Uber drivers. They're being targeted, too. Drivers people pay to take them places."

"But why *my* car?"

"They choose random cars. Did you lock your doors?"

Had I? "I must have."

"No offense, but your car is a piece of junk. Even if you locked it, any thief would have no trouble breaking into it. Easy."

"You said thief. I thought he was a serial killer."

After a pause, she repeated that I could leave. Now.

It hit me then. The inconsiderate killer had stranded me at the Safeway. Gutierrez realized the same thing, because she motioned the older patrolman over.

"Stockton, give her a ride home."

"Um, my groceries are in the back of the car."

Officer White gaped at me.

I held up my hands. "What? I just put them in there. They aren't evidence. And they didn't touch anything icky."

"You'll have to leave the car as it is, ma'am." Officer Stockton said it kindly. So kindly I pushed my luck and made them wait while I redid my shopping from memory. Officer Stockton even loaded the bags into the patrol car's back seat. At least he told Officer White to do it for me.

My first joyride in the back of a police car wasn't a joy. With so much on my mind, I'd hoped for privacy, but instead of opaque mesh, thick glass separated us. The see-through kind.

All the way home, I considered how to tell Dymphna about the body. She'd notice I wasn't driving my car. Explaining that a serial killer had dumped a corpse in my back seat at random didn't hold water. Gutierrez must think I'm a dope.

I'd only spoken to Mr. G once in the emergency room waiting area. The conversation had lasted a few minutes. That was my only connection to him...except Bowers. Was his body left in my car as a warning to my fiancé? Since he was unconscious right now, it didn't seem like an effective warning.

The corpse in the car couldn't have been meant for me. I'd only talked to a geeky, video game player and a farmer, and I didn't think I had ticked either of them off enough to take action against me. My connection with Bowers had to be the reason behind the threat. I sank lower in my seat. Did the person who pushed my fiancé suspect I was onto him? That I knew Bowers' accident wasn't an accident?

Craning my neck, I searched out the back window. Was I being followed? Did the pusher assume I would investigate Bowers' fall? Why?

Over the past year or so, I might have developed a reputation for nosing around. That was the fault of a certain jerk of a reporter who kept running articles that made fun of my pet psychic business. Was I in danger because of an idiot reporter? When I growled, Officer White glanced back, so I coughed a few times and cleared my throat.

"Allergies."

One thing was certain. My looking into Bowers' accident had annoyed someone, and I suspected that someone had pushed my honey down the hill. All I had to do was continue to poke and the snake would show himself. At that point, I'd skitter away and let the police handle it. But I wouldn't stop until then.

SEVENTEEN

When we arrived at my house, a dark red Chevy Suburban sat in my driveway, telling me Dymphna had figured out my door lock. I thanked the officers, who waited until I was inside before driving away.

As I entered the front door, my arms full of grocery bags, my guest, seated on my couch, looked up from her magazine. "Do you recognize me now?"

I cringed. "Sorry about that. I was worried about Bowers' surgery and didn't want to get held up."

She smirked. "Understood. I would have done the same. I forgive you, but Windy might not."

From Dymphna's lap, the poodle gazed at me with unblinking eyes.

"Tell me how Marty's doing. The surgery went well?"

As his fiancé, I should be able to give her a report. That I had less than nothing to tell her embarrassed me. Rather than explain my unease over Dr. Lerma's mixed messages, I told her the surgeon seemed super pleased with the titanium he used.

She stood and set the dog on the floor. "Good stuff, titanium." She glanced at my bags. "I picked up a few things on the way home. You were a long time coming."

"I ran into some...trouble." Instead of diving into details about the dead body, I told her I'd been in an accident.

"Ouch. You're obviously not hurt. Did the car suffer any damage?"

"It's not drivable."

"Ouch again."

She followed me into the kitchen and helped me unpack the groceries. Windy and Emily watched us from opposite corners of the kitchen. They might not be buddies, but at least they weren't fighting.

"We'll get an early start tomorrow and camp out at the hospital until we get the okay to see him. I'll have to leave Windy here. If you don't mind, we'll crank up your air conditioning. She's heat sensitive."

Bowers' sister deserved fair warning.

"The thing is, Dr. Lerma is being cautious. You might not get to see your brother. Or talk to him. I haven't."

"I'm his sister. They'll let me in."

Maybe they would. They shared the same last name and blood type. Type B, for Bowers. My hopes rose, but not too much. Something weird was taking place at Holy Cross. Something I didn't understand.

Using a light, casual tone, I informed her I had a few things to take care of before I drove to the hospital. "Things to do with our canceled trip."

As I popped the last items into the cupboard, she watched me with a disconcerting, unwavering gaze. "Is there anything you'd like me to pass on to Marty? If he asks."

I turned to face her and leaned against the counter. "That I love him and miss him."

"Noted." She nodded at a pot on the stove. "I've already eaten. Sorry, but I was starved. I've already fed your cat."

While she talked about the unfair pet policies at Holy Cross Hospital, I tucked away two bowls of chili with cheddar cheese and crackers sprinkled over the top. Once the dishes were cleared and leftovers secured in the refrigerator, I moved to the hallway and pulled out extra blankets I had stored in the closet that held my linens, medicine, extra candles, old notebooks, and things I didn't remember putting there, like a tin of cat food.

Once I understood Dymphna was too tired for girlish bonding, a twinge of disappointment caught me by surprise. Slumber parties weren't my thing, probably because no one had ever invited me to one. My pet psychic tricks backfired there. Other girls found me spooky. Not that I cared. I was raking in the dollar bills for pretending to know what their animals thought.

I reminded myself that I didn't want to talk to Bowers' sister, anyway.

After I brushed my teeth, I had a dilemma. As the guest, Dymphna was entitled to my bed. That's how I was raised. However, she wasn't an old, arthritic woman, so maybe she'd be okay on the couch. What was she? Aggie was a few years older than Bowers. Was Dymphna next? That made her mid-to-late forties. Hmm.

While I wrestled this point of etiquette, Windy decided it. Entering my bedroom to change into my jammies, I found the pup curled up together with Emily on my pillow.

"Isn't that cute?" Dymphna said over my shoulder.

"Cute. That's exactly the word I was looking for." Unsanitary and disgusting were up there, too. "You sleep here. I'll take the couch."

"Are you sure?" She inched her way to the head of my bed.

"It will give me a break from the animals."

She ran her fingers over the bedspread. "You've got clean sheets, right?"

We woke the animals to switch out the linens. By the time I got everyone settled, let Windy out for a last tinkle, I was on the couch with the sheets from my bed and a lap blanket woven by my great-aunt Dorothy.

The sleep fairy was on vacation that night. Imagined scenarios of Bowers' fall fought for attention with a plethora of questions.

Assuming the killer left Mr. G's body in my car, how had he done so? Easy. There were so many retired people in Wolf Creek, it wasn't unusual to see a relative or caregiver assisting someone into a car. Nobody would have questioned it.

I wasn't buying Gutierrez' explanation that a serial killer of taxi drivers chose my car at random. Mr. G had shown up at the hospital after Bowers' fall to check on his... he'd said my fiancé was more of an acquaintance. I had lots of acquaintances. I wouldn't visit them in the hospital.

It was possible that Mr. G, having pushed Bowers, wanted to make sure he'd done a good job, but I had faith in my ability to spot menacing body language. A possibility wriggled into my mind. Was Mr. G a witness? Is that how he'd known about Bowers' fall? Why hadn't he just volunteered to tell what he knew to the police? I'd pointed them out, so he had the opportunity.

Had the killer wanted to stop Mr. G from telling what he knew? I hadn't told anyone I was looking into Bowers' fall, but Del Bennett knew. At least he knew that I'd wanted to see the spot where Bowers had suffered his injuries. That was a natural move for a fiancée to make. Not threatening at all.

Gator. I'd talked to Gator. Had the little rat fink made a call after I'd left him? But if he was a serious suspect, Gutierrez would have taken him in for questioning.

And what about Gutierrez? If she'd mentioned meeting me at Bennett's Grazers to someone else, another police officer... I shivered. It wouldn't be the first time a member of the force had taken a bribe for information.

The final possibility left me unable to breathe. What if the killer had followed me from the hospital, hoping I'd lead him to...what? I knew nothing. An idea hovered at the edge of my mind but wouldn't make itself known.

Just as I drifted into an exhausted slumber, the nightmares began, featuring a disembodied hand and Mr. G.

EIGHTEEN

If I was going to hunt a killer, I needed wheels.

Dan Driver of Cavalcade Rental Cars maintained his fleet of vehicles with the loving attention of a collector. And he *was* a collector of sorts...of crappy, older model cars. Because he kept the fluids fresh and topped off, massaged the insides with butter, or baby oil, and buffed the paint jobs until they glowed, the cars survived.

He had a Ford Fiesta. A refurbished AMC Pacer. At least that's what the advertisement said. Rumor had it there was a Yugo stored out back for emergencies.

If I'd been in the mood for a laugh, Cavalcade would have met my needs. However, my back ached from sleeping on my floor, my eyes were crusty from lack of sleep—Windy snored—and I'd dressed in a hurry. It was possible I'd put yesterday's underwear back on.

Dan, whose bald head shone as brightly as his cars, walked me over to a sky-blue Geo Metro.

"A metro?" I squished up my face.

"It looks economical," Dymphna said, bored with my indecision.

Dan patted the hood. "It is."

In another life, I dated a mechanic. Jeff laughed himself silly when a friend bought a Metro.

"That's because it only has three cylinders. Can't you give me something with at least four?" I pointed to a silver SUV. "What about that one? In the corner?"

"Ah, a Dodge Nitro. Lots of room." With his hands on his hips and his eyes darting everywhere but my face, he said, "I heard about the body."

"Body?" Dymphna said, suddenly alert and standing tall.

Clutching his arm, I led him away, calling out to Bowers' sister as I did so. "We're talking price."

As soon as we were out of earshot, I dropped his arm. "My sister-in-law doesn't know about the body."

"If she doesn't now, she will."

"I'm sure she will, but I'd like to break it to her in my own way." After I'd heard from the goat and put her and my fears about a repeat to rest.

Dan wrinkled his brow. "I'm sorry It's just, well, once there's been a dead body in a car, it loses value. No one wants to rent it anymore."

"And you know this from personal experience?" I held up a hand. "Don't tell me, or I'll assume every stain I see is blood. Or worse."

"My cars are spotless!" He narrowed his eyes. "And I'd like to keep them that way."

I glanced back at Dymphna and gave her a small wave. We *were* out of hearing range, weren't we? She leaned against her ride, relaxed, so I assumed we were.

"Look. The body had nothing to do with me."

"Then how did it wind up in your car?" He folded his arms across his chest and lifted his chin in condemnation.

"People don't just deposit dead bodies in other people's cars. It's rude. There must be a reason."

I couldn't remember Gutierrez telling me not to repeat what she'd said. I crooked my finger to beckon Dan closer.

"The thing is, and this is privileged information, so don't share it." I took a deep breath and released it. "The police are looking for a serial killer. Someone who targets taxi drivers and Uber drivers. Just drivers." When his skin lightened by three shades. I held up my hands. "Not people named Driver. People who transport other people. They chose my car for no reason. They could have dumped the body in the car next to me. I was unlucky." I glanced at the SUV. "So, what do you say?"

When he quoted the rental price, I said I'd take the Geo. Just as he handed me the keys, one of the Great-tailed Grackles that had been squeaking its head off from the fence that lined the property swooped low and pooped on the car, almost as a warning.

"It's not as if you're in a hurry to get anywhere," Dymphna said as she climbed back into the Suburban. "It's safer to drive slow. Too many people zip around, paying no attention."

Funny, especially coming from the woman who'd set a speed record driving to Wolf Creek.

"I'll see you later at the hospital?"

For a moment, I wavered. What was the point of scrambling to find out what happened to Bowers when he might be awake and chatting right now? I should dump the Geo, go with Dymphna, and wait in the lobby for news.

Except I wasn't a good waiter, and if my phone call to the hospital was any indication, Bowers could turn cartwheels, and the doctor still wouldn't let me talk to him. Besides. The hand I saw in my vision came from behind, which meant my fiancé hadn't seen it coming. Bowers never would have turned his back on a suspect, which meant he had no idea who pushed him down that hillside. It was up to me to find out.

"I'll be there. Absolutely."

Bless her for never asking what was more important than waiting for news on Bowers. Or judging me when I said I had appointments and stuff to take care of. I would help Bowers best by finding out who did this terrible thing to him.

NINETEEN

Bowers lived in the northeastern part of Wolf Creek in the Mountain View Townhouses. The landscaping suggested a small-scale resort to me, with desert plants between winding sidewalks that lit up at night with tiny security lights shaped like bells.

About three months into our relationship, he had given me a key for emergencies. His hospitalization at the hands of a fiend qualified in my book.

Before unlocking the front door, I picked up his unclaimed deliveries of *The Wolf Creek Gazette* and brought them inside.

The morning of his attack, Bowers had pulled shut the drapes to keep the heat out, so the atmosphere inside was cool and dark. Peaceful. If I hadn't known he was fighting for his life, I might have taken a nap on his leather couch.

Since my mission was secret, I left the drapes closed and turned the switch on the closest lamp. Though I saw no signs of disturbance, the police must have searched his place for notes on his latest case. But I knew something they didn't.

The elusive idea I'd had last night smacked me in the head this morning.

Bowers had a diary.

Last Christmas, I'd given him a little girl's diary covered in adorable puppies and kittens. It included a lock and a tiny key. I meant it as a joke in reference to the regulation notebook he carried on the job. Though I never expected him to take it to work with him, he'd bucked my belief that it would sit, ignored, on his desk. I'd witnessed him writing in it.

Since my fiancé wasn't prone to examining, reveling in, or privately expressing his feelings any more than his fellow men, I assumed he was jotting notes about his job. The way I saw it, the police would take one look at the cartoon animals and the ridiculous lock and assume it belonged to me.

When I tossed the papers on his coffee table, ready to begin my search, a headline caught my attention. Snapping it back up, I groaned. Paul Simpson, evil, unethical reporter and general buffoon, had taken another potshot at me.

WHY DO CORPSES FOLLOW FRANKIE CHANDLER?

Once again, Wolf Creek's own crank pet psychic is in the middle of a murder investigation. This time, she supplied the corpse.

The body of George Dakos, a resident of Apache Junction, was discovered last night in the back of Ms. Chandler's Toyota Corolla, the victim of a shooting.

Ms. Chandler's fiancé, Detective Martin Bowers of the Wolf Creek Police Department, is hospitalized

> *with injuries that occurred on the job. He was unavailable for comment. The staff at Holy Cross Hospital are unable or unwilling to state the nature of his injuries.*
>
> *Police have no current suspects.*

That hyena! I crumpled the paper into a ball and lobbed it across the room before remembering it wasn't mine to destroy, though with a front-page story like that, Bowers should be grateful he wouldn't have to read it.

Since my fiancé kept his place tidy, I deposited *The Gazette* into the wastebasket in his kitchen before beginning my search.

The first place I looked was his bedroom. By the time I reached the second floor, my breathing was just shy of labored. I'd either have to work out or insist we move into a one-story home after the wedding. Like my house.

He'd left his bedroom in perfect order. I could have bounced a quarter on the brown bedspread stretched tight over the mattress. He didn't have little doodads taking up space on his six-drawer walnut dresser. Just a picture of us in one corner, taken at a company picnic. Someone had snapped the photo right after I'd taken a bite of hot dog. My cheeks puffed out like a hamster. Bowers, of course, looked perfect.

Even though I had every right to be here, I squirmed as I dug through his drawers. It felt like I was violating his privacy. When I didn't find the book, I gave myself a mental forehead slap. Bowers wasn't a teenage girl. He wouldn't keep the diary tucked away in his underwear drawer, safe from the prying eyes of siblings.

Downstairs, I headed straight to his office, where work

things belonged. He'd never banned me from this room, but we had an unspoken understanding that it was his private space. That, and I couldn't imagine anything of interest lurking amidst the filing cabinet, credenza, and desk. Until now.

Like everything of his, Bowers kept the top of his desk tidy. For a moment, I wondered how he'd get along with my sloppy habits. We'd find out. My lower lip trembled. I hoped.

The first drawer resisted my gentle tug. And my harder yank. He'd locked his desk.

At first, unreasonable anger popped up. Who locks their desk drawers at home? When you live alone? That emotion made way for excitement. People only lock drawers when they contain something important.

Without a handy bobby pin in my hair, one I wouldn't know how to use anyway, I couldn't decide how to proceed. His garage might hold some fine wire, the kind they used in television shows. I could insert it into the lock and whirl it around until I heard a click. Right. A hammer it was.

In his garage, I found something more useful than a hammer. A crowbar. But then I couldn't get the thinner end into the space between the drawer and the desk to pry it open. Plan B. A screwdriver. And a hammer.

By hammering the fat end of the screwdriver, I created a wedge and threw my weight behind it. The front of the drawer popped off.

Panting from the effort, I searched through his papers. Since I intended to keep his trust, I avoided reading any of the correspondence, even turning his bank statements face down without peeking. Once it became obvious the book wasn't there, I went to work on the next drawer. By the time I confirmed he didn't keep the diary in his office, I had all five drawers in splintered sections on the floor. It wasn't my fault. He was the one who'd locked the dang thing.

Back in the living room, I scanned the furniture. On the lower ledge of the coffee table was a heavy volume on the paintings of *Caravaggio,* a Catholic artist know for *The Calling of St. Matthew* and *The Beheading of John the Baptist.*

Disgusted by his neatness, I wandered into his kitchen. Two leather place mats sat on the round, wood table, and everything on the counter perched in its appointed place.

While there, it occurred to me he might have something rotting in his silver refrigerator. One glance inside showed he'd emptied it of anything that might go bad. Except the half-eaten candy bar on the second shelf. It would be a shame to waste it.

Still chewing, I returned to the living room. The sight of his brown leather armchair brought tears to my eyes. *The Throne.* I called it that because only Bowers was allowed to sit in it.

When I first noticed the bulge, I chastised my eyes for playing tricks, but when the vision didn't clear after a few eye blinks, I pounced on the armrest and yanked the diary from a side pocket located underneath. As I plopped into the coveted spot and held up my prize, I tsked. If only my fiancé weren't so possessive of his favorite spot to sit, I might have realized it had pockets.

When I pulled on the cover, the book didn't open. He'd locked it with the tiny key. Cute. Since I'd already wasted enough time searching, I felt no qualms about pulling his trusty screwdriver from my pocket. We needed to have a heart-to-heart about trust, I thought, as I sent the lock flinging across the room. And then I got a twinge of conscience.

What if he'd used it for personal stuff? It wasn't any of my business what the man I proposed to marry thought about me. *If* he'd written about me in his little book. And if he hadn't, what did that say? Wasn't I worth the ink? Wasn't I on his mind every moment, just as he was on mine? Maybe not every moment.

I glanced at my watch. Time was ticking, so I knocked Neurotic Frankie aside. Who was I kidding, anyway? Guys didn't pour out their deepest feelings into cute little books. If they even acknowledged those feelings, they hid them under grunts and jokes about football stats while bonding with other guys. I dove into the diary.

My suspicions were confirmed. These were notes about work. Bowers, the organized goof, had even dated the entries. God love him. I flipped to the most recent date, a week ago last Wednesday, and stared at the page.

"Oh, sweetie." He'd covered the edges of the page with doodles. Doodles of diamonds. I wiped away a tear. Even when hard at work, our engagement was on his mind.

When I saw the list of names on the page, I got over myself. If this was a work diary, the diamonds must relate to his latest case. In pride of place, topping the list, was Mike's Auto Body. Underneath was some guy named Luther Mendoza, followed by Enrique Salazar. Enrique. He must have meant Gator. Why else would Gutierrez visit the gamer unless he was related to Bowers' case? That made me growl. She knew what Bowers had been up to when he visited Bennett's Grazers. Maybe. The goat farm wasn't on the list.

When I got to the name George Dakos, I paused. Mr. G. The man said he was friends with Bowers. If I put Penny's name on a list, I wouldn't include her married surname, Mohr. She'd just be Penny. And why would his friend's name be on this list of suspects? Maybe Gator and Mr. G were witnesses, like I first thought.

A gigantic question mark loomed over the list. He'd underlined it several times, emphasizing its importance. What was Bowers confused about? A brilliant notion tapped me on the shoulder. What if he wasn't sure who was a suspect and who was a witness? That might explain how he wound up at the foot of a rocky slope. By trusting the wrong person.

That begged one question. Suspects and witnesses to what? Gutierrez said he was working on an old case. Was it *his* old case? Or was my hardworking fiancé cleaning up someone else's unfinished mess? Man, I wished I'd paid more attention to Bowers when he chatted about his day instead of focusing on the way his mouth moved when he spoke.

I flipped through the next couple of pages and found another reason to love my organized sweetheart. There were two columns, one with the names, and one with their addresses.

Reluctantly, I closed the diary. I'd already talked to Gator, and Eric White was MIA. Mike's Auto Body in Gilbert seemed like the best bet. I'd pretend my car needed service. Except I wasn't driving my car.

"Oh, oh!" I'd tell them I had a rental because my own car needed work. Which it did. Pleased that I had an excuse to drop in at Mike's, I tucked the diary into my purse, and after a few failed attempts to put the desk back together, left.

When I opened the door, a uniformed police officer greeted me.

"Who are you, and what are you doing here?"

"This is my fiancé's home. I needed to water his plants." Did Bowers have plants? I hoped so.

He stepped aside to let me pass. "I'm really sorry about Detective Bowers. He's a good guy."

My eyes misted over. "He is."

I hurried to my car, and when he stepped inside Bowers' home, I took off as fast as my Geo Metro would take me. Once he found the busted drawers, he might have questions. Questions I didn't want to answer.

TWENTY

Mike's Auto Body shop was in an industrial section made up of windowless buildings. Across the street, workers moved flats of what looked like theater scenery through a rolling door. The next building over, a semi-truck sat backed up to a loading dock. The truck had *Super Stuff* written in orange on the side. Everyone knew Super Stuff was a drop shipping company with loads of discounted products for sale on the internet.

I pulled into the shallow parking lot. The discreet sign on the door to the left of the double garage doors had *Mike's Auto Body* written in thick, blue letters under a picture of a double-sided hammer. A tall man with sandy hair and a full beard dressed in a blue jumpsuit that matched the lettering leaned against one of the closed garage doors, smoking a cigarette. The jumpsuit strained against a large chest, and he kept the zipper down to allow room for his thick neck.

Next to him sat the largest tabby cat I'd ever seen. Its gold-striped fur stuck out as if it had run into an electrical storm, adding to its size. If I shaved him, I bet he still would have weighed eighteen pounds.

As I exited my rental car, the man frowned at me and stood straight. The cat responded in kind, and I saw it was an American Bobtail, which would explain why it was keeping close company with a human being. I knew the breed as the Golden Retriever of the cat world.

"Good morning."

On the way over, I decided on a simple approach. I'd tell him I needed to make an appointment. While scheduling said appointment, I'd show him my engagement ring and ask if he knew a jewelry store where I could take it for a cleaning.

I turned up the wattage on my smile. "I need some help with my car."

His glance grazed the Metro. I laughed.

"This is the rental."

After taking a final drag, he tossed the cigarette on the cement and ground it under his work boot. He opened the door and motioned me inside. The cat led the way.

Overhead lights illuminated the enormous interior. Three cars parked inside were in various stages of undress. A sporty vehicle was missing both doors, another bulkier model didn't have a hood, and the third, an older model Jaguar, looked all right but had paper covering the windows, including the side mirrors. Forest green paint covered the edges of the paper, the same color as the car.

It must have been break-time. Six employees in matching jumpsuits sat around a large, unvarnished wooden table. A family-sized bag of chips was making the rounds. One man resembled my late grandfather, with his beaked nose and white buzz cut. His contemporary, a man with a black knit cap on his head, stopped talking and stared at me. Since he left his mouth open, I got a look at a crooked incisor that bent inward.

Three of the men were middle aged, one dark and skinny and one blond and stocky. The third man was dark-skinned with short-cropped curly hair. He was built like a bear.

The youngest, in his early twenties, had long brown hair pulled back in a ponytail. While the rest merely looked up at our entrance, he offered me a small wave.

The large room reeked of pastrami, paint, and something undefinable. From the temperature in the stuffy room, I guessed body odor. I wondered why they didn't throw the garage doors open.

The cat jumped on the table and flopped. The young guy scratched his belly, while The Bear stood. "What's up, Mike?"

"Customer," said the guy who'd led me inside. "What's wrong with your car?" His concern seemed disingenuous, and the strained atmosphere left me feeling I had interrupted an important conversation. Also, he hadn't offered me coffee or a chair. Or a smile.

"A lot," I gushed, adding a giggle.

He picked up a clipboard off the wooden counter. "Let's have a look."

"At what?"

"Your car."

Was he going to demand I take him to my car right now? What would he say when we pulled up in front of the police garage, where technicians were likely scouring the back seat for clues? Swiveling my head toward the parking lot and back at him, I let out another giggle, this one nervous.

"I told you. That's not my car. That's a rental."

"Is it drivable?"

"With three cylinders, it doesn't have a lot of power, but it'll do until I get mine fixed."

Thank you, Jeff, for my limited knowledge of automobiles. I could have an intelligent conversation with car people. A few of the men snorted laughs at my answer, but it satisfied Mike. He walked around the wood counter and pulled over a pad of paper.

"Not the rental. Your car. I'll need to see it."

"You can't."

He glanced up.

"I-I mean not yet. The insurance company has it."

"Where at?"

Would that be something I'd know? The pause went on too long. "They didn't say. They just told me to get quotes."

He set down his pen. "I can't give you a quote until I know what's wrong, can I?"

It might have been a mistake walking in here without a more detailed plan. I certainly couldn't work my engagement ring into *this* conversation. It seemed best to make a quick escape.

"Can't I make an appointment? I'll tell the insurance company to bring it here. You can take your time figuring out how to fix it because they're paying for my rental."

"What happened to it?"

My face got stiff remembering the body in the back seat. Mike would expect something more than upholstery damage. With my brain still frozen around the image of the dead Mr. G, I blurted out a familiar car part.

"The bumper is coming off."

He picked up his pen and jotted a note. "Which one?"

"Both?"

He circled the bumpers on a small drawing of a car on the form. "Any other damage?"

I shrugged my shoulders. "That's too technical for me."

One of the grandpas chuckled. "At least she's honest."

"How fast were you going when the accident happened?"

Bowers had been training me to always tell the truth to him. It was becoming an unfortunate habit. "Um, it was parked."

Internally, I cringed after I said it, but the scenario didn't faze Mike. "Ah. You were rear-ended and pushed into the car in front."

Beaming at him and meaning it, I said, "You clever man. That's exactly what happened." I clapped my hands together as if he had performed an amazing trick, which to me, he had. Mike had untangled my tongue before I tripped over it. A new sensation.

The next few questions were all about my car. Make. Model. Year. I had those answers ready. And then he asked the casual question that caused the catastrophe.

"How'd you hear about us?"

It slipped out. Or maybe I subconsciously wanted to test them with the information I'd learned from the diary. "My friend, Luther."

Conversation at the table stopped. Mike set his pen down. "Luther?"

Chair legs scraped against cement as the men at the table stood. All except the young guy, who wore a shocked expression.

"Luther Mendoza?" When he squeaked out the name, he clenched his hands. The cat hissed and swiped, leaving four trails of blood on his arm. The guy jumped to his feet, knocking over his chair. "You saw Luther?"

"Randy." Mike snapped out the guy's name like an order, and the young employee zipped it.

I took a step backward, towards the exit. "That *could* be his last name. We only use first names, which I suppose makes us acquaintances instead of friends."

"Luther is a friend of ours." Mike exchanged a glance with The Bear. "We've been looking for him. When did you talk to him?"

The Bear took a step forward.

I pressed my fingers over my mouth to stop my lips from trembling. "Gee. When was it? Last week? I'm horrible with time."

"When did your accident happen?"

"Last night."

Mike let out a dry laugh. "The Luther I know didn't have a crystal ball. So, either he's become a psychic, or you're lying. Which is it?"

"I'll come back later." When I turned, Randy stood in front of the door, blocking my escape.

"Look, lady. We only want to talk to Luther."

Taking a deep breath, I turned and arranged my face into a friendly smile. My expression slipped. While my back was turned, they had crowded forward and were now standing ten feet from me. They stared like shipwrecked sailors who'd been offered a lottery ticket for the last seat in the lifeboat, and each of them meant to win. I spread my arms with my palms up.

"There's been a misunderstanding."

Mike came out from behind the counter. Even the cat dropped gracefully from the table and sauntered up to join the line facing me.

"My friend's name might be Linus, not Luther. I have tinnitus and don't always understand people."

Randy snorted. "They're not even close. Just tell us where Luther is."

"That's all we want to know," Mike added. The Bear growled.

When Randy cried out, my shoulders scrunched as I turned, waiting for the attack. He stumbled forward and landed on his hands and knees, sent there by the motion of the front door flying open. Blinking against the sunlight streaming in, I made out a woman's silhouette. She stood with her legs slightly apart and her shoulders squared, like she had a mission, and nobody better get in her way.

One thing her outline couldn't tell me. Was she friend, or foe?

TWENTY-ONE

As she strolled inside, her gazed scanned the entire room, taking in every detail until it came to a stop on our little gathering. "Who drives the Geo Metro?"

From her fitted red t-shirt to her black exercise pants and matching trainers, she gave off the impression of an athlete. When she stopped next to me, her fit figure stood a few inches taller than my five foot seven inches. A black beaded bracelet and leather watch adorned one wrist, and a simple gold cross hung around her neck. Long, dark, wavy hair with streaks of gray refused to stay put in her ponytail.

Everyone stared.

"The metro?" she repeated in a scratchy voice that reminded me of *Charlie Brown's* Peppermint Patty.

Her gaze roamed over the men frozen in place. When her roving eyes landed on me, she pursed her lips. "Of course. It must be you." She wrapped her long fingers around my upper arm in a solid grip. I winced. "You're coming with me."

Randy looked at his boss. "But—"

Mike held up a hand, keeping his eyes on the intruder. "Is there a problem?"

"Nothing I can't handle." She kept me in a firm grip, so I felt her tense.

Before the men could respond, she pulled me outside. She swept her gaze over my car with a disappointed sigh. "A Metro? Wasn't a Pacer available?" She snapped her fingers and opened her palm. "Your keys."

"Wait a minute. Who *are* you?"

She let go and looked toward the doorway where the employees of Mike's Auto Body gathered, wearing grim expressions. "Would you rather go back in there?"

"Um, no."

"Then hand me your keys."

I fished them out of my pocket. With efficient speed, she snatched my keys from me, unlocked the passenger side door, and shoved me inside. As she rounded the front of the car, I played with my door handle. If I jumped out and ran, how far would I get before this crazy person caught me? Before Mike and his gang caught me? I slipped a glance at the very large employee. Even bears were capable of sprinting short distances. I stayed where I was but kept my fingers wrapped around the handle. Once she drove to a populated neighborhood, maybe somewhere near a bus stop, I'd make a break for it.

She didn't go far. Two blocks down, she turned the corner and pulled up to the curb. My heart lifted when I recognized the red Suburban. As she put the Metro in park, I turned in my seat.

"Who are you?" I repeated.

Before answering, she took a moment to study me. What she saw didn't satisfy her. "Edith. Edith Bowers."

I gasped and scrunched back against the door, hitting

my head against the window. Every single time I mentioned Edith's name, Bowers flinched. Since she was *his* sister, I trusted his judgment.

Though in her late forties, Edith seemed like a younger woman by her confident carriage and blank expression. On closer inspection, creases and lines marked her face, as did a pale scar traveling from her upper lip to her cheekbone.

When I met her eyes, I gasped again. She had Husky eyes. One was iceberg blue; its partner chocolate brown. This was the woman I'd dubbed Scary Sister, and I wanted her out of my car.

"Well, thanks for coming to my rescue."

"I love wasting my time cleaning up messes made by stupid people."

I cocked my head, irritation making me bold. "Did you call me stupid?"

"What would *you* call walking into the unknown without preparation or backup?"

"Brave?"

She snorted.

"I...you're right." I rubbed the sore spot on the back of my head. "I got excited and didn't think it through. How did you know I was there?"

"You left a broad trail." She tsked. "Desecrating Marty's desk? For shame."

I screwed up my face. "I forgot about that."

"What were you after?"

Crossing my fingers behind my back, I told Scary Sister my first lie. "My checkbook?" I may lie a lot, but I'm not good at it.

"Try again." She said it with the patience of a teacher encouraging a particularly dull student.

Heaving a big sigh, I pulled the diary out of my purse.

"It's embarrassing, but I like to jot my feelings and thoughts about the love of my life in this little book. Isn't it cute?" I ran my finger over the sweet puppies and kitties on the cover. When she reached for it, I jerked it back and mumbled about private, innermost thoughts.

"Well. I take back any credit I was willing to give you. How is Marty doing?"

"Ask Dymphna. She's at the hospital with him."

"I'm asking you."

"I don't know."

She licked her finger and rubbed at a smudge on the steering wheel. "Why not?"

"The doctor is being vague."

"What do you mean, *vague*?"

"As in not telling me any details."

"Maybe you didn't ask the right questions."

And with that, she got out of the car. I climbed over the console so I wouldn't have to face her again, but she rapped on my window. It took a minute to figure out the power controls.

"You should go straight home and stay put until this is over. Jot your feelings in your little book."

"That's not a bad idea," I said, fluttering my eyelashes.

She must have thought I was a mutt. As soon as she pulled away from the curb, I counted to three and followed her.

TWENTY-TWO

To my surprise, Edith led us to the Wolfe Creek police station. I parked in one of several available spaces in the lot next to the building. Before following her inside, I hesitated.

Did I want to talk to Bowers' coworkers? Did I want Edith to know I followed her? Did I want to encourage another Bowers sister to take up my time and interfere with my plans? Especially the scary one? Curiosity won out.

Just inside, to the left of the front glass doors, the small waiting area sat empty except for a teenage girl slumped into a chair next to a woman. The girl was part adult but mostly child, with none of the confidence of a grown woman. She chewed on a strand of hair as if sucking the final bit of flavor from a piece of gum. From their matching round faces and red hair, I assumed the woman was her mother.

"But I wasn't speeding," she whined in a low voice just above a whisper.

"Tell it to the judge," answered the mother without sympathy.

I caught up to Edith as she faced off with Denise, the

desk sergeant. Voices from the offices down the corridor buzzed in conversation. Detectives occupied those offices. Detectives who had more information than I did and should be out searching for Bowers' attacker.

"I'm afraid Detective Gutierrez can't see anyone right now. If you tell me what it's about, I can direct you to someone who can help you." Denise's blank cop face spread into a smile when she saw me. "Frankie."

Ever since I'd walked into the station with a license plate number they'd been desperately searching for, my stock had gone up with the Wolf Creek police force.

"How is Bowers doing?"

The sergeant's gaze met mine straight on. Maybe the doctors were keeping the police in the dark, too. I gave myself a mental slap for doubting Bowers' coworkers. For wondering if they hid him in a back room just to persecute me.

"The doctor is cautious. He won't let me see him or call him," I added, feeling I needed to explain why I wasn't at his bedside.

Since I wasn't pals with anyone in the department, but Denise knew I had some sort of relationship with Gutierrez through Bowers, she guessed who I had come to see. "I'll tell Juanita you're here."

Edith spared me a glance and said, under her breath, "You may come in useful after all."

The sergeant stepped into the hallway and entered the second doorway on the right. The first was Bowers' office. She reappeared a minute later to wave us in.

Juanita Gutierrez sat in her chair, her elbows on her desk. A painting of an Arizona landscape on the wall directly across from the detective provided the only view of beauty, as her window faced the parking lot. A vase of flowers sat on her desk. The bold purple irises and shocking red tulips reflected her personality. Beautiful, but in your face.

She leaned back when Edith followed me in. Scary Sister's gaze darted to the marksmanship award on the wall behind the detective before traveling around the room.

"Who's your friend?" It occurred to me Gutierrez might be more forthcoming with Bowers' blood relative.

Edith sat. She kept her feet tucked under her chair, resting on their toes, as if she might need to spring forward.

"This is Bowers' sister, Edith. His *favorite* sister." That sister's eyebrows inched up. "The one he's closest to. There are no secrets between them. They share *everything*. When God formed Eve out of Adam's rib, the original plan was for them to be brother and sister, and He had Edith and Bowers in mind. But then God decided He wanted little Adams and Eves running around and, well, that would have been gross, so He switched to man and wife."

My introduction called for an acknowledgment. Gutierrez stood, leaned over her desk and shook Edith's hand, forcing the latter to remove her baffled gaze from me. She made a quick recovery.

"My brother's fiancée has been trying to get me up to speed. I assume you have the details. I want to know what happened to Marty."

"Wouldn't we all," Gutierrez murmured, toying with the pen on her desk. "What has Frankie told you so far?"

A sudden, horrible thought occurred to me. What if Edith began the conversation with the amusing story of what happened at Mike's Auto Body? Gutierrez would kill me. Plus, she'd know what I was up to. I had to get in there first.

"I can answer that. Not a lot." I folded my arms.

"Because *the police* haven't told me anything." Meaning her.

Edith rested the ankle of one foot on the opposite knee. "I can't help wondering if his fall had something to do with his job. What was he working on?"

"A case." Gutierrez left it there, but that wasn't good enough.

"What kind of case?"

Gutierrez leveled her gaze at me. "An official case."

I leveled mine back. "There are so many to choose from. Murder? Rape? Robbery? A hi-jacked liquor truck? Kidnapping?" I chortled. "I'm joking, of course. That last would involve the FBI, wouldn't it?"

The detective's eyes narrowed. "If you want to play detective, you can sign up and take the same training your fiancé went through. The same training *I* went through."

Stubborn Frankie reared her head. Bowers wouldn't have doodled gemstones in his diary for nothing. "Did his case have anything to do with diamonds? Or jewelry?"

My entire body jerked as the detective threw an electric charge my way. Bullseye! My celebration dampened as I realized I'd revealed too much. Before she ordered my water boarding to discover how I'd come up with the information, I softened my features and tried to work up some tears. I settled for squishing up my eyes.

"I guess I have diamonds on my mind." I held up my hand, showing off my ring. "Because of our engagement. We were supposed to visit my parents this weekend. Will you at least tell me how he's doing? They said he couldn't take phone calls. Is that your doing?" This time, I didn't have to fake the tears stinging my eyes.

Gutierrez relaxed, tapped her desk twice, leaned back,

and let out a sigh that I would have believed if I hadn't known her. "It's the doctor's call. All we can do is wait."

Edith leaned forward, her elbow on her knee and her chin resting on her palm. "But I don't want to sit around and wait. You say the doctors aren't releasing information about his condition. We could get a better idea of the state he's in if we knew what happened. Where he was when he fell. What he was doing. We could piece it together if we had some place to start." She flashed a quick smile. "I bet if we looked at Marty's phone, we would see who he called last, or if he has notes."

"That's a shame," Gutierrez said, not meaning it. "His cell never made it to the hospital." She shrugged. "It's lost."

The detective stood.

"It was nice to meet you, Ms. Bowers. I'm afraid I must get back to my job." Meaning it wasn't our job.

At the front desk, Denise looked up from her conversation with the mother and daughter and waved. The girl slumped against the counter, her chin resting on her arm.

Before we exited the lobby, Edith pulled her cell phone from her back pocket and hit a speed dial number. She didn't raise the phone to her ear, which was odd. When I heard the theme from *Dragnet* drift out of Gutierrez' office, I froze. Bowers used the *Dragnet* theme. He found it hysterical.

Edith disconnected the call and smiled. "Naughty girl."

Turning back to stare down the short hallway, I sputtered. "She has Bowers' phone. That liar has Bowers' phone!"

Sergeant Denise looked up.

Intending to confront the detective, I took one step before Edith gripped my arm and shuffled me out the front doors. I shook her off. At least I tried to. She had iron fingers.

"She has his phone, and I'm going to demand an explanation."

"No. You're not."

"Why wouldn't I?"

"Never let the opposition know how much you know."

"Opposition? She's the police. He's a fellow cop. They stick together."

Leaning her head down, she glanced up through long, dark lashes. "Are you sure?"

That stopped me. So did staring into those Husky eyes. How well did I know Gutierrez? She and Bowers were both in line for a promotion when Captain Joe retired. They had both been up for the Sergeant's position, but Smitty had won that prize. Would she hinder the investigation into his accident, or at least drag it out, just to keep her competition sidelined?

Edith patted my back. "You need to rein in your emotions. They'll betray you every time, French Fry."

French Fry? Did she just call me *French Fry?* The gloves were off.

"Oh yeah? What about your emotionally impulsive call to track down Bowers' phone? That wasn't too smart. Gutierrez will recognize your name on the caller ID. Now she knows we know she has the phone. So much for keeping it a secret."

She didn't even do me the courtesy of looking impressed by my bold outburst. "Don't be naïve, French Fry. It's a burner phone."

My retort stuck in my throat. "Who carries a burner phone other than drug lords on television?"

"I always come prepared."

"Prepared for *what*?"

"Follow me," she said as she unlocked the truck.

"Where to?"

"U-Behave."

She knew where I worked. What else did she know about me? I didn't like it, but I did as she instructed so I could find out.

TWENTY-THREE

We parked on Maricopa Drive, where the front entrance to my shop was located. Normally, I entered through the back entrance by cutting through the Prickly Pear Bistro, stopping for breakfast with Penny, but I didn't want my best friend to make Edith feel welcome. In fact, I hoped to make Edith as *un*welcome as possible.

As I approached the door, Dymphna strolled out looking so unlike her usual ethereal wood nymph self, it stopped me in my tracks. Her broad smile showed teeth, and her crocheted vest in moss-green swung jauntily over her floral bell bottoms as she walked. I expected her to do a Mary Tyler Moore spin and toss her floppy brimmed hat in the air.

Ghost Woman carried Windy tucked under one arm. The other hand held one of my high-end doggie beds and a shopping bag bearing my store's logo. The fluffy, white dog wore a desert rose cable-knit sweater even though the temperature was in the low nineties. Those sweaters also came in mint green and haystack yellow, but Dymphna had chosen well. The rose made Windy's white fur pop.

A rhinestone collar, one I kept in stock for silly pet owners who liked bling, sparkled from around the dog's fluffy throat. When Windy stared at me with her big, brown eyes, I swear she would have snapped her fingers and ordered something cool to drink if she'd had fingers.

"The hospital won't let me see my brother, so I took a break."

Dymphna tossed the bed in the back of the truck and held out her hand to Edith for the keys. She wiggled her fingers, showing impatience.

"I have to drop Windy off before I go back. Those callous guards won't let her come inside. Don't they realize how much she loves Marty? A visit from her is all he needs."

Penny waved to me from the door, and I moved closer to confer.

"Dymphna said Edith said that *you* said it was all right for Dymphna to go on a shopping spree while Edith used the truck. I gave her lunch, too." Penny snickered. "That might have saved some of your inventory from her clutches."

I sighed and looked back at Dymphna. "What's in the bag?"

"Dog bowls, bones, three kinds of treats, a few items of clothing, and CBD tablets."

"Nope. Looks like she got one of everything I sell."

My friend frowned. "I hope it was all right. I assumed Edith had your permission to give Dymphna permission."

"Sure. Why not? It isn't as if I'm open for business, anyway."

"Don't worry about that. We're all banding together to help. Charlie and Bethany are taking shifts."

Charlie, a student at Scottsdale Community college, was worth her weight in dog biscuits as Canine Camp's bookkeeper. Her boyfriend had designed my logo and my shop's new window sign. Before then, I'd settled for a handwritten name on a piece of cardboard. Anything would have been an improvement, but the sign was cool. A silhouette of a dog sat pretty under the dash in the name, which was now a bone.

As Dymphna drove off with a wave, I covered my disappointment. She hadn't taken Edith along with her. Scary Sister sized up my friend and headed our way.

"I'm Edith Bowers. You must be Penny."

Penny rushed to her with arms spread wide for a hug. Edith stood still and took it until my friend stepped back. "It's so great to meet you. I can see the family resemblance."

Surprised, I inspected Edith's face. Her dark hair was a shade lighter than Bowers', but then I noticed her nose was straight like my fiancé's, not short and round like his eldest sister June's. Her lips were fuller, and her jaw more rounded, but there was a definite resemblance.

"Frankie and I should get going," Edith said.

"Not so fast. I need to look over my inventory and see if your sister left me anything to sell."

"Perfect. I'll take your car, and you stay here and tend to business. If I'm not back by five, you can call Dym for a ride."

I snorted a laugh. As I led the way inside, Edith had no choice but to follow. I had the keys.

"U-Behave," Edith mused as she strolled inside. She glanced around the shop. "Cute."

It *was* cute, but her comment irked me because I didn't sense sarcasm, but I knew it was lurking. I scooted around the counter and pulled out a spiral notebook.

"How did the surgery go?" Penny asked, joining me.

"The doctor was vague."

She huffed. "Vague? It either went well or it didn't."

"You would think."

She called out to Edith, who was snapping a leather leash between her hands as if testing the strength. Maybe she planned to strangle someone. "I'm so glad you're here to help Frances. She needs someone to watch her back."

"Penny," I warned.

One corner of Scary Sister's mouth raised in a smile. "Watch her back? Sounds serious."

"It is. Most ranchers don't appreciate it when you approach their livestock, and Frankie needs to get close to talk to the goats." Penny turned to me. "Or do you? I've never asked. Can you talk to an animal long distance?"

On Penny and Kemper's wedding cruise, I'd used my gift to track down a missing calico cat. A murder witness in hiding. Now wasn't the time to mention it.

My friend folded her arms on the counter and leaned forward, sharing a confidence. "You have nothing to worry about, Edith. Frankie will find out what happened to your brother."

Bowers' sister hung up the leash. "I'm so relieved. Thank goodness for Frankie."

Penny grinned at me, confident all would be well. My fingers twitched with a desire to grab Edith's hair and yank it out by the roots. My friend was too good-natured to realize that Scary Sister was mocking her.

Fortunately, Monica, the younger of the Prickly Pear waitresses, knocked and leaned in my back doorway, the one that led to the bistro's rest rooms.

"Table three is at it again."

Penny squinted her eyes, recalling customer placement. "The Knights?"

"You got it."

"I'll be right there." She returned Edith's frown with a sheepish grin. "Knights of Columbus. They're regulars. The retired Grand Night and the current Grand Night fight over the bill, every time. Each one thinks they should pay it. I better go before the pancakes start flying."

As soon as she left, Edith leaned against the counter. "You want to talk to the goat?"

My guardian angel decided to toss me a bone. A woman in her forties appeared at my door and received an effusive welcome from me that my typical clientele wouldn't recognize. In her arms, she held a solid-black French bulldog. When she set the animal down, the little guy filled the room with piercing yaps.

"Oh, darling," she said, picking it back up.

The animal stared at me through bulging eyes, his bat ears swiveling when Edith muttered, "He reeks of gardenias."

The woman beamed. "I have his shampoo made special for him by a woman who only uses flowers gathered from virgin forests. She caters exclusively to celebrities. Boswell is the exception." Remembering why she'd come in, she put on a suitably concerned face. "I need your help. Boswell is frightened of everything. He barks nonstop."

Boswell seemed like a spoiled little runt to me. He didn't show typical signs of fear. His ears stood alert, he held his head high, and he had no trouble making eye contact with me or Edith.

"Set him down, please."

She frowned. "You saw what just happened. You'll traumatize him."

"I doubt it."

When she said, "I hope you know what you're doing," it carried the conviction of one who was certain I didn't.

The pooch lunged forward and barked at Edith as ferociously as a Frenchie could manage. He swung around and started bouncing like a ball, begging his owner to pick him up. When she moved to comply, I told her to leave him, sending her lower lip into a frenzy of trembles.

"Edith, stomp your feet."

His pet parent shrieked. "Are you trying to torment him?"

Happy to take part in torture, Edith marched in place. Loudly. Boswell eyed her, delivered a few more barks, and then rested his forepaws on "mommy's" legs and trembled. She responded by snatching him up to safety, cooing all the while.

I rolled my eyes, but before I delivered the verdict, Edith took care of it.

"You're training him to climb your leg. If you keep it up, he really will be afraid." She reached out and scratched his ears. "You're not afraid, though, are you? Little devil."

Though he winced when she reached for him, as soon as the first finger scratched his round skull, Boswell closed his eyes and relaxed.

"But—but you're touching him! Boswell hates to be touched by strangers." The owner sputtered some more, and I suspected her anger had more to do with her pooch showing another being affection. "This is not what I expected. You don't care about your clients. Instead, you want to scare them to death."

When the customer stormed out the door, Edith shook her head. "Are all your clients that dumb?"

I hated to say yes, but I thought it. At least they tried to help their pets. And pay my bills. My frown lifted into a smile. I had an idea. A *great* idea.

"You have wonderful insight into animal behavior."

She refused the bait. "It's common sense."

"True. But not everyone has it."

"Obviously. It's so rare, when they see it, they think it's magic. Or psychic." She gave me a pointed look.

Resting my elbows on the glass counter, I delivered my best smile. "I have a few errands to run. Maybe you could—"

"No. I didn't come here to play games with you. I came here to help Marty."

I felt as if she'd smacked me on the nose with a rolled-up newspaper. It must have made it to my face, because she softened her tone.

"You look like a smart woman."

"Thank you."

"At least I know my brother wouldn't choose a moron."

"Thanks," I said with less enthusiasm.

"You're trying to ditch me, which means you have an idea. Let's hear it."

Well. That was blunt. She was right. I'd already wasted enough time. I grabbed my purse and headed for the door.

"Let's go."

Outside, she barred my way to the driver's side of my car, gestured to the passenger door, and held out her hand, palm up.

"I'll drive."

When I tried to get around her, she made a subtle move, angling her body. Unless I wanted to topple her, which I wasn't sure I could do, I'd have to take a stand.

Edith wanted to steal my only means of independence. She might as well ask to borrow my underwear. Both deserved a firm no, something I stink at. "Why would I let you, a stranger, drive my car?"

"Because I asked nicely."

"No, you didn't. You didn't ask at all."

She put on a high falsetto with a British accent. "Oh. How rude. May I please drive your car?"

"Oh for—" I held out the keys. Mother always said choose your battles. She also told me never to endanger my health unnecessarily. Though Edith hadn't damaged anyone at Mike's, except maybe Randy, I had the feeling she was not only capable but might enjoy it.

"Where to?" I asked, getting in on the passenger side.

"I want to see where my brother fell."

"Okay." I readily agreed, because that was exactly where I was headed. And because it was the compassionate thing to do. "But we need to make a stop on the way."

Edith started the car and glanced at the gages. "You have half a tank."

"I don't need gas. I need pastries."

TWENTY-FOUR

Armed with a sweet cream roll from the grocery store bakery, my chances of getting information from Pierre were a certainty. If I survived Edith's driving.

She took corners and yellow lights at speed. When the blue Mazda in front of us wasn't up to the challenge of making it through the intersection on the yellow, Edith passed on the right and shot through before the light changed, narrowly missing a cyclist.

"It will be hard to help your brother from jail, which is where we'll be if we kill someone."

"Civilians are collateral damage."

I gasped. Her eyes left the road to send an eye roll in my direction.

"It was a joke."

On the way to Cave Creek, I explained my process of eliminating the first two goat farms and arriving at Bennett's as the place where Bowers fell. Edith listened without comment, not even when I mentioned the fainting goats. I was tempted to embellish the story with the goats turning rabid, followed by the screams and chaos of their fleeing fans just to get a rise out of her.

Of course, I made the only object of my quest the desire to discover the location of Bowers' *accident*. I had no intention of sharing my plans for delving into the memories of four-legged creatures.

"Bennett's Grazers is off Interstate 17. Another thing. When I asked Gutierrez where they found Bowers, she started to say something that started with a "C" and changed it at the last minute. Bennett's Grazers is off Cave Creek Road."

"Not bad, French Fry. I'd say we're headed for the right place." She set her jaw. "If there's a farm, there's a farmer. Maybe he saw what happened."

"Del Bennett said he knew nothing about an accident until he saw the ambulance arrive. The police said the call came from someone who preferred to remain anonymous."

"It still might have been the farmer. People don't like getting involved." She said this in the same disappointed, accusatory tone Bowers would use for citizens who didn't step up and do their duty.

While she ruminated on the failings of her fellow human beings, I tried the hospital again. Call me an optimist. I asked for Martin Bowers' room, and when the operator transferred me without an argument, my hopes rose.

"Nurse's Station," the woman answered.

"Which floor? Am I speaking to the ICU?"

"Please state your business."

"Connect me to Martin Bowers, please."

"That's not possible."

My molars ground together. "Define not possible. Are you unable to press the transfer button? Maybe you have a new mechanical arm and haven't mastered finger movement. Or have you run out of phones and can't spare one for his room?" I might have shouted this last bit because she hung up.

"You lost your cool again. Seems like a bad habit with you."

She had a point. Usually, I kept my constant irritation with my fellow human beings under wraps. With Bowers in danger, my tolerance threshold had taken a deep dive. I had to get myself under control.

"Isn't it strange they won't let my calls through to Bowers?"

Edith kept her eyes on the road. "If there isn't a phone in the room—"

"But the nurse keeps telling me he *can't* take calls. Or they *can't* let me speak to him. He should be awake by now. And if he was unconscious, or in a coma or something, they would tell me, right?"

"You would think so."

"I don't get it. That doctor is like Jekyll and Hyde. One minute he's bragging about his success and the next warning me not to get my hopes up." I closed my eyes and voiced an embarrassing fear. "I want to see him, but I don't. Not with tubes and wires, unconscious and unable to recognize me. Machines doing his breathing. But I would take it if they let me. Does the side of me that doesn't want to see him helpless make me a bad fiancée?"

This time, she looked at me. "It makes you human. And we're here."

When she drove past Bennett's Grazers, I glanced over my shoulder. "You missed it."

"I don't know what you have planned, but I don't want an audience."

"Didn't you want to talk to Del Bennett?"

"I've changed my mind."

She turned the car around at the end of the road and pulled up opposite the abandoned, burnt-out construction site. When she got out, she left the keys in the ignition. I snatched them before locking the car and joining her.

Before heading to the farm, Edith made a detour to the house skeleton. Charred two-by-fours littered the ground. What was left of the walls reminded me of burnt matchsticks. The place smelled like a campfire, but worse.

When she stepped over a few boards and entered, I asked if we should be trespassing. "The place might collapse around our ears."

Edith dug the toe of her shoe through the debris on the floor, then leaned back and squinted upward. Curious, I followed her in and looked up. Nothing but more burnt wood.

"What are you looking for?"

"Nothing that's here."

Walking along the edges of what should have been the living room or an office, she stopped at a spot where the wood seemed darker than the rest. She crouched and poked around. After studying it for a few minutes, she abruptly turned and walked out.

Her long legs and fast pace made it necessary to jog to keep up with her. As we came parallel to the dreaded hillside, Edith halted and studied the drastic angle cluttered with boulders and the occasional cactus. "This is where my brother fell."

She wasn't asking, so I didn't answer. Instead, I focused on the yellow bursts of desert marigolds popping out of the rocky slope. I wondered if Bowers had noticed them before he fell. Or if they comforted him on the way down. Probably not.

Since our plans no longer included talking to the farmer, we avoided the gravel drive as we picked our way through the scrub, desert grass, and the occasional flowering plant. While Edith headed around the back of the pen, I made my way straight to the goats.

"Stick to the south side," she said with a nod at the barn, which stood between us and the house, blocking the view of anyone at home. I nodded back.

Fifteen faces looked up with interest on my arrival. Goats are curious creatures. Wandering around a pen provided little amusement. While I wiggled my fingers at them, Edith waited for me.

Resting my hand on the fence, I leaned forward and put on a droopy expression. One that might make a person assume tragic thoughts had overcome me. "You have a look around while I compose myself."

She didn't need me to say it twice and strode off along the hill's closest flank. As soon as she rounded the back, I pulled the pastry from my pocket. Pierre left his girlfriends in the dust to come stand before me. He snatched it from my hand and chewed, savoring his treat.

"Quid pro quo," I whispered.

Opening the doorway to my mind, I sent a mental highway between us and posed my question with an image of Bowers standing on the crest of the hill. I replayed the hand giving him a push. As I waited for a response, the chirps of a desert wren and the soft, whispering breeze went silent. Then the sun ran away, and it was night.

Short movies and choppy images flickered in front of me accompanied by background noise. Children's screams mingled with adult voices. An announcement over a loudspeaker. Eerily perky music. Confusing as those noises were, the visuals concerned me more.

A stocky cowboy, his face covered by a yellow bandana.

His arm around the shoulder of another man with scraggly blond hair wearing a bloody white t-shirt.

A trampled daisy on a strip of grass.

At a burst of noise, I clapped my hands over my ears.

Pink light reflecting off a knife blade.

I called out.

The blade thrust between ribs.

A red wheelbarrow overflowing with hay.

An arm with a black panther tattoo.

A cactus wren fluttered past, and the connection broke. I gaped at Pierre.

"What in the name of Billy Goat's Gruff was that?"

I lay there, frozen, until Edith grabbed my arm and hoisted me to my feet.

"What happened?"

Breathing hard, as if she had run to me, she scanned the area, searching for an explanation. As she did so, Normal Frankie skittered away, and I've-Had-Enough Frankie barged in.

Volcanoes are just pretty mountains until they blow. Days of worry, of not knowing Bowers' condition, the refusals to allow me to *speak* to him, the schizophrenic messages from the doctor. And now, my hopes of information that would lead to a reunion dashed against the same hillside where Bowers had taken his tumble. I'd had enough.

Panting, I yanked my arm from her grip, leaned over the fence so far that my feet dangled, and grabbed the goat's face in my hands. "What about Bowers? Quid pro quo. You know what that means you four-legged garbage pail? I gave you your treat. *I want to see what happened to Bowers!*"

Pierre nibbled on my jacket. Searching his eyes with their disconcerting rectangle irises, I saw a wall of stubbornness. He wasn't going to give me more. At least not right now.

To nail home this point, he sent me a barrage of images. Almond paste. Bavarian cream. Chocolate ganache. When my mouth filled with cheesecake—a dessert I can't stand—I sputtered and coughed.

Edith yanked me off the fence by my shirt collar. "Is there a problem?"

She might have meant the way I was scraping my tongue with my fingernails and spitting on the ground. Or my verbal assault on an innocent animal.

Stomping my foot didn't have the desired effect. It made a soft thud and scattered dust and pebbles. I jabbed a finger at Pierre and let loose. "I gave this brat his bribe. He promised!" For good measure, I shook my fist at the goat.

"Promised what?"

I whirled to her, not caring if she thought I was a maniac. Then sense returned. I checked my words in time and struggled with rephrasing my complaint, omitting any mention of the goat. "I want to know what happened to Bowers."

"We all do."

"I want to know what happened to Bowers," I repeated, my voice rising to a shriek.

"I know," Edith said reasonably. "But what's that got to do with this dumb animal?"

Pierre bleated.

She leaned back and crossed her arms over her chest. "Wait a minute. Is this about that pseudo-psychic business you run?" Her hands moved to her hips, and she shook her head. "I'm disappointed in you. Don't get me wrong. I'm happy to use any tool to get to the truth of what happened to Marty. But trying to get an answer from a goat? I can't believe you're surprised he said nothing."

With my hands balled into fists, I gritted my teeth. "I got worse than nothing. I got to see some man I've never met get a knife between his ribs."

Edith dropped to a crouch and turned a complete circle, scoping out our surroundings. Her movements were quick and limber. "Who?" She snapped out the single word.

I threw my hands in the air. "I don't know, and I don't care."

By now, disappointment had me sobbing. Using my sleeve, I wiped my nose. Then I launched my body at the fence again. "It's not fair, you little rat."

Behind me, Edith snapped out my name and ordered me off the fence.

"You owe me!" The goat licked his foreleg, ignoring me. "I hope a mountain lion feasts on your entrails."

Two hands gripped my arms and tugged at me. I strained against them to get in one last word. "Okay. I don't want that last thing. Not until you give me what I want. But I hope that roll gives you gas."

The bang of a door slamming brought me out of my frenzy. I was already moving when Edith hissed, "Go!" She beat me to the car by a few steps. Maybe twenty.

"The keys are gone." She glared at me. "And some idiot locked the car."

I fished them out of my back pocket and handed them over. By the time we drove past the goats, Del Bennett had made it to the pen.

He watched as we passed. I only hoped we were far enough away that he couldn't recognize me.

TWENTY-FIVE

"How was the hospital?" I called out as I entered my home and tossed my purse on the couch. I'd ignored Edith's questions about my experience at Bennett's all the way home, and when she pulled into my driveway behind Dymphna's truck, I jumped out before she had the rental car in park.

No way was I going to share what I'd witnessed with Bowers' sister. The one who'd referred to my skills as a pseudo-psychic phenomenon. After watching the horror movie Pierre shared, I didn't have it in me to brush off jokes about talking with animals. Also, I wanted to ruminate over what I'd seen, something that would be difficult with two Bowers women in my house.

I paused. Unfamiliar smells assailed my nose. Savory smells mixed with the buttery scent of baking.

Following the trail, I found Dymphna in the kitchen, seated at the table and flipping through a clothing catalog, something she must have brought with her. Clothing companies gave up on me a long time ago and removed me from their mailing lists.

A chorus of yips greeted me, and from the way Windy's

dark eyes held me without blinking, I assumed she had a complaint about Emily. Sure enough, my feline strolled past the dog, bumping into her as she passed. I lifted my fur baby into my arms.

"You need to be more polite to our guests," I whispered in her twitching ear.

When Edith walked in, Dymphna barely glanced up. Not the effusive greeting I expected from a woman who'd been given carte blanche to my store.

"I see you still drag that ball of curls everywhere."

Dymphna lowered the magazine. "You keep away from Windy. She's never been the same since the wastebasket incident."

"You can't watch her all the time," Edith said with an evil grin.

I raised my hands. "You two can maim and torture each other all you like, but no one touches an animal in my house." Dymphna's lips twitched, vindicated, and Windy shook herself, her curly ears slapping her face, as if to say, *"So there!"*

The timer dinged, and she removed a pan of triangle pastries.

"What kind?" Edith asked.

"Cherry."

What a coincidence. Just when I needed to bribe an irritating goat. Yes, I planned to have another conversation with Pierre. He'd shown me something unbelievable. Maybe Del Bennett had brought out a television to amuse the goats and left the station on a crime show. But that was wishful thinking.

The murder hadn't happened at Bennett's Grazers. I doubted the farmer had taken Pierre on a field trip. So, when had the goat gotten loose? Except he wasn't loose. I'd seen the murder through his eyes, and those eyes had watched through the bars of a fence.

Pierre held the answers in his little brain, and it was up to me to work them out. My difficulty would be in keeping Dymphna and Edith from asking questions or, in the case of the latter, following me.

Edith lifted the lid off a pot on the stove. "What is it?"

Dymphna plated the last turnover. "Chicken and dumplings. Unless you'd rather make something else?"

"It'll do."

When Edith pulled out the chair closest to the door and sat, my insides twisted. That was Bowers' chair. His stay in the hospital marked the first time since we started dating that I hadn't at least talked to him daily. Usually, we ate a meal together. Something Bowers picked up on his way over while I handled dessert. Cookies. I hadn't mastered more complex recipes like pie or cake. Or turnovers.

TWENTY-SIX

By the time I'd changed into my comfortable gray sweats, Dymphna had dinner on the table.

Before I sat down, my land line rang. I snatched the phone off the cradle, hoping for news of Bowers.

"How's Martin?"

"Mom!"

"You sound shocked. Did you forget you had a mother?"

I turned my back on the two curious faces watching me. "No. And he's fine. Well, you know. Not fine, but coping."

She launched into a recitation of canceled events and good wishes offered by friends and relatives. "Except Tracy Flynn. You remember Mrs. Flynn? She's head of the Women's Guild. Always was a snoot. She suggested I should reimburse her for the cookies she ordered for our lunch."

"We were having lunch with the Women's Guild?"

"It was a surprise. Anyway, I told her, 'Ordered my butt. If the Christmas potluck is anything to go by, you picked them up at the grocery store.' You know those plastic boxes they set out in the bakery section? You don't have to order those. They just sit there, waiting for someone to take the poor things home. So, I told her to donate them to the homeless shelter. Homeless people would love a cookie. Even store bought."

"Mom. I kinda hafta go. I've got company."

"Is Martin there? Let me talk to him."

"Um, he can't come to the phone, but I'll give him your best."

She paused, and I held my breath. Replaying the conversation, I didn't spot any direct lies, but mothers have detectors that can suss out nuances.

"If you tell me a more *convenient* time, I'll call back."

"Things are messy right now. I promise to keep you updated."

"You do that."

Drat. Mom didn't know the details, but I was certain she had sensed *oddities*. She wouldn't rest until I confessed the whole truth and nothing but the truth to her. So help me, God.

As soon as I disconnected the phone call with Mom, raised eyebrows met my gaze. Fortunately, the Bowers women were too well-mannered to ask for details, though my use of the phrase *he's fine* would stick with them until they got an explanation. Which I wasn't ready to give.

This was another example of why I needed to get loose of Bowers' sisters. As it turned out, I didn't have to work hard at steering them away from my plans. The opportunity came after dinner.

None of us realized how hungry we were. At first the only sound was the scrape of our spoons against the bottom of the bowls as we scarfed the best chicken and dumplings I've ever had.

"Do you ever get sick of chicken?" June and her husband, Carl, raised chickens, and Bowers and I ate a lot of them during our stay at her house.

"A meal serves one purpose," Edith said. "If I'm not hungry by the end, it has done its job."

Dymphna snorted. "You're so full of it. You were the pickiest eater of the bunch."

"Just because I didn't stuff my face like you doesn't make me finicky. I ate what I needed to fuel my body."

"Oh, brother."

Serving after dinner coffee turned into a chore. With three of us, I had to dig through my cupboards to find three mugs. With all of them being free promotional items I'd collected over the years, I gave Bowers' sisters the two most similar in size and held onto my favorite from Art's Service Station. It had a cute picture of an old-fashioned gas pump on the front.

After we cleared our dishes, Dymphna asked me to set up my laptop on the kitchen table.

"Oh. Sure. Did you need to email someone? Or are you going to video call June?"

My hopes were on the latter, since I might glimpse my dog, Chauncey, who I left to live on the farm with his new best friend, Hero. I needed his comforting gaze right now.

"We have a Zoom meeting in half an hour," she announced.

"We?"

"All of us." Dymphna glanced at the kitchen clock. "But there's still time. Give us a minute"

Time for what? Five minutes later, Edith and I received a summons to gather in the living room for a doggie fashion show. The pet parent forced us to crowd together on the couch while she pranced her little pup past us, wearing a brand spanking new U-Behave pink leather harness and matching leather leash.

"So cute," I murmured, ignoring my loss of profits with effort. No one asked how much Windy's windfall had cost me. This confirmed my inferior status in Bowersland. I served a purpose. Supply them with cute doggie stuff—and the clothes *were* adorable on Windy—and provide them with a butt for their jokes. They saw me as someone to fill a chair at June's huge dinner table to keep the numbers even. Seven sisters plus Bowers, plus three spouses and Agatha's kid... I counted on my fingers and came up with an even number. Was Mary married? Doubtful. Martha would have a spouse. There. An odd number. I was a placeholder.

When Dymphna disappeared into the hallway and reappeared with her furry fashion model wearing a camouflage raincoat and matching hat, a new item I'd only unpacked last week, my gritted teeth kept my lips from forming a smile.

Edith snickered, a quiet breathy sound that reminded me of the cartoon dog, Muttley. "Where's her umbrella?"

Dymphna spun toward me, pulling Windy with her. "Do you have umbrellas? I didn't see them."

"No." I sighed, more of a growl. "No doggie umbrellas."

"Oh, you should," Edith said in a dead-on imitation of her sister's whispery voice. "It could connect to the harness and keep Snookums safe from raindrops."

That earned her a glare from Ghost Woman. The ten-pound dog, picking up on Dymphna's vibe, stared with unnerving intensity at Edith, as if plotting revenge for past wrongs.

"Fine." Dymphna picked the fur ball up and snuggled her. "You don't deserve to see the rest."

The rest? I jumped to my feet and made my excuses before my hands clamped around Ghost Woman's neck and shook my store inventory from her. The sisters tagged along and announced it was time for the meeting.

TWENTY-SEVEN

And so, I faced the Bowers Girls once again. All of them. We arranged the chairs so that Dymphna sat center screen, with Edith and I on opposite sidelines.

Once I logged in, I invited the guests into the meeting and moved to my chair. Faces popped up. First came Agnes with her sleek, dark bob. She sat in a home office and looked as if she were calling a board meeting to order. She was closest to Bowers in age and rather protective. Martha and Mary arrived in a close tie, followed by Cecilia. June joined last, and there was no sign of Chauncey.

Mary and Martha suggested the sisters from the Bible, Mary being a dreamy lazybones and Martha focused on housework. This Martha had a sweet and cheery disposition and wore her greying hair in a bun, while Mary, hyper-focused on women's issues, came with a bit of snark.

Cecelia, named after the patron saint of music, played the organ. As the second oldest sister, she looked like she should get top billing with her white hair. Except June, all the Bowers Girls, as I called them, were named after saints.

As I gazed at the faces gathered on the screen, I had a

moment of weakness, where I decided to spill everything and join forces with them. Maybe I'd been a loner for too long. But then we got distracted.

"What's Dymphna doing there?" Agnes demanded. "June! You said we should wait to hear about Marty's condition before we made plans. That it would overwhelm poor helpless Frankie if we all showed up."

"Let's stay on topic," June said. "Marty had surgery on his leg. How is he?"

When Dymphna shrugged, Cecelia called out, "Frankie?"

I leaned my head in. "Um, it's hard to say."

Even easy-going Martha found that answer unacceptable. "I don't understand. What's hard about it? He's either peachy or he's in trouble. Which is it?"

"I bet they'd tell her if she were a man." That was Mary's two cents.

Edith came to my rescue. "The doctors aren't forthcoming. Neither are the cops. We know he's recovering from surgery, but that's it. His body will heal in its own time. More important, we need to consider the possibility that Marty had help falling down that hillside."

Her appearance shut them up, at least until Agnes said, "Edith gets to be there, too?"

Edith scooted forward to give Agnes a better view of her riveting stare. "I didn't ask permission. My appearance was unannounced."

Martha, typically the pleaser, snorted. "Aren't they always? It wouldn't hurt you to RSVP."

Edith made a t'cha noise. "That wedding was four years ago. You had plenty of food to go around. Let it go."

"Girls!" June used an angry mom voice. "This call will

take forever unless you agree to get along for twenty minutes. That's not too much to ask."

Chastised, they all apologized, though without enthusiasm.

"If someone pushed Marty, what can we do about it?" Dymphna had returned to whispering. She held Windy on her lap and fed her table scraps gathered from our dinner plates. She tore off a piece of breast meat and held it up. The dog sniffed, looked at the rest of us with an expression that said she suspected us of trying to poison her, and then, like a martyr headed for the lions, accepted the offering in a delicate bite.

Edith pushed her chair back. "No one gets away with attacking my baby brother."

"You mean no one but you," Dymphna said, a little louder.

Agnes slapped her desk. "I agree with Edith."

"We don't know he was attacked," June said with admirable calm.

Edith gave a dry laugh. "Marty fell. *Our* Marty fell. This was the boy who raced me on the edge of the foothills. He's as sure-footed as that goat Frankie attacked."

Silence.

"You attacked a goat?" Cecelia's reasonable tone made it a quest for information. Not a hint of condemnation.

I cleared my throat. "Not attacked. More gave it a good scolding. You know how annoying goats can be." I leaned my head back, offscreen, so they'd miss the evil glare I slapped on Edith.

"True," June said. They all nodded agreement. Edith shoved her face into the screen again.

"Marty did *not* fall." She let that statement hang in the

air before adding the dramatic finale. "Someone pushed him."

My head jerked up. How did she know?

"How do we find out who?" Martha said, glancing around at her sisters. Since she was on the left side of my screen, part of the time she was looking at my kitchen sink. "Frankie?"

"What are you asking *her* for?" Mary snapped. "No offense, Frankie, but you're a *pet psychic*. This is a *real* problem that requires *solid* solutions. Not airy-fairy wishes."

Mary's comment smarted. I cleared my throat, ready to show the Bowers Girls I had a brain. Maybe I'd work out a complicated math problem in front of them. Before I could speak, Edith stepped in.

"First, we find out what the police know. They're not sharing much information. Yet." Her words implied a threat, but I didn't see what she could do to the entire Wolf Creek police force.

Cecelia, always reasonable, got to the point. "Can't you just ask Marty?"

"I've tried to talk to him," I said. "The doctor refuses to put a phone in his room. We don't even know if he's—"

"He's a prisoner!" Agnes slapped her desk again. "He has rights."

"To be fair," June began, "we're not even sure he's conscious. He has a concussion."

"Of course he's conscious." Edith seemed to realize she'd spoken with too much certainty. "A concussion wouldn't keep Marty down."

"What's your plan, Edith?" Mary said. "This is a tough problem, one that needs a woman in charge."

"I'm a woman," I muttered, but no one paid me any attention as Mary warmed up to her theme.

"I bet it was a man that pushed him. Nasty beasts. Not that a woman isn't capable of pushing a man down a hillside."

They all leaned forward, eager to hear Scary Sister's idea. Even Agnes.

I cleared my throat. It was time to ask for their help. "When I was out there, there being where he fell, I saw something."

Agnes stopped me. "Let Edith handle it, Frankie. That's a fun parlor trick you can do, but we need action."

I gaped. Is *that* how Bowers' sisters saw me?

"That wasn't nice, Aggie. Apologize to Frankie." June being motherly again.

"She needs to toughen up. Haven't we got enough on our minds without worrying about *poor* Frankie? We've got to find out what happened to Marty and catch the SOB who did it, and that means stepping on some feelings."

June flushed. "I don't care what happened to him, as long as he recovers."

While Edith expounded on her theoretical approach to solving the mystery, my expression changed to one of admiration. Not because she said anything worthwhile. No, the lightness that stirred in my chest came because I'd come up with an excellent point.

If I went along with the gang and let them assume Bowers' fate rested in Edith's capable hands, they'd leave me alone to follow my own path. Now that I knew they rated me equal to the guy who makes doggie balloons at children's parties, I was one hundred percent in favor of being left alone.

After some pontificating about the type of person who would attack their darling brother and the shockingly unpleasant things the sisters wanted Edith to do to the culprit once she caught him or her, Scary Sister said she needed time to plan. They all seemed confident in her ability to do so and would have hopped off the call if I hadn't covered a yawn with my left hand. As soon as they saw my engagement ring, chaos broke out.

"Is that mother's ring?" Agnes demanded.

Dymphna grabbed my hand and inspected it.

"It is," Mary said with more offense than she had a right to. If any one of the Bowers sisters was destined for the single life, it was Mary.

After wrestling my hand back from Dymphna, I stuffed it in my lap and sent June a desperate glance. I'd grown to love this ring, and I'd fight them all to keep it.

She had my back. "It was mine to pass on. Since I couldn't choose one sister over the other, I gave it to Marty, for his fiancée."

Since berating their unconscious brother was out of the question, and June's point was valid, they let it go.

By the time the meeting ended, I was a non-entity, as far as the Bowers Girls were concerned. Finding out what happened to my fiancé was up to me. So be it.

TWENTY-EIGHT

After hiding out in my backyard for twenty minutes, the guilts hit, and I returned to the living room to perform hostess duty.

"Anyone need anything?" Always good to keep it general.

Dymphna had spread silk flowers, paper, ribbon, scissors, and a vase on my dining room table, all items she bought on the return trip from the hospital.

"I dislike fake plants, but since we don't know when Marty's coming home, I wanted to play it safe."

Ghost Woman worked for a florist. I knew the arrangement would be stunning.

Edith didn't have a hobby. At least not one she was willing to mention. After refusing my offer of several books on animal behavior for pleasant reading, as well as my suggestion that she watch television in my bedroom, she followed me into the kitchen and sat.

"We had a busy day." I began with a casual approach to find out what Edith had stored in that stoic head. "Did we learn anything?"

"I did."

When she left it at that, I pressed. "Care to share? We're on the same team. You know. Team Bowers?"

"What do you want to know?"

I sighed. "Are you going to make me pull it out of you piece by piece?"

"No, but you need to reason it out for yourself. What did *you* learn?"

Annoyed as I was over being treated like a student, I took the question seriously because it meant moving a step closer to seeing my honey.

First, I learned Bowers had a list of names in the diary I'd given him. Not something I cared to share, at least not until I knew my future sister-in-law better. The second revelation was that Bowers had been pushed. Again, I'd keep that to myself. No need to sound crazy this early in our relationship, especially after hearing the Bowers Girls' opinion of pet psychics. And then there was the whole murdered guy thing.

"I learned Gutierrez is a liar. She had Bowers' phone the whole time."

"Only natural. She's a police officer, which means she's going to keep anything she learns to herself."

"If she can." I smirked when I said it. When she raised an eyebrow at me, I gave in to the desire to brag, something I rarely did, as there was never anyone around to listen. "I followed her to this guy's apartment. Gator."

One corner of her mouth curled up. "You conjured that idea up on your own? Well done."

For a moment, I debated whether to be insulted or pleased. Since I was too tired to work up a convincing snit, I thanked her.

"Anyway, Bowers was asking about a guy Gator knew. Chopper."

"A friend? Or a colleague?"

"They weren't friends. More like a work acquaintance. Gator seemed happy Eric had exited the picture because he didn't want his sister dating him."

"Exited the picture?"

"He hadn't seen him in a while."

"What's this Gator like?"

"A nerd. He plays video games, and get this. He owns a ham radio. Didn't ham radios disappear with the invention of the internet?"

"It's a hobby. Kind of a cult with some people." Her eyes gleamed with interest, and I wondered if she were one of those people.

"Anyway, Gator did side jobs in tech. Eric was one of the gang. Not a criminal gang. Just a bunch of guys who did side jobs together."

"I never asked. Why were you at Mike's Auto Body?"

The bragging stopped. "Um, because I needed work on my car. You know, because of the body. Or maybe you don't know."

I brought her up to speed on the corpse in my car. What did her lack of surprise say about her? Did dead bodies pop up regularly during Edith Bowers' day?

"Mr. G? That was his name?"

"That was the only name he gave me, but the newspaper identified him as George Dakos."

"When I first arrived, the guys at Mike's seemed... intense. And you were nervous."

I chuckled, which helped push out the lie. "I never was any good with cars."

She kept staring with those Husky eyes, forcing me to give her additional information.

"They were interested in a mutual friend. I mentioned Luther Mendoza, just in passing—"

"Luther Mendoza? Who's he?" She kept her gaze fixed on me.

"A friend of theirs. They seemed desperate to find him. That's why they got worked up when they assumed I knew where he was."

"And do you?"

"Nope. They assumed."

Her eyes narrowed to slits. "Anything else you haven't told me? Like an explanation of what happened at Bennett's Grazers?"

That was off the table. Other than the news from Pierre that someone had pushed Bowers and the fact that I had my fiancé's diary in my purse... "Not a thing. Unless you know something I don't."

When she didn't offer a comment, I continued. "There doesn't seem to be any connection that links them together. And nothing any of them said points to Bennett's Grazers. And that's all I have."

Still nothing from Scary Sister. This felt like a monologue. "I wish I knew what case Bowers was working on when he fell. That's an important detail. You're his sister. I assume the two of you would enjoy chatting about handcuffs and tasers."

"We're not that close."

"You don't discuss his cases at all?"

"Never."

"Was there a falling out?"

An argument, leaving a residue of bad feelings, might

explain why my fiancé twitched any time I mentioned Edith's name.

She blew out a long breath. "We drifted apart like most people do when they become adults." Her expression made a pit stop at regret before she assumed indifference.

When she offered no other comments, I gave up and left the room. Conversation with Bowers' sister was exhausting.

The living room was empty. A very pleased Emily stretched her furry body across the couch. Sensing a presence next to me, I jumped. Edith had followed me in without making a sound. I covered my surprise with a nervous laugh.

"Where'd everyone go?"

"If I know Dym, she's planted herself in the bathroom for the duration."

I scanned the room again. "Where's Windy?"

"Dym's evening ritual includes cleaning the dog's teeth and bottom. I know. Disgusting. More important, what are your plans for tomorrow?"

I looked up from scratching my cat's ears, hopeful. "If you want to hang out at the hospital and wait to hear about Bowers, er, Marty, you should drive in with your sister. I have some work errands to run."

"Dym has that covered. Anyway, you're supposed to be on vacation." She crossed her arms over her chest and cocked her head. The interrogation had begun.

"Somehow, word got out I was still here. Things have come up. Important things I need to take care of right away. By myself."

"What do you really have planned?"

Afraid she'd see through me, I averted my eyes. "I didn't see your car. How did you get here?"

"Uber. That means you're my ride."

"Where's your luggage?"

She motioned toward a navy-blue backpack that wouldn't hold my toiletries.

"How did you find out about your brother?"

Her expression turned into a blank. "Word gets around." Bored with the question-and-answer session, Edith ran her gaze around the room, stopping on Emily. "It's been a long day. Where do I sleep?"

"I already offered Dymphna my bed. You can have the couch. It's old, but comfortable."

"I've slept in worse places."

Why wasn't I surprised?

When Dymphna and Windy made way for Edith to use the bathroom, I followed Ghose Woman into my bedroom and pulled my pajamas out of a drawer.

"So, what's the deal with Edith?"

Dymphna sat on the edge of my bed in a sleeveless white nightgown with the dog on her lap and grabbed a steel comb from my nightstand. The comb was for the dog, and she proceeded to work the knots out of Snuggums' curls.

"I don't know what you mean."

"Sure you do. The way she acts charges around like she's on a mission, running over anyone who gets in her way. She's not intimidated by the police, either. What's your sister do for a living?"

One corner of her mouth curved up.

"You don't know? Or are you warning me off."

"Edith's just Edith."

"Come on. Is she law enforcement herself? Does she work for a government agency? Or is she a criminal?"

Windy yelped when her pet mom tugged on a vicious knot.

"I find it's better not to ask."

That answer didn't comfort me.

TWENTY-NINE

That night, I didn't sleep well, and it wasn't just because I lay on the floor between two fitted sheets. Thoughts of Bowers alone in a hospital room made me twitchy. I kept seeing him waking up confused and scared. Or at least worried.

When I did sleep, the figures from Pierre's home movie popped into my dreams. The cowboy with the bandana over his face, as if he were expecting a sandstorm. A leopard tattoo, slinking up a bicep. Did it belong to the cowboy or the victim? I strained to recall without luck.

What was the meaning of the pink light that enveloped the scene? It followed a loud boom. Lights and booms meant fireworks. Did the murder take place on Independence Day?

Saddest of all, but only because I didn't know the victim, was the crumpled daisy, once stretching its petals to the sky, now flattened by shoes.

In the dead of night, I woke with a start. Something moved. I lifted my head. Emily? Not Emily. Edith. She crouched in the corner by the couch and reached for my purse.

"Do you need something?"

She crept next to me. "An aspirin."

"Why didn't you look in the bathroom?"

"I didn't want to turn on the light and wake you up."

I had no reason to distrust Bowers' scary sister. I just did. "Top shelf of the medicine cabinet."

As soon as she cleared the doorway, I shot across the room and slipped the diary out of my purse. By the time she returned, the precious book was under my sheet. I slept with it wrapped tightly in my arms.

The next morning, I'd begged off accompanying Dymphna to Holy Cross, saying I had phone calls to make about our canceled trip to Loon Lake. As the words came out, they sounded lame. I could just as easily make those phone calls from the hospital.

Ghost Woman placed her hands on my shoulders. "Frankie, I know you love Marty and would move mountains to help him. You do what you need to do and don't worry. I've got the hospital covered."

My lower lip quivered. "I'll join you as soon as possible. I promise."

Her faith in me took a pressing weight off my psyche. And no, I didn't feel like I was shirking my fiancée duties. I'd already phoned the hospital. The doctor, probably encouraged by the police, had erected a barrier around Bowers, one I couldn't bypass with tears or screaming. It would be more productive to find out what really happened at Bennett's Grazers.

As soon as Dymphna left, I sprang into action. I threw on a pair of jeans and a short-sleeved t-shirt advertising

Seamus McGuire's *Canine Camp,* slipped my feet into a pair of tennis shoes, and ran a brush through my hair.

That goat had information about my fiancé's fall, and I was determined to get it. Before I left, I took a detour to the kitchen and slipped a cherry turnover into a plastic baggie.

Just as I zipped the bag shut, a car engine turned over. A quick glance at the empty hook where my car keys *should* be hanging explained whose car was making noise. I grabbed my purse and fled out the front door.

Edith had the Geo backed onto the street. As she straightened it out, I raced in front of the car and planted my feet, praying she wouldn't run me over.

She didn't. After hitting the brakes, she leaned her head out the window. "Please move."

"That's my car."

"I'm borrowing it."

"No, you're not."

We held our positions, neither one budging. Sweat trickled down my back. I suspected Edith was weighing the penalty for running me over against the benefit of a Frankie-free drive.

She smiled and offered an incentive. "Why don't I drop you off at the hospital? I'll let you know anything I find out."

"I don't need you to find things out for me," I said, tamping down panic. If we had to wrestle for the car keys, Edith would win. "I told you; I have errands. Work stuff. Things I need to do. Alone."

She eyed me as if she were sizing me up for the first time. It felt like she was plundering through my psyche, and I wondered if my clients felt this way when I connected with their tiny brains. What had changed overnight? I wrote it off as she had been too tired from travelling to pay much attention to me yesterday. She gave a brief nod. "Let's go."

"Sure. As soon as you get out of the car." I didn't trust her not to take off the second I moved from her path. "It will be faster if I drive, since I know the area."

After putting the car in park, she got out and moved to the passenger side as if she hadn't a care in the world. She wore the same clothes she had on yesterday, along with a black jacket made of that stretchy material that repels wrinkles. Her underwear was clean. I knew this because she'd washed them in the bathroom sink and hung them over the shower rail to dry.

Next to Edith, I seemed girlish. Soft. Like I should star in a commercial advertising a kitchen mop. But the mop lady won this round.

As soon as I had my seatbelt buckled, I told Edith we were heading back to the goats. The goat farm. To the farmer.

Brushing me off, she held up her phone. "I looked up this Luther Mendoza and narrowed it down. I have his address."

I had Luther Mendoza's address in Bowers' diary. How was Edith so sure she had the right one? There were a lot of Mendoza's in Maricopa County.

Once I evaluated the situation, I realized talking to Luther Mendoza was on my list anyway, so I might as well have company. At least it wouldn't slow me down.

To my surprise, Edith's directions led us to the address I had, through a neighborhood in Scottsdale to a street lined with old duplexes. The neat front yards and large side-by-side garage doors seemed a far cry from auto body shops in warehouses and Gator's low-income condo. Before she exited the car, Scary Sister ran her fingers through her hair and pulled it back into a sleek ponytail at the base of her neck.

My eyes refused to stray from the white SUV parked in the driveway. "We should come back."

"What for? We're here."

And so was Detective Juanita Gutierrez. That didn't bother Edith. She strolled to the door. Since I refused to wait in the car like her chauffeur, I followed.

A short man with gray hair and a map of lines in his weathered face answered the door.

"Nestor Diaz?" She barked out his name in an official tone.

Diaz? Leaning my head back, I doubled check the house number.

The man nodded at Edith. Over his shoulder, Gutierrez looked up from the couch and... To say she frowned wouldn't cover it.

Tugging on my companion's sleeve, I melted into a polite smile. "Pardon us. We can come back later when you're not busy."

"We're with her," Edith said with a brief nod, daring Gutierrez to make a scene. The detective's eyes narrowed to slits. As Nestor gestured to the living room, Edith added, "If you could bring us up to speed, I'd appreciate it."

I wound up in an armchair across from the detective. As I met her cool expression, it took all my self-control not to grab the lapels of her suit and shake her, demanding to know why she was keeping me from Bowers.

Edith pulled a notebook from a small purse I hadn't noticed. I did a double take. It was the same regulation notebook carried by all the detectives.

"Your relationship to Luther?" Edith flashed a brief smile. "I know the answer," she held up the notebook, "but anything that goes in here needs to be official. You can keep it short. I'm sure you understand."

From his puzzled expression, he didn't. "As you already know, my name is Nestor Diaz. I'm Luther's uncle. He came to live with us when he was seven, after his mother died. She was my wife's sister. We adopted him. Did our best to make him feel he belonged, but he never referred to us as Mom and Dad. Once he came of age, he switched back to his mother's surname." He spread his hands. "That's as far as we got."

While Gutierrez recovered from her desire to throttle us, Edith slipped in another question. "When was the last time you spoke to Luther?"

"It's been almost a month."

Gutierrez beat Scary Sister to the follow up. "Is that unusual?" Even though the detective's nostrils flared with suppressed irritation, she used the same soothing interview voice that Bowers had tried out on me when we first met on a case. I told him it made me want to smack him. Luther's uncle didn't seem to mind.

"Actually, it is. Luther changed his last name to honor his mother, not spite us. He usually dropped in on weekends, though his visits tapered off after he got fired. He was embarrassed because he needed to borrow money."

"Fired from Rings and Things," Gutierrez clarified.

"He loved that job." Nestor rubbed his face with his hands. "It's my fault. I was too hard on him. I told him, '*¡Qué tonta eres!*' And I meant it. Last time he came, I said he'd get nothing unless he stopped hanging around with *esos alborotadores* at Mike's."

Though I didn't speak Spanish, Nestor made his meaning clear. He wasn't fond of the guys at Mike's. Edith and I exchanged a glance.

"The auto body shop?" I asked so Gutierrez would assume Luther's connection with them was news to me.

"That's them. I used to be pleased he spent time there. I thought he might learn some useful skills. Now? I don't know."

The detective flipped a page in her notebook. "Rings and Things lost ninety thousand dollars' worth of inventory right before they fired your nephew."

"Yeah, yeah. They got robbed." His voice grew weary, and I suspected the police had already grilled him about it. He leaned forward. "The owner never accused my nephew of taking part. A few weeks later, he let him go. I'm sure it was those friends of his that made his boss suspicious. Luther isn't perfect, but he'd never stoop to robbing somebody." He raised a finger. "And he liked his boss."

"Mr. Diaz, do you think the employees of Mike's Auto Body had something to do with the burglary at Rings and Things?"

Confronted with a direct question, he backpedaled. "I can't say for sure." He made a noise of disgust. "My nephew had a good job. Why couldn't he be happy with that? I blame his friend, Randy. He works at Mike's, and Luther started spending his spare time *hanging out with the guys*. A waste of time. My nephew has a talent for fixing jewelry. It's a respectable trade."

The detective made a note in her regulation notebook. "Do you know Randy's last name?"

"No. He didn't come over here and play video games or whatever young people waste their time on these days. When I was young, we'd work on the car. Do something productive."

"The reason I'm asking about Luther is he seems to be missing."

His brow furrowed. "And I'll tell you the same thing I told that other detective. The man. Detective Brewster."

I didn't correct him because it's impossible to hold your breath and talk at the same time.

"My nephew got some girl pregnant and ran off to escape his responsibilities."

"You know this for certain?" Gutierrez' tone barely hid her disappointment.

"Which part? I know he got some girl pregnant. He told me. Then he stopped coming around, and I put two and two together."

"Do you have the name of his girlfriend?"

When he told us it was Lola Falana, I almost choked. He smiled.

"She was a looker. A talented lady. I have no idea if this young woman is anything like her, but I doubt it. The original is gorgeous, a talented singer, and a sexy dancer. That's a high bar to meet."

Once outside, Edith took charge before Gutierrez scolded us. "You're following my brother's trail."

Gutierrez tucked her notebook into her purse. "I'm cleaning up odds and ends of a case he was working on."

"Do you have *anything* about Bowers you'd like to share with us?" I made the question a combination of sweetness and accusation. Now that Edith had planted the idea, I wondered if Gutierrez was playing for Team Bowers. Was she happy my fiancé was in the hospital? It gave her the chance to clean up his case and shine for the bosses.

The detective stepped closer. "It's a small world. But it's big enough that I shouldn't run into the two of you again." And with that witty remark, Gutierrez left us. But not for as long as she would have liked.

THIRTY

"We need to talk to Lola Falana."

I'd had the same idea but cooed over Edith's brilliant suggestion. My enthusiasm helped me convince Bowers' sister she had superior research skills and my cell phone data connection stunk. She reluctantly accepted the shotgun position in the car, so I was free to drive to Holy Cross first to check up on Bowers' condition.

"Marty was working on the burglary. The one Nestor Diaz told us about." Edith stated it as fact, which made me want to argue...except I agreed.

"It doesn't sound as if Luther were involved."

She gave me a raspberry. "Says his doting uncle."

"Okay. So, what does any of that have to do with a dead man in my car?"

"The names on Marty's list included Luther Mendoza, Enrique Salazar, and George Dakos. George Dakos is dead. I wonder if the big question mark at the top represents Bennett's Grazers."

My hands squeezed the steering wheel so tight they

trembled. "And how do you know about his list and the question mark?"

"It's in his diary. The one in your purse."

My teeth clenched, and I felt a tiny pulse in my jaw. "You stole the diary from my purse."

"I put it back. If I'd stolen it, I'd still have it. He also mentioned Mike's Auto Body. Did he mean the place? Or the employees?"

That fink! There she sat, casually talking about digging through my purse and snatching Bowers' diary as if she had every right. But did she? She was his sister. I pulled into the Holy Cross Hospital parking lot and slipped into the closest spot. Jamming the gearshift into park, I faced her.

"You could have asked."

She grinned. "But you had so much fun hiding it. Just like Dymphna when she squirreled away her love letters in high school. Bad poetry. The first place anyone looks is under the mattress. She should have given it more thought."

I aligned myself with Ghost Woman. "You're saying we should have expected you to go through our things. Invade our privacy. Maybe we gave you more credit than to assume you'd rifle our drawers when we weren't there. Or peek under our mattresses. Or hunt through our purses. We assumed you had more self-respect than to stoop so low."

I set my voice on full censure, so I'm not sure why she laughed throughout my spiel.

"Nothing in this world is private. Haven't you noticed? At least Dym had an excuse. She was fourteen. I doubt she'd make the same mistake now. In fact, I know she wouldn't. Look how long she hid her relationship with Duane."

Arguing seemed pointless. Edith Bowers had no conscience. Or softer feelings. When she glanced up at the hospital entrance, she asked why we were wasting our time here.

"Until I check on Bowers, my mind refuses to commit to the investigation."

A wave of guilt crossed her features. "Good idea."

Coming here might be pointless. I didn't expect they would set out runway lights leading up to Bowers' room, but I was tired of being rejected over the phone. Let them do it to my face.

Dymphna must have gone for coffee because she wasn't in the lobby. Or maybe she'd run home to check on Windy. Gary, the father-to-be, wasn't around either. I wondered if his wife had recovered and left the hospital. Lucky guy.

Edith halted inside the door and scanned the room.

Rather than approach the welcome desk myself, I nudged Edith forward. "Ask for your brother's room." Her intimidating aura and persistence might pay off. I should have known the welcome ladies were made of sterner stuff.

She leaned her arms on the counter and glanced down at the seated women. "I'm Edith Bowers and I'm here to see my brother, Martin Bowers. Could you tell me his room number?"

A fresh team was on duty—two elderly women with pleasant faces. Doris, according to her name tag, accepted old age and let her short hair go gray. She wore her glasses on the end of a rope around her neck made from colorful beads. Her partner, Mimi, planned to battle Death until she met him face-to-face in her coffin. She had dark brown hair with pink streaks, and from the startling blue eyes that met mine, a blue not manufactured by nature, she wore colored contacts.

Doris got efficient. "Visits to Mister Bowers are restricted."

It would have been interesting to study Edith's tactics as she finagled a way up to Bowers' room, but the back of my neck tickled. I turned to find the cause.

"Bruce."

When I said his name, the therapy dog wagged his tail. His handler, Stan, beamed.

"Have you two met before?"

Crouching, I rubbed the canine's wide face with my palms, massaging behind his ears with my fingers.

"Sort of. I saw you arrive the other day."

I made a connection. While Stan talked about his work, Bruce showed me examples. A group of children, most of them bald, crowded the bully with delighted cries and showered him with affection.

Reaching for his hindquarters, I gave him a vigorous scratch at the base of his tail and ran my fingers up his back. He wiggled with pleasure. Now that I had him prepped to accept requests, I sent an image of Bowers.

He immediately responded.

A hospital room, with a view from the doorway. From Bruce's height near the floor, naturally. Bowers in bed, propped up on an angle. His eyes closed. His head drooped to the side so I saw his dark lashes. Dark stubble covered his face, but not enough to hide the bruise on his cheek. Wires led from under the white thin blanket covering him to a heart monitor.

Suddenly, he opened his eyes and smiled directly at me. His hand worked itself out from under the sheets, and he stretched out his arm and wiggled his fingers. My butt wagged, and I wriggled with pleasure before I disconnected from the dog.

Falling from my crouch to my fanny, relief welled until it spilled out in tears. Bowers wasn't near death. *Bowers would be okay!* At least I thought he would be okay. If he was awake and in his right mind, why hadn't he called?

I reconnected to the dog mid-scene. Bowers looked over my head as someone taller walked into the room. Was it Sam, Bruce's handler?

A woman with long, dark hair wearing a black suit moved to the head of his bed. Gutierrez. That double-crossing banshee!

"We're headed to the community center," Stan said, pulling me out of my plans to confront Gutierrez, preferably with barbed wire and a knuckleduster. "Kids are going to read books to Bruce. Aren't they, boy?"

With a last pat, I let him go.

My thoughts slithered into a dark crevice. If Bowers was awake and receiving visitors, why wouldn't they let me see him? There must be a conspiracy to keep my fiancé away from me. No. That was silly. These people didn't know me well enough to take pleasure in my anguish. There had to be a purpose.

Sometimes, concussions came with memory loss. Would the shock of seeing me kill him? Had he forgotten our engagement? More likely, they were keeping him isolated from outside stimulation until he remembered what happened. The Wolf Creek police were good. They might suspect he had help down that hill, and they'd be right.

If that was the reason, I could expedite Bowers' release by wrenching that information from Pierre the Picky Goat. My heart expanded in my chest as I saw an end to our involuntary separation. Find out what the goat saw, relay that information, and bring Bowers home. If he remembered who I was.

"Are you going to sit on your fanny all day?"

Edith helped me to my feet, and I stared at her, hard.

Only then did I notice the dark circles under her eyes. The pronounced worry line between her brows. Maybe the frown wasn't her usual expression but one of concern for her brother.

Right then, she didn't seem scary at all. Just an older sister worried about her baby brother. It wouldn't hurt to work together, as long as I led the way. She might even come in useful. And being kind to Bowers sister was the right move. I decided to give her a break.

Though I preferred to see Pierre alone, I made a sacrifice and hooked my arm through hers. As difficult as it was for me to invite a witness to my reading, I would attempt to bridge the gap between us and make her part of the process. Without telling her what I was doing, of course.

"Let's go see some goats. Maybe torture a farmer."

She rewarded me with a grin.

Figuring out the truth behind my fiancé's accident might be the only way I'd see him at our wedding. Once I contacted Pierre, I wouldn't let go until I'd wrung every detail, every nuance, and even the goat's personal opinion from his temperamental, horned head.

THIRTY-ONE

It crossed my mind to tell Edith her brother was awake, but I feared she might struggle for the wheel and turn the car around. So, on we drove.

Forty minutes later, forty minutes of me asking Edith how she was holding up and her replying with stoic silence peppered with the occasional grunt, we pulled up in front of Bennett's Grazers.

Edith jerked forward and peered through the front window. "He's pulled a runner on us."

"Runner? As in run away? Why would he do that?" And then I saw the goat pen, which was only a *goat* pen because it once held goats. Right now, it was just a pen. Empty. No goats. No Pierre.

As I scurried out of the car in a full panic, my feet skid to a stop when the tall farmhand came out of the barn carrying a heavy, metal rake. His broad shoulders held up a pair of denim overalls, and a long, dirty brown ponytail hung to between his shoulder blades from under a straw hat. He wasn't wearing a shirt over his well-muscled arms.

I waited to see what purpose he had planned for the rake, and when he stepped into the pen, I made my approach.

"Where are the goats?" I asked, wincing when my voice cracked. "What have you done with the goats?"

He leaned against the rake and narrowed his honey-colored eyes, a confrontational move. Honestly, if I didn't need the money, it's how I would greet most of my two-legged clients. People were not my favorite animal.

"Who wants to know?"

"Me. I mean, I'm Frankie. Nice to meet you."

After taking a moment to decide, he wiped his hand on his dirty jeans and shook my outstretched hand. "Jacob. Not that it's any of your business—"

Baas drifted out from the barn, and my shoulders relaxed.

"I was interested in buying Pierre."

His eyebrows shot up in surprise. "First I've heard of it."

"I just decided."

"That's something you'll have to discuss with Del." He swept the rake over the ground, pulling back matted straw.

"Sure. It's his farm. But can I take another look at the goat?"

"Nope. He's working at MALG."

"Who is? Del, or Pierre?"

"Both."

I kept my expression blank while I considered what task the farmer had assigned the goat. Was he a performing goat? He had done nothing worth watching when I'd seen him. Not toppling over. Not attempting to leap on my back and massage me. Not even juggling, which was something I'd pay to see.

"Doing what?"

"Promotion. Advertising. Call it what you will. He took Pierre with him."

"Advertising? You mean he's selling the goats?"

He snorted at my stupidity. "Bennett's Grazers. It's not just the name of the place. That's their job, woman. Clearing land of overgrowth and weeds. Feral vines."

An image of a fanged vine snarling at homeowners popped into my head. I shook it off. "For how long?"

"As long as it takes. Why? You have some land you need cleared?"

His voice dripped with condescension, and I longed to say yes. However, if he called me on it, I'd have a bunch of goats crammed into my patio area. "Um, no." And that's when I remembered Penny's promise to do whatever I asked. Or something like that. "But my friend is interested. I told her about Bennett's, and she'd like to see the goats."

"Tell her to come when Del's here."

"She wants to see them today. It's the only day her husband has off from work."

"Come back tonight. After seven." Glancing toward the road, he said, "How did you get here?"

Following his gaze to the end of the driveway, I noted Edith had absconded with my rental car.

"A friend dropped me off. She's shy." Something warned me against making my next statement, but since when have I listened to my inner voice? "My car's in the shop. Mike's Auto Body. I had an accident, and I heard they do good work."

His expression didn't change except for his lips. They tightened. "I work on my own cars."

I smiled. "Guess I should have paid better attention to my dad when he fixed ours."

Edith had moved the car about half a mile down the

road. Sweat plastered my shirt to me by the time I reached her. Once I slid in, she immediately confronted me, if you can call an unblinking stare of death a confrontation. If I said nothing, would she eventually ask? It might be fun to see how long she'd hold out, but getting to Pierre took priority.

"Del's taken a few of the goats, but he'll be back after seven. He's not pulling a runner."

"You shouldn't have left the car. That guy—"

"Jacob."

She raised an eyebrow. "*Jacob* will tell his boss about your visit, and he'll be on alert when we come back later."

"Why wait until then? I say we track him down now." By *him*, I meant Pierre.

"I know why I want to get a look at Del Bennett. Why do you?"

An excellent question and not one I planned to answer. Not directly. "Oh, I don't care about the farmer. I want to see the goats." Before she could make a wise comment about pet psychics, I put enthusiastic goo in my voice. "It's a great opportunity for researching their behavior for U-Behave. You remember. My animal behavior business. You may be on vacation, but I still have a job to do. It's not as far-fetched as you think. I had a session with a turkey and a duck last Thanksgiving. Yep. Gotta keep current with potential clients."

She started the car. "Since I've got time to kill, I can indulge you. Do you have an address?"

I gave her the address of the Prickly Pear.

"Del's in Wolf Creek?"

"No. We're going to Penny's bistro."

"Home of the dueling knights?"

"And the best corned beef hash around."

"If you're hungry, I'll hit a drive-through here in Cave Creek."

"But a drive-through wouldn't tell us where to find the goats. I mean Del."

THIRTY-TWO

For a person who isn't social, let's use me as an example, there's only one way to remain aware of the comings and goings in Wolf Creek and the surrounding cities. To be best friends with the nicest woman alive.

If a frown lurked in Penny's vicinity, she would track it down and pelt it mercilessly with good cheer until it surrendered. Strange as it sounds in the current climate of unfriendly, ill-mannered, judgmental idiots, my best friend's approach disarmed people into responding.

Customers, upon entering Prickly Pear Bistro and seeing her welcoming grin, shared things with her unprompted. Sometimes horribly personal things, but just as often interesting, useful bits of information.

As we walked into the restaurant, Edith took in the room's logistics, something I noticed she did whenever she entered a new place. If the brightly colored booths that lined the walls, or the perky centerpieces bursting with pinecones and fake fall foliage, or the seasonal waitress uniforms, now an eye-catching orange, annoyed her, she didn't comment.

Once she'd taken in the front counter and open window to the kitchen, the back hallway that led to the bathrooms and my shop's back entrance, and the friendly faces of the diners, she walked to the empty booth in the corner, one that had a view of the front door and the hallway. She slid into the side that gave her a wall to her back and the front window to her left.

"I've never seen the place from this angle," I said, sliding into the bench next to her just to annoy her. "It looks bigger."

Ann approached us for our order, but Penny shooed her away.

"Are you here for lunch?" our hostess asked. "Or just coffee?"

"I have a problem.'

She plopped her butt on the bench opposite us in record time. "Shoot."

"I need to find the goats—"

Edith interrupted. "We want to talk to Del Bennett."

"And the only thing I know is that they're at MALG."

Penny leaned back. "MALG? Oh! The expo. Maricopa Livestock and Garden expo. It's a smaller version of the county fair held at the Arizona State Fair Grounds. People love a fair, and they came up with this one to fill the gaps."

"So, Del Bennett is showing his goats?"

She wrinkled her nose. "Not likely. The only livestock are at the 4-H competition. They limit the adult categories to rabbits and chickens."

"Then why would he go there? And why would he take some goats with him? His employee mentioned advertising."

"Bennett's Grazers. I assume he rents the goats out to clear land."

"He does. Feral vines and that sort of thing." I felt a twinge of pride over my new knowledge.

"Then he's probably got a vendor booth. You know, to drum up business."

Remembering the bright lights and noises that accompanied Pierre's vision of murder, I asked, "Would they have carnival rides? Fireworks? Games?"

"Oh, sure. One of those traveling carnivals sets up. Kemper won me a bear bank last year. The bank is his tummy. It's cheap plastic. I use it to store paper clips and rubber bands."

When had the murder taken place? "That won't work," I mumbled, which caught Edith's attention.

"What won't work?"

Avoiding a direct answer, I asked Penny if the fair lasted all week or just this weekend.

"It's every weekend during the month of September. That's why they don't allow the large livestock. It might get too hot in the barns."

That meant the victim had died during the last two weeks, since this was the third week of September. While I *could* look up the address and drive to the expo, approaching a relatively small vendor booth without being seen presented a problem. One I hoped Penny would solve.

"I have a favor to ask."

She clasped her hands together in front of her chest, just like a princess presented with a frog who claims to be a prince. "You need our help." She whipped out her cell phone. "Right now?"

Nothing on earth is more determined than an optimistic woman on a mission.

"As soon as possible would be good, but I don't want to bother Kemper if he's at work."

After hitting a speed dial button, she held her phone to her ear. "It's happening. How soon can you get here?" She nodded and ended the call. "He's on his way."

"Uh, Pen, you don't even know what we want you to do."

"It doesn't matter." Penny firmed up her chin. "Friends do whatever their friends need." She spoiled the somber moment with a squeal. "This is so exciting. I can't believe we're helping the police."

"The Wolf Creek police department is not officially involved," Edith said. Since she didn't know what I was after, she wisely limited herself to that statement and then kept her mouth shut. For the moment. Her Husky eyes reflected curiosity with an edge of wariness, one emotion for each eye color.

Penny leaned forward and patted her hand. "Don't be a spoilsport."

"Actually, Pen, do we need Kemper? Maybe you would work better alone."

Her jaw dropped. "And deprive my husband of the opportunity to play detective? Something every little boy dreams of? Shame on you Frances Chandler."

"The only thing Kemper ever dreamt about was an organizer for his toys."

The front door burst open. Kemper Mohr halted inside the entrance and searched the room for his wife. On his lanky body, he wore a medium-brown suit that matched his medium brown hair. The bland, solid dark brown tie and off-white shirt were suited to his job as an accountant.

His long legs brought him across the room in a minimum number of steps, and he gazed down at us expectantly. His eyes gleamed with interest, and the corner of his mouth twitched. If possible, the prospect of helping me excited Kemper, which was a shock. His typical reaction to me involved fear.

He held out one hand to me and then Edith. "I'm sorry to hear about Martin's accident. As Penny said, we'll help in any way we can."

By the time I finished explaining, his enthusiasm had waned, especially when I told him he'd need to change.

"You're going to a fair, not a business conference. Your suit will stick out."

He adjusted his black-framed glasses. "Why? If I'm supposed to be the owner of a large property in Scottsdale who needs the services of his goats, how would I afford that property without a decent job?" He spread his jacket open. "This suit will assure the man I'm a serious customer."

Penny had warned me that arguing with her husband would be an enjoyable experience only if I relished slamming my head against adobe brick houses, so I had to trust his way would work.

With the newly married couple in the back seat of my rental car, we headed to the fair grounds.

THIRTY-THREE

One quarter of the large parking lot at the corner of 19th Avenue and Encanto Boulevard was dedicated to the carnival. The remaining three-quarters was packed with cars, but I finally squeezed into a space. As soon as I stepped out of the car, I knew we were in the right place.

The children's screams were just as loud during the day as they were the night of the murder, most of them emanating from a Ferris wheel with swinging seats and a suicidal contraption that flung its occupants in nauseating loops.

A girl, about eight, struggled with an oversize hammer, attempting to hit the target and win a massive stuffed unicorn. She raised the implement of doom over her head, teetered, and fell back on her keester.

A mixture of people from tween to adult perched on stools and aimed squirt guns at passing ducks. A teenager with raven hair shaved close on one side leaned against the inner wall of her stall. She gazed around as if wondering how her dreams of joining the carnival had brought her so low. When she held out a handful of golf balls and raised her eyebrows in my direction, I understood she was above begging me to try her game. Out of pity, I paid five dollars to aim three balls at goldfish bowls. My tosses were half-hearted because the bowls contained goldfish. I didn't want to injure them.

Halfway across the blacktop, Kemper removed his jacket and slung it over one shoulder. When I gave him an *I told you so* look, he moved to put it back on. Penny stopped him.

"Let it air out."

Her command gave him the excuse he needed to keep the jacket off and save face.

"I hope this works." Edith strolled at my side, her face pointed forward as if, by avoiding eye contact, she could remain aloof. "Whatever *this* is. You want your friends to distract Del Bennett while you observe the goats. Why can't you observe them without a distraction?"

"Because he'll recognize me and try to talk to me. I need to focus."

"Focus on the goats."

"Yes. I told you. For my business. But the *real* reason for our visit," I said, lowering my voice, "is to let you get a good look at Del Bennett. I didn't want to mention it to Pen and Kemper. As good as their intentions might be, they might give you away."

Edith accepted that load of manure. She seemed more interested once she thought I was providing a diversion so she could lurk to her heart's content.

We paid our entrance fee and paused on the other side of the ticket booth to plan our route. The tri-folded brochure that came with my purchase showed the major competitions. Judging for the pies, jams and cakes took place in the Home Arts Center. The bakers shared the space with the gardening show, which was divided by flowers and edibles.

The Arizona Plaza had the 4-H, rabbit, and chicken judging. That seemed the most logical place for a vendor to set up a booth with a couple of goats, so we marched forward.

Along the way, food trucks offered a variety of edibles, most of them fried. The vinegary smell of fried pickles tingled my nostrils. The rest just smelled like old oil. Fried cookies. Fried candy bars. Fried elephant ears. When I spotted the last booth, I went back, bought one, and wrapped it in a napkin, dumping the smushed, gooey turnover I'd grabbed that morning into the next waste bin.

Screaming children ran past with cotton candy. Because of the heat, the truck selling flavored ice cones boasted the largest crowd. By the time we entered the plaza, the smells of grease and sugar coated my nostrils and smothered my tastebuds, though I hadn't sampled the yummies.

We arrived in time for the best-dressed pet competition. The honors went to a Yorkie in a vampire outfit.

Penny stood on her tiptoes and scanned the room. "I don't see any trade booths here."

We backtracked until we found an area covered in tents in a grassy spot known as The Backyard. It was located near the entrance where we started, something Kemper pointed out to me several times. Admittedly, the return trip wasn't as exciting. Several of the food truck employees were snatching fresh air out their back doors. Sweat tickled my armpits.

When we finally made it to our destination, I took a

moment to get my bearings. Two long sections of tents stood in double rows, with the tents in each section placed back-to-back. A wide path traveled between the canvas walls to allow vendors to slip out to use the facilities or get something to eat without being seen. I knew the moment I saw that corridor this was the place.

Seed companies, lawn care services, and nurseries all vied for our attention, luring us with offers of peppermint candies and free pens bearing their logos. All tactics to get us close enough to shove flyers in our hands. Though Edith and I didn't fall for it, Penny, with her generous spirit, slowed us down, speaking with each one.

Just as I was tempted to lie down on the trampled grass and take a nap, I spotted a tent about twenty feet long and ten feet deep. The entire area, except for the table, was lined with wire fencing. I recognized Pierre right away. The other two goats, both females, I hadn't met. One had brown and black markings. The other was solid black. Unlike Pierre, both had been dehorned.

We had found Del Bennett.

I grabbed Penny's arm and pulled her away from a tree removal service, careful to keep my back toward Del's tent. "There he is."

"Where?" Kemper's voice carried.

"Don't be so obvious! Right behind me. Four tents down on this side. You know the plan?"

Embarrassed by my criticism and irritated by the heat, Penny's husband developed an attitude. "We talk to him and hold his attention so you can play with the goats. We can handle it."

"Good. Don't hurry over. Just wander up and start talking. Act natural. I'll wait for you to get started before I slip in. And for goodness' sake, don't look in my direction. Or at the goats."

When I turned to ask Edith her plans, she wasn't there. Relieved that she wouldn't be hovering while I communicated with Pierre, I slipped between the closest two tents, determined to get some answers.

THIRTY-FOUR

Except for me, the passage was empty. It was long past the lunch hour, but if the women vendors were anything like me, they'd have to tinkle again soon.

Three tents down, a woman with straw-colored hair slipped out the back of the tent on my left. Dropping to one knee, I fumbled with my shoelace. As she passed, I glimpsed a blue apron with pink writing on it and a border of daisies. A flash of a pathetic wilted daisy, trampled on the grass, entered my mind.

The next tent down on my side belonged to Bennett's Grazers, so I remained where I was and leaned forward to peer past the edge of my current cover.

Penny and Kemper stood in front of the table. I could hear every word. Kemper's voice carried as he introduced them as Mr. and Mrs. Decimal.

"He's not going to buy it."

I jumped at Edith's voice in my ear but covered my yelp in time. She crouched over my shoulder and watched the happy couple with a grim expression.

Adjusting my volume to a whisper, I attempted to stop

the pulse in Edith's jaw muscles. "Penny grew up on a farm. She'll do fine. Kemper will be her ignorant, pretentious husband. Perfectly realistic." My assurances were for both of us. Though Penny had tested her acting chops at the local theater production of *A Christmas Carol,* Kemper didn't strike me as a talented improvisational actor. "Why aren't you positioned to observe Del Bennett?"

"I can see him just fine from here." Edith adjusted a small pair of binoculars with a rectangle on top and leaned forward. I rolled my eyes.

"Are those high-caliper, special agent issue? Can you see through walls?"

"Left that pair at home."

We both winced as Kemper delivered his next line. Now that the greetings were over, he got straight to the point.

"We want to see your gang of goats," Kemper said, trying to sound like a man in charge. "All of them. In action."

"You'll have to meet me at Bennett's Grazers. As you can see, this is just a sampling." Farmer Del sounded as gruff as ever. When he turned and gestured to the goats, Edith and I leaned back in unison.

"Idiot," Edith mumbled.

Penny, who would never bruise Kemper's ego in public, gently took over. "We would like to hire your herd to clean our property."

"Whereabouts are you located?"

We'd discussed the details beforehand so my friend had her answer ready. "South of Shea. It's three acres with two horses and some chickens."

"It's an extensive property," Kemper confirmed. "Huge. Overrun with...stuff. Uh, that's why we need the goats."

"Do you have any brochures?" Penny asked, her voice dripping with honey.

While Del handed her a single-page flyer, I crept closer to the fence. After unwrapping the elephant ear, I waved it in the air, spreading the scent. All three goats moved forward and leaned against the chicken wire. As they were perilously close to knocking it down, I tore off two pieces and tossed them away from the fence, all the while holding the biggest piece in front of Pierre's eyes.

"The horses haven't met goats before," Penny said. "The Appaloosa will be fine, but the Thoroughbred mare is skittish. I need to see your herd in action before I decide whether to go ahead with your services."

Thoroughbred? Penny couldn't help but brag, even over an imaginary horse.

"A Thoroughbred?" It was as close to friendly as I'd ever heard Del. "Do you race her?"

"Never." Penny's curt answer expressed her opinion on racing horses professionally. Uh-oh. Hold on to that temper, Pen.

"Or breed her?" he persisted. "Because I know some folks who would be interested."

"I ride her. For pleasure. Both hers and mine. I don't run her until her nose bleeds, and I don't rent her out to stud farms."

My friend was getting worked up over the welfare of an animal she didn't own. Because it didn't exist. I willed the conversation to move on.

"So do I," Kemper blustered. "Ride her." I figured he wouldn't know a saddle horn from a stirrup.

I carefully rose to standing and held out my hand. In a flash, Pierre yanked the pastry from me and devoured it, paper and all. Stepping back to my cover, I winced with each crinkle until he finished. His bizarre eyes met mine. A wave of reflected pleasure filled my chest. Before I had time to lick the powdered sugar from my fingers, the sun disappeared along with Edith, and it was night.

This time, the vision showed me more detail. The same cowboy headed my way, wearing the same bandana. This time, he had his arm in a tight grip around the shoulders of someone I recognized.

I strained to make out the cowboy's face, knowing how important that information was, but the broad brim of his tan Stetson covered all but his pointed chin, as he had his head bowed to say something in Mr. G's ear.

In a fear response to what I knew must happen next, I scrunched my shoulders to make myself smaller, which was ridiculous. The men couldn't see me. Their shapes lit up in a pink glow as fireworks snapped and boomed. Both lifted their heads to watch, revealing the cowboy's thick eyebrows.

The cowboy proved to be a versatile killer. He pulled a snub-nosed gun from his pocket the same time he shoved Mr. G to the ground. His victim rolled over and held out his hands, pleading for mercy, but the killer aimed for his head and shot once. If I hadn't been watching, I would have mistaken it for another firework.

Another cowboy, this one taller, slipped out from the back of a tent with his wheelbarrow of hay, stuffed the corpse inside, covered it, and went on his way. Before he turned, his honey-brown eyes seemed to meet mine. Panicked, I jerked back, breaking the connection.

As my world came back into focus, I fell to my hands and knees, panting hard. Another man murdered in front of me. And nothing about Bowers. Throwing back my head, I cried out in a hoarse voice that didn't sound like me.

"Be quiet," Edith hissed, but she was too late.

"Who are you?"

A woman stood next to me, her hands on her hips. The writing on her apron said Daphne's Daisies. She wasn't the only one watching the spectacle. Del came to the back of his fencing. Something told me another story about missing Bowers wouldn't do the trick.

Kemper watched me with the wide eyes of a cartoon fan viewing his first horror film. Penny's tight smile showed she wasn't sure how to proceed.

"That woman looks injured," Penny said, her usual chipper tone edged with worry.

"Do you know this person?" Del demanded, without removing his gaze from me.

Penny's glance flickered over me. "Never seen her before in my life."

"Me either," Kemper added, happy to have an excuse to ignore me.

"Let's go," Edith said, placing a hand on my shoulder.

"It's not fair." I brushed her hand off, holding onto the tent to help me to my feet. "I'm staying until I get answers."

"She's distraught," Edith said to no one in particular. "Out of her mind."

"Look," Del said. "I'm really sorry about what happened to your fiancé, but you need to move on and stop harassing me." He patted Pierre on the head. "And stop upsetting my goats."

Pierre didn't look upset to me. He looked hungry.

Lurching across the path, I jerked open the panels at the back of the tent opposite Del's. A startled teenager, seated behind a table, looked up from her magazine. Samples of daisies and other flowering plants surrounded her. On the table, packets of seeds and brochures were spread out in fans.

The woman in the apron skirted around me and blocked my way. "You don't belong here."

Searching the space, I said, "Where is it?"

"You're scaring my daughter."

A second chair sat in front of the table. Aside from empty boxes for the seeds and brochures and trays of flowers, the tent held nothing of interest. No wheelbarrow. No scary-looking cowboys.

"Sorry," I mumbled as I stepped back into the walkway. Del had his attention on another potential customer. I strode past his tent, stopping on the other side of the fenced area. Edith followed close behind.

"You need to stop this," she hissed.

"Stop what?" I asked, feigning ignorance. When I assumed the woman's tent was the one exited by the man with the wheelbarrow, I hadn't considered that Pierre moved around his temporary pen. That meant I had two more tents to choose from, depending on where he was standing when he witnessed the murders.

"We need to see who is in those tents." I motioned toward my two choices, and Edith slapped my hand down.

"No. What we need to do is pull back and reevaluate the situation. That means get out of here."

"You don't get it. It's important I find out—" A handcuff snapped shut around one wrist. "What in the—"

"Let's go."

Though I knew Edith could take me in a fight, I still underestimated her full strength when she put her mind to it. She held my arm—the one with the handcuff—pinned to her side as she steered me out of the fairgrounds and through the parking lot to the car.

"Why in the world do you have handcuffs?"

"I always come prepared."

She released me next to my passenger door. After one last glance toward the vendor tents, I got in the car. Turning my head to fish out my seatbelt, I yelped when she palmed the crown of my head and shoved it between my legs.

"What the flying Fritos are you doing?"

"Stay down," she hissed, shoving me again and leaning sideways to join me. She raised her head enough to see the side-view mirror, and after a minute, sat up. "Okay. You're good."

"I don't believe you. Who do you think you are?"

"I'm the woman who's keeping you safe."

"From what?" Following her gaze, I looked over my shoulder and thanked my stars for her quick action. A brown pickup truck turned as it reached the end of our row. On the side of the truck, in blue lettering, it read *Mike's Auto Body*. "Oh."

"Yeah, oh."

I could tell Edith was furious by the way her nostrils flared. Just like a horse. Or Gutierrez.

"Why did you stop me back there? You don't even know what I was after."

She cocked her head. "Really? You wanted to get inside the two tents across from Del Bennett's. While he watched."

"But I was looking for something. Something related to the murders."

"Murders?"

"Yes. Pierre showed me—"

She held up a hand. "So help me, if you bring up talking goats again, I'm going to lose it."

The back door opened and the Mohrs slid into the car.

"That was pretty freaky," Penny said. Kemper chose to pretend I wasn't there.

"We'll talk about it later, Pen."

The couple remained silent after that. Scary Sister didn't want to talk, either. She didn't say another word on the drive back to Wolf Creek.

As for me? One question occupied my head. Now I knew where the men were killed, but what did that have to do with a hillside in Cave Creek?

THIRTY-FIVE

"Can I drop you off anywhere? Shooting range? Camping supply store? A nice little camouflage clothing store?"

After returning the Mohrs to the Prickly Pear, Edith remained in the driver's seat, which made her in charge of any dropping off. However, I had an appointment, a real one, and I didn't need Scary Sister's commentary while I did my job. Naturally, Edith declined my offer. "I'm sticking with you. Just tell me when to turn."

She understood something happened at the fair. In her attempt to reconcile what she'd seen with her logical mind, she expounded on her theory that I had information buried in my skull, but believed it came to me through the goat. It was my turn to be the stoic one. To give Edith her due, she worked hard at convincing me to talk.

"If we're working as a team, I need to know what you know."

A snort slipped out. "We're a team? Team members share things, like the car keys."

"Team members have designated jobs that match their skill set. One of mine is driving."

I shifted to face her. "What's my skill set? My designated job."

"You talk a lot. It's distracting and gives me a chance to accomplish things without being noticed."

"What things?"

"Things."

"Since you're driving, and I wouldn't want to distract you, I'll shut up now."

It wasn't in Edith's nature to beg, so she stewed instead.

Someday I'd wrestle my keys away from her and hold on to them. For now, I gave her directions to an area west of Phoenix surrounded by farmlands and ponds. An area where duck hunters gathered to lure waterfowl to their deaths for sport. Calling it sport didn't sound fair. In my mind, sports involved competition between evenly matched competitors. Duck hunting seemed more like trickery.

Once Edith stopped asking about my meltdown, it took some of the fun out of keeping the information from her. Which made me want to talk. She kept the conversation light, or light for Scary Sister, which meant saying nothing. Not when I asked if she always wanted her own car and maybe that's why she enjoyed driving mine so much. Not even when I asked who did her hair, which was pulled back in a single braid down her back.

After getting lost three times, we found the right pond. As we slowed to maneuver around a pothole, the crack of gunshots echoed around us. Even with my window up, I heard them. Then all would go eerily silent until the next round began.

Hunting was necessary to thin out the herds when the population grew too large. A quick death seemed preferable to disease and starvation. I also didn't mind hunting for food if hunters ate what they caught. And they hunted in season and kept within the quotas. And they chased down anything they injured. That didn't mean I wanted to witness it.

A guy dressed in a camouflage jumpsuit hailed us. Once we parked and I got a closer look, I realized it wasn't a one-piece outfit. His synthetic overalls were tucked into high boots. Underneath, he wore a long-sleeved shirt in a slightly different pattern, more greens than the browns in his waders. Over it all, he had a brown vest with a zillion pockets, and he topped it all off with safety glasses and a brown baseball cap.

He carried his shotgun broken over his arm. I approached and introduced myself. He responded by grabbing my hand so tight my knuckles cracked.

"I'm Dave. Boy, am I glad to see you. Jingle needs your help." He gestured to the black Labrador sitting calmly at his side.

"What's the problem?"

"He refuses to retrieve." Dave frowned his disappointment. In response, the pup wagged his tail.

It took no time to connect with Jingle. The dog showed me an image of a bloody Mallard duck corpse. My face puckered, reflecting the canine's opinion. When my mouth filled with soggy feathers and blood, I bent in half and gagged.

Jingle's brows shifted as if to say, "Tell me about it."

Dave took my elbow and asked if I was all. right, while Edith looked on, not as amused as she'd been the first few times she'd witnessed me read an animal.

"It's not as if he doesn't recognize a duck. He keeps bringing back the decoy. Maybe he's just dumb."

This wasn't the right time to snort out a laugh in the

hunter's face. In my defense, the chuckle came to me via Jingle.

"Sorry about that." I gave the dog an inconspicuous wink. He wagged his tail. "The thing is, Dave, Jingle knows exactly what he's doing."

His face reddened. "If he knew what he was doing, he'd bring me the duck, not the decoy."

At his feet lay several duck corpses tied together. The most recent had not yet joined the string-gang. I pulled a tissue from my pocket, wrapped it around the neck of the duck corpse, picked it up, and held it out, grimacing as I did so. "Put that in your mouth."

He stepped back. "Are you nuts? That's disgusting."

I dropped the duck. "That's how Jingle feels about it."

The hunter stared at his furry friend. The dog stared back and whined. Stan rubbed his chin, considering.

"Are you serious?" He directed the question to me, not the dog.

"I'm afraid so."

"He's a retriever. It's his nature to go get things and bring them back. That's what he does."

"Except with the ducks. Is that right?"

"B-But he loves coming with me. He gets excited when I pack up my equipment."

"That's because he loves being with you, Dave. He loves being in the fresh air. He enjoys running through the rushes and even jumping in the water. What he doesn't like is mouthing dead animals."

Jingle woofed his agreement.

"And what would he rather do instead?"

I asked.

"Those drives you take with him in the early morning, just as the sun is rising. You drive to—" I turned back to the dog to get confirmation. "Someplace with a red-and-yellow awning. You go through the drive-through and get him a burger. He says burger, but if it's morning, I imagine it's sausage. He likes that way better than slogging through cold water to snag a dead duck. Way better." I shook my head. "Sausage isn't good for him, Dave. And you should settle for the single sausage biscuit for yourself instead of the double with bacon, egg, and cheese. Too much cholesterol."

He gaped. "He said all that?"

"Not in words." I shrugged.

"Aw, shoot. The whole reason I hunt is to be outdoors with my dog at my side. The hunting part—well, to tell the truth, I never cared for it."

"You don't?" I glanced at his outfit. "You seem really into it."

When he broke into a broad smile, the skin on his face creased. "It doesn't take much to look the part. Just the right outfit."

A rifle shot exploded nearby. I flinched. Edith merely turned her head to glance in the noise's direction.

Dave crouched and took Jingle's head in his hands and rubbed his ears. It warmed my heart.

"I used to do it with my father. I guess it's a tradition."

"Maybe it's time for your own traditions."

"What do you say we get out of here, Jingle? Go for a ride? There's a Burger Hut on the way home." His gaze flickered up to me. "Maybe I'll get a salad."

The Labrador hopped and twirled in a frenzy of joy.

"You got your answer."

As we returned to the car, Edith kept her eyes on me. "What?"

"You convinced that man his lazy, poorly trained dog didn't want to hunt."

I stopped and stared. Her tone carried an accusation, like she was angry over my success. What did it matter to her?

"That's not a fair description of Jingle."

"Fair doesn't come into it." She glanced back at Dave, loading his equipment into the back of his truck while Jingle waited in the cab. "And he handed you money for it. Amazing."

"Call it what you will. It pays my bills."

"You peeked in his truck and saw fast food wrappers." Edith said this with certainty, as if it settled the matter.

"If you say so." I had gone nowhere near his truck.

"Any more appointments?" she asked, unlocking the passenger door for me. "You don't need to tell some old lady that her dog's overweight because she feeds it six times a day?"

"Jeepers. Let it go. I don't make fun of the way you skulk around, playing secret agent, or superhero, or whatever fantasy plays out in your head while you're standing there looking threatening."

"I don't skulk."

Pressing my lips tight, I did a rapid nod. "You do. Skulk. Lurk. Call it what you will."

She straightened her shoulders. "I do *not* skulk."

"Fine. Whatever. To answer your question, no, I don't have another appointment right now. We can skulk to wherever you like."

"Good." She moved around the front of the car and held up her phone. "Because we're not that far from Lola Falana."

As I buckled up, I thought, "*My life is strange.*" And my pet psychic skills are not the weirdest part.

THIRTY-SIX

Apparently, Lola Falana, the performer, had several fans in Maricopa County who had named their children after her. Edith said it had taken three phone calls before she struck lucky and got Lola's roommate.

"The woman said Lola's at work. Pretty stupid to give out that information to a stranger."

"When did you call her? I didn't see you use your phone."

"You were busy pretending to talk to the dog."

Not that busy. But I let it go. For now.

"Where does she work?"

"Nemo's."

Nemo's was a seafood chain one step above fast food. "Did you ask which location?"

"I'm not the stupid one."

As Edith pulled into a parking spot a few blocks from Gilbert's town square, I cautioned her about our approach.

"Nestor Diaz said this woman is pregnant, so she's in a delicate state of mind, amped up because the father of her child skedaddled. Take it easy on her. Besides. She's at work. Bowers wouldn't be happy if you were arrested." To be crystal clear, I added, "She's not the enemy. She's suffering."

Edith rolled her eyes. "She's a dunce for hooking up with Luther in the first place."

Since the lunch rush was over, the restaurant was empty except for a smattering of customers, but the smell of seafood and grease hung heavy in the air.

A replica of a ship's anchor hung over the hostess booth. We asked the scrawny woman behind the podium, the one dressed in a white sailor's outfit, to seat us in Lola's section. She led us to a dimly lit booth in the back of the dining area and handed us menus.

"Is the food here any good?" Edith asked, scanning the selections. "I'm hungry."

I snatched her menu away. "It's better if we don't order. Once we talk to her, she may ask us to leave."

The woman who approached us, in her mid to late twenties, had a bulging belly under her blue sailor costume. She was pretty in a natural way, with her brown hair pulled into a bun, smooth brown skin that glowed, and green eyes that sparkled with humor.

"Welcome to Nemo's. I'm Lola, your server for today."

Her pregnant belly threw me. I'd assumed hers was a recent condition. It made me sad to think Luther had abandoned her so close to the birth of his child.

"Hi. I'm Frankie, and this is Edith. We wanted to talk to you about Luther."

Instead of hurling her order pad at our heads and demanding we leave, Lola's eyes opened wide. "Is he all right?"

"We don't have any reason to believe otherwise. We're

trying to track him down for his uncle. Can you tell us what happened? Why he left?"

She lowered herself to the edge of my bench. When I offered her my glass of water, she declined. "My feet hurt."

Edith didn't care about her feet. "Where did your boyfriend run off to?"

These booths were spacious, which meant Edith's foot was out of kicking range. "Luther's uncle suggested he might have, um, run from his responsibilities."

"No way. Luther was ecstatic when I told him I was pregnant. Sure, he was scared, but he looked forward to being a dad. Then he disappeared. He never called. He hasn't written." Tears sprung up in her eyes. "I'm really worried about him."

She had a right to be worried.

Please don't be dead, Luther. Please stay away from fairgrounds. Please don't show up in my car with a bullet in your brain.

"Are you sure he hasn't tried to reach you?"

"Positive."

"Maybe he's written, and the letter got lost."

She frowned. "Luther isn't much for writing notes. Though he did write me some poetry when we were first dating."

"Have you checked your messages? I have a land line, and my mother is always complaining that my message box is full."

She picked up on my worry. "I've checked. I'm certain I've checked. Maybe I should look again when I get home."

"Can you guess where he might have gone? Could it have had something to do with the guys at Mike's Auto Body?"

"You mean Randy? No. Randy's looking for Luther, too.

Besides. Luther promised to find something stable." She rubbed her belly. "Something that would support us. He won't find that in an auto body shop. He's terrible with cars." She turned her green eyes on me. "Luther had dreams."

"You mean premonitions?"

"Ambitions."

Edith looked like she was sleeping with her eyes open until she spoke. "Like what?"

But Lola refused to share. "It would be bad luck to talk about them before they happened."

My face grew warm as I followed my train of thought to a new station. "You're, um, pretty pregnant."

She rubbed her belly. "Seven months."

"Luther's only been gone a short while, right?"

"Four weeks."

"So, you'd been pregnant for a while before he left. Um..."

She put me out of my misery. "Luther didn't tell his uncle right away. He didn't want him to know about our baby until we were married, but he didn't want to get married without a way to support us."

"Quite the conundrum," Edith said, earning my glare.

A dark thought slithered into my head. I'd never seen Luther Mendoza. Maybe he was a blond Spaniard, like the first unfortunate fellow Pierre showed me. "Do you have a picture of Luther?" When she asked why we didn't have our own picture if we were looking for him, I said we wanted a more recent photo.

"You know how men are about having their picture taken. Can you see Luther and his uncle posing for a Christmas snapshot?"

She giggled and reached under her neckline, pulling out

a chain with a cheap, stainless steel, heart-shaped locket. When she flipped it open, the subject of the tiny photograph had brown hair that flopped over his right eye and too many teeth. Not the guy I'd seen in my vision.

"Very nice looking. Your baby will be beautiful. Or handsome. By the way, and I only ask because you brought up the robbery—"

Edith piped in. "Burglary."

My molars ground together. "Burglary. It made me wonder if Luther ever did anything...unethical?"

Her face flamed red as she glanced down at her belly. "I know our timing wasn't the best—"

"No! Not what I meant. Besides. You're thinking immoral, not unethical. Not that I'm judging." My face burned hot. "I just wondered if Luther had a criminal past."

"Criminal? Are you saying Luther is a criminal?"

Her volume rose with each word. The waitress serving the section across the room looked over, concerned. I smiled to let her know this was a friendly conversation.

"I'll have you know, Luther is a saint."

"A saint?"

Her eyes narrowed. "A saint. One time, I wanted to stay in the seats after our movie ended and watch it again. Luther said no way. That would be cheating the movie theater."

"Okay. He's a saint. But were his friends all saints, too?"

She relaxed. "I see what you're getting at. I wasn't happy with some of them. He hung out with this one friend-of-a-friend. Chopper. The guy had a record. Luther said it was in his past and I wasn't to worry."

"How about his other friends?"

"His friend Randy is nice. I don't know anything bad about him."

Before we left, Edith asked if Lola could think of anything that might help us in our search.

"I've been over our last week together again and again, looking for a hint. Something that would tell me why he left or where he went." She turned thoughtful. "In fact, he said that soon I wouldn't have to worry about anything."

Uh-oh. Was he talking about the spoils from the burglary?

"Do you have a pet?" I blurted it out. Edith stared, but Lola giggled.

"The baby is enough for us to look after."

On impulse, I rested my hand on her arm. "Don't worry. We'll find him. I'm sure there's a reasonable explanation for his sudden departure."

And I hoped it wasn't the reason I had in mind. Because the killing I'd seen was impersonal. Professional. I didn't know if hired killers got paid by the body, but I was certain they didn't stop at one. Or two.

THIRTY-SEVEN

Lola convinced us to take fish tacos to go. She said they were the best in the entire Phoenix area. Fish tacos didn't sound appetizing, but she had so much enthusiasm for her restaurant's product. It's hard to resist an employee who loves their job.

I got mine without sauce. The idea of a taco made without ground beef—and did I mention it didn't come with cheese?—was difficult enough to wrap my brain around without wondering what was in the white stuff they wanted to drizzle over it.

"You're too picky," Edith said, shoving the last of her lunch into her mouth as we walked. "You should eat what you can when you can. You never know what lies ahead, and your next meal might not be as soon as you hope."

"Yeah. I'll take my chances and eat it sitting down like a civilized person." Not that I never ate on the run, but I was familiar with what I was shoveling into my mouth. Fish tacos demanded my attention and inspection before I tasted them.

She clicked the key fob to unlock the door for me. After

sliding in, I sniffed. Holding the container to my nose, I sniffed again. No way was I going to eat food that smelled this bad. Funny, I hadn't noticed the stench in the restaurant when I'd peeked inside the container.

Edith got in, and before she got comfortable, I stuck my lunch under her nose. "It stinks."

She took a whiff. Her eyes opened wide, and she whipped her head around to look in the back seat. "Get out."

I started to turn my head to see who was in my car. She pushed my jaw forward with her fingers. "Don't look. Just get out."

After taking a shaky breath, I sighed. "It's not my lunch that smells, is it."

She was already out of the car and on her phone. My fingers clenched and broke through the Styrofoam box. Edith didn't want me to see, but for the love of Mike, it was my car. At least it was my rental. I kept my breathing shallow to control my intake of stink and repeated a new mantra. *Please don't be Luther. Please don't be Luther.*

Get it over quick, I thought. My head wouldn't cooperate. I explained who was in charge and forced it to turn.

"Oh, no. Oh, no."

The car door opened, and someone jerked me out. Fish tacos scattered on the sidewalk, and I landed on my butt.

Gazing up at her, dazed, I said, "How did he get in there?"

She rubbed a hand over her mouth. "I'm more concerned about who he is and who put him in there."

I gulped. "I can answer the first question. *That* is Gator. Gamer extraordinaire."

THIRTY-EIGHT

"What do you mean you've met Enrique Salazar before?"

Edith and I stood on the sidewalk several yards from my car. The police and medical people had taken over the Metro. The question came not from Edith but from a furious Detective Gutierrez.

I sniffed. "He was Gator to his friends."

"And you were his friend?" The detective glared at me, waiting for a response.

"Is that an official question?"

Gutierrez pulled out her notebook. "Yes." Edith groaned and rubbed her hands over her face.

"I ran into Gator a few days ago while I was—" Did I want to tell her what I was up to? I thought not. Instead, I flipped the conversation, pretending to be angry about my alleged ignorance of Bowers' status. "You wouldn't tell me *anything* about Bowers. Not what happened to him. How he was doing. You still aren't saying anything. As his fiancée, I have a right to know." As an afterthought, I added, "And his sisters do, too."

Gutierrez wasn't impressed. "You interfered with a police investigation."

"What investigation? You said he fell."

That got her. "Yes. And since Martin is an officer of the law, we need to investigate any irregularity."

"How is he doing?" I moved forward, daring her to let it out that he was conscious. "If you want me to share what I know, you need to give a little."

She sighed and closed her notebook. "He's doing as well as can be expected."

"Is he hooked up to machines?"

"For now."

Liar. "A ventilator?"

"Yes."

Drooping my face in a hang-dog expression, I pressed her further into her false statement. "IV drips?"

"Yes."

I gasped and winced. "A catheter?"

"There are lots of wires and tubes coming out of him, okay? Don't make me describe it."

Gutierrez glanced down at the fish tacos. Then she looked up at the smiling sailor inviting one and all to eat at Nemo's. "What were you doing here?"

"Eating. The fish tacos are fabulous. Best in the valley. Right, Edith?"

My sidekick remained silent. She wasn't talkative in the best of circumstances, but her added glower in my direction surprised me.

"And that's why you drove all the way from Wolf Creek. For takeout. It had nothing to do with Lola Falana waitressing at Nemo's."

"Our waitresses' name was Lola." I gaped. "You mean

that was the same Lola Luther Mendoza abandoned? What a coincidence."

"Isn't it?" Gutierrez waved over a patrol officer and told the woman to give us a ride home. As Edith straightened up from leaning against the detective's car, Gutierrez blocked her path. "I've been lenient because of your personal relationship with Detective Bowers. I'm drawing the line here. Don't cross it."

A shriek made all three of us turn toward the car. The noise came from a tiny woman in her eighties wearing a dark blue polyester pants suit with a yellow scarf around her throat. Her wedge heels put her at five feet tall. She waved her hands over her head. Her long, pink fingernails fell under the registered weapons category.

"Don't touch him!"

Gutierrez took one look at the Catholic priest hovering behind her and sighed. Stepping forward, she identified herself, and the woman broke into Spanish. I only understood the interspersed English words, like *heathens* and *hell*.

To my surprise, the detective leaned in and talked to the guy from the coroner's office, who was himself Hispanic. He glanced over the body, nodded, and moved aside for the priest after first warning him not to touch the body.

The priest hung a purple stole around his neck and recited some prayers from a book, ending with the sign of the cross over Gator. It did the trick, and the old woman's breathing returned to normal.

Once the cleric finished, he led the sobbing woman away.

Gutierrez hadn't forgotten about us. Her eyes were moist, and the show of emotion made her cranky. "So, do we understand each other? Go home and behave yourselves."

Edith glared not at her, but at me. "You know, if you

won't tell me what happened at the fairgrounds, maybe you'll tell the nice detective."

"Tell her what?" I tried for innocence, but the way I choked on the words ruined the effect.

"There's only one person I care about, and that's Marty. Something happened at MALG. If you don't trust me, fine. Tell her." She jerked her thumb at Gutierrez.

Without a mirror, I couldn't be sure I'd pulled it off, but the death stare I sent Edith was an imitation of the one I'd seen Windy give Dymphna after her *mommy* pried a chicken bone out of the dog's mouth.

Team Bowers had suffered a split, with Edith sacrificing me to the Wolf Creek Police.

The detective eyed me, wary. "Well?"

"Well nothing. I fell. Clumsy me."

Edith felt the need to clarify. "And screamed. That was after you shouted *Look out for the gun*."

"Gun?" Gutierrez took a threatening step forward. "If you know something..."

I definitely didn't *know* anything. Not for sure. The goat may have misinterpreted what happened, though since the results of at least some of his visions wound up in my car, it seemed unlikely. Backed into the proverbial corner, I responded with an attack.

"You wouldn't be interested."

"I'm all ears, but it would be better to take this information at the station."

THIRTY-NINE

I'm not often furious. It takes too much energy. However, Edith's betrayal stung. So, I punished her by avoiding eye contact as we sat in the chairs facing Gutierrez's desk. Also, I hoped her head would explode.

When I finished giving the detective a description of my time with Gator, emphasizing the time spent discussing vampires, she turned the topic to my embarrassing performance at the fairgrounds. I had a dilemma.

If I wanted the murdered men's killer captured and brought to justice—and I did—then Gutierrez needed the details of my "talk" with Pierre. Telling Gutierrez all I knew might get me mocked, but it wasn't like we saw each other at parties. However, I was not prepared to ride the ridicule train with Bowers' family.

"Can we speak privately?"

Edith sat up straight. "There is *no* possibility I'm leaving this room."

Gutierrez' evil smile waned, probably as she considered the fallout of wrestling with her hospitalized colleague's sibling. Not much sympathy in that scenario.

"Your sister-in-law mentioned a gun."

My glare marked the first time I'd looked at Edith since entering her betrayal. "If she says so. I don't remember saying anything."

And there we were. I would not bring up my visions in front of Edith. Gutierrez sure the heck would not ask. Shortest interrogation ever.

The detective took a roundabout approach. "If there is anything either of you knows about these murders, you need to tell me."

What did I know that Gutierrez didn't? We both knew there were dead bodies, though that first guy might not be on her list. She didn't know about MALG. Or the cowboys. Or that someone pushed Bowers. Seems I had the upper hand.

"You both have been poking around. Is that why someone keeps leaving bodies in your car, Ms. Chandler?"

Edith's hand shot out and clamped onto my arm before I could answer. "If we knew who was leaving those bodies, we might answer your question. Do you have any suggestions?"

It took all my strength, but I regained possession of my limb. If Scary Sister thought she could use me to extract information from Gutierrez, she had another thing coming.

"I'm not here to answer questions, Ms. Bowers. You are. Both of you." Then Gutierrez showed me she was made of sterner stuff than I'd imagined.

"Just give it to me straight. What did you see?"

The detective's direct approach surprised me. I expected a game that involved telling my story without touching on visions or psychic abilities. It would have been refreshing to tell it straight, but with Edith present, I obfuscated.

"Has Bowers ever mentioned—"

"Yes." The detective's gaze flickered over the third party in the room.

"You know about the two dead men I found in my car?"

"Enrique Salazar and George Dakos."

"Look for a third. Please, God, don't let him wind up in my car."

Gutierrez grabbed her notebook and pen. "Who?"

Bowers' diary mentioned four names. Chopper, Mr. G, Luther Mendoza, and Eric White. The picture in Lola Falana's locket didn't resemble my blond guy. I took a shot. "Eric White."

She set down her pen and stared. "Where did you get that name?"

"It's a long story."

Her fingers drummed on the desk. Then she stood. "Wait here." She closed the door behind her.

The trembling had subsided, but my insides twisted in a knot. I shut my eyes and rested my head in my hands.

The detective returned with a photograph and slid it across the desk. "Is this who you saw?"

Edith leaned in to get a closer look.

His hair was neatly combed back from his face, and he smiled at someone off-camera, showing a gap between his top front teeth that made him look boyish and friendly if you discounted the predatory gleam in his light-brown eyes. He wore a baggy, mustard-yellow sweatshirt, which was a poor fashion choice. It made his skin tone pasty.

A flash of the arm sticking out of the wheelbarrow passed before me. "Do you know if he has a panther tattoo?" I rubbed my bicep. "It looks like it's crawling up his arm."

She answered with a grim expression.

"That's him." Seeing his face made his death more real. My stomach gurgled a warning.

"You're sure?"

"Positive."

Gutierrez snatched back the photo.

"Just to be clear," the betrayer said, "you're accepting Frankie's word about something she says was witnessed by a goat." Edith persisted, ignoring Gutierrez's growing scowl. "What if she just said that was the guy to make you happy? Or to make you believe?" She looked at me. "Funny that this dead guy hasn't shown up in your car yet. Or is that still to come? If you weren't about to become a relative of mine, I'd think *you* were the killer."

Both fixed their gazes on me. I'd seen what I'd seen. Tired of feeling like I had horns coming out of my forehead over an ability I hadn't asked for and, most times, didn't want, I bristled.

"Seriously? You think I'm messing with you? And give me a reason to give a goat's butt if you believe me."

Scooting my chair to face my future sister-in-law, I grasped at my ever-evasive courage. "You have a lot of nerve, accusing me of lying. I never met you before—" Gutierrez didn't need to know about my foray into Mike's Auto Body. "You only met me a few days ago, yet you assume you know all about me. I certainly don't know you very well, and that was my mistake. I thought you had my back."

She growled a warning. "The only thing that matters is finding out what happened to Marty. Your feelings don't count."

"Ah, Marty. You think your brother is dumb enough to hook up with a scam artist. That I fooled him into believing I'm whatever you believe I am."

As I criticized Bowers, her face turned crimson, and she got a dangerous look in her eyes. I backed off with a weak, "So there."

When she lunged forward, I yelled. Instead of killing me, she gripped me in a tight hug. Just as quickly, she grabbed my shoulders and pushed me away.

"You're right. If you're good enough for Marty, you're good enough for me. Even if you are a charlatan and a fraud."

It wasn't a great endorsement.

The door opened, and Sergeant Smitty leaned in. "Everything okay?"

Gutierrez joined him and lowered her voice. The only words that jumped out at me were *BOLO* and *Eric White*.

Gutierrez turned back and strolled to her desk, pulled open a drawer, and took something out. She tossed. Edith caught. "I believe that's yours."

Scary Sister smirked at the small device in her hands. "Busted."

"What's that?" The little black rectangle reminded me of a thumb drive.

Edith held it up and admired it. "It's cheap, but it works."

Just then there was a knock on the door. Captain Joe leaned his head in and told Gutierrez to report to his office. We knew better than to delay the detective's exit, so we slipped out the door before her and headed outside.

"*Quid pro quo*. I just unraveled another clue for you. What did Gutierrez give you?"

She tossed her toy in the air and caught it. "Tracking device."

"You put a tracking device on a detective's car?" I lost a little respect for her internet searching capabilities. She hadn't chased down Luther's uncle or Lola Falana. She'd kept track of where Gutierrez was going and looked up the addresses online to find out who lived there. "Why aren't you in jail?"

"Because, deep down, the nice detective wants our help."

FORTY

That night, as I brushed my teeth, I made a decision. A monumental decision, considering my lack of confidence.

I had a talent. An ability. I could read the thoughts of animals. Sometimes. When they let me. I'd honed my control with practice, but there were still surprises. Not always the good kind. Still, my success rate had risen.

As I stared into the hazel eyes in the mirror, they sent back a question. Was I ready to stop hiding behind my animal behavior business and declare myself a pet psychic? To own it without apology. It might mean losing the respect of Bowers' sisters, but if they couldn't accept the entire Frankie Chandler package, what was their approval worth?

To be fair, I'd give them time to accept the notion without shoving it down their throats. But I was through apologizing and finished deferring. After an unsteady nod at my reflection, I spit out my toothpaste and hurried to let Dymphna and Windy take their turn in the bathroom.

Once everyone was asleep, I snuggled down under my flimsy sheet with the diary and a flashlight. By laying on my side with the book open to the important page and the beam pointed over Bowers' writing, I could study the clues to my heart's content without shifting position.

It seemed silly to go through all this effort to hide Bowers' diary, knowing that Edith had already seen it, but I felt violated. And I wanted to punish her by not sharing. Let her steal it again if she wanted another peek.

As I gazed at the list of names, searching for a connection, a soft footstep landed on the carpet near my head.

"Reading the diary?"

Flipping off my flashlight, I pulled the covers from my face and looked up at Edith's chin as she stood over me. "What do you want?"

She made a gimme motion with her fingers. "Let's move to the kitchen table."

Since there was no point in feigning embarrassment, I followed her out of the living room. This wasn't my party, so I didn't play hostess and offer tea or cookies. Instead, I slumped at the table, clutching the book.

"Just so you know, I'm still mad at you."

She grinned. "Eventually, you can tell me how you knew about Eric White. Are you investigating on the side? No. I haven't let you out of my sight. Maybe before I got here. That's it. I'll give you credit. You got onto it fast." She nodded at the diary. "You hang onto it. I memorized the pages. If Enrique, Eric, George, and Luther were in on the burglary at Rings and Things, we need to figure out the connection between the men and what role they each played."

Before I had a chance to agree—or disagree—she moved on. "Assuming you're right, Enrique, who worked in tech, knew Eric White. Do we know what Eric did for a living?"

"If Gator did side jobs with him, I assume he also worked with computers." I insisted on calling Enrique by his preferred name to honor his memory. "And why wouldn't I be right?"

Her eyebrows raised. "He might have lied to you. Since we have no way of checking right now, let's move on. George drove a taxi. Luther worked at the jewelry store. Obviously, he tipped the rest of them off. Told them something tasty had come into the store."

"I disagree." Though I didn't have an ounce of proof, I didn't want to believe that Luther's idea of supporting his family came through criminal activities. Call me sentimental. "I'm more concerned with the fact that Gator, Mister G, and Eric White are all dead."

"We don't have proof that Eric White is dead," she said, dismissing my vision. "He's just missing. Like Luther." She pursed her lips. "Has Lola's honey been naughty?"

At first, I stifled my laugh, but since it was at her expense, I let it out. "You're suggesting he killed off his cohorts? Isn't that short-sighted? How would he be able to pull off other jobs if his teammates were dead?" Folding my arms on the table, I narrowed my eyes, hoping to appear insightful. "I'm trying to imagine all four men crowded into the store and robbing it in broad daylight. Maybe Mister G was an innocent bystander who had come in to purchase a delightful gift for his wife. He was a witness."

"That's not how it happened."

I propped my chin on my fist. "You were there? Tell me. I'm all ears."

"The articles referred to it as a *burglary*. Not a robbery. They broke in at night and stole at leisure."

"At leisure. *Leisure.* Hmm. What if one of them suddenly remembered he'd left the stove on at home? He would have hurried. Or were there signs they used the company coffee pot? Of course, they would have brought their own snacks."

"It's a figure of speech."

I sat up straight. "If it happened at night, Luther might not have been there. Unless he helped them get inside. Did he have a key?"

"The security system was disabled, and the lock melted."

"Melted!"

Dread chased my sarcasm away. A disabled security system needed a disabler, and who better than the employee with the code?

"But what about Mike's Auto Body? Why would Bowers mention the place? Luther only hung out there with his friend, Randy. Since your memory is apparently photographic, you'll note that Randy's name wasn't on Bowers' list."

"Maybe he didn't single him out because everyone at Mike's Auto Body was involved."

"Okay. But you still haven't explained Mister G's connection."

"Getaway driver."

Unfortunately, that made sense. "But if he was involved in the robbery—excuse me—burglary, why would he visit Bowers at the hospital? His body language screamed his concern."

With my eyes closed, I recalled that day in Mike's Auto Body. Randy, as well as the rest of the men, were interested in Luther's whereabouts. Very interested. I'd assumed they had nefarious reasons for wanting to track the future father down, but Randy was Luther's friend. And then it hit me.

"Another thing. Mike and his employees were nervous, bordering on...scared?"

"Maybe they were scared Luther would give them up."

I conceded. "Let's say you're right. They were all involved. Luther told them about the jewelry. Mister G waited in the car. What did Eric and Gator do?"

"I know nothing about Eric White, but Enrique disabled the system."

"I thought Luther let them in."

"A ham radio can interfere with an alarm system. If Enrique was into tech, he'd figure it out. And he just happens to own a ham radio. Then they melted the lock, probably with the same blowtorch they used on the safe."

"I thought burglars blew up safes."

"Not according to the newspaper. They might have used a portable plasma cutter."

Sounded far out there to me. "Let's say that's even possible."

"It is."

"Then what? They'd need to give the jewelry to someone. A fence, right? That's what it's called?"

"If they were smart, they'd keep the stolen items off the market for a while. I'd like to know what triggered Marty to look into the case again. Right now, the only people with that information are the police."

That made me laugh. "I can't see Gutierrez opening up to us just because we ask nicely."

"We'll have to find another source."

I knew another source, but I'd rather feed my eyeballs to Emily than talk to Paul Simpson, unethical reporter.

FORTY-ONE

Dymphna insisted we attend the earliest Sunday Mass on the schedule. It was a punishment. Last night, she'd turned snippy when Edith and I, by tacit agreement, chose not to give her the details of our day, especially the part about the dead body. She, in turn, described her time spent studying the walls of the hospital lobby and demanded a break. We promised to cover for her this afternoon.

Since the police had impounded the Metro, we had no choice but to go to church with her if we wanted a ride to Cavalcade Rental Cars. Besides. With all my recent prayer requests, one of which had been answered by my vision of Bowers awake in his hospital bed, it seemed bad form not to go to church and give thanks.

Since weather forecasters expected temperatures to reach the mid-nineties, I wore tan linen slacks, a short-sleeved yellow blouse, and leather sandals.

And then I discovered Edith owned clothes other than her t-shirt and exercise pants. When she strolled out of the bathroom dressed in black slacks, a black short-sleeved turtleneck, and black boots, her hair knotted into a bun, I wondered if she had a ski mask tucked in the paper sack she carried to the truck. Helpful in a reconnaissance mission.

The second the priest left the altar, Edith strode out of the building.

"Always in a hurry, that one," Dymphna said before getting in a line that stretched around the patio to greet Father Damien. Edith looked furious by the time we all crammed into the front seat of the Suburban. As least Dymphna left Windy at home.

Cavalcade Rental Cars was closed on Sundays, but Edith tracked Dan Driver down at home and emphasized our dire situation. And she suggested he add a convenience fee to my bill.

Dan wasn't happy to see me, but the rental agent finally agreed I couldn't control strangers depositing bodies in my car and let us have a 2004 Dodge Dakota, also on Jeff's list of vehicles he would never drive. My ex-boyfriend wasn't someone I would rely on for good advice, but as he was an excellent mechanic, I assumed he should know.

When Edith held out her hand for the keys, Dan should have argued that I was the one who paid his exorbitant fee and given me first call. Instead, he took one look at her grim expression and handed them over. She shot out of the parking lot and drove us back to Cave Creek at high speed.

Frankly, I was tired of seeing dead bodies—both in visions and in person—and I'd forgotten to bring a treat for Pierre. And I couldn't stop thinking about Bowers. Maybe, if we swung by the hospital, I'd sneak up the service elevator and track him down.

"Del Bennett wasn't happy to see me at the fair. I don't expect he'll be too chatty. He may even call the police." I slipped her a nasty look. "Or do you plan on cuffing him?

Maybe follow up with a few toothpicks under his fingernails?"

"Relax, French Fry. We won't bother Del. He'll be at the fair. Remember?"

I smacked my forehead. "It's Sunday. I've lost track of the days."

"We just went to Mass. That should have tipped you off."

"Haven't you heard of weekday Masses?" I snapped, embarrassed that the entire service was a blur. I might have nodded off. "Anyway, why do you want to go if Del's not there?"

She sped past the cornfield, his house, the treacherous hill, the burnt construction site, and made a sharp left at the end of the road.

"Hey!" I wasn't up to losing three cars in one week. Though she avoided the shrubs, most of them, she hit a few solid mounds of desert needle grass that thumped the bumper and scraped against the undercarriage. She finally brought the SUV to a stop in a spot that put the hill between us and the farm.

"What are we doing here?" I grumbled. "Besides ruining my car."

She got on her knees and reached over the back seat to rummage through her backpack. When she returned to sitting, she had a pair of binoculars that she rested on her lap. "Let's just say we don't know enough about the farmer named Del."

We walked along the base of the hill facing the road. She seemed content to inch forward before dropping into a squat.

"Are we spying on his employees?"

"I prefer the term watching."

"Watch them do what? Feed the goats Del left behind? I know he feeds them because they're still alive. Do you know how many employees he has? Because I don't. They're always working in the barn. Speaking for myself, I can't see through walls."

"Yes, they do spend a lot of time in the barn."

The way she said it, laced with suspicion, made me snort. "Del might have horses, or cows, or something. Well, maybe not. We would have heard them. A workshop then. That's it. If my dad had a barn, he would spend all his time there instead of in the garage."

"Then there's no harm in checking it out."

But she didn't check it out. Not then. A rickety truck, the faded green paint rusted and peeling, rattled up to the entrance of Bennett's Grazers, slowed down, and turned up the drive. I crouched and followed her forward.

Scary Sister dropped to her belly and crawled toward the goat pen. Slithering on my belly fell outside of my skill set, so I dropped to my hands and knees and crawled up next to her. She put a hand on my shoulder and yanked me flat.

By peering between the goat's legs, I caught sight of the truck. The visitors had parked in front of the barn.

Edith had her binoculars pressed to her eyes. "Looky there. He brought the party to his place. Nice."

Three men squeezed out of the truck. They had on blue-jean overalls and straw hats with large drooping brims. Perfect for keeping the sun off their necks. The clothes were right, but something was off. Their skin looked too pasty for people who labored outdoors. When a barn cat rubbed against one man's leg, he jumped, which added to my suspicions.

Del stepped out of the barn.

"Dang it. He *is* here."

Raising myself a few inches from the ground, I searched the pen for the familiar brown handprint marking Pierre's hair. I couldn't see faces, but when a doe moved, I spotted him.

Pierre occupied a corner of the pen, separated from the other goats by temporary fencing. Was the goat being punished because of my interest in him? Not fair!

"Well, well, well," Edith murmured.

The farmer approached the three men with his hands stuffed into his pockets. He stopped about ten feet from them and nodded. The guy on the left said something and gestured, and Del pulled his hands out and held them up, palms open, before shaking the hand of the middle guy.

"What's he doing here?" I hissed. "I thought you said he'd be at MALG."

"He's not. Deal with it."

"What do we do now? He's not going to invite us in for a tour."

"We wait."

When the four of them entered the barn, Edith lowered her binoculars and motioned me to follow her at a crouching run back to the truck. Once there, Edith connected her binoculars to her phone. In a few seconds, she had closeup photos of the men from the truck and Del as they greeted each other.

"What are those for?"

"My album."

Smart aleck. Resting my head against the headrest, I flipped the visor to keep the blazing sun off my face and considered the best approach to get back to Pierre. Now that I was here, and he was here, I'd see if he'd give me a freebie.

Pierre. The stubborn goat who held the answers to Bowers' presence on this rocky mound of dirt. Monsieur Pierre and his pastries. What was his favorite? He'd thrown me everything from cheesecake to eclairs, but maybe there was a flaky crust or fruity filling that would entice him to answer my questions.

I jerked at the rattle of a motor on the move. Del Bennett's visitors pulled out of the driveway and turned right. A few minutes later, the farmer followed in a much nicer Dodge RAM. A dark blue one. He had Jacob with him.

Edith was already out of the car. "I want to see what's in that barn."

When we got to the gravel driveway, Pierre bleated from his small enclosure. Pleased that the goat recognized my scent, my steps slowed.

"You go ahead. I've seen the inside of plenty of barns. No thrill there."

She gave me an inscrutable look. We split up, with Edith cautiously approaching her target. Every few steps, she'd stop and listen, her head swiveling to take in any changes in her surroundings.

Too much work for me. I trudged to the makeshift pen and hung over the top rail, wiggling my fingers toward Pierre. He captured my pointer finger and gnawed until I pried it out of his mouth.

I studied my objective. No candies. No cookie. Not even a breath mint. I hoped the goat would be amenable to a promise. He wasn't. As soon as he realized food would not be forthcoming, he turned away and—

"Holy cow!"

Pierre had twisted himself into a pretzel position and—

and—he tinkled. Because of his current arrangement, urine streamed all over his face.

"Stop it!" I shrieked this several times until he stood there, dripping wet, and looking very pleased with himself. A couple of does moved in on the other side of his prison. Apparently, goat standards in the cologne department scrape the bottom.

"Aw, jeepers. Oh, man." I fled from the scene and caught up with Edith in the barn, shaking my entire body to rid myself of the images of Peeing Pierre. "Brrr."

Edith told me to close the door behind me, as that was how she'd found it. Doing so left only a few cracks of light coming from between boards in the old roof and walls, just enough to give me a shadowy idea of the contents.

The temperature in here was slightly cooler, and the air had a musty smell mixed with oil and something unpleasant.

Movement came from ten feet to my left. Edith flicked on her flashlight and let the strong, narrow beam travel over the tools leaning against the wall along with a pile of burlap sacks, bales of hay for the goats, and bags of feed. Several stalls stood empty.

A piece of machinery stood in the center of the room. It resembled a miniature plow.

And then I saw it, tucked into the corner.

"What?" She sensed my tension because she kept her voice to a whisper.

Instead of answering, I pointed at the red wheelbarrow.

She let out her breath. "So? It's a barn. On a farm. We have one just like it at June's."

"But it's red."

"Find me one that isn't." She walked to it, flashing her light over the inside and out. "It's just a wheelbarrow."

Coincidence? Possibly.

"Let's go."

As the beam of light passed over the ground, I cried out. "Go back. To the left."

While she followed instructions, I crept forward until I found the bloody rag. I shook my finger at it. "You were looking for proof of nefarious goings-on. There it is."

She wasn't impressed. "Please. This is a farm. People get hurt every day. June keeps a year's supply of bandages on hand for Carl."

Edith led the way outside, and since she had the light, I followed. As she walked, she kicked at the rocks on the driveway. I didn't have to be a parent to recognize a sulk. She hadn't discovered a Tommy gun or wanted posters in the barn. I thought it might cheer her up to hear about my horrors. When I finished my tale, she stopped walking, threw back her head, and laughed so hard she doubled over.

"It wasn't funny. It was gross. Why would Pierre do that?"

She patted my shoulder. "It's fall, French Fry. Mating season. Pierre was sprucing himself up for the ladies."

"They *like* that? Oh, that is so disgusting. I'm going to be sick."

"Nature isn't all butterflies and bluebells. It's cruel. Sometimes gross."

Just as we got to my car, Edith yelled, "Duck!"

Del was back, and he had company. The van that followed him up the drive had white paint with a pattern of red, white, and green on the side. Black cursive lettering read *Venito's Meats*. Underneath, in smaller letters, it said *Keeping Traditions Alive since 1960*.

"Traditional meat?"

Edith squinted. "Your friend might be in trouble."

FORTY-TWO

The van backed up to the goat pen. Jacob led Pierre, a small female, and her kid to the open doors and loaded them on.

"They're going to eat him?" I squeaked.

"It happens."

I grabbed Edith's turtleneck collar in my hands. "If that goat goes, so does our chance of finding out what happened to your brother."

She believed me. At least she believed in my panic. This time, there was no argument over who would drive. Without waiting for the truck to leave, she tore off, headed for Cave Creek Road.

She thrust her phone into my hands. "Call them and find out where they're located." Flexing her photographic memory, she gave me the number.

My fingers shook, but I got through on my second try. A woman with a thick Italian accent answered.

"Hello. May I have your address please?"

My voice, high and hysterical in pitch and tone, might have put her off answering my question.

"Why? You no need. We deliver to you."

"I'm in the area and want to pick it up."

"Your name?"

I hung up. "She wanted my name."

"Dial this number and put the speaker on."

I pushed the buttons as she called them out.

"What."

I recognized that whispery tone.

"Dym. Edith. Get the monster and meet me in Cave Creek."

"I'm on my lunch break and am clipping Windy's nails. I can't leave her half clipped."

"It's life or death."

Silence. Then rustling, the slam of a door, and the rumble of an engine starting. "Where's Cave Creek?"

Edith gave a description of our current location. "How soon can you get here?"

"Twenty minutes."

"Only if you fly," I said.

"Who's that? Frankie?" Dymphna snickered. "You haven't seen me drive." The call disconnected.

"Why did you give her our current location?"

"As soon as Dym gets here, grab the goat."

"Seriously? Excuse me, can I open your van and empty the contents?"

We'd reached a stretch without houses. Without warning, Edith slammed the brakes and jerked the steering wheel to the left. As the rear of the car skidded right, she took her foot off the brake and turned into it. My body strained against the safety belt, then flattened against my seat until the SUV came to rest across the road, blocking passage for anyone behind us.

I let out my breath. "What the—

She popped the trunk and shot out of the car. I followed. Dan Driver had left us with extra coolant and oil.

"That was nice of him."

Scary Sister snorted. "I brought them along. You should—"

"Always be prepared. I get it." Looking back in the direction we'd come from, I whistled. "That's a beautiful set of skid marks."

"Get back in the car."

"It's safer out here."

She took a step forward.

"I'm going to wait in the car." And I stayed there, even as I watched her empty half the coolant under the engine. She returned it to the trunk and slammed it shut just as the meat truck came into view.

The driver pulled up behind us and leaned his head out the window. "What's the problem?"

Edith gave a frantic cry. "Something's wrong with my car. The thermometer thingy suddenly shot into the red."

He got out of his truck and approached the front of the car. When he glanced down, he took a step back. "You've got a leak. A big one. It might be a cracked hose, but that's a lot of coolant."

She wrinkled her face, preparing to cry. "Would you check on my friend? I think she's injured."

Taking my cue, I slumped against the passenger door. The driver, a middle-aged man in jeans and a blue button-down shirt, leaned his head in my window. "She looks okay to me. I'm not a doctor."

"I'll call an ambulance. You talk to my friend. Keep her awake."

"Lady, I got a delivery to make."

Peering through my lashes, I watched as Edith pulled

herself up to her full five feet ten inches and lowered her voice, transforming into Scary Sister. "You're not leaving. You're a witness. Now tend to my friend."

He didn't question what exactly he witnessed or why it bore repeating to the authorities but did as she ordered. A typical male reaction to female barking, I've noticed. Anything to avoid the bark.

It was difficult to remain passive while he tapped my face and poked my side, so I mustered up a moan and slapped his hand. I'm certain Edith's frantic call for an ambulance was a one-way conversation. When she hung up, she reached next to the driver's seat and popped the hood.

The guy backed out of the car. "What are you doing?"

"Checking the engine." She lifted the hood and leaned inside. "Do you know anything about cars? Why don't I take off the radiator cap?"

"Don't touch it!" He glanced back at his van. "Just wait for it to cool off. You got any extra coolant? Never mind. With a leak, it won't help. You better call for a tow truck."

In the distance, an orange shape moved toward us at speed. I slipped out of the car.

"Your friend is up and moving. Looks like you don't need that ambulance after all."

I could make out June's truck, but Dymphna was still a few minutes away. We needed a diversion. By leaning against the car with my hands on the roof, it appeared I was supporting myself while I overcame a dizzy spell.

"She's going to tumble," Edith warned.

Like a gentleman, he rounded the car and helped me into a sitting position. Warily, he eyed me and said, "You okay?"

Dymphna slowed the truck and leaned out the window. Windy rode shotgun. "What's the trouble?"

He eagerly jogged to her. "Can you stay with these women until help comes? I have to get going."

"Just let me navigate around you." She looked my way. "The one on the ground doesn't look so good."

He came and stood by me with his hands on his hips, his frown leaning more toward annoyed than concerned. Just as I was wondering how to get him to leave my side, Edith let out a bloodcurdling cry. That got him moving.

"I told you not to touch it." When he got to the open hood, the exposed engine emitted a tractor beam that latched onto his Y chromosome, specifically the gene that controls a man's inability to resist tinkering with anything broken. He rested one arm on the car and leaned in for a better look.

I crouch-walked to the back of the van. Dymphna had the Suburban flush with the open back doors. Pierre tossed me a sulky glance. The driver had tied all three goats to rings on the wall. Fortunately, Venito's Meats hadn't anticipated an escape attempt, so I climbed in and undid the knots with minimal fumbling.

Ducking my head, I led the little goat into the back of the Suburban. Dymphna had lowered the seats to make room. His mother followed. To my surprise, Pierre came, too, sticking close to the others in a stiff, protective trot. I closed the back doors with minimal noise and hissed, "Go."

"Where to?"

We didn't have time for a considered answer. "My place. Put them on the patio."

Driving with one hand—she held the leads in the other —she maneuvered the vehicle back onto the road in the direction from which she came, while I scurried back to

Edith, slowing my steps as I approached the hood on the shoulder side.

"I feel dizzy again." I swooned, and the driver caught me before I fell. He was too busy fumbling with my dead weight to notice Dymphna's cargo as she drove past. Once he lowered me to the ground, Edith searched through the SUV and found a water bottle, which she sloshed on my face until she'd squeezed out every drop.

"Thanks," I said through gritted teeth, sliding a glance at the road. Dymphna's truck blended into the horizon, with no possibility of identifying her passengers. Once the driver helped me to my feet, his eyes fixed on my soggy shirt, I said, "I'm feeling better. Thanks for your help."

He glanced down the road. "That ambulance is taking a long time."

"Yeah," Edith said with regret. "I'll just drive her to the hospital."

In record time, the driver climbed into his van. "Good idea," he called from the cab, his subconscious missing the point that our vehicle was disabled. Or he didn't care.

"Will he notice his van is lighter?"

"Don't care," Edith said, slamming the hood. "We need to get moving."

The Dakota started, and she headed back to Wolf Creek.

FORTY-THREE

When Edith rolled onto the 101 Loop, I thought nothing of it. Not until she passed the Shea Boulevard exit.

"That's okay," I said, peering over my shoulder at the missed ramp. "We can take Frank Lloyd Wright."

"We're not going back to your place."

"There are goats waiting there that need my attention."

"Dymphna knows what to do with them."

My pride kept me from asking our destination, but once we got to the neighborhood of dingy apartment buildings, I knew. As Edith turned onto Alpaca Street, cars were parked up and down the block, indicating a neighborhood party. We finally found a spot when a brown station wagon pulled away from the curb.

Before she exited the Dakota, Edith reached into the back seat and grabbed the paper sack she'd brought with this morning.

"What's that for? BYOB?"

"Enrique's family."

"His family?" I frowned. "How do you know they'll be at his apartment?"

She glanced at the surrounding vehicles parked bumper to bumper. "Lucky guess." She dusted the barnyard dirt from her knees and strolled across the street.

As soon as I spotted a group of men in suits crowded on Gator's patio, smoking cigarettes and drinking from bottles of beer, I turned back to the car. Edith grabbed my arm in a vice-like grip and dragged me forward.

The two gentlemen closest to the open patio door stepped aside for us. One waved his curling smoke away.

The little woman who'd brought the priest to bless Gator now stood inside the entrance surrounded by women her age. She—and they—were dressed in black dresses and shawls.

Scary Sister hailed her in Spanish, and the woman nodded and responded in kind.

"This is Enrique's grandmother."

I took her small hand and shook, receiving a disapproving frown before she enveloped me in a hug. Edith got the same treatment.

Everyone was dressed in suits and dresses, mostly black. With thirty pairs of eyes staring at us, I was glad I hadn't changed into jeans after Mass, though my color scheme of beige and yellow made me stand out.

The couch where Gator had sat reviving his vampire character now held three people once the grandma shuffled over and took her seat. An elderly man in a dark gray suit slumped a little, his shoulders bowed in grief. Next to him sat a gorgeous young woman, maybe twenty, with lush dark brown hair and dark eyes. She had a camisole on under her buttoned jacket to block the view of her cleavage. The fourth spot seemed to be reserved, since there were plenty of people standing who might have snagged it.

Occupied kitchen chairs and several folding chairs lined the room. Two tables held places of honor in front of a gas fireplace. On the first, the family had set up a display in memory of their loved one. Several pictures of Gator were surrounded by knick-knacks that must have been important to the young man in life. The tassel from his cap hung over the corner of his high school graduation photo. A dinged-up metal toy car sat in front of a childhood picture of him and the young woman on the couch posed for a Christmas photo. A quick sob escaped when I spotted his game controller.

Also on the table were several statues of saints. I recognized St. Jude, the patron saint of lost causes. My mother had a similar statue at home and asked regularly for the saint's intercession on my behalf.

The second statue looked like a little girl seated on a wooden chair. She held a basket of flowers in one hand and a staff in the other.

"Is that Little Bo Peep?" I whispered.

Edith punched my arm. "*Santo Nino de Atocha.* The Holy Infant of Atocha."

Rubbing my arm, I took a closer look. If she said so.

While the photos on the first table were fun, candid shots of Gator, the second table was serious business. The framed photo had all the earmarks of a high school yearbook photo. The young man was posed in front of a dark gray background, and the photographer had captured him from the shoulders up in a blue dress shirt and tie. His smile held the awkward joy of a teen closing in on adulthood but not yet confronted by bills and office politics.

On either side of the picture frame stood a crucifix and a statue of Our Lady of Guadalupe, both accompanied by burning candles. Behind it all, white, yellow, and purple flowers burst from a glass vase, forming a canopy over the photograph.

Edith approached the elderly man seated between the grandmother and the young woman.

"*Señor, mi nombre es Edith.*" She gestured to me. "*Esta es Frances. ¿Dónde está la madre de Enrique, por favor?*"

"My mother is in the kitchen." The girl studied us, curious.

Edith smiled kindly. I didn't recognize her. She reached into the bag and drew out a set of white candles in glass with an image of Jesus on one side and the Lord's Prayer on the back in both Spanish and English. "Then she's busy. I don't want to bother her. We were only acquaintances of your brother." She set the candles on the coffee table to the approval of grandma and grandpa. "These are for her." She pulled a thick greeting card out of the bag. "As is this."

The girl took the envelope with thanks and handed it to her grandfather, explaining in Spanish. He glanced inside at a nice-sized packet of bills and bowed his head.

Edith returned the girl's unblinking stare. "May we speak with you outside?"

A short woman with dark hair in a black skirt and vibrant orange jacket came out of the kitchen. She spotted us and waved us over to join her next to a dining table covered with buffet items.

"Come. Have something to eat." She swept a hand over the table. "We have beans and rice, tamales, taquitos, *arroz con pollo*. For your sweet tooth, there's tres leches cake and pan dulce." She flicked her fingers over the last items on the table, dismissing them. "And mac-n-cheese and store-bought cookies, if you like that sort of thing."

Her disappointed gaze identified the culprits who brought the last two dishes. A couple of young men and women Gator's age formed a circle in one corner, their eyes glued to their cell phones.

"We only stopped by to give our condolences," I began, but Edith elbowed me in the ribs and my words ended on a grunt.

"Thank you," Scary Sister said, accepting a plate.

"Um, thanks," I added.

My fears that I had nothing to say to Gator's family were put to rest by his mother. She talked nonstop about her son while I listened as respectfully as possible while stuffing a taquito filled with tender chicken and diced peppers into my mouth.

One of the older ladies, a buxom woman with thick arms, called out in Spanish. All chit-chat ceased. In the silence, I set down my plate and told Edith we should leave. To my surprise, she dropped to her knees and pulled me with her.

"Nobody leaves during the novena."

"Novena?" Every hand in the place clutched a rosary.

"I don't suppose you—" Edith huffed. "Here. Take mine."

She handed me an emerald-green rosary with an image of St. Michael the Archangel on the connector and rolled the black beaded bracelet from her wrist. It was a rosary decade bracelet.

"You carry two rosaries with you?"

"I always come prepared."

After the Rosary, which I mumbled in English, came a litany. I followed Edith for the responses since I knew neither Spanish nor the litany involved.

Once the prayers ended, a loud wail pierced the air as one of the women by the sliding glass door held a lace handkerchief to her face and rocked. Her friends comforted her with pats and kisses.

A woman of comfortable size with a white pageboy spoke from the closest chair. "Don't worry about Catalina. It's just her way. Not that she doesn't have reason to be upset. Enrique was her nephew." She held out her hand. "I'm Jan. A neighbor. Are you Isabel's friends?"

"Would that be Enrique's mother?" Edith asked.

The woman's smile faltered. "I'm sorry. No offense, but you look too old to be her son's friends. How did you know Enrique?"

"We're gamers."

She raised her finely plucked eyebrows, and I squirmed. "Um, I—we got into it late."

"Through your children?"

"No kids yet, I'm afraid."

Gator's sister extracted us before I confessed to crashing the party. She led us to the now empty patio, where she folded her arms over her chest and lifted her chin. Her posture showed defiance, but her hands, clenching her forearms, trembled. "Who are you and what do you want? I knew my brother's friends, and you weren't among them."

"You must be Marta," I said. "I only met your brother once, but he seemed nice. This is Edith, and I'm Frankie."

When she heard my name, a laugh escaped. All anger drained out of her. "You helped him with *Elder Scrolls*. His vampire problem." Her lips trembled. "You helped make his last days happy. Thank you."

"Sure." I gave her a minute to remember his final happy days before asking a question. "It's not surprising he liked video games. Your brother mentioned he worked in tech."

"He worked at Computer Emporium, fixing computers. He would have made more money as a programmer, but he found repairs more challenging." She glanced over her shoulder. "He bought his ham radio used. It didn't work. He was so proud the first time a voice came over the speaker. You'd have thought he invented it, not repaired it."

"Is that where he met Eric White? At work?"

Her smile drooped. "Eric... Oh, right. Eric was a friend of Randy's."

"Randy at Mike's Auto Body?"

She nodded. "Enrique and Randy hung out together at college. Enrique was getting his bachelor's in computer science. Eric and Randy were in the trade school."

"Does Eric work at Mike's?"

"No. At least, I'm not sure. He's a welder."

Edith smirked at me as the final piece fell into the burglary puzzle.

"I guess they use welders at an auto body shop," Marta continued, "but I thought he worked in construction. I don't really know. Are you a welder, too?"

"Definitely not. I'd be too scared of setting something on fire. Especially me."

She nodded but didn't laugh. Neither did I because I was focused on the disconnect. A woman madly in love with a guy usually knows what he does for a living.

"It must have been difficult when Eric went away."

Her face was a blank. "Why?"

"Because you were in love with him."

She gasped. "Who told you that?"

"Your brother. He said he was glad Eric had disappeared because he wasn't good for you."

She waved off my suggestion. "Enrique was my older brother. Protective. I was only alone in the room with Eric once. We were talking. I was being polite. My brother might have misunderstood the situation and put his own interpretation on it." She rolled her eyes. "We weren't holding hands or snuggling. Not even whispering sweet words." Shaking her head in wonder, she laughed until reality slapped her. I saw the notion that she'd never roll her eyes at her big brother again cross her features. She took a small gasp of air, covered her face with her hands, and let the sobs come.

With six sisters and a baby brother, I would have thought Edith Bowers would excel at handling emotions, but she abruptly said, "Thank you for your time," and walked away.

I, the one who didn't care for people, also didn't like to see anything living suffer. Patting her back, I told her that Edith and I were going to find the people who'd hurt Gator and make them pay. As the words came out, Gator's mother approached the door.

Instead of being grateful, Marta said, "No. Revenge is wrong."

Her mother had different views. "Good. You let me know when you find them. I want to watch them suffer."

And on that cheery note, I left.

FORTY-FOUR

"You brat!"

I snatched the keys from Edith's hand and stormed to the car. It took until I pulled away from the curb before I calmed down enough to confront the evil one. Once I got started, the words rushed out with plenty of heat.

"You *knew* Gator's family would be gathered here today."

She angled the rear-view mirror to peek at her face. "It was a good guess."

"It was more than a guess. You dressed in black, for the love of Mike. *And* you brought gifts. If I'd known, I could have brought a gift, too, and not looked like a bumbler."

"I said it was from both of us."

"But you kept the important bits to yourself." I threw my hands in the air. The crappy SUV with bad alignment swerved left as soon as I let go, so my dramatic demonstration was short-lived. "I can't believe you dragged me into a house in mourning without warning."

"You have brains. At least I thought you did. You could

have come to the same conclusion I did if you put out the effort. Don't blame me if you're lazy."

"I give up."

Edith was a bonehead. I don't know how Bowers put up with having her as an older sister. Unfortunately, we couldn't choose our families, like the loved ones gathered to remember Gator. Would anyone bother with my funeral? Hopefully, my parents and aunts and uncles would be dead by then. Not that I wanted them dead, but I hoped to live to my nineties. By that time, if the elders were still around, they would be creepy.

My cousins might come, not that we were close. Penny and Kemper would be there, though husbands tended to die before their wives, so maybe just Penny. I gasped. Would I outlive Bowers? Not if I could help it. If I had my druthers, we'd die at the same moment. But not violently. I didn't want flailing arms and screams to be his last image of me... What was the question?

Since we'd promised to take a shift at Holy Cross Hospital to relieve Dymphna, I headed north.

After a few minutes, long enough to allow the air to clear, Edith said, "Do you believe her?"

"Who? Marta?" I gaped. "Crimony. I thought I was the suspicious one. Of *course* Marta's in mourning. Even if Gator was overprotective, even if he pummeled her dolls when she was little and read her diary when she was a teen, he's still her brother."

"I meant about Eric White."

I thought about it. "Her posture was open. She showed genuine distress about her brother but went blank at the mention of Eric's name. Not blank as in she was hiding something. Blank as in she didn't care. I think *she* told the truth, but why would Gator lie about it?"

"Don't be naive. People lie to cover the truth, like his work relationship with Eric." She pursed her lips. "It was smart to keep Eric's death from her."

"I didn't *keep* it from her. I was being tactful."

"Whatever kept your mouth shut, I approve."

"I'm so relieved." In the ensuing silence, unwelcome thoughts battered my skull, trying to take root. One of them made it in. "Is it possible that Marta and her family are in danger?"

"I doubt it. Not unless they took part in the burglary. And now we know Eric's role." When I didn't respond, she said, "A welder? To get through the safe?"

"So, the four of them did the job alone. Three if Luther wasn't involved. I vote for three."

Edith swore. "We should have asked Marta if she knew Luther and George Dakos. That would have given us corroboration from an outside source. Right now, it's all theory."

"She was a little busy crying her eyes out over her dead brother."

Edith shrugged. "It would have been good information to know." She fiddled with the rearview mirror again. "Turn left at the corner."

"But Holy Cross is straight ahead."

"Just do it."

"Left? That's heading downtown." I put on my signal.

"Don't use your signal."

I flicked it off.

"It's too late now. Go straight."

Jerking the wheel, I pulled out of the left turn I'd started. "Make up your mind."

As I approached an alleyway, she grabbed the wheel and tugged hard. "In here."

I smacked at her hand, finally pinching it to make her let go. "Don't—do—that!"

"Why did I let you drive?" she mumbled.

By now I was furious. Swerving to the curb so hard I bumped it, I put the car in park. "Geez Louise, lady. You might have killed us."

And that's when the dark blue Dodge RAM passed us, driven by Jacob, the farmhand.

Edith unbuckled her seatbelt. "Get out, now."

She was already halfway around the hood, and I didn't want to get left behind, so I crawled over the console. Once we switched places, she tore away from the curb, tires squealing.

"He's turning left."

"I see him," she growled, taking the corner in a skid.

"What are you going to do when you catch up with him?"

"This." Edith floored the gas pedal and cut around the truck. As she passed, I returned the terrified gazes of a man and his passenger in the tiny Scion headed directly for us. When the crash seemed inevitable, Edith cut hard to the right and slammed on the brakes. Tires squealed until we stopped at an angle, blocking the truck. I covered my eyes and prepared for impact.

But it never came. The SUV was still rocking from our quick stop when I heard the car door open. Peeking through my fingers, I watched Edith stroll to the Dodge RAM and lean against the window. Jacob wisely stayed in the vehicle.

When he didn't pull a gun on her, I got out and joined them, ignoring the honks from the waiting line of cars.

Jacob looked cool. Amused, even. His lips twitched as he nodded at the vehicle blocking his path. "Since you came from behind, it looks like *you* were following *me*. At least that's how the cops would see it."

With all the witnesses glaring at us, a surge of courage coursed through me. "Have you been leaving bodies in my car?"

He gave my rental a startled glance. "Are you serious?"

I crossed my arms. "As a heart attack."

Edith shook her head at me. "French Fry. What did we decide about sharing information?"

"He's been following me. Whoever has been leaving corpses in my back seat has to know where I'm at, which someone who was following me would know."

"Report me," he said. "I dare you."

Edith studied him for a long minute before abruptly returning to the car. His smirk didn't leave his lips as he watched her, but his eyes told a different story. But was it wariness? Or fear?

About those eyes. As they met mine, their honey-brown color gave me a shock. I scurried back to the car.

"He's got the eyes of the killer. Or, not the killer, but the guy who helped cart the body away."

She started the car and straightened it out. "His eyes are light brown."

I grabbed her wrist. "I'm telling you I recognize those eyes. The disposal guy, the one with the wheelbarrow had eyes just like his."

After considering my shocking revelation, she told me to relax. "I can guarantee that man is not your killer."

FORTY-FIVE

By the time we made it to the hospital, dusk had fallen. A glimpse through the glass doors revealed Doris and Mimi at the welcome desk. As I approached, Mimi's jaw set. She was ready for me, so I hooked a U-turn and headed for the sofa against the wall. I hate being predictable.

Inhaling, I imagined his unique scent. It wasn't something I could describe, but it was *him*. I'd know it anywhere. Musky with a hint of citrus. After growing up on June's farm, it shocked me he didn't smell like chicken. Anyway, I could pick him out of a lineup blindfolded.

Edith sat next to me and slumped back. After five minutes of inactivity, she stood. "I'm going for a walk. Maybe find the doctor. He might have something new to tell us."

Using both hands, I grabbed her wrist and yanked her back down. "He doesn't." It wasn't fair to keep her in the dark, but how much should I share? "I want you to know that your brother will be fine."

"Of course he will," she said, her voice gruff.

"I'm serious. This isn't wishful thinking. Bowers will be fine."

Not one to take a relative stranger's word for anything, Edith gave a slight nod to be polite and assumed a position of watchful stillness.

Just then, the perfect opportunity to confirm how well Bowers was doing stepped off the elevator. As Stan and Bruce the Therapy Dog passed through the lobby, I made a connection.

Bruce glanced at me and wagged his skinny tail. Before I could send him an image of Bowers, the dog looked over his shoulder at a man in blue scrubs who waited for the next car. When Bruce cocked his head, the smells of Old Spice and mustard filled my nostrils.

As I attempted to decipher the dog's message, an image of Doctor Lerma appeared before me accompanied by the scent of disinfectant wash and other less pleasant odors, like blood.

So, the doctor didn't smell like a doctor. Maybe he was a nurse. Who else would dress in scrubs and wander the hospital?

As the elevator doors opened, people stepped out. When the man turned sideways to let them pass, I saw his eyes and nose over his mask. It was Gary. What was his wife's name? It started with a T. Why would Gary dress in scrubs?

"Oh, my," I muttered. It must be for his baby's delivery. Men joined their wives in the delivery room these days. How far along was his wife? Three months. Too early for a delivery.

Gary had been in the emergency room when they'd brought Bowers in. He'd been in the lobby during Bowers' surgery. A disagreeable sensation passed up my spine. Was the alleged father-to-be watching Bowers?

Without consulting Edith, I took off at a jog for the elevator banks, reaching them just as the doors closed. As Stan pulled on Bruce's leash, the dog leaned toward me and barked. He approved of my suspicion.

I ran back to the welcome desk. "You need to tell me what floor Detective Martin Bowers is on. Now! It's an emergency."

When she hesitated, I sprinted past the elevators to the stairwell beyond and took the steps two at a time until I reached the second-floor landing.

The door wouldn't open. I pounded until a puzzled nurse peered out. I leaned over her shoulder and watched the elevators long enough to confirm that this wasn't the scheduled stop. Back up the stairs I went.

By the time I made it to the third floor, only adrenaline kept me moving. My heart pounded against my ribcage, and my lungs demanded overtime pay.

Using both fists, I pounded on the door, and when it opened, I got a surprise. Sergeant Smitty stared back at me.

"Where is he? Where's Bowers?"

"Now, Ms. Chandler. No one has access—"

That's all he got out before I shoved him on his rear end. Vivid memories of what this killer did to his victims assaulted my brain.

The elevator doors were open, which meant Gary must have stopped on this floor. Smitty called after me, but I stayed on task, searching the faces of the medical personnel. So many scrubs passed me by, entering rooms, pushing carts, but none of them had caterpillar eyebrows.

As I jogged down the hallway, I searched each room. Empty. All of them empty. When I reached the nurses' station at the end, I followed the short path around and made a pass along the second corridor.

A nurse stepped out of the station and blocked my way. "This area is off limits."

"Grab her," Smitty called out, limping to catch up. The nurse stared at him contemptuously. No mere police officer was going to order her about. I shimmied past while she thought up a witty rejoinder.

Unlike the first corridor, patients occupied every room on this side, most of them in their prime. They glanced at me, curious, as I passed. I kept running, bouncing like a pinball from door to door on each side of the hallway.

I almost missed him. Bowers had his head turned to accept a glass of water from Gutierrez. When her eyes met mine, I sagged against the door frame, panting while I wheezed out my question.

"Where did he go?"

"Frankie?" Bower's weak voice melted my heart, but I didn't have time for sweet emotions.

"He got on in the lobby. He's in blue medical scrubs and got off on this floor."

The detective's hand moved to the gun holstered at her waist.

"I didn't pass him. Maybe he slipped into a patient's room to blend in."

Suddenly, a feral cry resonated down the hallway. I twirled around in time to meet the eyes of Gary, the allegedly worried husband. No longer friendly and concerned for my fiancé, he lifted his shirt and reached for a black, menacing gun grip. I threw myself across Bowers and heard a grunt of pain. If this was *it,* I wanted to face my end and turned my head so I could see it coming.

But it never came. Edith, the source of the cry, flew

through the air and performed a perfect tackle. The high-pitched squeal of skin on tile pierced the air. By that time, Gutierrez had her weapon drawn and joined my crazed sister-to-be over the man's prone body.

Police officers poured out of the patient rooms, tearing off the flimsy hospital gowns covering their uniforms as they joined in the arrest. A blond nurse scooted past and trotted into the room to check on her patient. I gaped at Bowers.

"Were you expecting this?"

He smiled. "Not exactly this." He wrapped his arms around me and hugged me tight, whispering in my ear. "I've missed you."

His warmth enveloped me, as did the stench of unwashed sweat.

I pulled back my head and looked down on him. He hadn't shaved in days and was well on his way to a beard. One that traveled down his neck. "Just how injured are you?"

The nurse answered for him as she took his pulse. "Detective Bowers has a mild concussion, a fractured collarbone, a broken rib, and a fractured tibia." She shook her head. "Your pulse is racing."

He raised one eyebrow. "Someone just tried to kill me."

"There is that."

"And I've seen my fiancée for the first time in days."

She smirked. "It's good that elevates your pulse."

The cops in the hallway argued over who got to escort Gary to the police station. They finally did rock, paper, scissors, and the winner and her partner, a lanky man in his thirties, smirked at their prize. "We've got some folks who want to meet you."

Gary growled, and I wondered how I missed the evil behind his eyes.

But that evil now wore handcuffs, and my fiancé was safe.

FORTY-SIX

Once the nurse left, I rested one hip on his bed and lowered my head to Bowers' good shoulder. "I've been worried about you."

"I'm sorry. They wanted to keep everyone away in case, well, in case someone came after me."

"Do you know who he was?"

He sighed. "No. I don't."

"He told me his name was Gary and that he had a pregnant wife in the hospital. The last time we spoke, he asked how you were doing." I gasped. "Oh, my gosh. It's my fault."

"If it hurried things along, I'm grateful. I'm going stir-crazy." Even though he looked okay, his speech was tired, and he kept furrowing his brow to focus on his words.

Edith walked into the room. "Have you remembered who pushed you off the hillside?" She dabbed blood from her nose with a tissue.

"Nice tackle," he said in greeting. She shrugged, but his praise pleased her. The corners of her mouth twitched to hold back a grin. "I don't remember. I know I went..." He struggled to name the place but gave up with an exasperated huff. "Somewhere. To verify some piece of information. Some fact. But I can't remember."

Gutierrez strolled in and nodded at Edith. "Nice."

All this praise was going to inflate the scary woman's ego.

The head of Bowers' bed was raised on an angle. Using one arm and the opposite leg, he scooted upward. Edith pulled on a lever located on the side of the frame, while I adjusted the pillows behind his back until we had him sitting.

He rested a hand on my shoulder. "How did you know?"

"Bruce."

He frowned. "I'm afraid I can't remember knowing any —" His expression cleared. "The therapy dog."

At that, Gutierrez and Edith started talking about techniques for subduing suspects. I lowered my voice.

"The dog said the doctor didn't smell like a doctor. And when I saw who it was..."

Speak of the devil, Bruce trotted into the room, his tongue lolling. He headed directly to Edith. She scratched his ears.

Suddenly, flashes of Edith tickling his belly filled my head. They weren't hopeful dreams on the dog's part. In the vision, she had on the outfit she'd worn the first day.

The room grew hazy, and my blood pulsed in my ears. "You knew. All this time, you knew." Tears stung my eyes. "You knew your brother was okay. You've been amusing yourself at my expense."

She gave me one of her condescending head shakes. "You're letting your emotions take over, French Fry."

"Shut up."

"Frankie," Bowers said, reaching for my hand. "It's my fault."

My anger, now at a rolling boil, took over. I turned on him and snapped. "You trusted your scary sister, but not me?"

"Scary sister?" she said with a grin.

He closed his eyes and sighed. "Not my call. But after Juanita told me about the body in your car," his jaw pulsed, "the *first* one, I wanted someone to look out for you. So, I called Edith."

"You trusted your sister, but you didn't trust me. It was fine for Edith to know you were all right, but I could think the worst and be damned." I spun on Gutierrez. "And you. What? You thought I'd blab that my fiancé was alive? Maybe call up my favorite reporter and share the news?"

"We weren't willing to take a chance. You would have acted different. It would have been impossible for you to hide your feelings."

Rubbing my forehead, I put the brakes on the flow of bad words itching to leap off my tongue and turned back to Bowers. "The important thing is you're all right."

"Maybe not at the top of my game, but I should be all right by our honeymoon."

If I didn't calm down, we'd be spending our honeymoon in separate beds. "So, what now?"

My fiancé and his sometimes partner in crime-solving exchanged a glance at the same time Captain Joe entered the room.

"Well, that's that."

"You mean it's over?" I held my breath, waiting for the downside, and noticed that Edith, perhaps disappointed to see her role as hero to her brother and sisters end, frowned her disagreement.

"You're going home, Martin, and I'm sure it's a relief."

"I'm afraid you need to explain it to me, sir. My head—" Bowers shrugged and then winced at the motion.

"Oh, right. The man we just arrested was Paul Burgio."

Gutierrez set her expression on blank, which meant this was important information.

Bowers moved to shrug again and thought better of it. "Should that mean something to me?"

"He's a rough character. I suspect by the time we get through with him, we'll have solved a dozen crimes in Wolf Creek. Phoenix is after him, too, along with half the police forces in Maricopa County." He smiled. "But we got him first."

I raised my hand. "What does Paul Burgio have to do with Bennett's Grazers? I mean, that's where Bowers' fell. I assume he followed this Paul out there."

Captain Joe's eyelids came down to half-mast. "Why would you assume that? I don't believe his fall had anything to do with Paul Burgio."

"Then why would Paul attack him?"

"It's my belief the case he was working on—"

"Which case exactly?" Edith smiled when she asked.

"Martin's fall and consequent hospitalization provided an opportunity for Burgio to remove an inconvenience. A coincidence."

"Then why was Bowers at Bennett's Grazers?"

The man didn't become captain of the Wolf Creek Police by being slow on his feet. "We might never know why Martin was out there, but I will tell you one thing that should put your mind at ease. Del Bennett and Bennett's Grazers were never part of the investigation."

FORTY-SEVEN

While we debated where Bowers should stay for the duration of his recovery—my house, of course—he fell asleep. I hoped it was because he felt safe and relaxed in our presence and not because we bored him to snores. Captain Joe escorted Edith and me to the elevators but stayed behind to cleanup some details. Or at least supervise his underlings while they cleaned them up.

The colossal relief that came from Paul Burgio's capture did little to soothe my fury over Edith's betrayal, but I played it cool and kept my hands off her throat as we made our way to the car. Once there, I set aside my carefully planned diatribe to discuss an important point.

"Paul Burgio wasn't in any of my visions."

She glanced my way as she started the car with the same keys she'd lifted from me in Bowers' hospital room. "Let it go, French Fry. The good guys won."

"But he wasn't in Bowers' book," I protested.

"Maybe Marty didn't have time to add him."

I shifted to face her. "Please turn the car off and give me your attention."

She didn't switch off the ignition, but she removed her hands from the steering wheel and looked at me.

"Do you seriously believe this is over? That the capture of Paul Burgio means we can gorge on June's baking and plan for a family vacation to Wisconsin Dells?"

She looked away. "No. I don't."

Surprised that she hadn't fought me on the idea, I said, "Well. Good. Very good."

"But it's time we parted. Things might get rough, and I don't want the responsibility of exposing Marty's fiancée to danger."

After a moment to confirm she wasn't kidding, I threw back my head and laughed until I cried.

"What?"

"Did you hear yourself?" I lowered my voice to a martyred growl. "*I will bear this cross alone. Save yourself while there is still time. Mwa-ha-ha-ha!*" The last bit of theatrics ended in a coughing fit.

"It's serious. *I'm* serious."

I snorted. "Maybe that's your problem. You should learn to laugh. Look. I appreciate how you want to keep me from soiling my hands, but these hands," I held them up, "have been slobbered on, pecked, bitten and worse. I don't want to look over Bowers' shoulder for the rest of his life making sure the police have it right. I won't rest until I see a play-by-play of what happened on that hill and reveal everything that led to his presence at Bennett's Grazers. I'm going to figure it out with you or on my own. Your choice. But I ought to warn you. This is my car and I'm taking it with me."

She glowered at me, but when she saw I wasn't intimidated, she gave it up and sighed. "Okay. We work together. Fair warning. I'm used to working on my own."

"Me too. So, we'll work on our own, but together." Leaning my head back on the headrest, I closed my eyes. "First stop, home to check on the goats and make sure I have clean sheets and another blanket for your brother."

"Dym will take care of that. We haven't talked to this Randy character. He seems to be the center of our gang of misfits. He knew Eric, and he knew Luther."

"*Randy* pushed your brother? He looks so young. And nice."

"I don't know. Do you?"

By the time she pulled into the parking lot of Mike's Auto Body and turned off the engine, I'd relived the embarrassing scene of my last visit about twelve times.

"I don't want to go back in there."

Edith practically clapped. "Great. You wait in the car. I'll go in alone."

If the men in the shop were killers, it would be irresponsible to allow Bowers' sister to approach them by herself. I may not be a fighter, but I had the fingers to dial 9-1-1.

I let her lead the way inside. The crew had left for the day. The cars were in shadow, and the only light came from over the counter, where Mike stood, flipping through paperwork. Unfortunately, the humongous black man I'd nicknamed The Bear stood by his side.

When the owner glanced up and spotted us, I gave him an A-Plus for self-control. He closed the file, leaned his elbows on the counter, and folded his hands.

"Don't tell me. You want your rental car repaired."

Edith caught him off guard with a bark of laughter. "What number rental are you on, French Fry?"

"Three, not counting my original car," I mumbled.

The Bear spoke. "Some people shouldn't drive."

"It's not me," I snapped. "Someone keeps leaving dead bodies in my vehicles."

The two men exchanged a glance, and it wasn't one of surprise. Either Edith didn't catch it, which I doubted, or she ignored it.

She rested her elbows on the counter. "Is Randy around?"

The Bear moved forward and growled. "What about Randy?"

"I take it that's a no. Let's talk about Luther Mendoza. Are you trying to kill him, or save him? We need to know before this conversation moves forward."

They weren't the only ones shocked by the blunt question. "Have you lost your mind?" I murmured.

"Because, depending on your answer, this meeting will go one of two ways."

As Mike studied our faces, his arms dropped to his sides, where they were blocked by the counter. It made me nervous. Was he pushing a button to summon the police? The rest of his gang? Or was he reaching for a weapon?

Don't get me wrong. His eyes had a hard expression in them, but they didn't seem mean, prompting my next words.

"Lola misses him."

He raised one eyebrow. "You've talked to Lola?"

I nodded. "At Nemo's."

He exchanged a glance with The Bear and put his hands back on the counter. "How much do you know?"

Edith leaned in. "Rings and Things."

Head-nodding accompanied his resigned sigh. The Bear put his hands on his hips and let out a stream of air. "Bunch of morons."

"Why don't you start at the beginning?" Edith walked

to the table, pulled out a chair, and sat down. I preferred my current spot, with its closer proximity to the exit.

After a bout of throat-clearing, Mike began his story. "Luther mentioned his job at Rings and Things. Why shouldn't he? That kid loves working with his hands. I let him do a few jobs here, but it didn't work out. He found his niche in jewelry, and like anyone else who falls in love with their work, he liked to talk about it. The question came up about how much jewelry regularly stayed in the shop."

"Who asked?" Edith held up a hand. "Let me guess. Eric White."

"I told you he was bad news," The Bear said.

"About fifty times, Jake. I got it."

Jake wasn't a very scary name for a bear.

"Did Eric work for you?"

"He subbed when one of our welders took a vacation." Mike's jaw clenched. "One day, when Luther wasn't around, Eric told the fellas he knew a guy who could help them make big money for little work. They'd just have to give the guy a cut."

"Did Luther know?" Please, please let Luther be innocent.

"Not according to Randy."

A sigh of relief.

"Who did he talk into it?" Edith asked. "And if it makes it easier, we know about Enrique and Mr. G."

"Enrique?"

I took a tentative step forward. "Gator."

Mike tapped the counter. "Gator? Are you messing with me?"

"That friend of Randy's," Jake said. "Kind of a geek."

"That's him, Mr. Bear—um, Mr. Jake."

They both gaped at me before bellowing with laughter. "You *do* look like a bear," Mike said, wiping away a tear.

Jake motioned at Mike's beard with his finger. "If I'm a bear, that makes you Grizzly Adams."

I like to see people enjoy themselves, but my impatience kept me from enjoying the comedy routine. Finally, Mike got serious.

"I only met the kid a few times." Mike jabbed his finger at us. "Randy wasn't involved. None of my guys were. They thought Eric was joking. Talking big."

"Did you believe him?"

"We didn't find out about any of it until after the fact."

"That's right." Jake shook his head. "Fools."

"They were smart enough to keep quiet around me. I would have knocked some sense into them." Mike passed a hand over his mouth. "One day, Randy came to me scared out of his mind. Showed me an article about a guy trying to pawn jewelry stolen from Rings and Things. He also hadn't heard from Luther in a while. He panicked, especially when someone tried to kill him."

"Kill Randy?" I tamped down my panic. Randy hadn't become backseat fodder for my latest vehicle. Yet.

"Someone tried to run the kid off the road," Jake said. "Then Eric went missing. When Randy tried to contact Luther to warn him, Lola said he left without saying goodbye. . The final straw came when someone Randy knew turned up with a bullet hole in his head. They found him in some lady's car."

I raised my hand. "That would be mine."

Mike's hand moved back under the counter. "Why your car? Are you involved?"

Explaining about Bowers would take too long. "I don't

know why he used my car. And the dead guy's name was George Dakos. Mr. G. How did Eric know him?"

Jake glowered. "Mike and me didn't know about him."

Edith spoke. "You should know that Gator is dead."

Jake swore.

My hand went to my temple. "Wait a minute. If Randy wasn't killing anyone, and Eric was innocent—"

Mike challenged my assumption. "We don't know that."

Edith gave me a glare that said the vision Pierre showed me better be right. "Eric's out of it. Permanently."

The owner of the auto body shop paled. "That leaves Luther, who had no reason to hurt anyone, and Eric's contact."

"Does the name Paul Burgio mean anything to you?"

It was too much for Mike. He came from behind the counter and took a seat at the table. "That was their contact? Those stupid sons-of—"

"Paul won't be bothering anyone for a long time." Edith smiled, most likely reliving her famous tackle. "What can you tell me about him?"

Jake took over. "Word on the street is he's muscle for hire. There's nothing that dude won't do for money. Nothing."

Doubt crept in. "Maybe he's responsible after all. Maybe Bennett's Grazers is just a random, isolated location he picked to lure Bowers."

"Detective Bowers?" Mike and Jake exchanged a glance. "He dropped by a few weeks ago to talk to Randy. He was nice about it. Didn't make the kid feel guilty for being stupid."

My heart rate picked up. "Did Randy tell him about Paul?"

Jake gestured toward the back corner of the room. "Why don't you ask him yourself?"

The young employee stepped out of the shadows. "I didn't know this Paul guy's name or I would have. I just knew Eric had a friend. A former cell mate. He talked about the guy as if they worked together all the time. Bragged about knowing him. It creeped me out." His gaze flickered over Mike. "Eric never mentioned the guy's name. He enjoyed keeping it secret."

"What were they in for?" I asked.

"It seemed better not to ask."

"And Luther? Do you have any idea where he's at?"

Randy stared at the floor. "I wish I did, because then I'd know he wasn't dead."

FORTY-EIGHT

We argued all the way home about Paul Burgio's role in recent events. I thought he sounded like an evil genius. Edith didn't credit him with the brains to organize a jewelry heist.

"You heard what they said. Paul has a reputation for being muscle. Muscle carries out orders. Like killing Marty. Muscle does *not* come up with new crimes on his own."

"How do you know?" I demanded. "Is there a handbook? You can't tell me when Eric White presented Paul Burgio with the opportunity for easy money, he passed on it because it fell outside his job description."

"Fine. He may be behind the burglary, but I guarantee he didn't do it without permission."

"From who? His mommy?"

"Trust me. A guy like that has bosses."

The temperature in the car dropped a few degrees, and it wasn't the work of the crappy air conditioner. I wrapped my arms around my middle. "Then we keep looking for whoever was responsible."

"That we do, French Fry."

When we entered my home, we were met by Windy's frantic barking. Edith raised her voice. "Dym, control Princess Yap-Yap or I will."

My sliding glass door opened, and Dymphna scooted inside, pushing back the goats with her rump. After a final yank to pull her crochet vest from the mother's mouth, she slammed shut the door, straightened her clothing, and pulled a piece of hay from her hair. As soon as she came in the house, Windy's bark lowered to a whine.

"They're fed and watered, but the buck won't eat."

I turned to Ghost Woman. "He prefers pastries if he can get them. And cookies."

We hadn't yet sampled any of the teas I'd purchased, which meant I hadn't opened the vanilla wafers. When I returned with a handful of bribes, Edith nodded at the hairy faces staring at us through the glass. "They can't stay here."

The first burn of rebellion warmed my chest. "They're staying here, where they're safe."

"I have an idea. It's a temporary solution." Scary Sister directed the comment over my head to Ghost Woman, as if I wasn't standing between them.

"This is *my* house, and I say they're staying. We'll close the drapes. Your brother won't even know they're here."

"Marty's coming home?"

While Edith explained what happened at the hospital, the baby goat chose that moment to hop onto a potted plant, one too small to support his weight. I winced at the crash but held my ground.

"They're staying. Seeing Pierre might jog your brother's memory. Besides, I need time to get through to him. He's the only witness to what happened to Bowers."

Edith chortled, as if I'd told the best joke ever. Dymphna did not, as she once told me she understood

Windy perfectly. Animal communication was no big deal to her.

As I brushed off Edith's negative energy, my toes wiggled with excitement. I had cookies in my hand, full access to the creature I most wanted to talk to, and my fiancé was coming home. It was almost too much to bear.

Half an hour later, my excitement had waned into irritation, and not just because eating another vanilla wafer would make me ill. Pierre, surrounded by his loved ones, refused to talk about anything but the kid. *His* kid, I assumed.

I sent him a movie of Bowers walking up the hillside followed by a nefarious shadow.

He showed me the baby goat hopping around the pen back at Bennett's Grazers.

An exaggerated video of Bowers bumping down the hillside watched by a faceless question mark inspired the same type of response, only this time the kid was having dinner, courtesy of momma goat. Didn't he have an admirable appetite? Momma goat bleated her approval.

Pierre strolled over to the empty cake pan, former home to June's goodies, and nudged it.

"You're going to turn into a diabetic," I complained.

The goat responded by leaning into my wall to scratch his side. My heart leaped in my chest with frenzied joy. Too much joy for a simple scratch.

I lunged just as the little bugger rebounded off Pierre's back and took flight. His front feet made it to the top of the wall, but my hold on his back legs kept him from going over. He bleated his frustration, and just as I set him on the ground, the doe headbutted my rear end. I admit I gave her a target.

The back door slid opened, and Dymphna strolled out. "Do you have any chicken wire handy?"

Two hours and one trip to the feed store later, we'd goat-proofed my patio. Chicken wire blocked the baby's access to the world outside, and we added a makeshift covering that predator-proofed my patio. Thank goodness I didn't have a homeowners' association.

As I twisted the final piece of wire into place, Dymphna brushed her hands on her skirt. "Perfect timing. Dinner's ready."

"Let me guess. Chicken."

"No, silly. Marty's coming home tomorrow, so we're having a roast tonight."

The correlation wasn't clear to me, but I was too tired to question it.

FORTY-NINE

Bowers' homecoming the next afternoon happened with the fanfare of a royal visit.

Edith and I drove to the hospital to do the honors right after we exchanged the Dakota for a 1983 Ford Fairmont Futura in a burnt orange color with a white top. It looked like a creamsicle, but it had four doors to make it easier to transport him.

Dan Driver rejoiced when I told him the exchanged had nothing to do with bodies.

Dymphna remained at home to put last-minute touches on her flower arrangement.

A man in blue scrubs with dark hair and a goatee peppered with gray pushed Bowers through the front doors in a wheelchair. My fiancé gestured to us. "Martin, this is my sister, Edith and my fiancée, Frankie. Frankie and Edith, this is Martin."

"Egads. There are two of you?" Edith joked.

As we took turns shaking his hand, I tore my gaze from Bowers long enough to be polite. "Are you my fiancé's nurse?"

Martin and Bowers both chuckled.

"I'm a porter."

"You mean like a hotel porter?"

"And I'm the luggage." Bowers grew serious. "He was my guardian angel. Knowing you're headed for surgery and tests is unnerving, but Martin would show up with a few terrible jokes—"

"Hold on. They weren't *all* bad."

"He even sang to me, which was surprisingly comforting, considering he's tone deaf." Bowers held out a hand. "Seriously, I can't thank you enough."

Embarrassed, Martin bowed when he took his patient's hand. "We aim to please at Hotel Holy Cross." His gaze landed on my new ride. "Woah."

When my fiancé noticed the Fairmont, he cracked the broadest grin I'd seen in a long time, even before his accident.

"You sold your car and bought this Fairmont for *me*?"

Had he mentioned loving Ford Fairmonts? It didn't matter. He was happy. "Yes. Yes, I did." With Edith's approving glance, that settled it. I'd make Dan part with this car if I had to tie him up and tickle his feet with feathers, which is not as erotic as it sounds.

Dr. Lerma joined us. "No excitement. This man needs time to heal. And *don't* jostle him."

Bowers let us help him out of the wheelchair. As soon as he was standing, my fiancé shrugged us off, shook hands with Dr. Lerma and Martin, and limped to the car with the aid of a crutch, using the open back door to steady himself. He turned his back to the car and lowered himself in, with me hovering and making noises every time he winced. Edith came through the opposite door, hooked her arms under his pits, and dragged her protesting brother until she had him stretched out across the back seat. Then we were off.

When we arrived home, Edith once again opened the back door, wrapped her arms around his chest, and tugged him backward.

"Edith! Stop it." His pleas had more to do with embarrassment than agony. She ignored his protests and continued to tug. When he bent the fingers of her left hand back, she yelped and bit his shoulder.

"Dammit! That hurt." He rubbed his shoulder. "You probably gave me rabies."

Tension made me raise my voice. "Jostling. The doctor said no jostling."

We both watched him navigate the threshold, and once he made it across, my lips trembled, and a tear escaped. We helped him to the couch, placing a pillow under his foot so he could keep it elevated on the coffee table.

While I stood back to admire the results, I sniffed the latest aroma to grace my home and leaned toward Edith. "Is she cooking another pot roast?"

"Stovies is a Scottish thing. Leftovers from the stove. Dym was going to make Rumbledethumps, but she couldn't find turnips at the store."

After thanking God above for this failure, I voiced my surprise. "You're Scottish?"

"On our father's side. German on our mother's side." Edith snickered. "That's why we're such boneheads."

"Speak for yourself," Dymphna said, entering through the kitchen doors with Windy tucked under one arm and a vase of fake flowers in the other hand. For the time being, she'd given up whispering. "Nice to see you," she said to Bowers, depositing the small dog in his lap. He jerked forward with an *Oomph*.

"Stop complaining. Snuggums doesn't weigh that much." She plunked down the vase. "I made these for you."

Getting a closer look at the arrangement, it wasn't something I'd brag about. The petals hung in limp strips. Some leaves had tears in them. As the explanation settled on me, I caught her glare.

"Your *cat* added her own touches."

Bowers snorted a laugh through his nose.

The animal situation wasn't that simple. Emily, who was as fond of Bowers as a feline could be of a two-legged creature, sprang to the armrest and stared at Windy, her tail twitching and her eyes filled with disdain. The latter was normal.

The dog had snuggled into the dip between Bowers' thighs, which was Emily's sweet spot and rightful place. I tensed, waiting for the battle.

When she shrieked MINE, I winced and covered my ears, waiting for action. However, animals can sense pain and illness. After a speedy review of the situation, Emily dropped onto the couch cushion and stepped delicately onto Bowers' leg. Windy looked up and attempted a growl, but coughed. Emily rapped her on the nose, but it was a half-hearted effort. With a bit of wiggling, they wound up crammed together, side by side, neither one willing to give up Bowers' company.

Dymphna had kept busy while we were retrieving her brother. She returned to the kitchen and came back with a plate of cookies. Oatmeal raisin.

All the activity seemed to happen in a vacuum, while I stared at my fiancé and took in his presence on my couch. I'd spent so much stress-time on him, first worrying about his recovery and then busting my hump to find information that might get him home. It was hard to take in the joyous reality. Bowers was sitting on my couch. Bowers would be fine. Eventually. He still had a dazed look about him, but I attributed that to the pain medication administered at the hospital. Mostly.

It was then I noticed Edith was watching him, too. He had his head back and his eyes closed. He looked so peaceful. Too peaceful. Oh, my gosh. Had he had a stroke? Was he dead?

I plopped onto the couch next to him with extra oomph, relieved when the jostling jerked him awake. Edith boxed him in, taking a seat on his other side.

"Are you sure you're all right?" I said. "This isn't too much for you? Coming home? All these people?"

He leaned back again and closed his eyes with a sigh. "It feels good to be out of that hospital room."

"And you don't remember your accident?" Edith asked.

"No, but I'm not sure I want to." He rubbed his eyes and dropped his hand onto Emily's back, digging his fingers into her fur. Delighted, she stretched and kneaded his leg. When she flopped sideways to bask in Bower's attention, her massaging paws landed on Windy's side. The dog looked up, surprised, and then shifted her chubby body to direct Emily to a preferred spot.

"That's a lie. I do want to know what happened. In fact, it's driving me nuts trying to remember."

His eyes opened, and the worry and fear were back.

"No stress. The doctor said no stress. That means you relax and heal and let us take care of you."

Though I didn't know how I'd find time to do that *and* confirm the police had the right killer behind bars.

My mother was right. A woman's work is never done.

FIFTY

Dymphna announced dinner was ready. In concession to Bowers' lack of mobility, we served the meal on the coffee table and gathered around him on the couch and a dining room chair I pulled over. When he attempted to move his leg from the coffee table to make room for his plate, his sisters surrounded him, objecting loudly.

"No need for that, Marty." Ghost Woman carried in his food on a blue-green plastic dinner tray. I'd no idea when she'd bought it.

He thanked her. It was a considerate gift, but Bowers needed more than a dinner tray. He needed peace. A peace that wouldn't come until he knew what had happened to him.

Dymphna had inherited the same cooking skills as her sister June. The pot roast fell apart when I speared it and then melted in my mouth along with the mashed potatoes, bits of onion, and garlic infused gravy. Mid-chew, I paused and wondered if I'd ever cook this well. Then I chuckled, almost choking. Bowers had eaten my cooking. He knew what he was facing and would certainly give me a handicap, like they gave to the subpar players in golf.

Once we cleared up the dishes, and I'd made and served coffee, the pent-up stress from the last few days found an escape in giddy humor, with Bowers as the butt of his sisters' jokes.

"So, why did you fall?" Dymphna asked, hand feeding Windy scraps of roast as the dog perched in her lap, leaving Bowers' lap free for Emily. "Did you forget how to tie your shoelaces?"

Edith smirked, but her eyes stayed serious. Watchful. "My guess is Nero was so caught up investigating, he forgot to look where he was going."

"Nero?" I glanced at Bowers. "Is that your middle name?"

The sisters guffawed.

"He's Martin James Bowers," Dymphna said. "That was Edith's nickname for him."

"Was it because he liked to play detective?"

"She called him Nero because he was chubby." Dymphna frowned. "It was cruel."

"Aw, Dym," Bowers said. "She was only joking."

"She might have hurt your feelings. That was her goal."

"Now you read minds?" Edith snapped. Her lips spread in a slow grin. "Maybe you can take lessons from French Fry here."

"Oh, is that your nickname for Frankie?" Dymphna's tone suggested it wasn't a compliment.

"You are salty," Bowers said, and when his sisters chortled, he blushed. "As in spunky."

Ghost Woman shook her head. "Bull. Edith calls you that because, in her mind, she's the main event, and you're just a side order."

My jaw dropped. "Seriously?"

Sensing my frownie face might lead to harsh words, Bowers broke in with a topic meant to capture our attention. "It was a lucky thing you ran into Bruce, or I might not be here."

"You mean Bruce, the therapy dog." Edith frowned. "What about him?"

"You mentioned mind reading and Frankie and..." Bowers let it drop.

Edith strolled to my chair and dropped a hand on my shoulder. "I was talking about the goat. Right, Frankie?" Apparently, shaking me until my teeth rattled was a sign of friendship.

"The goat." Bowers lowered his chin. "Explain."

"Better still," Edith said, "why don't I show you?" A smart aleck grin on her face, she whipped open the curtains, startling the dozing threesome.

My poor fiancé didn't register surprise, which was telling.

"Frankie, I know we haven't discussed pets, and I know you miss Chauncey—"

Unable to hold back my excitement, I jumped up. "Do you recognize any of them?"

"Recognize them?"

While Bowers studied their faces, faces now plastered against the glass, I held my breath. Would seeing Pierre jog my beloved's memory? Would the horrible episode come rushing back? Would this nightmare finally end?

"No." He laughed. "I'm sure they're nice goats. Alpines, aren't they? But I don't believe we've met."

Disappointed, I tried another tactic. "Maybe, when you're feeling better, we should go to the fair."

Edith shot me a warning glance.

"If you'd like, though we'll have to take it slow." He patted his leg.

Disappointment made way for excitement as I realized the fairgrounds might not have slipped Bowers' memory. His investigation might have ended before he made that discovery, which meant Edith and I had information to share. Which made me eager to come up with more goodies for Bowers.

I stood and snatched a few cookies from the plate. "I'm going to give our guests a treat." Windy considered herself a guest, too, so I broke off a piece and waited a minute and a half before she condescended to take the treat she'd just begged for.

Instead of closing the door behind me, I left it open about ten inches. The setting sun reflected off the glass, and I wanted Pierre to have a good view of Bowers.

First, I shared the oatmeal cookies I'd snagged between the three of them. With Pierre focused on chewing, I made a connection and showed him Bennett's Grazers, including the rocky slope beyond. Then I grabbed his face in my hands and pointed it to the gap in the doorway, where he had a perfect view of my fiancé.

At first, my pulse sped up with recognition, surprise, and pleasure that the guy who fell down the hill had survived. I found the goat's concern touching.

While Pierre had Bowers' face in view, I showed him Paul Burgio standing alongside him. He pushed my sweetheart down the hill and looked directly into Pierre's eyes.

My stomach gurgled. I leaned my face into the crack and snapped my fingers at the one person in the room who didn't find my gift surprising. Dymphna. "I need treats. Please."

She complied without question. Soon, I pulled Paul's

face up again. Pierre made a snorty sound and scoured the ground for cookie crumbs. After making a wide-angle shot of Bennett's Grazers, I inserted Paul in different locations, popping him next to the goat pen, then in front of the cornfield. Finally, he hopped to various positions on the hill.

At first, the scenery remained still. Undisturbed. Bowers appeared, standing at the base of the hill. When I tried to move him to the top, Pierre shifted him back to the bottom like a chess piece. Without warning, the hillside shrunk, while Bowers grew to gigantic proportions. A golden glow surrounded him, illuminating him as if he were the patron saint of goats. Shuffling my feet back to avoid being crushed by Mega Bowers, I noticed the hillside had shrunk to where I had to squint to see it. And then it all stopped.

"What in the name of Buster Brown does that mean?" I whispered.

The kid leaped up and down, squeaky baas sounding out each time he landed. As the connection broke, Pierre bit the little guy's rump. His final bleat came out as a squawk, and he ducked between his mother's legs.

In desperation, I played word association and threw out whatever came to mind. "Huge. Larger than a hill. Bowers the giant." I had a thought. "Are you saying the hill doesn't matter?" Rubbing my forehead, I tried to see the scene from the goat's perspective.

"What does the hill represent to you? Grazing?" I snorted. "Right. Why graze when you can get free pastries? Anyway, goats browse for tasty leaves and stuff. It's sheep that graze."

Pierre belched.

"At least you're healthy," I mumbled.

Edith slipped outside and closed the door. "What's up?"

"Just chatting with the goats."

She stared, then returned to the living room. I gave up and followed. She stopped in front of her brother. "I hate to break up all this family fun, but you're ripe, Marty. You need a bath. The hospital sent over a stool for the shower. I'm going to have to wrap your leg in a plastic bag. Maybe you can hang it over the edge. Anyway, I'll be there to help you balance."

Bowers froze. "Uh, I'll be fine."

"I changed your diaper and wiped your bottom. I've seen it all."

Dymphna giggled. "Me, too. And we certainly can't expose you to Frankie before your wedding day."

Both sisters became still. It reminded me of two dogs right before they launch into the fray. They pounced, tickling his sides.

"You're helpless," Dymphna cried. "You have to do what we say."

All joking ceased when he twisted away from her and shouted with pain at the movement in his shoulder.

Scary Sister clapped her hands, demanding obedience. "Let's get to it."

My fiancé sent me a pleading glance, but I held firm. "Edith's right. My hair curled when I hugged you."

Before he could argue, I grabbed the dirty plates and carried them to the kitchen. From the laughter filling my living room, the sisters were assisting Bowers to his doom.

FIFTY-ONE

If my fiancé thought he could relax after his bath, his sisters had different plans. Edith confiscated my laptop and set it up on the coffee table, logging in with my password.

"Are you a hacker? Did you hack me?" I demanded.

"I watched you enter the password when we had our last meeting."

Note to self. Never *ever* do anything in front of Edith I didn't want her to remember.

Soon the sisters crowded around Bowers on the couch. Edith had my password to my online meeting account, too, and she welcomed the rest of the sisters into the chat room. I moved to another chair outside of their circle. I felt an unfamiliar surge of jealousy watching them snuggled together and laughing with the same straight noses and the same square chins. Same dark, slightly curled hair in various shades. Scottish/German faces.

Chandler was Norman French and meant someone who sold household goods. Maybe, centuries ago, my family had conquered his family. Or sold them candles.

"Marty." June's voice cracked, and she pressed her lips together. "You scared the life out of me."

"Aw, Junie." He held his hand out toward the screen. "Don't cry. It's just a scratch."

"Will you listen to him?" Cecelia cackled. "I'm sorry I haven't called. It's been crazy around here ever since Peanut Butter foaled." Cecelia and her husband, Joe, lived in Texas. Joe was a farrier, which meant he shoed horses. I assumed Peanut Butter was a mare.

June's spread her concern to include her sister's animals. "No one's sick, I hope."

"No. Just a handful. That colt reminds me of some of my former students. Full of curiosity and oblivious to the needs of others."

Bowers' initial excitement at seeing his sisters gave way to the sleepiness that follows a hot bath. He leaned back on the couch and closed his eyes. When he missed a question and Agnes shouted his name, his eyes snapped open. "Sorry. I drifted off."

That set off general cooing about how tired he must be. Not that they would let him out of this call to get some sleep.

As they babbled about how good he looked, I listened with a tinge of envy. As an only child, I'd missed out on having a support team at home. Penny was my best friend, and her older brother Robby would have defended me against a pack of wild dogs, but it wasn't the same.

Of course, having seven sisters would also have meant sharing Mom and Dad, bathroom time, and my childhood bedroom. I should be grateful for my lot.

"Edith," Martha said with dignity. "I owe you an apology. You came through and brought Marty back to us."

Martha's Lazarus complex must have come from her

namesake. It wasn't as if Scary Sister had raised her brother from the dead. Not to mention the substantial part I played in his return home.

Edith simply nodded without explaining, but Dymphna reached over the armrest on the couch and pulled me in front of the screen, forcing me to kneel at Bowers' feet. "Frankie has been working on his release since this all started."

Bowers objected. "My release? I wasn't in prison. I was in the hospital."

They ignored him.

"I'm sure you helped to the best of your abilities," Martha said, trying to be kind.

"Tell us what happened," asked Mary, the uber-feminist. "Were you pushed by a man or a woman? I have money riding on this."

A look of intense focus and worry worked its way across Bowers' features. His forehead wrinkled, and he pressed his lips together. I thought he might cry. Finally, he let go a stream of air and rubbed his temples. "I can't remember."

"Don't stress about it," Agatha said. "It will come to you. Happens to me all the time. I'll try to remember if that dress I want to wear to a work function is at the dry cleaners, and in the middle of the night, it comes to me I packed it away with the winter clothes."

"Me, too," Martha agreed with enthusiasm. "At least once a week I forget important things. My phone number. What I walked into a room for. Whatshisface's name. Maybe more often than that. Possibly daily."

Mary didn't admit to any faults, but she added her own comforting words. "Until then, Edith has you covered."

"Sure." Edith agreed as if it were a given that she would

follow little Marty and watch over him forever. Once we were married, we'd have to set up a spare bedroom.

June turned the conversation to practical matters. "What *can* you remember? If it's not too stressful to talk about."

He hesitated. "I've been told I was working on a case that had gone stale."

Was he being coy? Or had he forgotten the jewelry store burglary?

Agatha made a sound like tuh. "They're working you too hard. No wonder you fell."

Edith glared at the screen. "He didn't just fall."

"They were connected somehow," Bowers continued, more to himself. "But why I went to Bennett's Grazers, I can't tell you."

After chastising myself for ignoring an obvious source of information, I said, "What does Gutierrez think?" Now that Bowers wasn't in hiding, he was free to tell me all about their conversations.

"We haven't discussed it."

It was as if the man had slapped me. He was lying, his first direct lie ever. At least to me. Gutierrez had been in his hospital room, and she hadn't come to discuss the food. However, he might want to keep that information from his sisters. I'd tackle him later. Alone.

June wrapped up the meeting with a directive. "You leave Detective Gutierrez to deal with it. She's a competent lady, or she wouldn't have her job."

Edith and I exchanged a glance. Whether Bowers listened to June or not, we were still on the case.

FIFTY-TWO

Once Edith, Dymphna and I washed and put away the dishes and leftovers—leftovers of the Scottish leftovers dish—I retrieved some pajamas from my bedroom. I pushed open the door and heard a man swear an endless chain of creative curses.

Bowers avoided a full crash by throwing his body sideways onto my bed. I shrieked, and the posse of sisters were at my side, pushing past to help him to his feet.

"I'm so sorry. I thought you were in the bathroom."

Edith righted him, and Dymphna handed him his crutch.

"No harm done." He smiled for emphasis. My fiancé looked boyishly handsome in his burgundy cotton pajamas and gray suede slippers. Since he hadn't gone through his grooming routine after his bath, his hair had extra curls, which Edith ruffled with her fingers.

"That was the fun part when you were little. Playing with your curls and pinching your chubby bottom."

He swatted at her hand as she tried to reenact the latter memory.

"Where are you going?" Dymphna asked him. "You're sleeping in here tonight."

"I will not let you ladies sleep on the floor while I'm comfortable in bed."

She let out a whispery laugh. "Maybe we can get a priest over here and you can share with Frankie."

My face burned, especially when Bowers said, "The last thing on my mind is sex."

"Who said anything about sex?" she responded, with extra innocence. "You have a dirty mind."

"Anyway, I'm not tired," Bowers insisted. "I'll just sit with you all for a while."

Though he said *you all*, his gaze was on me. Dymphna snickered and Edith said, "Sure, little brother. Join us on the couch. I call dibs to sit next to Marty!"

"Me too!" Dymphna joined her sister in teasing us, which I didn't mind because they left us to claim their spots.

Suddenly, I felt shy.

"Come here," he said, his voice husky.

I did as he asked, and he pulled me in for a one-armed hug and kissed the top of my head. When I looked up, he put his lips where they belonged. On mine. After a minute of slow, careful kisses, he sighed and rested his chin on my shoulder.

"Right about now, your mother should be introducing me to her friends at the church potluck. I was a bit terrified at the thought of her contemporaries interrogating me, but I'm sorry we missed out. I hope you're not too disappointed."

"You're the only thing that matters." I buried my face in his jammies and he held me in silence until I lifted my face for another kiss.

He adjusted his crutch and put an arm around my

shoulder, and I helped him to the couch. Once we got him settled between Edith and Dymphna, with Windy in his lap, he turned serious.

"What did you find out about what I was doing at the time of my fall?"

Edith pursed her lips. "Why are you sure we didn't spend every moment prostrate on a couch in the lobby, waiting for news?"

"I had access to the security footage. Besides, I know who I'm talking to. Tell me about the goats. Bennett's Grazers."

She nodded. "The site of your alleged accident. Owned by Del Bennett. Behind the pasture, pen and buildings, there's a rocky slope."

"Which I tumbled down."

"I scoped it out. Flat on top. Not too bad a climb. There's no way you just fell."

"But I might have. No one witnessed it. There's no reason Paul Burgio would follow me to a farm. Maybe I got distracted and didn't watch my footing."

Since Bowers' tone was sinking into depression, Edith moved the conversation along. "I peeked in his barn. The usual, though it was cleaner than any barn I remember. Also, he had a mini skid steer."

"You mean that piece of equipment?" I frowned. "What would he need that for?"

Bowers answered for her. "Landscaping. Maybe he plans on planting a small garden."

"There's a cornfield next to the house."

He ran his fingers through his hair. "I wish it would come back to me. It's frustrating."

Catching my concerned gaze, he patted the couch next to him. Edith scooted over and I wedged myself between them, while Dymphna grabbed her pup and moved to a chair.

Bowers put an arm around my shoulder and kissed my head. "You smell good."

"Knock it off," Edith said, rolling her eyes. "I assume you know which case you were working on, but in case you pinkie-swore secrecy with Detective Gutierrez, we'll tell you. The burglary of Rings and Things. Three months ago. Dead end all around for the police. Employee Luther Mendoza suspected," and here she sent an amused glance my way, "but Frankie assumes he's innocent. Then, a few weeks ago, one of the gang brings some of the stash to a pawnshop, and the alert broker recognizes it. The reappearance of stolen items opens the case again." She raised one eyebrow. "How am I doing so far?"

My fiancé had on his poker face, which meant we'd nailed it. "Interesting."

"Would you like us to fill you in on what's happened since your fall? Just in case your partner missed something?"

"Why not?" He kept his voice casual, but I saw the spark in his deep-blue eyes.

"Luther is missing. Gator, known to you as Enrique Salazar, is dead. George Dakos, aka Mr. G, also dead. Eric White, if you believe your fiancée, takes the death toll to three."

He adjusted his position to face me. "You saw his death? Juanita mentioned that Eric White was presumed dead."

"I did. And Mr. G's, too."

Bowers pulled me in tight and leaned his head into mine. "I'm so sorry."

Edith's brow wrinkled. I could tell she never considered

that witnessing murder wasn't a joy-filled experience for me. Dymphna just listened.

"What I don't understand is why Mr. G stopped by the hospital to see how you were doing. He arrived right after I did."

Bowers closed his eyes, finally expelling a frustrated breath. "I don't know. What did Pierre have to say about it?"

My fiancé had an aversion to conversations about my *psychic thingy*. "You must be desperate," I joked.

"I am." He squeezed my shoulder. "If I'm going to rely on your ability to help me solve this case, I'll do you the courtesy of speaking plainly. So, did he show you anything?"

I puffed up my cheeks and blew out, ignoring Edith's frown. "Not much. I understand he used to belong to a pastry chef in Scottsdale. Apparently, I haven't given him the right bribe yet." I clasped my hands and stared at my knuckles.

"I need the details of what you saw."

My head jerked up. He had his blue eyes fastened on me. Again, a direct request.

"Marty, you've had a tough week, and you're not thinking straight." Edith's mismatched Husky eyes gave off an *I'll burn a hole in your face* intensity. My face, not Bowers'.

Mortified, I glanced from sister to sister. Dymphna looked back with interest. And doubt. Reading a news story that made fun of your future sister-in-law's penchant for talking to animals was one thing. Listening to her repeat what a goat showed her required a level of belief I didn't expect. My earlier vow to own my abilities slipped out of the room.

"The thing is..." I shook my head. "I'll tell you later."

"Oh, come on." Dymphna leaned back in her chair. She looked like a queen pronouncing judgement. "Don't treat us like children. If it has something to do with what happened to Marty, I want to hear it no matter how bad it is."

When I hesitated, she continued. "We're all family here, Frankie." Dymphna had the same sharp expression in her eyes she'd worn when holding a gun on the man who had killed her boyfriend. "You can tell us anything. We won't judge you."

Wouldn't they? And then I locked onto her first sentence. *We're all family here.* Did that mean they wouldn't disown me because I was a freak? Should I get it in writing? Insecure Frankie was starting to annoy me.

I began at the beginning with Eric's murder, including every detail down to the colored lights from the fireworks. Then I repeated the same process with Mr. G's death.

"I still can't figure out what any of this has to do with Bennett's Grazers."

"The place where I climbed a hill and trip over my own feet." Bowers made a noise of disgust.

My voice lowered to a whisper. "I *know* you didn't fall. I saw a hand push you."

When I made my pronouncement, Bowers' grip on me tightened. "You saw someone push me? Who?"

Edith scrutinized me with clenched teeth and a pulsing jaw, and I knew what was on her mind. That I was messing with her injured, confused baby brother. I'd sleep with one eye open tonight.

"Pierre only showed me a hand reach out and shove. No face."

"Does Juanita know about this?"

I lowered my chin. "Seriously? You want me to tell her about a hand in an image sent to me by a goat?"

"Not a good idea, Marty." Edith rested her chin on her fist.

"I know, but it's too important not to share. She might find the information useful."

Dymphna leaned forward. "Marty, you've been through a lot. Maybe you should rest before discussing...things."

Edith snorted. "Things that might affect your career if you repeat them."

He held up a hand to stop further discussion, pinning me with his gaze. "Two of the men who were murdered. The killer put them in your car. Why?"

"Got me. Unless... Jacob was following me and Edith. He's an employee at Bennett's. It was just the once, but maybe it wasn't the first time. What if it's just the first time we spotted him?"

"No one could have followed us without my knowing."

At Edith's boast, Dymphna stood and plucked Windy from the floor. "Windy has to pee." But first she strolled to the couch and held out her dog. "Say goodnight to Snookum's." She waited until Bowers kissed the dog's fluffy head.

"You said Pierre had a previous owner. A pastry chef. Any idea who?"

I gasped. "Do you think he's involved?"

Bowers smirked. "I thought he or she would be able to suggest an incentive that would get the goat to—to refresh his memory."

So logical, yet I hadn't thought of it. Narrowing my eyes in Edith's direction, I said, "Did Gutierrez visit him before she removed your tracking device? Maybe you have the address."

"You put a tracking device on Juanita's car?" Bowers

threw back his head and shouted a laugh. He held up a hand and they hi-fived.

"I'll get the address," Edith said as she settled down from her emotional display.

While she typed into her phone, Bowers leaned his head in. "Did you sneak into my room at the hospital?"

I gaped. "Did I what?"

"It's just ... I'm positive you were talking to me that first night. Teasing me about being on the case." He put air quotes around that last bit.

The night of his fall. I remembered reaching out to him. Great goats above, he'd *heard* me.

"I know it's crazy. The meds. The head injury. It just seemed so real."

If I acted on the idea I had, would he hate me forever? On the plus side, it would save time.

"It must have been wishful—"

I grabbed his hand in both of mine and opened my mental doorway. As soon as our hands connected, electricity shot up my arm and my grip tightened. Snippets of Bennett's Grazers flashed in front of me from Bowers' point of view. The hillside as he climbed. The view from the top. The burnt-out house across the street. A figure waiting for him by the goats. I felt his determination just before my muscles tightened in response to a yell. "Behind you!" A thump in the center of my back, sending me forward into a free fall.

The connection broke when I landed on my face at Edith's feet. Twisting my head, I knew Bowers had seen it all by the way his eyes struggled to remain in his skull.

Both of us were breathing hard. Dymphna stood inside the sliding door, clutching Windy to her chest. Edith, well, Edith sat perfectly still.

"I'm so sorry. But it was for your own good."

He flinched when I reached for him and the flurry of emotions crossing his face...well, none of them were good.

"I'll just—" I moved to the kitchen.

"Frankie, wait."

Fighting back tears, I kept walking. Why did I feel as if I'd attacked my fiancé? I only wanted to help. All I'd done was confirm he had climbed the hill. I'd alienated my fiancé for a worthless bit of information.

I ran a washrag over the clean sink and scrubbed at an imaginary spot. As I turned off the faucet, it occurred to me I could access his memories, even though he couldn't. And I'd learned something new. Someone else had been there. Someone on his side. Someone who'd called out a warning. Most likely the same person had dialed 9-1-1.

Staying in the kitchen the rest of the night was not an option. I squared my shoulders and returned to the scene of the mental crime. Edith and Bowers looked up from their conversation.

"Come here."

He patted the couch cushion next to him. Edith got up and strolled to the back door, staring out with her hands on her hips. I sat as far from him as possible. When he held out his hand, I shrank back.

"You need to do it again. See what else is in there."

"No." I shook my head. "It was an impulse. A bad idea. I'm so sorry."

"I'm asking you to help me."

My lower lip trembled. "What if I see something you don't want me to?"

"Like what?"

"I don't know. You with an old girlfriend."

He made a strangling sound. "I wish you hadn't said that."

"Or details from an especially horrid case."

"Stop giving me ideas. You're making a difficult situation worse." After hesitating, he reached for me again. This time, I took his hand.

WHEN BOWERS YAWNED, I told him he should get some sleep. My second attempt to access his memories bombed. After ten minutes of nothing but sweaty palms, I gave up. The poor thing tried to cover his relief. Not that I blamed him. I wouldn't want me rummaging through my head, either.

Maybe I succeeded the first time because I caught him by surprise. Or because I was determined and emotional. Was it possible to apply my pet psychic methods to humans in times of overwhelming stress? Next time I was ready to pass out from anxiety, I'd give it a shot. Or not.

When I went to get the bed ready, Dymphna lay in the middle fully dressed and snoring. The television played a sitcom rerun on low. Windy's head drooped off the edge of the bed. She looked like a wet noodle. I pulled the extra blankets and sheets that Dymphna had purchased out of the shopping bag, tossed one to Edith, and dropped one on the floor for me.

As I unfolded the final blanket, I said, "Looks like it's the couch for you after all, mister."

After I'd tucked him in, Bowers took hold of my wrist. Not my hand. "Where is it?"

"Where is what?"

"I need to see my diary. Would you get it for me?"

He knew me so well. Squashing the impulse to inform him as to the condition of his home office, especially the desk, I left that news for later and retrieved his book.

When it wasn't in my purse, I took advantage of Edith's visit to the washroom and found it in her backpack. Holding the book just out of reach, I said, "Promise you'll share any insights that come to you."

"Don't I always?"

Either he was joking, or his memory impairment was much worse than I thought.

After flipping to the middle of the book to his last entries, he scanned the page. Then he scanned it again, chewing on his bottom lip.

"Don't stay up too late."

He was so absorbed in the diary that he didn't respond, but he didn't have to say anything. As he flipped between the last few pages, his forehead wrinkled in thought, I tingled from the top of my head to the tips of my toes. Bowers was here. Not tucked away in the hospital, but here. In my living room. And still speaking to me.

The happy tingles subsided. But was he happy? Bowers once told me it wasn't my job to solve his problems. His memory loss was a problem, but to overcome it, he had to know what had happened on that hill. Gutierrez was working the case along with others in his department, but as far as I knew, none of them considered the goat a serious witness. Therefore, they'd ignore their best source of information.

In this case, he was wrong. It was my turn to take care of him.

FIFTY-THREE

Bowers fell asleep long before Edith or I did. Seeing him snuggled under the covers on my couch reminded me of the first time he'd spent the night at my place after I'd stupidly placed myself in a dangerous situation. He had a change of clothes in his car's trunk and slept on the same couch. It felt like ages ago.

After adjusting his blanket, I got a glass of water from the kitchen. Edith followed.

She held out a hand for a cup. I pulled two out of the cupboard and passed one to her. She made an *after you* motion, so I filled mine from the dispenser on the refrigerator.

"I've been thinking."

The idea of Edith Bowers volunteering information shocked me into blurting out, "You've what?"

"Your water's overflowing."

Jerking the cup back, I took a few swallows while I considered my approach. If I looked interested, would she clamp her mouth shut like a dog refusing to release a chicken bone? Or did she *want* me to prod her into sharing more?

Though I'd never admit it, Edith had impressed me with her tough, fearless approach. And she knew things. Like how to put a tracker on a police car. It wasn't as if I cared if she respected me or not. It wouldn't have a tremendous impact on my life. Still, it would be nice if she didn't see me as a complete dunce. So, I took my time responding. Too much time.

"If you're not interested—" She turned away.

"I'm interested."

After a curt nod, she took a seat at the kitchen table, careful to lift the chair so it didn't scrape against the linoleum. I followed suit after grabbing a few of Dymphna's cookies to share.

She broke off a piece and popped it in her mouth. "So, Luther Mendoza. Nobody knows where he is right now. No one we've talked to so far," she clarified. "Since he hasn't turned up in your car, he might be alive."

"You mean he's just an irresponsible creep?" I clenched my hands. "I wish I'd had a photograph of Luther when I talked to..."

Edith raised both eyebrows.

I'd been about to mention Pierre. After what happened in the living room, I thought it best to stick to tangible facts.

"Gator wasn't worried about Eric. In fact, he was happy Eric was out of his life. Since these guys all knew each other, wouldn't they know if one of them showed signs of being a homicidal maniac? And if they thought they were in danger, wouldn't they be worried when one of them disappeared? Randy was, but wouldn't the rest of them talk to each other?"

"True. Luther's uncle wasn't worried about him, but if

Luther is the one killing his friends, he wouldn't be, would he?"

I objected. "Lola Falana thought her boyfriend's disappearance was unusual but not suspicious."

"She seemed..." Edith searched for the word. "Gullible. Women who dream their bad boy lover is going to turn a new leaf for love are...naïve."

She'd been about to say stupid. I was sure of it. "Another thing." I hesitated, uncertain how she'd take the next bit of information. Gratitude wasn't on the table, but I hoped she wouldn't walk out and make her next mission to get Bowers to dump me.

"Luther, and I'm not saying he isn't involved in the killings, but Luther didn't pull the trigger. Or the knife. I saw it."

"Did you see the killer's face?"

"Well, no. But I saw his eyebrows. That's why I'm sure it was Paul Buglio."

"So you say after the fact."

Scooting my chair back, I winced at the noise. I lowered my voice to a whisper to make up for it. "I'm going back to bed."

"Not so fast, French Fry. What's the story with George Dakos? How did he know Marty was in the hospital?"

"He heard it on the—" It hit me. The police were keeping Bowers' accident quiet. Mr. G wouldn't have heard it on the radio. Or television news. How *did* he know?

"He must have been the witness."

"Exactly. And now he's dead. I don't get why you keep sticking up for Luther Mendoza, but your instincts may be right."

"They are?"

"They might be. Maybe George Dakos wasn't the only witness to Marty's fall."

As her meaning sunk in, my tummy twisted. "You mean Luther was there, too?"

"That might explain why he's...unavailable."

He wasn't there. Not unless he had wandered out of view. I groaned. Not unless he was behind Bowers, ready to push him down the hill. "You think he's dead?" I preferred him dead to being a killer.

"We need to consider the possibility."

No. I would not accept that Luther was permanently out of the picture. Nor would I accept he had pushed Bowers. That man would return to his woman and child if I had to drag him back from the netherworld.

"That's a lot to digest," I said, standing. Instead of following suit, her hand shot out, and she twisted my wrist until I was forced to bend close to her.

"If you cause a setback in Marty's recovery, there will be no wedding. Because you won't be around. Understand?"

I sunk my teeth into her hand until she let go with a yell. "He's my fiancé. I would never hurt him. If you don't get that, you're an idiot."

Still rubbing my wrist, I stepped through the swinging door. Two hands pushed my shoulders, and I went sprawling.

"Son-of-a—"

On my knees, I lunged for her leg and wrapped my arms around her ankle, pulling hard. She swore as she landed on her fanny.

"Frankie! Edith!" Bowers struggled to his feet.

I stood and dusted off my knees. "See what you did you horse's rear end?"

"He's already traumatized from whatever you did to him." A hand slapped the back of my head. I whirled and wrapped a handful of Edith's long hair around my hand and yanked hard. It's nearly impossible to navigate when someone has hold of your hair. Unless you kick them in the knee.

When Dymphna ran into the room, I smothered my cry with the hand not holding her sister's hair. Edith's release depended on my ability to untangle my engagement ring.

"Marty, are you all right?"

When she ushered him, limping, back to the couch, the fight ended, though it took Dymphna's help to free her sister's head from my hand.

Bowers, breathing as hard as if he'd taken part in the fight, pressed his lips together in a thin line while Dymphna rubbed his arm and made soothing noises.

"Explain. Now."

Edith and I looked at each other and drew the same conclusion. Explaining would make us sound like fools.

"We're only concerned about you, Marty."

"You have a funny way of showing it. Attacking my fiancé."

It had been a while since I'd seen him so angry. To calm him, I fell on my sword.

"It's my fault. I asked her to show me some moves so I could protect myself."

"I know some moves," Dymphna murmured.

His anger dissipated. "Oh. It's not a bad idea."

Edith nodded. "She did well for her first lesson."

When I replayed the "lesson" in my head, the corners of my mouth wouldn't stay put. A laugh snorted out my nose. Edith quivered, trying to hold it in, but suddenly, we were both laughing. Hysterical, tears-streaming-down-our-faces laughter.

"You both are nuts. I'm going back to bed." Dymphna left us with a disgusted glare.

We got Bowers situated again and got ready for bed ourselves.

After Edith's breathing evened out in sleep, I searched the internet on my cell phone. I'd had an idea. Granted, it was a silly idea, but it was better than accepting Luther might be dead. After I sent a few carefully worded emails, I shut off my phone and settled under my covers. It was my last shot at finding Luther, and I hoped it worked.

FIFTY-FOUR

Between us, we got a little sleep that night, but not much. Bowers refused his pain medication, so every time he groaned, two heads popped up in the dark and stared at him to make sure he wouldn't wake and need something. Like the pain medication he refused to take. Edith and I resembled whack-a-moles except for the missing teenager with a bat.

By six a.m., I had given up on sleep. Edith was curled up in a blanket tucked between the couch and the coffee table, and Bowers snored lightly from the couch.

Noises originating in the kitchen pulled me out of my semi-conscious state. When I investigated, Dymphna was humming a tune and fixing a breakfast worthy of a lumberjack. Thank goodness one of us cooked.

After slipping into jeans and a gray t-shirt, I joined her in the kitchen. My hairy guests were still quiet, but I thought checking on them might send them into a cacophony of bleats and wake Bowers.

Edith followed me in wearing blue sweatpants with her original red t-shirt.

"Do you need to use my washing machine?"

Dymphna chuckled. "When she gets ripe, we'll tackle and strip her."

"Hilarious," Edith mumbled, joining me at the table. We devoured the salty bacon, buttery potatoes, and Vermont maple syrup covered pancakes in record time. It helped that neither of us engaged the other in conversation. Dymphna followed up with sourdough toast and two fried eggs for each of our plates.

"I'm going to need an elastic waistband." That didn't stop me from finishing. "You need to give me your grocery receipts."

Of course, she declined.

When the doorbell rang, Edith said she'd get it. Since it was my house, I foolishly thought the visitor was for me. She wasn't. At least not at first.

I found Bowers awake and sitting up. He had a guest. My fiancé had folded his blankets and put on sweatpants and an Arizona Cardinals t-shirt. His stretched-out leg rested on the coffee table. Gutierrez sat next to him, and when I walked in, she crossed her arms and sent me a glare.

"Martin said you have something you want to share with me. Something you didn't tell me before. You remember. When I asked if you knew anything."

"I do?" My fiancé ignored my pleading glance. Edith plopped onto the only spot left on the couch and squeezed her brother's shoulder in the manner of one anticipating an entertaining movie. The motion startled Emily from sleep, and she launched off Bowers' lap.

Sweatpants don't protect you from kitty claws like jeans do. While he swore, Gutierrez caught her mid-flight and pulled her in for soothing words, running her fingernails down the cat's back. That move is second only to catnip.

Emily met her gaze and smacked her face, minus claws. It was a warning smack. A surprised Gutierrez dropped her, and my cat strutted into the kitchen. Mission accomplished.

"Cats usually love me," she muttered.

"Not when you smell like a Bernese Mountain dog-Labrador mix," I mumbled, repeating Emily's thought out loud without meaning to.

The *zing* from Gutierrez hit me dead center, so hard my chair flipped. My backward somersault ended with me on my butt.

Bowers struggled to get up, so I held out a hand and hopped to my feet. "No damage."

Bowers looked from Gutierrez to me. Wariness etched his features. I shrugged and pointed after Emily. He hid a smirk.

The detective stood. "I don't have time for this."

"Hold on, Juanita. It'll only take a minute."

Unable to refuse a request from her injured colleague, the detective resumed her seat. "Well? I have things to do. Spill it."

One way I avoid looking like an idiot is by not volunteering information. If Gutierrez wanted me to share what Pierre told me, she'd have to work for it. "Tell me what you want to know."

"Frankie." Bowers sounded tired and not a bit amused. "Just tell Juanita what you told me last night."

"Bowers was pushed." There. I'd said it.

Her perfectly plucked eyebrows disappeared into the mass of curls sweeping her forehead. She busied herself extracting her notebook from her purse to cover her shock.

Taking a steadying breath, I let myself relive the vision. "He was standing on the edge of the hill next to Bennett's

Grazers, looking down at something. A hand reached out and pushed him."

"What kind of hand?"

"One with five fingers."

She growled. "A man's hand with dirty, spatulated fingernails? A woman's slim hand with polished nails?"

Her vivid descriptions helped me zero in on the details. "No nail polish or dirt. Thick fingers. I assumed it was a man, but it might have been a hardy woman."

"Did you get a glimpse of a shirt sleeve?"

Good question. "Funny, I hadn't thought of that. But no."

She exchanged a glance with Bowers. "So, our guy, if it was a guy, was bare-chested, or wearing short sleeves, which doesn't help. Not on a farm."

When he spoke, Bowers sounded only slightly less irritated than Gutierrez, though I suspected his was self-induced. What's wrong with pain pills? "When you say I was looking down, be more specific. At the ground at my feet? Something on the hillside? The burnt-out mess across the road?"

"You remember the construction site?" Gutierrez asked.

Hoping to spare Bowers from reliving last night, I stood. "That's enough for now."

But it wasn't. Gutierrez made me repeat my other two *vision-thingies,* interrupting with questions. How tall were the men? What color hair? Did either of them limp? I told her what I recalled, but between the fireworks and their wide-brimmed hats and bandanas—and the fact that I was seeing them from the eye-level of a goat—my information didn't amount to much, except I did stress I thought the one who did the killing was Paul Burgio.

"Hard to miss those eyebrows. One more thing. George

Dakos witnessed the fall. He tried to warn Bowers and most likely was the person who dialed 9-1-1."

That led to another round of questions. Gutierrez gave me a lingering look before she left. Like she was trying to figure something out. Which she was. How I knew she'd been in contact with a Bernese Mountain dog-Labrador mix.

Edith sat with her arms crossed and her features compressed in an angry stare, which she sent my way.

"I don't see why you should believe I can communicate with animals. I didn't. At least when it started. I thought it was a brain tumor. But it's not. It's my—how did your sister put it?—my party trick. Except it's real. Sometimes it's inconvenient. Sometimes it's horrible. But it's always right. At least as far as the animal sees it."

She gestured toward the backyard. "Then why don't you just ask Pierre who did it?"

"Because I live for challenges," I snapped.

One eyebrow lifted up to acknowledge my sarcasm. "So? Why don't we have an answer?"

"Because animals don't speak in complex sentences. Sometimes a word. Usually an image that makes sense to them, but not to me. At least not until I look at it from their perspective. And he's distracted by the kid right now."

"That's convenient."

"Edith," Bowers began, but I held up a hand.

"I got this. If you're so smart, decipher the meaning in Pierre's latest message. I showed him Bowers standing on that blasted hill. I showed him Paul Burgio. You know, hoping for a reaction. Do you know what he gave me in return? Bowers standing at the *base* of the hill, which suddenly shrunk as Bowers turned into a giant Gulliver. So, Miss High and Mighty, what does it mean?"

"Where was Paul?"

Edith's question showed great insight and attention to detail. Did that mean she took me seriously?

"He wasn't there." I frowned. "He wasn't there."

The three of us considered the implications in silence.

"I was at the base of the hill?" Bowers asked. "Maybe that means I was standing in the wrong place to find whatever I was looking for."

I crossed my arms and dug the toe of my shoe into the rug, looking for the words to express myself without coming across as a mystic maniac. "A glowing light surrounded you. I wondered if it was because Pierre seems to like you. A lot."

"Like me?"

"He was really happy to find out you weren't dead. There is another possibility. I've found animals like to do things for people they like. What if he was trying to light your way to the solution?"

Edith cocked her head at her brother. "How would Pierre know what you were after? Also, I've walked along the base of the hill. There's nothing there except shrubs and dirt. And why did the hillside disappear? Erosion?" She added a snarky lift to her upper lip.

"Exactly," I agreed, placing my hand on my cheek. "Which will take thousands of years. Pierre is seeing the future. And since Bowers is there, he's telling me my fiancé is immortal."

"We're wasting time. Marty? What do you think?"

"I like the sound of being immortal."

Edith threw up her hands.

"So." I upped my volume to override whatever smart-mouthed comment she had ready. "What is Pierre trying to tell us?" I craned my neck to get a view of my temporary guests, as if looking at them would bring clarity. "I've been sending him images of that hill and—sorry honey—your fall."

He grinned. "Did you at least have me fall gracefully?"

"Uh, sure. He typically responds with a murder. I guess I should be grateful he skipped that show this time."

"But the murders didn't happen near the hillside."

"No. At the fairgrounds."

He spread his hands. "Maybe the hill has nothing to do with the murders."

Edith glanced at her brother. "Huh."

When it became obvious we'd tapped the well of ideas, Edith and I prepared to leave for some alleged errands. Bowers, now tucking into his own breakfast, called us over. He knew I had an appointment, and Edith planned to tag along. He also knew we wouldn't come straight back because he was familiar with both our habits. After I kissed his forehead and Edith patted his head, he grabbed his sister's wrist. "Watch out for her."

She gave him a curt nod and held out her hand for my keys. Again, it wasn't worth an argument, so I handed them over and kissed my fiancé's forehead once more. "Don't worry. I'll keep Edith safe."

His snort set off a coughing fit that brought Dymphna into the room. We left her to minister to her baby brother.

FIFTY-FIVE

As soon as I saw Sampson and Delilah, I wanted to kill them. Not from animosity, but to put them out of their misery. I'd never tried talking to a fish. Following the owner down a hallway of a one-story stucco home, I contemplated how to achieve underwater communication.

Jared, just out of his teens, took us to a spare room used for storage. When he opened the door, darkness met us. He kept the drapes pulled shut, treating his pets like the victims of a crazed kidnapper.

I'd already opened the doorway to my mind. The minute I stepped into the room, my stomach heaved with queasiness.

When the kid flicked a switch, I expected a light to snap on. Instead, pounding music came from the side of the room that I assume held speakers. My heart clenched.

"Turn it off! Turn it off!"

He did so, though he complained that the fish enjoyed it.

"They do not," I snapped. "You're vibrating their water

and stressing them out. Try some ambient music if you must."

"Fine," he mumbled, flipping the light switch. I curled my lip and gasped when I saw the bowl and its depressing contents. The two goldfish floated in a large fishbowl, the kind you see in cartoons. There wasn't room to move.

Sampson should have been gold, and Delilah had hints of red on white, but both had the pale pallor of the undead. They hovered around the surface of the water, gasping for oxygen.

"Okay, buddy. First things first. The only reason Sampson is terrorizing Delilah is because he can't pummel you with his fins."

"How do you know they aren't mating?" He said it with a sneer, but by then I knew that was his natural delivery.

I crossed the room, skirting an electric guitar, a pile of clothing, and several cardboard boxes. Edith, who I'd introduced as my assistant, followed me inside. Sticking a finger in the water, I said, "Too cold. And mating season, under the right conditions, is in the Spring." My words carried my own sneer, though some of it was natural repulsion from the condition of the water. I scrubbed my finger against my jeans.

Edith leaned over the bowl and sniffed. "Their chances would be better if we dumped them in a lake."

She was right, but I shushed her. "Let's start with the obvious. You need a tank. Twenty gallons minimum. You need a filter, lights, running water." I ran a skeptical gaze over him and corrected. "*Gently* running water. *Clean* water, which means you change it. When's the last time you switched out their water?"

"I just did it yesterday. Maybe the day before."

Goldfish can remember three months' worth of information. I sent an image of Jared doing as he said he'd done. Since I'd never met a fish capable of telling time, I had a dilemma.

"How often are you in here every day?"

"Once. To feed them." I narrowed my eyes. "And change their water," he added.

Replaying the movie of Jared changing the water, I accompanied it with the lights going on and off. They sent me back a black screen of darkness, indicating it had been many, many visits since their caretaker had given them fresh water.

These fish were in danger. Would Jared heed my advice? I thought not. He had his face buried in his cellphone, his attention already off his suffering pets.

"Why did you call me?"

He finished typing with his thumbs and looked up. "My girlfriend saw them and got scared."

Decision made. I was determined to escort these fish to a safe harbor, and that meant making things up.

"Under the 2019 Goldfish Act, I am hereby confiscating your fish."

Edith's eyebrows inched up.

"Okay."

I caught the relief, but I didn't trust it.

"And you must sign a form stating you will not purchase replacement fish when we're done."

"My dad says I shouldn't sign anything without reading it."

"Of course, you can read it. I don't have one handy. I didn't realize the severity of the situation. You can write the entire thing in your handwriting. But first, I need a large plastic bag."

When I left with the handwritten form in one hand and

the goldfish bagged up with fresh water in the other, the only thing I was missing was my fifty bucks. At the mention of money, Jared displayed a mental acuity and verbal dexterity that surprised me.

"You're taking the fish."

"I am."

"Then what am I paying you for? You're not helping me with my fish. They're *your* fish now. Charge yourself."

Edith said she'd be right with me. By the time she slipped into the driver's seat, she held three tens, three fives, three singles, and a handful of quarters. She dumped them into the cup holder. "I thought you should be paid."

I stared at the money, searching for bloodstains. Part of me wanted to go back to the house and make sure Jared was in one piece. She read my mind. "I didn't hurt him. Just pointed out his obligation to pay for services rendered."

"Thanks," I said, stuffing the money in my back pocket.

She started the car. "Where do we dump the fish?"

After dialing the number of a one-time client and explaining the situation, I gave my future SIL directions to Sampson and Delilah's new home.

FIFTY-SIX

After we'd dropped off Sampson and Delilah at a home equipped with a thirty-foot tank, Edith drove away as if she had a destination in mind.

"Care to let me in on where we're going?"

"The Back Room."

That didn't sound good. "What's that? A bordello? A den of drug dealers? A secret society of weapons dealers?"

"A restaurant."

"Oh." I frowned. "That's nice of you, but I'd rather not stop for a meal."

"We're not eating."

And that's all she'd tell me. This Scary Sister persona might be handy if we found ourselves locked in a toilet stall, barricaded against an invading army, but Edith's *strong and quiet* attitude was wearing on me. I reciprocated and refused to speak again until she begged me to. Which she never would.

Why would we go to a restaurant? We'd already met with Lola Falana at Nemo's. Were all our suspects restaurant employees? Suspects I didn't know about because Scary Sister wouldn't share information?

A name like The Back Room suggested a seedy dive with floor mats that smelled of stale beer and a resident drunk ensconced at the end of the bar. Maybe a rough biker gang hangout. Though, honestly, all the motorcycle riders I knew were courteous. And she was taking us through Scottsdale, which was cute and clean in a touristy way. And expensive. If we were on our way to confront evil doers, they were successful at their craft.

Just as I decided I didn't know *all* of Scottsdale, and maybe there were *neighborhoods,* a euphemism for pockets of crime, she turned off the main road onto a side street lined with a sushi house, an organic market, and a pub. Tucked into the corner of the block, down a short walkway surrounded by gravel and verbena shrubs, The Back Door welcomed tourists and businesspeople to enter through the open French Doors. A few late diners trickled in ahead of us.

On either side of the entry doors, bougainvilleas overflowed with fuchsia-colored flowers, showing off like the tarts of the plant world and shaming the bright orange-and-red birds-of-paradise, who next to them look skimpy. To the left, a framed chalkboard on a stand announced today's specials. Bison burgers with crispy Walla Walla onions and homemade bar-b-q sauce. Grilled salmon with a baby arugula and spiced, candied walnut salad. A vegetarian lunch with a fancy name, which, practically speaking, was just another salad.

The restaurant dedicated the lower half of the board to dessert. In pink and yellow chalk, someone with better handwriting than I could hope for had written *Baked Prickly Pears with fresh whipped cream, Crème brûlée oatmeal with handmade vanilla bean ice cream,* and *French strawberry and vanilla Charlotte.* I didn't know which was French, the strawberries or the Charlotte. Dessert cost more than the entrees.

"Not that way."

Edith led me around the corner to an alley lined with dumpsters. The back door to The Back Door stood open, and a guy in a white shirt, black pants and a white apron leaned against the wall, smoking a cigarette. He came to attention and tried to block our entry, but Edith bumped him with her shoulder, hard, and said, "We're friends of Charlie's."

He shrugged and stepped aside. Edith took hold of my arm and lowered her voice. "I'm only doing this because my brother seems to trust you."

Before I could thank her for this dubious compliment, she strode inside.

Since the lunch rush was over, the only busy employee aside from the dishwasher and an occasional server passing through was a round man in his thirties with a tiny mustache. He wore his brown hair short and slicked into a part on the left side of his head. He hovered over an explosion of color disguised as a cake. White frosting peeked out from between candied oranges, lemons, and limes. After placing the final orange slice in place, he stood back and admired his creation.

"Charles Beaumont?"

He turned to Edith and beamed. "A masterpiece. Wouldn't you agree?"

She spared the dessert a glance. "Sure."

Dissatisfied with her response, he looked to me.

"It's pretty."

His sigh carried the disappointment of one who has just

inherited Gainsborough's *Blue Boy* only to discover the person he most wanted to impress was colorblind. Shaking off his personal feelings like a wet dog, he became businesslike. "I'm booked solid through January. Anyway, Penelope handles all my bookings."

"We're here about the goat."

At these simple words from Edith, a transformation came over the pastry chef. His eyes brightened, his round cheeks puffed up, and a smile of pure delight took over his face. He grabbed Edith's arm with his pudgy fingers. "*Monsieur Pierre Petit Crutte?*"

He pronounced *petit* pe-tee, and the last word sounded as if he were clearing his throat.

So, this was Pierre's buddy. The one who turned a walking garbage pail into a connoisseur of fine foods. The one who set up the roadblock to accessing memories I desperately wanted to see.

The hostess, or possibly the manager, walked through the swinging door from the dining area in time to hear the name. She wore her blond hair pulled back in a severe bun and a form-fitting, black, sleeveless sheath over her compact body.

"Are you talking about that stupid goat again?"

Ah. The girlfriend.

He winced. "Pierre is *not* stupid."

"I'm glad to hear that," I murmured.

"How is my little dumpling?"

"I thought *I* was your little dumpling?" she snapped, approaching us with determined, clicking steps in her high heels.

"Of course you are, Penelope." If he meant to appease her, he should have thrown some emotion behind his words.

"The goat's fine," Edith said. "How long ago did you give him to Bennett's Grazers?"

"Eighteen days, six hours," he glanced at his watch, "and twenty-three minutes. I will never forget the betrayal in his eyes."

"Creepy eyes," Penelope added.

"Soulful eyes," he countered. "The eyes of an innocent."

"In fact," I added, "he's been such a good boy we wanted to offer him a treat."

Edith shot me a glance I couldn't interpret, which made me nervous.

Charles clapped his hands in rapid succession. "An apple tarte Tatin. So simple, but the magic is in my dough. Oh! Or a buttery Madelaine, one that would melt in your mouth." He closed his eyes and inhaled. "Maybe a blackberry clafoutis, a recipe of my own making."

Penelope stepped in front of her boyfriend. "Stop it. That—that—ridiculous, overbearing animal is all you talk about. Do you think Pierre would like this? I wonder what Pierre is up to? It drives me mad."

"Nonsense," her boyfriend soothed. "I have three loves. Pierre, pastries, and you."

"You named me last." She spun to face us. "Do you know he actually called out Pierre's name when we were snuggling?"

"Pierre. Penelope. They're easy to get confused when my mind is on my pastries."

"Your mind is supposed to be on me."

Edith ignored the percolating spat. "Do you have anything handy? Readymade that we could take with us? We're in a hurry."

With the exit of his opportunity to create something worthy of Pierre, the pastry chef deflated.

"There are some cookies in the front display," Penelope said, already on her way out the swinging door. "I'll get you a few and you can leave."

"But they're not fresh," he called after her. Fresh enough to sell to customers, but not fresh enough for *Monsieur Pierre Petit Crotte*.

FIFTY-SEVEN

Edith handed me the bag of madeleines. I accepted them with joy.

"Pierre is going to freak." Maybe he'd explain the minuscule mountain to me. "Why did you want to know how long ago Pierre and Charlie parted?"

"We've assumed the goat was in Del Bennett's possession when the murders happened. I wanted confirmation."

When a patrol car passed going the other direction, my excitement waned. "Do you think the farmer knows we've got his goats?"

"They weren't his when we freed them. As for if he knows about the theft, possibly."

"Is kidnapping goats a felony?"

"Probably."

"Because prison doesn't sound comfortable."

"Prison isn't so bad. At least in this country."

I gaped. Bowers' scary sister was a jailbird.

"It's funny that Del Bennett sold those goats at this particular moment," she said.

Angling in my seat, I studied her profile. She kept her face stoic, but the underlying censure in her tone irked me.

"It's my fault Pierre almost wound up barbecued. Is that what you mean?"

"You *were* making an obvious fuss over him."

"And goodness knows that's a reason to kill an animal."

She pursed her lips. "Makes me wonder why he considers you talking to the goat a threat. How did he know what you were doing? From the outside, you looked like a crazy woman lurking around an animal."

"You know Paul Simpson? The reporter? He's mentioned me a few times."

"Eleven times. I've read the articles. You're right. It was a coincidence that Del chose those three goats for the meat market." She grinned. "The articles weren't flattering."

But what if Del Bennett looked past the reporter's snide comments? Would he consider me a threat? I didn't want to be a threat to anyone, especially not someone who might have pushed my fiancé down a hill. So transfixed was I on the idea, I didn't realize we'd arrived home. A gold sedan blocked the driveway, so Edith pulled up in front of the house.

"Expecting company?"

"Maybe it's someone from work," I said, sounding more upbeat than I felt. His fellow detectives shouldn't put pressure on him. Not while he was still weak.

But it wasn't the police. A tall, sturdy African American woman in a navy-blue suit sat next to Bowers on the couch. She wore minimal makeup, no jewelry except small, gold earrings, and she kept her curly, shoulder-length hair loose. As we came through the front door, she snapped shut the notebook spread open on her knees, impressing me with the leather cover.

Bowers, whose regulation notebook had a flimsy cardboard cover, rested his elbow on the arm of the couch and rubbed his fingers over his brow as if willing his thoughts to come together.

His guest stood.

"I'll stop by again to see if anything new comes to you."

Crossing the room with determined steps, I held out my hand but skipped the welcoming smile. "Frankie Chandler. And you are?"

She took my hand in a firm grip. "Sonia."

The movement revealed a gun belt around her waist. I knew it was a gun belt and not just a sturdy leather belt because there weren't any belt loops around it to hold up her pants. And it held a holster. And a gun, of course. Law enforcement.

"I assume you're from another police department, come to get what you can on Paul Burgio. You may not realize my fiancé is recovering from serious injuries and shouldn't be stressed." I gave her the benefit of the doubt.

"Frankie. It's all right."

Keeping my eyes on her, I said, "No, it's not all right. You need rest. Later, when you recover, you and Sonia can spend hours and hours chatting."

She glanced at Bowers, then me, and finally Edith, who stood by the door, struggling to conceal her grin.

The woman shifted the purse on her shoulder. "It was nice to meet you." Turning her head to Bowers, she added, "I'll be in touch."

Once she left, Edith flopped onto the couch and snuggled up to her baby brother. "What did your *special* friend want with you?"

He twitched at her emphases of *special*. "She's not my friend. She's a colleague."

"What did she want?"

"You know I can't talk about it," he said, with no small amount of satisfaction.

"Were you having a natter about Del Bennett's naughty friends?"

His head jerked to look at her. "Where did you hear that?"

She grinned, triumphant. "I've seen it."

I looked from one to the other, confused.

As she tapped on her phone, I joined them on the couch and peered over her shoulder. Her photo album opened on a picture of Del Bennett with the men who came to visit him the day Pierre pulled his tinkle trick.

"Mario and Frank Scarpetta and their sidekick, Bruno Benetti." Names in tiny lettering hovered next to the faces of all those facing the camera, including Del's.

"Who are they?" I asked.

Edith answered. "Family members."

"The Scarpetta's are obviously related," I began, but Bowers shook his head.

"Not that kind of family."

My eyeballs froze, unable to look away from the photo. "What are they doing in Arizona? Mobsters live in Chicago and New York."

Edith broke out in peals of laughter. The skin around her eyes wrinkled in deep lines. "You are so innocent, French Fry. Don Bollis?"

"Who?"

Bowers picked up the story. "Just last June, *The Arizona Republic* ran an anniversary story about his death. He was an Arizona reporter working on an exposé that linked politicians to organized crime. They bombed his car."

"Ouch." My jaw dropped. "You don't suppose the mob,

or mafia, or whatever you call them attacked you, do you?" A lone killer didn't intimidate me much. A bunch of killers with organizational skills gave me the willies.

He frowned. "My case wouldn't have anything to do with organized crime. Not directly. That would fall under the FBI's jurisdiction."

"You mean like Special Agent Sonia?" Edith was pleased with herself. I was not.

My fists clenched at my sides. "How long have you known?"

For the first time, I saw guilt flash in her eyes. Just a tiny flash, but it was there. "About five minutes after I took the picture."

"And you didn't tell me? I've been trying to talk to the goat of a guy who associates with the mob, and it didn't occur to you to let me know? I can't believe you." My voice lowered to a growl. "You may be clever, but your mean."

Her body jerked. She was holding back a laugh.

Bowers locked eyes with me. "More to the point, you see why Juanita warned you to stay away from Del Bennett. He has dangerous friends, Frankie."

Closing my eyes, I replayed their greeting that day. "Not friends. His shoulders were stiff, like he wasn't pleased to see them. And when he shook hands, he leaned forward to do it, as if keeping his distance."

"That's interesting." Bowers scratched the stubble that had taken over his face in less than twenty-four hours. "Very interesting."

Edith sighed. "Del Bennett associates with mobsters. Is it any wonder you were attacked?"

"It doesn't feel right. I can't remember what I was doing, but I get feelings when I talk about it." A glance skittered in my direction. He coughed. "Call it instincts. No warning bells go off when you say mob." His gaze returned to me, serious this time. "But that doesn't make it less dangerous. From now on, I want you both to leave this case to the professionals."

Edith and I exchanged a glance. She spoke first.

"Sure thing, little brother. I haven't had time to visit with you and get to know your future bride." When she grinned at me, it reminded me of a painting I'd once seen of Mephistopheles, Faustus' dubious helper as he wrestled with the wisdom of selling his soul. "I want to know all about you."

Bowers relaxed back into the couch. "That's a good idea."

And so, she asked me all about the wedding and pretended to look interested. I answered her questions with brief responses because I wasn't as adept at hiding my distraction. It was as my thoughts wandered, I remembered I hadn't given Pierre his treats. And then I noticed the silence.

"Why are the goats so quiet?"

"Because they're not here."

Leaping to my feet, it took every ounce of self-control to keep from strangling Bowers' sister. I strode to the patio door and flung it open. The chicken wire and covering were still in place. Traces of hay littered the cement. The pans of food and water were gone.

With my hands clenched at my sides, I returned to the living room. "You had no right."

"I did what was best for everyone involved."

"You had no right!"

"Frankie." Bowers reached out a hand. He had to settle for holding my fist.

"You had no right." This time, the words came out low and quiet.

"When it comes to protecting those I love, I have every right. What if Del decided to look for the goats? What if he put the pieces together and came here? What if he brought his friends? I'm not willing to take that chance with my family."

She had a point, but I wasn't ready to listen. "How can you be so cold?"

"Frankie, that's enough."

Edith patted her brother's knee. "It's all right, Marty. I don't mind. Someone has to make the tough decisions. I don't expect to be popular."

I continued to glare. "Martyr. Self-righteous martyr. Self-righteous, *arrogant* martyr."

Dymphna, emerging from my bedroom to head for the kitchen, tossed out her opinion. "Don't forget smart-mouthed."

"You've made your point," Bowers said. "It's over. Drop it."

My stomach lurched. "Are you taking her side?"

"I'm taking my side. I'm getting a headache."

Edith considered this a victory. She smirked. When Bowers closed his eyes, I mouthed the word *smug*. She caught me off guard when she stuck out her tongue.

In a weird way, our fighting reminded me of something. The quarrels between siblings. We were acting like...sisters.

Fighting against a pleasurable flush that ran up my insides, I stalked out of the room in search of Dymphna. And the goats.

FIFTY-EIGHT

The argument with Edith threw a spotlight on my need to get the Bowers' girls out of my house. If my life didn't return to normal soon, I'd move out until they all returned to their own homes. Dymphna refused to help me reach my goal.

"I promised," she said, spreading butter over slices of freshly baked bread she had whipped up for our dinner.

"That's not fair. I wasn't in on the decision. Otherwise, I would have kept you from making that promise. It's only right to tell me where my guests have gone." With a quick glance toward the living room, I lowered my volume. "Dymphna, I *need* to talk to those goats."

"Like I said. I promised."

I growled.

She shook her finger at me. "No fighting in front of Marty."

"Marty is in the other room."

Bowers called out from behind the closed door. "But he can hear you."

Note to self. Never, *ever* say anything I didn't want Bowers to hear unless I was in the next county. Dymphna claimed victory in this round, but I wasn't about to forfeit the game.

After we ate dinner, which was the leftover leftovers that were even better the second time around, Dymphna served up the latest cookies. Some kind of crispy treat she deep fried on a branding iron of sorts. Must be a country woman thing.

"Delicious," I exclaimed after my first bite. Holding the cookie up, I said, "Desserts are an art form. You, Dymphna, are an artist."

"No. I'm bored. No offense, Marty. Rosette cookies are a specialty of June's. They're her mother's recipe. I gave them a shot."

"I would never have thought to fry a cookie. And it's so delicate. Not greasy at all. Bakers use so many tools. Irons —" I saw a chance to prod Bowers' memory. "And blowtorches."

He looked up, startled. "Eric White was a welder." After blurting this out, Bowers frowned. "Where did that come from?"

Keeping my face straight, as we hadn't discussed this point with my fiancé, I tapped my chin. "I forget. Who did he work for?"

"Bright Star Construction."

A thrill that coursed through me. Not only had he remembered Eric White, but he'd recalled the place of his employment. The name Bright Star Construction sounded familiar, but I couldn't place it. If Bowers' memory was returning, did I need to chat with the goat again? Maybe the solution would work itself out.

"Juanita mentioned another case that came up when she, um, met with you at the grocery store." He slipped a guarded glance toward Dymphna and lowered his voice to a whisper. "The serial killer."

Dymphna started. "Serial killer?"

Ignoring the sphincter clench that accompanied Bowers' step backward into memory loss, I made a dismissive motion. "No worries. He's only after taxi drivers."

Edith started to speak, but I held up a hand. Bowers needed to reason this out for himself. "What do you think of her theory? That these murders are the work of a serial killer and had nothing to do with Paul Burgio?"

"The man who attacked me. Well, serial killers have multiple victims," he said, wary. "This murderer certainly qualifies."

"That would make me the very unlucky recipient of his handiwork, twice. Too much of a coincidence?"

Dymphna hissed in a breath. "What is she talking about, Marty? You're the victim of a serial killer?"

Drat! I'd forgotten Dymphna didn't know about the corpses in my car. Cars. "Nothing important," I said, waving my hands.

"It may not be important," Dymphna said, "but it's much more interesting than discussing baking methods." She buried her face in the pile of fluff on top of Windy's head and planted a big smooch. "You was making Sweetums snore. Wight, Sweetums?"

She set the dog down. After a long stretch, the pooch headed for her water bowl. "Now, stop treating me like a hothouse flower and catch me up to speed."

I leaned forward and patted Bowers' knee. "Gutierrez made up the serial killer."

Both Bowers and Dymphna exclaimed, "She did?"

"She might have mentioned it to you, repeating the lie she told me. The only reason I'm telling you this is I don't want you wracking your brain trying to remember how you were hunting a nonexistent killer. Not that there isn't a killer, but it's not some maniac targeting taxi drivers. Okay?"

Bowers sank back into the mountain of cushions his sisters had surrounded him with for his comfort. "Thank you. I had no memory of going after a modern-day Ted Bundy. I guess it's going to take longer than I thought to get my head clear."

I don't know what clear heads had to do with families or phone calls, but Dymphna slapped her hand on her leg. "I forgot to tell you, Frankie. Your parents called."

Aw, double poop. "Did you answer the phone?"

"That's how I knew it was them."

Time for damage control. I grabbed my cell phone and dialed, moving to the privacy of my bedroom. Windy snored from the top of my bed, her furry butt positioned squarely in the middle of my pillow. Just as I raised my hand to swat her rump, my mother answered, and I sat on the edge of the mattress.

"Who answered your phone when I called?"

Would it be gutless to pretend I'd hired a maid? It would. "That was Dymphna. Bowers' sister."

"She came all the way from—where does she live?"

"Just north of here. She overreacts to everything and rushed down here as soon as she heard about his accident."

After a pause, my mom said, "There's something you're not telling me."

"Like what?" I made an exaggerated sigh sound. "Fine. If you won't believe me, ask Bowers."

"He's there? Why isn't he at home? I knew you were hiding something. He's an invalid, isn't he. Do you have to cut his food for him?" She lowered her voice. "Will he be able to have children?"

Once I finished blanching, I attempted to drag the conversation back to normalcy. Mistake.

"He and Dymphna are visiting me."

"So, he *could* get on a plane. If he wanted to."

I gave up. "Ask him yourself."

Before handing him the phone, I hit mute. "It's my mother. When I canceled, I told her you'd injured your leg and your ribs. I might have left out the bit about the head injury. And the attempts on your life. She now believes we'll have to adopt our progeny. Can you handle her?"

Fortunately, his injury kept him from running away. I took the phone off mute and handed it to him.

"Mrs. Chandler. So nice of you to check up on my recovery."

Edith opened her mouth to say something smart, and I silenced her with a death stare. If my mother heard additional voices, she'd assume I was having a party to celebrate the canceled flight.

Now that Mom knew I wasn't hiding his demise from her, she did most of the talking. Bowers responded with one-word answers, when she gave him a chance to speak at all.

I pulled Edith aside. "You are taking me to Pierre tonight. Your brother needs peace, and that's only going to happen if he understands what put him in the hospital. I am going to talk to the goat, yes, talk to the goat, and he's going to spill everything, or I'll roast him myself."

She glanced at Bowers and nodded her assent.

Once my fiancé disconnected the call, I covered an enormous yawn, stood, and stretched. "I'm going to hit the hay early tonight."

As hoped, my yawn led to a big mouth-stretch from Bowers. "I have done nothing but sit on this couch all day, but I'm exhausted."

I moved around the coffee table and kissed his forehead. "Healing takes a lot of energy."

Gently, he removed his leg from the coffee table and, with our help, stood. "I better get changed before Dym gets in there. She takes forever."

By the time I chased that sister out of the kitchen and put the dishes away, Bowers had returned to the couch. I checked my watch. Eight pm. Good thing my guests lived on a farm and were used to getting to bed early. Dymphna and Windy were already asleep in my full-size bed. As a precaution, I snuck in and grabbed Windy for a last-minute tinkle, sticking close to guard her against coyotes, bobcats, and hawks as she did her business in my backyard.

She demanded a reward for a job well done. After giving her half a cookie, I managed to slip her back under the covers without waking her pet mommy.

They looked so comfortable it made my eyes droop, and I yawned for real. Fortunately, Edith put on a pot of coffee, and I downed a cup before Bowers called out to tell us to turn off the lights and resume our positions on the floor.

FIFTY-NINE

The first time I tried to get up in the dark, Bowers stirred on the couch and mumbled, "Is everything all right?"

The stubborn mule wouldn't take his pain pills, which would surely have knocked him out for the night. Though I was grateful he seemed more alert than yesterday, my plans didn't include explaining that Edith and I were going for a midnight stroll.

I went to the couch, leaned over him, and kissed his lips. When I brushed my fingers through his hair, he took my hand in his.

"Not really my idea of spending the night with you," he murmured.

"Go to sleep."

After ducking into the hallway for a few minutes, I leaned my head into the living room and didn't reenter until I heard him snoring softly. As I tiptoed to the kitchen, my foot bumped into something soft but solid. Edith's empty pile of covers. The woman moved like a cat.

She wasn't in the kitchen where I left my slip-on tennis

shoes. I hadn't changed out of my sweats and t-shirt, so in a minute, I was ready.

Edith waited outside, and she wasn't alone. Dymphna, her hair disheveled from sleep, clutched a limp Windy in her arms. The dog was getting her beauty sleep, adventure be damned.

"You're not leaving me out this time. I've been the Holy Cross lobby monitor, stay-at-home nursemaid, and resident cook. It's my turn for some action."

After some discussion, we took the Suburban rather than risk the Fairlane's shocks and undercarriage on off-road driving. Dymphna and her pup sat in the middle, leaving me to stare out the window at the passing desert in silhouette. Without traffic, we got to Cave Creek in no time. The open spaces looked creepy in the moonlight.

When I figured out where she was taking us, I freaked out. "You took him back to the farm? How could you take those poor goats back to Del? If they're not on someone's dinner plate already, they will be soon."

"Relax, French Fry. Del doesn't know they're here."

Edith drove past Bennett's Grazers to turn the car around. She parked in front of the burnt construction site. The headlights illuminated the sign in front of the building. Bright Star Construction.

"I *knew* I recognized that name."

"Bright Star?"

"Don't tell me. You figured it out right away."

Her smirk told me yes.

"Edith prides herself on her memory." Dymphna lowered her mouth to Windy's ear. "But she's not the only one with excellent recall." The dog's ear twitched, and she yawned and stretched.

As we piled out of the car, Ghost Woman lay her pup

on the car seat, explaining there were too many nasty beasts that might find Windy delicious.

Once the car headlights were off, and we'd stepped out into the night silence, I expected coyotes, mountain lions, or even a lone serial killer of taxi drivers to leap out at us from the edge of the dirt road. The desert is creepy at night.

Bright security lights shone from the top of Bennett's barn, illuminating the area in front of the house. The peripheral light swept over the goat pen.

"They're in here." She jerked her head toward the ghostly skeletal frame.

"What were you looking for that first day?" I asked Edith. "You said you didn't see what you expected to see, or something like that."

"There weren't any conduits for the electrical wires. If there wasn't any wiring, what caught fire? Unless someone set it deliberately."

I'd had enough coffee that I put two and two together. "So, Eric White was an arsonist and a thief?"

"It makes sense."

"Why would Bright Star Construction want to burn down their own building?"

She gazed across the street at Bennett's Grazers.

My shoulders shivered. "Oh. Del had it torched to keep witnesses away. But witnesses to what?"

Edith didn't have an answer.

I had my mental doorway open, ready for Pierre, but at a sudden burst of static, I clamped my hands over my ears and whimpered. The back of my neck tickled from Windy's frantic attempts to get my attention, so I turned back to the car. The ball of fluff stood on the dashboard, her tiny teeth bared and ready to take on the threat.

Edith turned back. "What's the matter?"

"We've got company."

I felt it before I saw it. A low rumbling that vibrated in my chest. Out of the darkness, two glowing eyes stepped around the corner of the house and into the moonlight. The Doberman Pinscher lowered his head and moved forward in a stalking position.

Even as he threatened us, I congratulated his owners on not cropping his ears. Nasty business. Another rumble made me focus.

When I connected with the animal, he raised his head in surprise. I covered Edith, Dymphna and myself in non-threatening bunny outfits. He returned the favor, surrounding us with a swirling, black mist of doom. Clearly, he considered us a threat.

Edith spoke out of the side of her mouth. "Let me handle this."

"That's not a good idea."

Dymphna backed me up. "Let Frankie handle it."

When I brushed the mist aside and put us in dopey, bright outfits, red noses, and gigantic shoes, the dog gave me his opinion of clowns, grabbing our imaginary ruffled necks one at a time and shaking the life from us.

"You just need to show them who's boss," Scary Sister whispered.

"He is."

"Watch and learn, French Fry."

Dymphna remained frozen in place.

Before I could stop her sister, Edith drew herself up and took a deliberate step forward. "Bad dog."

An involuntary gurgle rose in my throat. The pincher considered *bad dog* high praise.

"Stop talking and let me handle this," I hissed.

"You go ahead, Frankie," Dymphna said.

Rifling through my animal behavior knowledge, I went with authority over bribery. I shot him an image of Edith in a circus tamer's outfit with a dangerous-looking whip in her hand.

The dog growled louder, showing an impressive set of choppers.

Showering him with raw steak and chew bones didn't set off more growling. Neither did it stop his forward movement.

With his fit form and clean teeth, the dog wasn't a wandering stray. The closest house was Del's. In a last effort to keep us from being eaten, I showed him a movie of Del, the Bowers' sisters, and I laughing together. He stopped walking. Del patted Edith on the back, joked with Dymphna, and shook my hand. Then he whistled for the dog, made him sit, and introduced us. We all patted him on the head and said, "Good boy."

While he digested this, I repeated the words out loud. "Good boy."

"I thought you told me to stop talking," Edith snapped.

His deep, answering growl buried her words. Since the dog was here to guard things, he needed a bigger threat to investigate. One he couldn't ignore.

Creating an army of men dressed in teflon and goggles, I sent them on a stealthy crawl onto Del's property from behind the house. I set them far enough back that it would take him a while to confront the danger.

After turning his head to consider the imaginary army, the dog continued in our direction. Catching sight of the plan formulating in his head, I admired the canine's efficiency. He felt addressing the immediate threat would give him plenty of time to take care of the army out back. Included in his calculations were the time to chase us down, dispatch us, and the number of seconds it would take the crawling army to stand once they spotted him.

"Sit!" Edith commanded, striding forward.

The pincher perked up. His prey was coming to him. I grabbed her arm.

"You're not helping."

She pulled loose. "These dogs are used to obeying commands. We just need to find the right one. Stay!"

"Will you shut up and hold still? You're going to get us killed."

"Listen to her," Dymphna whined in a high-pitched voice.

When his sinewy muscles contracted, my own muscles tightened. Panicked, I sent the army image again, doubling the number of invaders.

My voice joined his in a final throaty growl, and we sprung at the same time. His target was Edith's throat. Mine was the same, but with an intention to block.

I threw up my hands and flooded his brain with the scene from every military movie I'd watched. The leader standing, raising an arm, and shouting, *"Charge!"* The enthusiastic cries as his men rose and ran toward their destiny.

Mid-air, the lean body pivoted and landed in a run. He bounded away, headed to the open land beyond the house. His last thought was to save the weaker prey, meaning us, for last.

"We have to be quick," I said, heading for the crumbling entry.

"What just happened? Why did you yell *charge*?"

"Who cares?" Dymphna said, rushing past us.

Pulling out the bag of Madeleines as I jogged, I had a cookie ready when I made it inside the ruins. Pierre, along with his family, waited inside a high fence of chicken wire attached to burnt two-by-fours.

To make sure he knew what the stakes were, I slipped one through the wire. His eyes popped open, and he staggered back a step.

"That's right." I held up the bag and shook it. "Now, *Monsieur Pierre mon Petit Crotte*, you are going to tell me what I want to know."

Careful to make myself clear, I showed Bowers walking toward the hill behind the farm. He glanced around as if searching for something. Then I met Pierre's gaze and waited.

The first murder scene of Eric White slammed into me, and I grabbed a support beam to catch my balance. I persisted, repeating the scene. Mister G's demise sent me to my knees.

Either the goat didn't understand the question, or I was asking the wrong question. About to rephrase my query, the first murder scene played out again. Only this time, right after, a single light glowed in the desert that stretched out at the base of the hillside across the street. That light was joined by a second after Pierre replayed the Mr. G's murder again.

Now it was my turn to cock my head in confusion. I showed him the two lights to let him know I understood, which I didn't. A third light came on.

I scrambled to my feet and walked to the door, searching the landscape across the road as I played back the first murder, leaving the victim's face a blank.

Another light came on.

There were more murders? I turned my head. "How many," I whispered. My hands shaking, I held up four fingers, then added a fifth. Another light went on. I stopped breathing.

"Hold up ten fingers." I choked out my demand to Edith. "You, too." Dymphna complied. I joined them, raising my own ten digits.

Suddenly, lights popped on, one after another, until glowing lights carpeted the ground stretching forth from the hillside and reaching out toward the dead end. A golden glow, like the one that surrounded Mega Bowers.

I took a stumbling step backward, my breath coming in short pants. Another light. A whine crept up the back of my throat, but I tamped it down. Turning to the sisters, I opened and closed my mouth, trying to get the words out.

"What is it, French Fry?"

When a rumble in my chest joined the fear already there, I pulled in a bucketful of air.

"Run!"

SIXTY

Every light in my house glowed. When the front door opened, I cringed. Bowers came outside, fully dressed, and leaned on his crutch.

"What's the problem, Marty?" Edith strolled to the door without a hint of guilt. "French Fry was with me and Dym. She was perfectly safe."

You wouldn't guess that forty-five minutes ago we were panting from our race to the car. Just as Edith demanded an explanation for why she'd done a quarter mile in twenty seconds, the Doberman's face slammed into my window, leaving drool as he gnawed at the glass. All three of us yelled, while Windy, bless her, air-snapped from Dymphna's lap.

When Edith pulled onto the road, she did so slowly so as not to run over the dog, though when the upstairs lights in the house went on, she sped up.

We were silent on the drive home. I relived my memories, trying to make sense of what Pierre had revealed. Edith remained silent, no surprise. Dymphna was occupied calming down Windy. But now we were home, and silence wasn't an option.

The skin around Bowers' tightened lips was pale. Was he in pain? Or just angry. The way his blue eyes seemed darker than usual, and the way he jerked his arm aside when Edith patted it, he might have been both.

Dymphna passed him with Windy in her arms. "You two are so selfish. Poor Marty was worried about you." She looked up at him. "I thought they'd told you about our drive."

His glance took in the way she roughly stroked Windy. She was going to take off the dog's fur. I mean hair. Poodles have hair.

"I meant to check with you before making plans," Edith said, heavy on the sarcasm.

"We're sorry." I meant to sound contrite, but my voice still shook with leftover fear and adrenaline. My fiancé, instead of responding with loving concern, let loose a chain of swear words. The room went silent.

Without apologizing, he limped back to the couch and sat down. "Explain."

Edith tried to bluff. "What's to explain? I felt like getting out of here and Frankie and Dym came with to keep me company."

He locked eyes with me. "Frankie?"

It wasn't that he trusted me more than he trusted Edith. If I lied, he'd recognize my tells. I shrugged at Edith. "Sorry."

If the story was going to come out, Edith wanted to control the flow of information. "It wasn't any big deal. We found the guy who used to own Pierre, and he gave us some of the goat's favorite cookies. We wanted to pass them on without having to explain to the farmer in the dell what we were doing. And we got spooked by the guard dog. That's all."

Bowers raised his brows. "Is that all, Frankie?"

With everyone's eyes on me, I got shy. "Can I tell you in private?"

"Not after what we've been through," Dymphna snapped, contradicting our story.

Bowers realized that, underneath my cool exterior, I was freaked out. He held out a hand and invited me to sit next to him on the side without the broken rib and fractured collarbone. With his arm firmly pinning me to his side, he repeated his order, though in a gentler tone. "You're keeping something from me because you want to protect me. It's having the opposite effect."

With the way his jaw pulsed, he was suppressing some powerful emotions. I wasn't sure he could handle what I had to say. But what exactly did I have to tell him?

Pierre had shown me a new light every time I asked. Did he assume I wanted to see more lights? When Edith and I held up our fingers... Well, it wasn't as if the goat knew arithmetic. Had he lit up the desert landscape to please me? I couldn't be sure. Was it worth risking Bowers' health to present a massacre that might exist only in a goat's desire for sugary pastries?

"Boy, oh boy. That was some scary guard dog." I patted my chest. "I thought I'd have a heart attack when he hit my window. We made it in by the skin of our teeth." I added a chuckle that ended in a hiccup.

"Is that it? You're not leaving anything out?"

As a diversion, Dymphna held Windy close to her face. "Does Snookum want to tinkle?"

Glancing through my lashes, I noticed Bowers staring at

me. And Edith. My face felt warm as I stood and stretched. "I'm bushed. Don't wake me for anything but breakfast."

I proceeded to the kitchen to turn off the lights and slipped the rental car keys from the hook. After the lights were off and everyone snuggled in their beds, the only sound was the tick of the kitchen clock and the hum of the overworked refrigerator motor.

Since waking early without an alarm clock would be an impossible task for a heavy sleeper like me, I replayed the scene at the farm. Fear would keep me awake a few more hours.

I planned to be at Bennett's Grazers when the sun rose. This time, I would find out exactly why Bowers was on the hill.

SIXTY-ONE

Half an hour before dawn the next morning, I was climbing the back slope of the rocky hill where Bowers took his fall. Edith had referred to it as *not much of a climb*, but by the time I reached the flat area on top, I thought a tumble down the face might be a mercy.

My first three attempts to slip out of my house had brought Bowers to the brink of waking. He merely adjusted his shoulders and drifted off, but it spooked me enough that I didn't risk undoing my fancy front door locks to a series of clicks and beeps.

Instead, I'd slipped out the sliding glass door and climbed over my back wall. It was more of a roll and a thump, but I got over. That's all that mattered.

When I decided to return to the scene of the crime alone, it wasn't from a puffed-up ego. Or maybe it was. Bowers had already seen me at my worst, so I wasn't shy about pulling a boner in front of him. Now that I'd taken a bold stand and declared I was an honest-to-goodness pet psychic, fumbling Pierre's message wasn't an option. The only way to be sure I'd rightly interpreted that blanket of lights he'd shown me was to see for myself what Bowers had gazed on right before the fall.

It was still dark when I parked on the shoulder of the road past Bennett's Grazers. With the guard dog roaming around, I planned to approach the hill from the side opposite the barn. Before getting out of my car, I opened the glove compartment and grabbed my flashlight.

I stood still and let my eyes adjust to the dark, mentally scanning the area for signs of the Doberman. When nothing came up, I moved. As I trudged through the open land, I used the light sparingly, only flicking it on whenever I saw a short shadow ahead, usually a shrub, and cupping my hand around the light to keep it pointed to the ground.

Once the hill was between me and the house, I exercised less caution. By now I had my arms wrapped around me tight to ward off the cold. Actually, no one can call the seventies cold, but I refused to admit the goosebumps on my arms were my body silently screaming in fear.

When at last I stood overlooking the Bennett farm, I still had time before the sun made its appearance and revealed whatever Bowers had hoped to see that fateful day. But what if he had only climbed this hill because he'd been following someone? Or meeting someone? Then I'd left my warm, makeshift bed, driven miles down lonely roads, and made the arduous climb for nothing.

The sun peeked over mountains in the distance, highlighting them in pink. At least, they were mountains to me, as was anything larger than a sledding slope.

I stepped closer to the edge and looked over the open desert, now in hazy shadow, waiting for it to reveal its secrets. I watched the shadows recede as if my life depended on it. And suddenly, I knew.

Blinking a few times didn't make the scene go away.

Below me stretched open desert, dotted with desert sage, saguaro cactus, and ocotillo plants, as well as something unnatural. Man-made.

Mounds. Mounds of disturbed earth. Graves. There were dozens. Some, flattened by rains and wind, wouldn't have caught my eye except for the sudden absence of plant life. And some were fresh. Recent. I took a step back to distance myself from the horror, not realizing the real danger was behind me.

SIXTY-TWO

"Nice view, isn't it?"

I spun so fast I lost my balance, righting myself before I fell. Del Bennett watched me with a slight smile. That smile gave me hope.

"Yes. It's beautiful. The last thing my poor fiancé saw before he fell." My calm voice amazed me. "I had to see it for myself. Thank you for that."

"You can drop the act. How did you spot Paul? The Scarpettas were furious about that. He's one of their best men. You must be pretty good to catch him out. What are you? FBI? Or private?"

Standing there, putting his weight on his walking stick, he looked defeated. Tired. And a little sad.

"If you're asking what I do for a living, animal behavior."

"Is that why you were so interested in Pierre?"

"Yes. Yes, it is. In all the goats. Not just Pierre, though he is more interesting that the rest of your herd. Active. Intelligent."

He shuffled a few stones around with his walking stick. "I read about you. That you talk to animals. Is it true?"

"Depends on what you mean by talk."

"I suppose it doesn't matter."

I wanted it to matter. "If you like, I'll demonstrate on one of your other goats."

Interest crept into his eyes. It died out like an old ember. "Under different circumstances, I'd take you up on that."

I tamped down a wave of nausea with effort. When they found my body, if they did, I didn't want to give them a clue about how terrified I was in my last moments.

"Is Jacob a mobster, too?"

He laughed, showing square, yellow teeth. "He'd like that, but he's not, and neither am I. Just a farmer who couldn't make ends meet." He glanced down at his property. "That cornfield is the last crop I have. I keep it around to remember what it feels like to work the land."

"But you make your living renting out the goats."

"That helps, but it's not enough to keep up with the taxes. So, when I got approached by a few men with poor reputations asking if they could borrow some land, I had no reason to decline their offer."

Squaring my shoulders, I asked the question of the week. "Did you push my fiancé?"

He winced. "When I saw him climbing the hill, I panicked. Let's be clear. I have done nothing wrong. Just rented land out to other people. That's not a crime. But—" He passed a hand over his mouth. "He wouldn't have understood." He turned his thoughts inward and gazed at the horizon, perhaps debating my fate. I took a tiny step to my right. The movement brought his attention back, and his voice and manner turned brusque. "Enough talk. I will not enjoy this. I want you to know that."

When he took a menacing step forward, I inched back until I heard crumbling earth scatter down the hillside. I'd gone far enough. In fact, putting distance between me and the edge sounded like a great idea.

Shock kept anger at bay, but not adrenaline. After feinting to the left, I dug my shoes in and pivoted right. The arch I made to pass him wasn't big enough. He caught my arm and yanked me back.

As he pulled me toward the rocky, steep incline, I kicked and twisted and punched like Emily on her way to the bathtub. My blows bounced off his solid form.

Though the thought of putting his hand in my mouth disgusted me—I didn't know where that hand had been—I bit down hard on the flesh surrounding his thumb. He yelled, but he didn't let go.

The ground beneath my feet disappeared, and the only thing between me and a deadly fall were the hands gripping my arms. So, I gripped back. Grappling with his hands, I clutched at his shirt.

He wedged one palm under my chin and forced my head back, at the same time tugging my hand off his collar. When he slapped me, my hands let go. I fell.

As soon as my feet hit the incline, I leaned forward, clutching at dirt and stone. With great effort, I stilled my movements until I was flat on my stomach, spread eagle.

When his walking stick landed on my left hand, I yelled and pulled my arm back. The motion started my slide again. My foot hit a protruding rock, and a wrenching pain shot up my leg as my heel dropped and twisted. Crying out through gritted teeth, I focused on the positive points. Point. At lease I had my balance back.

Glancing up through my lashes, I saw Del Bennett

standing on the edge of the drop, his walking stick raised high. This time, he aimed for my head.

Suddenly, his eyes opened wide. His tummy bulged forward right before he went airborne, passing me before he landed. And bounced. And kept bouncing all the way to the bottom, where he lay motionless.

"What the—"

Two eyes with rectangle irises stared down at me. Pierre shook his head, bleated once, and turned away.

"Wait!" I paused. Even if Pierre could pull a Lassie for me, who would I send him to for help? Jacob wouldn't be sympathetic. Not if he was one of Del's goons.

I let out a sigh, but only a small one. Alone and unable to move without major consequences, well, it didn't look promising. Bowers wound up with a concussion and several breaks falling down this same hill. He was much hardier than I, so what would the fall do to me? Would it kill me? Maim me for life? Leave me paralyzed?

I tried to imagine saying my vows from a prone position. Being wheeled into the reception on a bed. Not a treat for Bowers, especially if he had to chew my wedding cake before feeding it to me through a straw. And then the honeymoon! Would I be functional?

Something tickled my hand. With my luck, it was a tarantula or a scorpion.

"Need help?"

Edith Bowers stood at the edge of the drop, a rope wrapped around her middle that she fed through her hands.

"I'm just admiring the scenery."

She grinned. "It's better up here."

Reaching for my lifeline, the earth beneath my feet shifted, moving me out of reach. Edith grunted as she released another two feet of rope. It wasn't enough.

Whispering a short prayer, I pushed off with my toes as gently as possible. My right foot slipped, and what began as a slow slide picked up speed.

"Son of a—"

Though I scrambled at the earth with my fingers, I couldn't catch hold, and the motion sent dirt into my face and open mouth. In an effort to control my descent, I pushed off with my right hand to angle my body onto my left hip. At least I'd see the obstacles in my path. Like that pointed fifteen-inch boulder ahead.

I yelled when my injured foot hit the rock. Just like the *Titanic*, what I saw was only the tip of something larger buried in the ground. In other words, immovable. My ankle twisted again, but I was distracted by the jagged pebbles digging into my side.

By swiveling my pelvis, I gained some control and was able to skirt the shrub to my left. Mostly. Dried branches scratched my arms, leaving tiny trails of blood.

Funny thing. As I skid down the rest of the hill, I *did* notice the cheery, bright yellow marigolds as I passed. Ten feet from the bottom, I jerked to avoid a vicious outcropping of basalt and went into a side roll.

Once the motion stopped, I rolled to my back and stared at the cloudless blue sky. I'd survived.

A hairy face came into view.

"Sorry, fella. I'm fresh out of treats."

"And he deserves one," Edith said, pulling me to my feet. I winced and hopped to take my weight off my sore ankle. "I saw the whole thing." She rubbed Pierre between his horns. "You're a hero."

We both turned and gazed over the impromptu graveyard.

"Quite a collection you've got here," she called to Del, who lay in a heap about twenty feet away. He groaned.

"What made you follow me?"

"You were obviously withholding something last night. I knew if I waited, you'd lead me to it."

She wrapped an arm around me. "Can you make it to the road, French Fry?"

"A little at a time." I gasped. "We'll never outrun the Doberman."

"I took care of him first."

"Tell me you didn't hurt him."

"He'll be fine. So will your friend Jacob." She grimaced. "It took longer than I anticipated. Good thing you had your own backup."

SIXTY-THREE

A welcome party of several police cars and one unmarked gold sedan awaited us.

And one lone figure leaning on a crutch. As soon as Bowers spotted us, his sister steadying me as I hopped along, he strode forward, limping. Edith called out.

"If you wind up back in surgery, I will never let you live it down." When that didn't stop his progress, she followed with, "Don't be a fool. We'll be right there." He stumbled but kept coming.

"Hang on, French Fry." She lowered herself, hoisted me over her shoulders with a grunt, and headed his way. I imagined this was the way shepherds carried lost lambs, though my weight put me in the grown sheep category.

An ambulance pulled up just as we reached my fiancé. Edith dropped me to my foot, and Bowers let go of his crutch and wrapped his arms around me. "I can't decide whether to yell at you or kiss you," he whispered in my ear, right before he squeezed the breath out of me.

"You're welcome," Edith panted. When she thumped

his back, we both lost our balance and landed in the dirt. Gutierrez' face entered my view of the sky.

"Del's down for the count." She grabbed Bowers' hand, and with Edith's help got my fiancé back on his feet.

"P—I killed him?" Unsure what penalty a goat would pay for killing someone, I intended to take the blame. I rolled onto my stomach and pushed off the ground to get to my hands and knees. "He's dead? But he made a noise."

Edith and Gutierrez hooked me under the arms and hoisted me up. "He's coming around now. Keeps mumbling about a beast from hell."

Special Agent Sonia strolled up to us. "Congratulations. You just destroyed six months' worth of work."

"There's another guy back there." Edith motioned to behind the barn.

"That would be Special Agent Erik Montoya. He was on the phone with me when you clobbered him." She flashed a quick smile. "Assaulting a federal agent carries jail time."

If Sonia planned to intimidate Scary Sister, she failed. Edith didn't even flinch.

"He shouldn't have let me catch him off guard."

A loud and angry curse word came from the direction of the pen. Pierre rounded the corner, a middle-aged patrol officer huffing to catch up. When the goat spotted me, he trotted over.

Scratching his ears, I asked if anyone had food on them. Gutierrez finally gave in and retrieved a banana muffin from her car. She handed it over with bad grace, mumbling about missing breakfast.

"Pierre appreciates your sacrifice." As if to agree, he bleated. A response came from the burnt-out house across the street.

Gutierrez scanned the landscape. "There are wild goats in the Sonoran Desert?"

Bowers put his arm around my shoulder, more to hold himself steady than from any romantic feelings. "Fess up, Frankie."

My lower lip trembled. "They were going to eat them."

The detective made a face. "Yuck."

"Anyway," Edith said, watching a white van screech to a stop in the middle of the road, "the owners are here to claim them."

Technically, the van wasn't all white. An image of Pierre adorned the side together with *Pierre's Pastries*.

The driver's side door opened, and Charlie spilled out. "Where is he? Where is my *mon peitit crotte?*"

"Your little poop is right here," Edith said.

"*Crotte* means poop?" I laughed. "I thought it meant darling. Or loved one. Poop's more appropriate."

When Penelope came around from the passenger side, I worried about the goat's fate. Her frownie face lacked excitement.

Pierre bleated and raced to the source of all the tasty yummies. When Charlie wrapped his arms around the goat's neck and showered him with kisses, Penelope's upper lip curled in distaste.

An officer led momma and her baby out of the construction site. Charlie gasped before awarding Pierre a fond grin. "You little devil!"

I thought Penelope would chime in with her opinion about Satan's spawn, but her eyes stayed fixed on the baby.

"Look at you," she cooed. "You sweetie-pie. Let's get you out of this nasty desert." When she put her hand on the kid's head to rub the bumps where his horns would grow, the nanny goat snapped her teeth perilously close to Penelope's hand.

For a minute, I thought we had a deal breaker, but the woman surprised us *and* the mother goat by patting her on the head. "You are right to protect your child. Let's get you both some water."

"What happened to The Back Door?" Edith asked.

The chubby chef pulled himself straight. Poor thing. It didn't make him taller. "I have taken the leap to bring my pastries to the world by selling direct. And now," he looked down at his best friend, "with my muse by my side, I cannot fail."

"And Penelope," Edith added with a smirk. "With Penelope by your side."

"Get a move on it, Charlie," the neglected girlfriend called out. "We need to feed these poor babies."

Charlie beamed at her. "Coming dear."

Some of the cops helped Charlie violate several health codes by moving the shelves in his van to make room for the goats. Before Pierre departed to a new life filled with his favorite foods, I wrapped my arms around his head and hugged him.

"Sorry I was so dense."

He nibbled on my t-shirt, and it required Gutierrez's help before I got loose.

When I turned back to Bowers, he was watching the paramedics load Del into the ambulance.

"That man pushed me."

I wrapped my arm around his waist. "He did. But if it makes you feel better, he didn't enjoy it."

Special Agent Sonia interrupted our moment. "We're taking things from here."

"And why is that?" Gutierrez said. If the agent could

have felt the fury behind the sentiment, she would have pulled her weapon.

"Because this is a small part of a larger case we're on. You can have Del Bennett when we're through with him."

Gutierrez said a naughty word.

Bowers frowned at the agent. "I'm glad my near-death experience was only a small part."

My giggle turned into a gasp when I shifted my weight.

"Let's get that looked at," Bowers said, and we moved the party to the ambulance.

SIXTY-FOUR

It turned out I had a sprained ankle along with a lot of bruises. Not the worst thing in the world, but now Bowers and I sat side by side on my couch with our legs up on matching pillows. At least it solved the lap problem. Emily had my fiancé to herself. I got Windy, who, once asleep, lived up to her name.

Once I'd repeated Del's conversation to the rest of the sisters, both those staying with me and those on the video call, everyone congratulated Edith on her fine work.

"You should have stuck with her, Frankie," Agnes said. "It would have saved Edith the trouble of rescuing you."

"Actually, the goat got to her first," Edith said. "Darndest thing. It somehow got loose and went after Del."

Dymphna, seated next to me, looked up from stroking Windy. "Almost like it knew what it was doing."

A moment of silence preceded hoots of laughter.

"You better stop hanging around with Frankie," Martha said. "She's rubbing off on you, Dym. Soon you'll believe that fluff ball of yours can talk."

Dymphna's eyes met mine, and she smiled.

As everyone exchanged goodbyes, I got a call on my cell from an unlisted number. Probably a recorded call about my car warranty. About to press the ignore button, I recognized the area code. Tucson. The location of The Southwest School of Jewelry Design.

"Hello?"

"Is this Miss Frankie Chandler?" asked a soft voice.

"Who is this?"

"Luther Mendoza."

"Luther?" I shouted, and the room went silent.

"I understand you've been trying to reach me, but the Dean didn't say what it was about. Is everything all right? Are Lola and the baby okay? I tried her first, but she didn't pick up when I called."

"They're both fine, but she's been frantic about you."

He paused. "She has? I told her I had a plan to support us. I wanted to surprise her with my certificate. Imagine me, a certified bench jeweler."

"You disappeared without a word. That's not a nice surprise."

"Oh, man. I didn't think she'd worry. I'll try her again right now."

As I disconnected, Edith shook her head. "Where was he?"

"After Lola repeated his promise to support her and the baby, I wondered if he might have enrolled in continuing education. Everyone said he excelled at working with jewelry. I called the closest schools that offered training."

"All's well that ends well," Dymphna sighed.

I took in the faces of the surrounding woman. The deceptively quiet Ghost Woman, Dymphna, and her curly sidekick; even Edith, the Scary Sister with secrets. Could I ever call them "sister" and mean it? Would I ever belong? It might take time, but I thought I'd enjoy the journey.

My gaze still on Edith, I tugged Bowers' shirt. "There's something I need to know. Every time I mention Edith's name, you twitch. Yet while she's been here, you're fine. What gives?"

"Oh, Marty," Dymphna said.

"What's the story?" A weak laugh escaped me. "What did she do to you?"

His shoulders hunched, and his face squished up at a painful memory.

"It's what he did to *her*," Dymphna said with a tiny smile.

Edith's hand moved to the scar that traveled between her upper lip and her cheek. "It's old news. Anyway, it was an accident."

"They were rough-housing," Ghost Woman explained. "Marty shoved Edith into a pile of hay. He didn't know there was a pitchfork buried inside."

He covered his face, and I winced along with him. "Ouch."

"No big deal," Edith said. "It didn't hurt much." She grinned at her brother. "You still feel guilty? That means I have power over you. Hmm. What should I make you do?"

He peeked at her from between his fingers. "Not that guilty."

Dymphna stood. "Speaking of guilty feelings, you need your bed tonight, Frankie."

"I'm fine. Really. My leg will be in the same position on the floor or in the bed. And this way, I won't accidentally jump up in the middle of the night."

"I'm getting sick of the couch," Bowers said. "Why don't you—"

"I have a solution. Not for tonight, but from tomorrow on."

Before I explained my plan, the doorbell rang. Dymphna grabbed the opportunity to take her pup out back, while Edith strolled to the door and swung it open.

"May I help you?"

Leaning forward for a better view, I fell off the couch when I saw who it was.

"Frances!" My mother pushed past Edith and rushed to my side. Bowers had caught hold of my ankle to keep it from slamming into the coffee table, leaving me in a pretzel position.

After my mother helped me back to sitting, and Bowers repositioned my leg on the pillow, my mother grabbed my face in her hands.

"What is going on here?" She looked to Bowers. "Martin?" She stuck out a hand. "Nice to meet you." Her gaze ran over him in a quick evaluation. "Frances didn't mention what a handsome devil you are."

Edith led my father, who carried two large pieces of luggage, into the room. He set them down and shook hands with my fiancé, waving off Bowers' attempt to stand.

"You're a little red in the face. Either you're sicker than I thought, or my wife has found time to embarrass you. She works fast. We *would* like to know what's going on."

Before I could come up with an explanation to fit the facts, Scary Sister took charge.

"You must be Frankie's parents."

"This is my mother, Beverly, and my father, Albert. Mom and Dad, meet Edith, one of Bowers' sisters."

Dymphna returned from outside, so I made additional introductions and invited them all to find a place to sit. Mother squeezed in next to me, while Edith sat on

Bowers' left. The rest of them grabbed chairs from the dining table.

"What an adorable puppy," Mom said as Dymphna set her in Bowers' lap before claiming a chair.

"Did you have a nice flight?" I asked to give myself time to come up with a story.

"Fine. Now tell us what's going on."

"Um..."

"As you heard," Edith began, "Marty suffered a fall at work."

My mother took a time out to ask if he was feeling better.

"Slow but sure," Bowers said.

"Did Frances fall down at work, too?"

"I'm afraid that was my fault, Mrs. Chandler." Edith was going to take one for the team. "When I arrived, I set my backpack down in the middle of the room and your daughter tripped over it."

Mother laughed, relieved. "You wouldn't believe the scenarios running through my head. I thought Martin had changed his mind about the wedding."

"Mother!"

She shrugged. "It's happened before. To other people, not you. Then I assumed his injuries were much worse than what you described. I had an image of Martin in the hospital, unconscious and hooked up to machines. It was terrible."

Dymphna met my panicked gaze. "Imagine that."

"Friends and family back home will be relieved. They all suspected something was up. I told them you both were fine."

"We better check into the hotel," my father said after a glance at his watch. He had on a light-blue golf shirt and tan slacks. With my mother's white capris and sparkly t-shirt, they looked like vacationers. "I'd say we'd take you to dinner, but the two of you don't look up to going anywhere right now."

"Actually," I said, slipping Bowers a look. "If you all could give me a few minutes alone with my fiancé, you're going to be busy tonight."

Intrigued, they headed for the kitchen.

"We have leftover Stovies," Dymphna said.

Mother took her arm. "Doesn't that sound delicious, Albert? We love trying new dishes."

I took Bowers hands in mine.

"Am I going to like this?" he joked.

"I hope so." I turned to face him. "Martin James Bowers, I don't want to spend another day not being your wife."

The corners of his mouth twitched in a smile. "Go on."

When I told him my plan, he rewarded me with a solid kiss that only ended when Windy passed gas.

SIXTY-FIVE

There weren't any flowers in the church except for my and Penny's white rose bouquets, picked from her garden. No carpet down the center aisle. The organist was a parishioner's grandmother who knew how to pick out the notes with two fingers.

When I rolled into the back of the church, Bowers waited for me at the altar with the priest. He'd yet to pick a best man, so at his side stood Detective Juanita Gutierrez. Technically, his best woman. I could tell she was pleased with his request, though he tried to play it down, telling her if he asked one of the male detectives the others might be offended.

Since the Catholic Church requires two witnesses but doesn't specify if they need to be male or female, Father Damien embraced the arrangement. It was he who got us special permission to be married in the Church. We'd already been through enough of pre-Cana to qualify for a dispensation.

In the front few rows on the left side of the aisle sat my mom and dad, my neighbor, Betty, and her beau, Bull.

Seamus McGuire brought his girlfriend, Bethany, who eagerly accepted our invitation. Perhaps she hoped seeing two people survive a wedding ceremony might prompt him to propose. And of course, Kemper, paying more attention to the bridesmaid than the bride, as he should.

On the groom's side sat his sisters, most of them, and the entire Wolf Creek police force.

Penny marched down the aisle first, wiggling her fingers at Kemper as she passed. With the first notes of the *Wedding March*, everyone stood and turned to see the bride, resplendent in the only white dress her mother could find off the rack—a long sleeved, knit turtleneck two sizes too large.

Then, with an initial grunt, my father pushed my wheelchair down the aisle. June and her husband, Carl, had made it down with a special guest. As I passed Chauncey, I reached out and rubbed his head. He rewarded me with a bark and tail wag, which sent Windy into a cacophony of howls.

By the time Dad handed me off to Bowers by parking my wheelchair next to his, the dogs were under control. My fiancé looked so handsome in a deep navy suit jacket, white shirt, and matching tie. They went pretty well with his sweatpants and leg brace.

Since I didn't have time to choose readings, Penny let me borrow the ones from her wedding last year. And when it came time for Bowers to slip the ring on my finger, his nervousness showed, and he fumbled and dropped it.

As it rolled down the aisle, Chauncey leaped from his pew and retrieved it. For a moment, I feared he would swallow it, but he trotted to me and spit it in my hand. Bowers slipped it on me, drool and all.

When Father Damien pronounced us man and wife,

Bowers grinned at me, which set off a fit of giggles. Our kiss was passionate but brief, as the wheelchair arms dug into our sides.

And then, for better or for worse, I was Mrs. Martin James Bowers.

HAPPILY EVER AFTER? To find out when the next Frankie Chandler novel is out and keep up with all the latest news, check out the website.

IF YOU ENJOYED THIS BOOK, please consider leaving a review. Reviews help readers discover new books, and the author, who socializes mostly with dogs, appreciates the human feedback.

A NOTE FROM THE AUTHOR

Transporters. Sounds like a super-hero film, doesn't it? Hospital transporters *are* heroes, usually unsung. They are the people who gently transfer you to that moveable bed or wheelchair without harming you or your dignity. They are the ones who accompany you to that operation, test, or treatment, often telling jokes or singing songs or praying with you to lift your spirits and calm your fears. It's a difficult job. Draining. They give of themselves every time they walk into a patient room and rarely receive back. So, thank you, Transporters, for all that you do.

ACKNOWLEDGMENTS

Writing can be a lonely business...unless you have friends! Thank you Kim Taylor Blakemore, Robert Gwaltney, and Tonya Mitchell for your support, jokes, and advice. They make the journey more pleasant.

Writers are famous for procrastinating. Thank you Kim Taylor Blakemore for keeping me on track with your advice, friendship, and friendly ultimatums.

Thank you Jennifer Bradley for allowing me to visit with your goats. They were a hoot. Readers, keep on the lookout for future author, Abbey Bradley.

Many thanks to Adrianne Lerma-Corcoran for sharing your insights into Mexican traditions surrounding death to keep me from making a fool of myself. Any changes, deviations, or exaggerations are mine.

And thanks to Adrianne Lerma-Corcoran and Gigi Chavez for their help with my Spanish phrases. If I got it wrong, it's my fault.

Finally, there are those who make the journey worthwhile. My husband, Foster, my parents, Al and Bev, and my sister, Andrea, who shares my warped sense of humor. (I think I caught it from her at a young age.)

BOOK CLUB QUESTIONS

A Scape Goat for Murder

1. When Bowers is injured, Frankie feels helpless until she comes up with a plan to discover what happened at Bennett's Grazers. Have you ever felt helpless in the face of misfortune? How did you respond?

2. When a person falls in love, their significant other's family is most often part of the package. Did you ever worry there was something about you that your "in-laws" might not like? How did you overcome obstacles? Be yourself? Try to change? How did that work for you?

3. The police and the doctors kept Bowers' condition from Frankie for his protection. Did they have a point? Or do you think they should have included her in their deception?

4. Edith gets all the credit for "saving" Bowers. Should she have pointed out Frankie's contribution? Or would it have made no difference, since the rest of the Bowers Girls seemed stuck on the notion that Edith can do anything?

5. According to Edith, she and her brother grew apart as adults, yet she's the person Bowers turns to when he wants Frankie looked after. Is there someone in your life you've lost touch with but would still trust if you needed help?

6. Frankie and Bowers wedding wasn't your typical affair, with flower girls and beautiful music and bows on the ends of the pews. If you were in Frankie's position, would you have put off the wedding until both she and Bowers were healed and then plan a perfect event?

7. Frankie observes that she and Edith are "fighting like sisters." How do you think sisters fight? Do you have any experiences to base this on?

8. Did you find the inclusion of Windy, Emily, and Chauncey distracting? Or did you enjoy their little bits?

9. In the beginning, Frankie feels she's on her own. True to her nature, she even prefers it at first. Do you think wanting to deal with tough situations alone is the best route? Or should everyone have someone they can rely on?

10. Frankie asks Penny to accompany her to the goat

farms, but her best friend has other obligations, including her husband. Do you think the dynamics between friends *should* change when one of them marries?

ABOUT THE AUTHOR

Jacqueline Vick writes the Frankie Chandler Pet Psychic Mystery Series about a woman who, after faking her psychic abilities for years, discovers animals *can* communicate with her. Her second series, the Harlow Brothers mysteries, features a former college linebacker turned etiquette author and his secretary brother. Her books are known for satirical humor and engaging characters who are desperate to keep their secrets. Visit her at www.jacquelinevick.com

ALSO BY JACQUELINE VICK

Frankie Chandler Mysteries
Barking Mad at Murder
A Bird's Eye View of Murder
An Almost Purrfect Murder
What the Cluck? It's Murder
A Scaly Tail of Murder
A Scape Goat for Murder
Some Like Murder Hot

Harlow Brother Mysteries
Civility Rules
Bad Behavior
Deadly Decorum

Standalone Novels
The Body Guy
An Unhealthy Attachment
Family Matters